Silverblind

TOR BOOKS BY TINA CONNOLLY

Ironskin
Copperhead
Silverblind

Silverblind

TINA CONNOLLY

A Tom Doherty Associates Book
New York

This is a work of fiction. All of the characters, organizations, and events portrayed in this novel are either products of the author's imagination or are used fictitiously.

SILVERBLIND

A Tor Book
Published by Tom Doherty Associates, LLC
175 Fifth Avenue
New York, NY 10010

www.tor-forge.com

Tor® is a registered trademark of Tom Doherty Associates, LLC.

The Library of Congress Cataloging-in-Publication Data is available upon request.

ISBN 978-0-7653-7514-8 (hardcover)
ISBN 978-1-4668-4540-4 (e-book)

Tor books may be purchased for educational, business, or promotional use. For information on bulk purchases, please contact Macmillan Corporate and Premium Sales Department at 1-800-221-7945, extension 5442, or write specialmarkets@macmillan.com.

First Edition: October 2014

Printed in the United States of America

10   9   8   7   6   5   4   3   2   1

For Dad,
who told me bedtime stories about girls who did things,
and for Andy,
with thanks for the explorer hat

Silverblind

Chapter 1

INTERVIEW

Adora Rochart had not called on her fey side for nearly a decade, except for the merest gloss of power that helped keep her unnoticeable: allowed her to slip onto trolleys without paying, to slip under the radar, and incidentally to keep breathing. When the fey had showed her how to extract the blue from her system, they advised her to keep the tiniest film of fey dust about her. There was no other creature such as she: no other half-human, half-fey, and on many things the fey could not advise her.

But the Monday morning she went to her job interviews—that morning, for the first time in seven years, she unlocked the copper box of concentrated blue, and dipped her fingers in it. More than the dusting she had had. Far, far less than her whole self.

The blue must have sparkled on her fingers before being absorbed. Surely it must have tingled. But mostly, we may never know—why that particular morning, did she decide to bring the fey back into her life? Was it for luck? Was there fey intuition at stake, telling her she was about to need it? Or was it somehow the fey themselves, desperate about all that was about to come, slipping their blue poison in her ear, telling her that she must side with them in the final war?

—Thomas Lane Grimsby, *Silverblind: The Story of Adora Rochart*

* * *

Dorie sat neatly on one side of the desk, hands folded on top of the dirt smudge on her best skirt, heart in her throat. This was the last of the three interviews she'd managed to obtain— and the most important.

The desk was sleek and silver—like the whole building, shiny and new with the funds suddenly pouring into the Queen's Lab. The ultra-modern concrete-and-steel space had opened a scant year ago, but the small office was already crammed with the books, papers, and randomnesses of some overworked underling. On a well-thumbed book she could make out the chapter heading: "Wyverns and Basilisks: A Paralyzing Paradox." A narrow, barred window was half-covered by a towering stack of papers, but there was some blue summer sky beyond it. Perhaps if you stood on that chair and peered around it you could see the nurses marching at the City Hospital. Not that she was going to do anything so improper as stand on chairs today. This was her last chance.

The door buzzed as the underling scanned his ID medallion and walked in. Late, of course. He was probably a grad student from the University, thin and already stooped, in a rumpled blue suit, with a brown tie that had seen better days. Dorie refused to let her heart sink to her feet. There was always the chance that this boy was better than the two men she'd interviewed with that day, even if they had been higher on the ladder.

The underling sat down in his chair and moved stacks of papers with a dramatic groan for his overworkedness. Took out a pencil and began adding up a column of figures on a small notebook he carried. He didn't even bother to look up at her. "Let's get this farce over with, shall we?"

No. It was not going to go better at all.

Dorie pulled her papers from her satchel and passed them over. "I'm Dorie Rochart," she said, "and I'm interviewing for the field work position."

He dropped the papers on top of another stack without a glance and continued adding. "Look," he said to the notebook, "it's none of my doing. I'm sure you had very good marks and all."

"I did," Dorie interjected. She found his name on a placard half-buried in the remains of lunch. "Mr. . . . John Simons, is it? Pleased to meet you. Yes, I was top of the class." She had worked hard for that, after all. Firmly squashed all her differences and really buckled down. "I have a lot of fantastic ideas for ways this lab could help people that I'd really like to share with you."

"I'm sure, I'm sure," said Simons. "But be sensible, miss. You must realize they're never going to hire a girl for a field work position."

And there it was. He was willing to say what the first two men this morning had only danced around, mindful of keeping up the appearance that their labs were modern and forward-thinking and sensitive to the current picketings going on around Parliament. She could almost like him for being so blunt.

"I'm very qualified," Dorie said evenly. Of course she could not tell him exactly why she was so qualified. Being half-fey was the sort of thing for which they might just throw you in an iron box for the rest of your life. If they didn't hang you first. "I grew up in the country, and I—"

"I know, I know. You always dreamed of hunting copperhead hydras and silvertail wyverns like your brothers."

"I don't have any—"

"Or cousins, or whatnot." Simons sighed and finally put his

pencil down. "Look, I don't want to be rude, but can we call it a day? I still have all this data to sort through." Finally, finally he deigned to look up at her, and his mouth hung open on whatever he was going to say.

This was the look Dorie knew.

This is what she had encountered twice before today—and more to the point, in general, always. The curse of her fey mother: beauty.

He stammered through something incoherent, in which she caught the words "girl" and "blonde." Finally he settled on, "I am very sorry. Terrible policy, terrible policy. Should be hiring girls right and left. You're not going to cry, are you?"

"Of course not," she said flatly. Dorie Rochart did not cry. She might, however, cause all those papers behind Simons to dump themselves on his head. It would be very satisfying. The fey in her fingertips tingled with mischief. She tucked her hands under her legs and sat on them.

He brightened. "Oh, good. I wouldn't know what to do." The mental wheels behind his eyes turned and Dorie braced herself, for now was the moment when they all propositioned her, and she didn't know what she would do then. The other two men that morning had done that . . . and her fey side had reacted.

Dorie had locked away her fey half for seven years. She couldn't trust herself with it. This morning, for the first time, she had retrieved just a trace. Just a smidge. It had felt so good, so *real*. Like she could face the day. Like she could sail through these interviews. A drop of blue, just to bring her luck.

But in seven years she had forgotten all her habits to control that part of her.

Her fingers had twitched, flicked, and had made a hot cup of tea "accidentally" spill on the first interviewer's lap. The second one, she had dropped a nearby spider down his collar. Simons had the misfortune to be third in line, and papers dumped on his head would be just the tip of the iceberg.

But to her surprise, he said, "Look, are you good at sums? There aren't any indoors research jobs right now, but I believe they're hiring more ladies to work the calculating machines. There's some girls in the physics wing crunching data."

Her fingers relaxed with this minor reprieve as she stood. He was safe for the moment. "I'm afraid not. Thank you for your—"

The door buzzed again. It swung open and a young eager face poked his head in. "Wyvern's hatching! Wyvern's hatching! Ooh, girl!" He blushed and left.

Perhaps Simons saw the light on her face, for he bended enough to say, "Look, I know you're disappointed, miss, uh, Miss Dorie." He blushed as he said her name. "I could . . . I could sneak you in to see the hatching before you go? As a, uh, personal favor?"

Dorie nodded eagerly. This was by far the most tolerable suggestive remark of the day, since it had the decency to come with a wyvern hatching.

"Stay behind me, then, and keep a low profile." His thin chest puffed out. "Top secret, you know? But they won't get too fussed about a girl if they see you—Pearcey brings in his latest bird all the time. I'll show you out when it's over."

Dorie followed Simons down the concrete hall to a room crammed with all the boys and men of the lab. He scanned his medallion and pulled her through behind him as the door opened. She caught a glimpse of the copper circle and saw a thin oval design there, its lines a faint silver glow. The same symbol was visible hanging on the lanyards of a few other men as well—some sort of new technology. Using electricity, she supposed. And a magnet, in that lock? She had not seen this sort of security before, but then she had been consumed with finishing her University studies this year.

She stood behind him, out of the way. She did not need to be told to stay to the back, as she felt conspicuous enough being the only girl. It was a clean, cold room, with metal tables and more rows of those narrow barred windows. The overhead lights were faintly tinged blue, and a smell of disinfectant hung in the air.

There was a small incubator in the middle of the room, made of glass and copper and lined with straw on the bottom. Inside was a grey egg speckled in silver. The top was thoroughly cracked and it was rocking back and forth. More chips from the egg tooth and a large piece broke off.

A man in a lab coat was making sure everyone was at their assigned station—from that and the murmurs she pieced bits together: one man was fetching a mouse for the new hatchling, another man was readying to seize the eggshell at the precise moment the wyvern was done with it and rush it to something called the extraction machine.

What was so important about the eggshell? Dorie wondered. In her childhood, she had made note of the elusive wyverns whenever she stumbled across a pair, crept in day after day in half-fey state to that bit of the forest and stared in awe. No one had been interested in them then, or their eggshells. But she was not supposed to call attention to the fact that she was here, and she did not want to be thrown out, so she did not ask.

Across the concrete room she saw someone in a canvas field hat and her heart suddenly skipped a beat. Tam had always worn a hat like that—he called it his explorer hat. She hadn't seen her cousin for seven years, not since they were both fifteen and in the fey-ridden forest and—well. She wouldn't think about that now. Dorie peered around shoulders, wondering if it could possibly be Tam. He would have liked this job, she thought. But the man turned toward her and she could see that it definitely wasn't Tam, not even Tam-a-decade-later. Of course, Tam had too much class to be wearing a hat inside.

Another crack, and the wyvern's wet triangular head came poking out. She heard an audible "awww" from someone. The man assigned to the task stood waiting, gloved hands out and ready to scoop up the apparently precious pieces of eggshell.

The egg broke all the way open and the little wyvern chick came wiggling out. Dorie barely noticed the process with the eggshell, as her attention was taken with the wriggly wet chick. They were bright silver at this age, and the sheen of liquid left from its hatching made it shine like a mirror under the laboratory lights. It stalked along, screeching for food. A short man swung a cage up onto the table, reached in with gloved hands to grab a white mouse by the tail. Dropped it into the incubator.

The little wyvern stalked along, its tiny claws clicking on the metal, its feet splaying out as it tried to learn balance. A man moved in front of her and by the time Dorie could see again the wyvern was comfortably gnawing on the mouse.

"Bloody-minded, aren't they?" said someone.

The short man brought a shallow bowl of water to set on the table and the wyvern chick stopped eating long enough to flap its wings and hiss, causing much laughter as the short man jumped back, spilling the water. A tall man in a finely cut suit said, "Doesn't like you much, does it?"

"Nasty little things don't like anyone," retorted the short man.

"And here I thought it was showing good taste," said the tall man in a pretend-nice way. The other scientists laughed sycophantically and Dorie thought this must be someone with power. She dropped her eyes as she realized he was looking back at her, and turned to Simons.

"What now?" Dorie whispered to her interviewer. "Will they return the chick to its parents?"

"Oh, no," Simons said. "We sell the hissy little things—to zoos and other research facilities, mostly. We're only interested in the eggs here, and they don't breed in captivity. Every so often someone makes arrangements with Pearce to purchase one as a pet—don't ask me why people want them. They don't like anybody. All they do is spit and scream at you, and when they're older, steam, too."

"Who's that man?" said Dorie, for Simons seemed to be in a question-answering mood. "The one looking at us."

Simons stiffened. Hurriedly he stepped in front of her as if to block the man's view. "Come on, come on, let me show you out," he said. "That's the lab director, and if he's cross about me showing you this I just don't even know. Hurry, miss."

Dorie started to the door, but stopped, Simons running into her. That boy, all the way in the corner, getting the wyvern chick more water. Wasn't that Tam after all? Or was her mind playing tricks on her now? She had not seen him for seven years, but surely—

"Dr. Pearce," said Simons, swallowing.

"Yes, this must be the one o'clock, correct?" The tall man was there, beaming down upon them in more of that faux-friendly way. "Showing her around a little bit?"

"Well, I—"

"Good, good. Miss Rochart, isn't it? If you'll come this way? I'd like to continue your interview in more comfortable quarters."

Simons looked as startled as Dorie felt, as the lab director escorted her to his office.

In stark contrast to the underling's office, this office was expansive and tidy. You could make seven or eight of Simons's office from it, and everyone knew that guys like Simons were the ones who did the real work. The omnipresent barred windows were replaced with a large plate-glass window. The new security building was across the street—a twin of this one, in blocky concrete and steel. And here was that clear view of the old hospital—and yes, the women with their placards attempting to unionize: FAIR PAY FOR FAIR WORK. A VICTORY FOR ONE IS A VICTORY FOR ALL. Dorie strained to see if she could see her stepmother, Jane, who was not a nurse, but liked a good lost cause when she saw one.

The other significant object in the room was a large glass terrarium. Its sides were made of several glass panels set into copper, including a pair of doors fastened with a copper bolt. The top was vented with mesh, and the ceiling above the whole shebang was reinforced with anti-flammable panels of aluminum. Inside this massive display was an adolescent wyvern chick, about the size of a young cat. It was curled up in a silver ball on a nest of wool scraps and looked very comfortable.

Dorie wondered how secure the copper bolt was.

Dr. Pearce pulled out the chair for her, and leaned down to shake her hand. She realized now who he was—she had heard all the stories of his tailored suits, suave manner, and ice-chip eyes. Her hope bounded upward—talking to the lab director himself was an excellent sign. She had not gotten this far with the other two interviews.

Dr. Pearce had her sheaf of papers with him—her stellar academic record, her carefully acquired letters of recommendation. He smiled at Dorie—they always did—and sat down across from her. "The lovely Miss Rochart, I presume? So pleased to finally meet you."

Dorie tightened her fingers together at the mention of her looks, but she did not stop smiling. *The Queen's Lab. Focus on the goal. With this position you could really start to make a difference. Don't drop spiders on the lab director.*

She knew what she looked like—the curse of her beauty-obsessed fey mother. Blond ringlets, even, delicate features, rosebud lips. She could put the ringlets in a bun—which she had—and put on severe black spectacles—which she hadn't; she couldn't afford such nonsense—and still she would look like a porcelain doll. She had several times tried to tease the ringlets apart in hopes they would turn into a wild mop, which she always thought would suit her better. But no matter what she tried, she woke up every morning with her hair in careful, silken curls. Even now they were intent on escaping the bun, falling down to form softening ringlets around her face.

"And I you," said Dorie. Her normal voice was high and dulcet, but through long practice she had trained herself to speak an octave lower than she should.

He steepled his fingers. "Let's cut right to the chase, Miss Rochart—Adora. May I call you Adora? Such a lovely name."

"I go by Dorie or Ms. Rochart," she said, still smiling.

"Ah yes, the diminutive. I understand—after all, I don't make my friends call me *Dr.* Pearce *all* the time." He smiled at his joke. "Well, then, Dorie, let's have at it. I understand this is your third interview today?"

"Yes," she said. The laced fingers weren't working as well as she had hoped. She sat firmly on one hand and gripped the leg of her chair with the other. It would be terribly bad form to make that porcelain cup of tea with the gold rim levitate off the desk and dump itself down his front. "I understood that information to be private?"

"Oh, there are so few of us in this business, you understand. We are all old friends, all interested in what the new crop of graduates is doing." He smiled paternally at her. "And your name came up several times over lunch today."

"Yes?"

"Again, Adora—Dorie—let's cut to the chase. My colleagues were most amused to tell me of the pretty young girl who thought she could slay basilisks."

"I see," said Dorie. "Thank you for your time, then." She began to rise before her hands would do something that would betray her fey heritage and have her thrown in jail—or worse.

"No no, you misunderstand," he said, and he came to take her shoulders and gently guide her back to the chair. "My colleagues are living in the past. They didn't understand what an opportunity they had in front of them. But I understand."

"Yes?" Her heartbeat quickened. Was he on her side after all? A rosy future opened up once more. The Queen's Lab—a stepping-stone to really do some good. So much knowledge had been lost since the Great War two decades ago, since people started staying away from the forest. Simple things like what to do with feywort and goldmoths and yellowbonnet. She could continue her research into the wild, fey-touched plants and animals of the forest—species were disappearing at an alarming rate, and that couldn't be good for the fey *or* humans. And then, the last several times she'd been home, she'd hardly been able to *find* the fey in the woods behind her home. When she did, they were only thin drifts of blue.

But Dorie could help the humans. She could help the fey.

She was the perfect person to be the synthesis—and this was the perfect spot to do it. The Queen's Lab was the most prominent research facility in the city. If she could get in here, she could solve things from the inside.

Surely even Jane would approve of that.

Dr. Pearce smiled, one hand still on her shoulder. "If you've met any of the young men who do field work for us, you know they grew up dreaming of facing down mythical monsters." He gestured expansively, illustrating the young boys' fervent imaginations. "Squaring off against the legendary basilisk, armed with only a mirror! Luring a copperhead hydra out of its lair, seizing it by the tail before it can twist around to bite you with its seven heads! Sneaking past a pair of steam-blowing silvertail wyverns, capturing their eggs and returning to tell the tale!"

"Yes," breathed Dorie. She put her hands firmly in her pockets.

"Those boys grow up," Dr. Pearce said. "Some of them still want to fight basilisks. But many of them settle down and realize that the work we do right here in the lab is just as important as risking your neck in the field." He perched on his desk and looked right at her. "Our country is mired in the dark ages of myth and superstition, Dorie. When we lost our fey trade three decades ago, we lost all of our easy, clean energy—all of our pride. We've been clawing our way back to bring our country in line with the technology of the rest of the world. We need some bold strokes to align us once more among the great nations of the world. And we can only do that with smart men—and women—like you."

She heard the ringing echo of a well-rehearsed speech, and still, she was carried away, for this *was* what she wanted, and more. "And think of all the good we could do with the knowledge we acquire in the field!" she jumped in, even though she had not planned to tip her hand till she was hired. "Sharing the benefits of all we achieve with everyone who truly needs them. Why, the good that can be accomplished from one pair of goldmoth wings! From a tincture of copperhead hydra venom! Do you remember the outbreak of spotted hallucinations last summer? My stepmother was the one who realized that the city hospitals no longer knew the country remedy of a mash of goldmoths and yellowbonnet. We worked together—she educating hospital staff, me in the field collecting. With the backing of someone like the Queen's Lab, I could continue this kind of work. We could make a difference. Together." She was ordinarily not good with words, but she had recited her plans to her roommate over and over, waiting for the key moment to tell someone who could really help her.

"Ah, a social redeemer," Dr. Pearce said, and a fatherly smile smeared his face at her youthful enthusiasms.

This was not the key moment.

"But more seriously, Dorie," he went on, and his voice deepened. "I would like to create a special position in the Queen's Lab, just for you. A smart, clever, lady scientist like you is an asset that my colleagues were foolish enough to overlook." He fanned out her credentials. "Your grades and letters of recommendation are exemplary." He wagged a finger at her. "You know, if you had been born a boy we would never have had this meeting. You would have been snapped up this morning at your very first interview."

"The Queen's Lab has always been my first choice," said Dorie, because it seemed to be expected, and because it was true.

He smiled kindly, secure in his position as leader of the foremost biological research institution in the country. "Dorie, I would like you to be our special liaison to our donors. It is not false praise to assert how important you would be to our cause. The lab cannot exist without funding. Science cannot prosper. We need people like you, people who can stand on the bridge between the bookish boy scientist with a pencil behind his ear and the wealthy citizens that can be convinced to part with their family money; someone, in fact, exactly like you."

Her hands rose up, went back down. A profusion of thoughts pressed on her throat—with effort she focused to make a clear sentence come out. "And I would be doing what, exactly? Attending luncheons, giving teas?" He nodded. "Greasing palms at special late-night functions for very *select* donors?"

"You have it exactly."

"A figurehead, of sorts," said Dorie. Figurehead was a substitute for the real word she felt.

"If you like."

"*Not* doing field work," she said flatly.

"You must see that we couldn't risk you. I am perfectly serious when I say the work done here in the lab is as important—*more* important—than the work done by the hotheads out gathering hydras. You would be a key member of the team right here, away from the dust and mud and silvertail burns."

"I applied for the field work position," said Dorie, even though her hopes were fading fast. In the terrarium behind him, the adolescent wyvern was awake now, pacing back and forth and warbling. The large terrarium was overkill—their steam was more like mist at this age. It could as easily be pacing around Dr. Pearce's desk, or enjoying the windowsill. All it would take was a little flicker of the fingers, a little mental nudge on that bolt. . . .

Dr. Pearce brought his chair right next to hers and put a fatherly arm on her shoulder. She watched the wyvern and did not shove the arm away, still hoping against hope that the position she wanted was in her grasp. "Let me tell you about Wilberforce Browne," Dr. Pearce said. "Big strapping guy, big as three of you probably—one of our top field scientists. He was out last week trying to bring in a wyvern egg—very important to the Crown, wyvern eggs."

Dorie looked up at that. "Wyvern eggs?" she said, trying to look innocent. This is what she had just seen. But she could not think what would be so important about the eggs— except to the wyvern chick itself, of course.

Dr. Pearce wagged a finger at her. "You see what secrets you would be privy to if you came to work for us. Well, Wilberforce. He stumbled into a nest of the fey."

"But the fey don't attack unless provoked—"

"I wish I had your misplaced confidence," Dr. Pearce said. "The fey attacked, and in his escape Wilberforce stumbled into the clearing where his target nest lay. Alerted, the mated pair of wyverns attacked with steam and claws. He lost a significant amount of blood, part of his ear—and one eye."

"Goodness," murmured Dorie, because it seemed to be expected. "He must have been an idiot," which was not.

Dr. Pearce harrumphed and carried on. "So you see, your pretty blue eyes are far too valuable to risk in the field. Not that one cares to mention something as sordid as money"— and he took a piece of paper from his breast pocket and laid it on the desk so he could slide it over to her—"but as it happens, I think that you'll find that sum to be very adequate, and in fact, well more than the field work position would have paid."

Dorie barely glanced at the paper. Her tongue could not find any more pretty words; she could stare at him mutely or say the ones that beat against her lips. *"As it happens,* I have personal information on what your male field scientists get paid, and it is *more* than that number." It was a lie—but one she was certain was true.

Shock crossed his face—either that she would dare to question him, or that she would dare talk about money, she didn't know which.

Dorie stood, the violent movement knocking her chair backward. Her fey-infused hands were out and moving, helping the words, the wrong words, come pouring out of her mouth. *"As it happens,* I do not care to have my time wasted in this fashion. Look, if you did give me the field job and it didn't work out, you could always fire me. And what would you have wasted? A couple weeks."

Dr. Pearce stood, too, retrieving her chair. "And our reputation, for risking the safety of the fairer sex in such dangerous operations. No, I could not think of such a thing. You would need a guard with you wherever you went, and that would double the cost. Besides, I couldn't possibly ask one of our male scientists to be with you in the field, unchaperoned. . . ." His eyebrows rose significantly. "The Queen's Lab is above such scandal."

"Is that your final word on the subject?" Her long fingers made delicate turning motions; behind him the copper bolt on the glass cage wiggled free. The silver wyvern put one foot toward the door, then another.

"It is, sweetheart."

The triangular head poked through the opening as the glass door swung wide. Step by step . . .

"Thank you for your time then," Dorie said crisply. "Oh, and you might want to look into the safety equipment on your cages." She pointed behind him.

The expression on his face as he turned was priceless. Paternal condescension melted into shock as a yodeling teenage wyvern launched itself at his head. Dorie was not worried for his safety—the worst that could happen was a complete loss of dignity, and that was happening now.

"I'll see myself out, shall I?" said Dorie. She strolled to the office door and through, leaving it wide open for all to see Dr. Pearce squealing and batting at his hair as he ran around the wide, beautiful office.

Chapter 2

A CUNNING PLAN

Unless there is a strong leader to shape and mold them, the fey are not by nature violent. But they *are* very fond of pranks, especially when irritated. They don't seem to be able to help themselves—or more likely, don't want to. Many of the stories I gathered—from the humans, at least—are based around some particular fey who tipped over someone's butter churn once.

—Thomas Grimsby, *Collected Fey Tales* (foreword)

* * *

"He was just so . . . argh," said Dorie. "Argh!" She had spent the last coin in her purse on an ale at The Wet Pig and was making it last as long as possible while she drowned out the horrible Monday. "All those years at the University. All that time spent preparing for real interview questions. All those *actual* plans of what I want to *do* with the kind of work they're doing, and I didn't even get to *tell* anyone about my ideas to help people. I even told him about the work Jane and I did on spotted hallucinations last summer, and does he care? No! Argh!"

"Tell me again how you sicced the wyvern on him," said Jack, and she gestured with a bit of charcoal pencil. With her other hand, she smeared a chunk of fried fish through the vinegar on her plate and popped it into her mouth, licking her fingers. "In loving detail, please."

"So I could see that the bolt was copper, so I knew I could finesse it," said Dorie. She looked longingly at Jack's last piece of fish, but pride forbade her from begging her roommate for food. The mustard greens she had scavenged in the park would hold her until she could stop by those wild blackberry bushes by the pond on the way home from the bar. She went through the story one more time for her best friend, stopping to thoroughly capture the expression on the lab director's face. Dorie snickered, then stopped, a little worried. "Is it terribly cold-hearted of me to say that that was the best part of the day?"

"No, any human would say the same," Jack assured her.

Jack was the only friend Dorie had entrusted with her deepest secret—that she was half-fey. There were only a few people in the whole world who knew. But Jack had been an old family friend since Dorie was little, and back then Dorie wasn't always as good at keeping her secret as she was now.

Jack—Jacqueline—was the foster daughter of Alberta, a friend of Dorie's aunt Helen. Jack's parents had died abroad, and Jack had gone to live with her aunt Alberta, who had raised her as her own. Jack was attractive, with dark skin and curly dark hair that she kept cropped about an inch from her head, and she mostly got along with her aunt except that her aunt wanted her to be practical. Alberta had been a musician long ago, but had given it up when she took in Jack, in order to settle down and have a stable life. She had transferred into the business side of things, and worked fiendishly hard, worked her way up until now she owned one of the very nightclubs she used to perform in. It had a sterling reputation for booking the very best established musicians—it was not a place you went to hear what was new, but a place you would happily take the new girl you were wooing, or your fiancée's parents, and everything would be beautiful and perfect and unobjectionable. This was the business Alberta wanted Jack to take over.

Jack wanted to be an artist.

"Anyway, surely it wasn't the *only* good part of the day," Jack was saying. "Tea on the lap? Spiders down the collar?" She held up the sketch she had been making. It showed a cartoon of a curly-haired girl knocking a baboon across the room with her uppercut. "Of course, that's what you should have done." Dorie chuckled as Jack raised her pencil to the bartender. "Another round, please."

"No, wait. I'm flat," interjected Dorie. "Completely stinking goners. And the rent is five days past, and I still owe you my half from last time—"

Jack waved aside these objections. "We're too far in, Dorie. If I don't sell a good-sized piece at my show tomorrow—or you come up with some way to make the whole rent—it's curtains for us and I have to go back to my aunt, who'll say I told you so and then make me learn how to do sums so I can figure out how to get the best price on bulk orders of tuna fish." She pulled a note from her canvas bag and slapped it on the table. "I have a tenner to my name and that's only because I caved this morning and drew a dirty picture for that laddie pamphlet that keeps pestering me. It's blood money that can never be used for the rent and only be used for buying drinks and fried fish."

"Well, all right," said Dorie with resignation. "If we're up a creek without a paddle we might as well enjoy it." The two of them had been scrimping for years. Jack had won a scholarship to her art school, and Dorie's aunt Helen had paid for her tuition, as her own parents had no money. But that still meant plenty of odd jobs for both of them to pay for room and board. And now here they were, a month post-school, and everything had finally run out, right down to emptying the old vase they had been throwing pennies in to save against a rainy day. Dorie sighed, for Jack *was* talented, if she could just get her foot in the door. And as for her, researching things that could potentially save thousands of lives was plenty practical—if someone would just *let her do it.*

Dorie pointed to Jack's cartoon. "I want that for my bedroom wall." She downed the last of her drink and grinned. "You know, if I *had* done that, it would never have come back to haunt me. If there's a perk to being a girl that might be it. That boy would never, *never* tell."

"An unexplained rash of men walking into doorknobs sweeps the campus," said Jack dramatically, gesturing with her pad as though she were reading a newspaper headline.

"And I did get to see a wyvern hatch," said Dorie. "That was also pretty good. Except . . ."

"What?"

"Well, it's interesting," said Dorie. "The Queen's Lab is clearly using the eggshell for something. Or, rather, the goo left inside the eggshell, right as it hatches. But what? This isn't something I've ever heard of—at least not from the herbalists in the village."

"What about from the fey?" said Jack, who knew that Dorie had spent some time as a child going quite wild in the forest, studying the fey and just being with them. She did not know all the details, though.

"Fey don't like the wyverns much," Dorie said. "I don't remember them talking about them beyond that." She pondered.

"Makes me want to go into the forest and get an egg, so I can experiment. Except I hate the idea of taking the chicks away from their parents."

"Ugh," said Jack. "If you want to mess around with wyverns. Aren't they, like, the baby great-great-grandchildren of basilisks?"

"If they ever existed," said Dorie.

Jack's fingers flashed over the pad again. Dorie zoned out and thought about how she would catch a wyvern, until Jack held up the pad to show another cartoon of Dorie staring lovingly into an enormous basilisk's eyes, each of them with bugged-out eyes hypnotizing the other. Little hearts floated above their heads.

"You goon," Dorie said with love.

The waiter brought over their drinks—ale for Dorie and some gin thing for Jack. He was rather stout, and had a funny walk—one leg was held completely straight. It didn't cause him to spill the drinks, though—he was obviously used to it and swung his leg along with a practiced gait.

Jack busied herself with her sketchpad, looking tactfully away from the boy and his stiff leg, but Dorie stared openly. "What's wrong with your leg?" she said.

The waiter looked up, perhaps surprised that someone was speaking directly to him, and not about him or past him. He appeared to be early twenties like them, with a wide, friendly face, and a thatch of ginger hair. "Just a brace, miss," he said. He scooped up Jack's empty fish plate. "Can I bring you something else?"

"An *iron* brace," countered Dorie, for she had seen it where it rested in his boot top.

"Dorie," hissed Jack, meaning, *this is not appropriate human behavior.*

Dorie flushed. She had only added a little bit of her fey side back into the mix this morning. Was that enough to undo seven years of trying to be human? "My stepmother wore iron for a long time," she said softly to the boy. "Usually when people wear iron there's a reason."

The waiter looked surprised to be having this discussion, but not angry. Perhaps a little sad. He lowered his voice, glancing from side to side. "If you know what iron's for, miss, you know they don't like me talking about it. If I want to keep my job, that is." He raised his voice to normal pitch. "Would there be anything else then?"

Dorie put a hand on his arm. "I'm sorry," she said. "I just wanted to help."

He smiled ruefully. "After twenty-odd years living with it? You'd deserve a medal, you would."

"Just tell me," said Dorie. "What's yours?" *What's your curse,* she meant.

"Hunger," he said simply, and limped away.

Jack raised eyebrows at Dorie. "What the heck was that?"

"He's ironskin," Dorie said quietly. It was the old name for those who had been wounded in the Great War two decades ago. Hit by fey shrapnel that contained a bit of fey—which left behind scarring and a curse on the victim that could only be contained by iron. Her stepmother, Jane, had been scarred on her cheek and cursed with rage. Rage that infected others if she didn't cover it with iron—rage that infected Jane if she did. The poor boy must be hungry all the time. And two decades of it! There were not many ironskin left that she knew of. But the ones left had lived with their curses a long, long time.

Jack shuddered. "Could you fix him the way you fixed your mom?" she said in a low voice.

Dorie shook her head. "I wish. My father and I did that together and he doesn't have the ability anymore." Besides, her mother *still* had fey in her face, so that had hardly been a perfect solution. Dorie rubbed her fey-tinged fingers, wishing she could wash away the guilt she felt at the sight of the boy. Every day she found something new about the fey-human rift to feel guilty about. If the fey hadn't driven humans away from the forests, the old cures wouldn't have been forgotten. If the humans weren't polluting the rivers, the fey habitat would still be pristine. And now add the ironskin to her list of things to fix. She sighed. "Where were we?"

They were interrupted by an extremely tiny, extremely curvaceous blonde with a ponytail lugging over a stool from the wall, climbing up it, and plunking herself down next to Jack. The movement made Jack's gin teeter precariously near the edge of the heavy wooden table, and Dorie imperceptibly scooted it back with a mental nudge.

"Stella!" said Jack, squeezing the girl's shoulders. "You made it."

"Soooo many bed sheets to wash," groaned the girl. "I swear it's doubled in the last month. And during this heat wave, too! My hands are like sausages. Wrinkled red sausages. May I?" She swooped down on Jack's gin and took a hefty swallow. She took her ponytail down and fluffed her hair till her heavy bangs fell in a curtain over one eye, causing her to go from laundry girl to glamour girl in a blink. "Much better," Stella said, and yawned. "The hospital laundry will be the death of me."

"The hospital laundry plus calculus tutoring plus your maths degree will be the death of you," said Jack.

"Plus modeling for you," said Stella. She had a thin cardigan draped loosely on her shoulders for modesty in the streets—now she shrugged it off to reveal a white sleeveless button-down and coral choker. "Even though you don't pay me." She pulled out a lipstick that matched her choker and slicked it on.

"Yes, but I let you sleep on the job," said Jack. "I bet those teenagers you tutor can't say the same."

"You'd be surprised," said Stella. "I think I can factor in my sleep now." She yawned again and smiled at Dorie. "How were the interviews?"

"Ugh," said Dorie, and ran through the story one more time, this time with many more drunken asides from Jack. "At least the boy at the Queen's Lab came right out and told me that I wasn't going to get the job because I was female. The first two kept stringing me along while they tried to talk me into bed."

"And then—this," said Jack. "Well. Metaphorically." She held up the cartoon for Stella, who laughed appreciatively.

"So the Queen's Lab boy flat out told you they wouldn't hire a woman for *daaangerous* field work," mused Stella, lingering sarcastically on the word. "Everything else was perfect."

"As far as I know," said Dorie.

"So all you have to do is be a boy," Jack said. She was quite happily drunk now.

Stella clapped her hands, flipping her heavy bangs out of her face. "Yes, a boy, a boy! I did it for a lark at a fancy dress party once. Everyone was supposed to come as someone famous, you know, and I didn't want to be the twentieth Queen Maud. So I wrapped my chest in cloth and tied back my hair and came as her very tiny pirate. It was oodles of fun. I bet we could do you no problem and you'd make a fine figure."

Dorie laughed and waved this off. "And then what, I go

back to the Queen's Lab and pretend I didn't sic a wyvern on him?"

Stella pondered. "No, you'd have to go somewhere else, I suppose. Unless your lab director happens to be nearsighted I don't think you could quite pull that off."

"Ditto hot tea man and spider collar man," said Jack.

"Unless you could change your face," said Stella.

Across the table Jack raised an amused eyebrow at Dorie. A sharp shudder ran from Dorie's heels to her head. She *could* change her face. Jack had seen her do it. Dorie hadn't done it in years—not since she was a child and playing some practical jokes that went too far. She had determined when she was fifteen that she would put away that fey side of her for good. No more pranks, no more mischief. No more dancing lights or moving objects or shape-shifting.

Of course, she hadn't managed to keep that vow today.

"Nose putty," said Stella thoughtfully.

"A chin wart," said Jack.

"Glasses," said Stella.

"Is there anyone else you haven't pissed off?" said Jack.

"There is one person," Dorie said slowly. "It's not really a real position. And everyone knows not to go over there if you're a girl, because he's a perv. So I didn't talk to him or anything."

"Who is it?"

"Wild animal fancier named Malcolm Stilby," Dorie said. "Pays piecemeal for anything you'll bring him. The boys were always doing it to fill in the gaps during school. Bar tab too high? Find Malcolm a winged squirrel."

"What does he do with them?"

"Sells them to collectors, mostly," said Dorie. "But these aren't pets—they aren't used to being in captivity. They sicken and die even if he gives the collectors proper instructions, which I'm sure he doesn't. Honestly, I wouldn't want to work for him even if I were a boy, unless I didn't have any other options. But even if I *could* disguise myself as a boy, I wouldn't have a degree or any recommendations, so I couldn't go back to the places I was today. So that really would leave Malcolm, because of . . ."

"The rent," finished Jack.

"The rent," agreed Dorie. "Say, why don't you sell a dozen paintings tomorrow, and then this will be academic? I can mooch off of my rich artist friend."

"If I sell a dozen paintings," said Jack grandly, "you can mooch for the rest of the year."

Behind the saltshakers Dorie suddenly saw Stella's fingers clutch the table. The front door flew open behind Jack. Three men all in black burst through. Their faces were covered, but their hands were bare. They held up their palms, flashing the same silver sigils that Dorie had seen on the hands of the boys at the lab. An oval with a circle inscribed inside, like an eye. The pub went silent as the men peered around for their target. Then a clatter from a table behind them as some university boy tried to run for the back exit. The men were on him in a second.

Two of the men pressed their bare palms to his skin—one gripped his arm, one his neck. They bore the boy down to the wooden floor. The third whipped out a fine mesh net that twisted copper and silver in the dim light of the bar. Dorie could not get a fix on it. The third man spread the mesh over the boy's face and then added his palm to a spot on the boy's chest.

"What is this?" whispered Dorie, but Jack put a silent hand on hers. *Hush.*

The boy squirmed under their grip. Then abruptly, went limp, his head lolling at an unnatural angle. His skin grew paler and paler as a fine blue smoke coalesced between his mouth and the mesh. Working with more care now, the men gathered the mesh around the smoke, trapping it. But no, not smoke—Dorie knew all too well what must be escaping from the boy's dying body.

A fey.

The boy slipped from under the men's fingers as they concentrated on the mesh; he fell to the floor in a silent heap, bleached white. The blue fully trapped, one man packed away the mesh in a copper container; another threw the body over his shoulder.

Noise resumed as the men pushed out into the mild summer night.

Dorie's hand on her ale was shaking the glass. She was not sure if it was rage or fear. She put her hands under her thighs just in case and turned to Jack. "What. Was that."

"The silvermen have been everywhere since that Subversive Activities Act snuck through over the winter hols," said Jack. "You've been shut up inside working so hard the last half-year. And then out in the country all the weekends on your research. I'm not surprised you haven't seen it." Her dark eyes held meaning: *I didn't want to scare you.*

"Oh, but there's nothing to worry about," said Stella blithely, stealing one of Jack's fried potatoes and gesturing with it. "That boy was as good as dead already. Those silver hand things of theirs only work on fey that have taken over bodies. Not regular people."

"I see," said Dorie. "And what, exactly, are the fey doing back in the city?"

But she was met with blank looks from her two friends.

"I think we need another round," Jack said at last.

Dorie agreed that this was a good idea. Still, it was a long time before she felt comfortable enough to take her hands out from under her thighs and drink her ale.

The conversation turned to Jack's gallery opening on Tuesday night—Jack made the two of them cross hearts and swear to attend—then to Stella's summer classes, gossip about mutual friends. Though they had all been at the same prep school, they had been on different paths for the last several years—Jack and Dorie had just finished their degrees at the nearby art institute and an elite women's college, respectively. Stella was at the main university—one of two girls in the math department—and still had another year left, due to a gap year spent working as a governess.

After yet another round of stories about someone who had been told she couldn't have the job because she'd just get married and have babies, and someone else who was using her political science degree to governess for a toddler, Dorie suddenly burst out, "It's like nothing's changed. My stepmother is always saying you can do anything and you just have to get out there and show them. But then what do you do when you just hit that brick wall?"

"But so much *has* changed," Stella said. "Heck, ten years ago women couldn't even be at this university, even if ninety-nine percent of my classmates look at me like a statistical anomaly. And that's not even counting that time a couple decades ago where they stopped letting *dwarvven* in for a year."

"You're doubly blessed," said Jack.

"Five years ago Jack couldn't have gone to her art school," continued Stella.

"Trailblazing, as usual," said Jack. "The first year we had

separate life drawing classes for the women, where the male models kept towels draped modestly over their naughty bits."

"But somehow it's okay for the boys to draw naked girls all day."

"Finally there was a big revolt—"

"—led by a certain young lady named Jack—"

"—that involved a sudden surprise confiscation of all the towels," finished Jack. "Thank you, thank you."

"Plus ça change, plus c'est la même chose," said Dorie. "The more things change . . ."

"The more they don't," rejoined Stella. "Hey, did you hear Madame Martine ran off with our geometry teacher?"

"No! Remember his ear hair?"

"The ear hair! Remember the *nose* hair!"

Jack bought more rounds until the tenner ran out, and Stella called for one more, that Dorie declined. Unsteadily she rose to her feet. Maybe Simons and the world in general were right. You couldn't do anything as a girl, a girl who had to slink around for fear of being noticed. But if you had another option . . . were you wrong to try it? What if you could change things from the inside? "I think I'd better head home and crash," Dorie said.

"I'll come," said Jack.

"No, no, you two stay and have fun," said Dorie. She knew that was what Jack really wanted to do anyway. Besides, Dorie needed to be on her own for this. She hadn't done it in years. Seven years, to be exact. "I'll see you in the morning."

Dorie sat cross-legged in the tiny top-floor flat she shared with Jack. She rather liked living with an artist—though the flat was crammed full of canvases, jars of brushes, turpentiney rags, and so on, its fire-hazardy disarray reminded her of home. Her father had been a sculptor, once. His hands were stiff from a long-ago accident, but he hadn't been able to give up his artwork entirely. He painted in oils on the top floor of their drafty house, and the studio was crammed with the same sights and smells as here.

Moonlight streamed through the thin sheet Jack had hung for a curtain. The window was open to the cool summer night, and the breeze blew away the lingering heat in the apartment.

Dorie went to her room. Pulled out a locked box of copper she kept secreted at the bottom of a trunk. On a long necklace hidden inside her blouse was the copper key. In seven years, she had not opened this box till this very morning, when she had cracked the lid a fraction and slid the tips of her fingers inside, hoping somehow it would bring her luck.

She unlocked the copper box now, flipped open the lid with enough force that it clanged against the outside of the box. The dense concentrated blue seemed to vibrate with its stored energy. Light streamed onto her face, her chest, her hands.

Her light. Her self.

Her missing half.

Perhaps she had always known that, once she tasted the addiction again, there would be no turning back.

Dorie plunged her hands into the box.

Chapter 3

COMPLETE AGAIN

How do you live with half of yourself missing? Is it like the pain of losing a brother, a child? How can you stand to diminish yourself, and then bear up under that self-punishment for seven years? The only possible answer is that it must be an atonement.

—Thomas Lane Grimsby, *Silverblind: The Story of Adora Rochart*

* * *

The blue flooded through Dorie, plummeting her, ricocheting from finger to knee to ear to toe. She felt powerful, alive. She felt as if she had been a covered plant, coiled and white without the sun. She felt as if she had had a seven-year-cold that dampened her taste and smell and touch. She felt as if she had not truly breathed in a long, long time.

In wonderment she stretched out her hand. The little pranks this morning were nothing now—jostling a teacup, nudging a bolt to fall. She had been able to do those things as a child. Now she crooked a finger and her entire bed on its heavy wooden frame sprang lightly up to the ceiling. Strange, hysterical laughter burst forth, and the bed wobbled in her mental grasp, the bedclothes sliding off and knocking over the apple crate that doubled as her bedside table. The thump of the box falling, her books sliding, registered only from a distance. Her ears and eyes were buzzing with the joy and blue that surged through her, and she made the bed right itself and spin a circle that tangled with the thin curtains, ripping one of them free.

A banging on the door recalled her. The cross, wheezy voice of their landlady: "What are you two girls doing in there?"

Hastily Dorie set the bed down—mostly in the right place— and ran to the door. She was shining blue with her self, her self, how she loved her whole self, and she stopped as she reached her shining blue hands for the doorknob, stopped herself and said as meekly as possible, "I'm sorry, Miss Bates, I knocked over a table on my way to bed. It won't happen again."

"See that it doesn't" was the rejoinder, but slow footsteps indicated the landlady was shuffling away. Dorie could hear the footsteps all the way down the stairs, all the way to the landlady's rooms, and she wondered how she had managed to track anything in the forest in the last seven years. Why, she had hardly been alive!

Dorie closed her eyes and breathed, trying to calm herself. There was a reason she had asked the fey how to extract her fey side, how to lock it away. She could not be trusted with the power. If she was going to do this, she had to hope that she had learned some measure of self-control in the last seven years. No, more than hope. She pounded a blue fist into her palm. She had to be damn well sure.

There was a reason she was letting her fey side free. And that was to disguise herself as a boy, so she could get that field work position. So she could pursue her goals, so she could help the poor and sick in the city. As her stepmother, Jane, was always saying: those in power had an interest in keeping things that way. That's why Jane was marching with the nurses trying to unionize, though the regular insults of "mannishness" were being hurled at them, as they were with most of the causes Jane joined. Her aunt Helen, too, worked for social justice, but for her own reasons and in her own way. Helen was much more empathetic than Jane or Dorie, apt to pick up a new cause because she had met some poor single mother facing it. And then, her method was to use her social and political connections to make changes at the top. Jane was always there in the trenches, fighting. Dorie despaired, sometimes, at the thought of living up to either one of them. She believed in their work, but she could not imagine putting herself out there so . . . openly.

Her brains. Her skills. And in secret. It was all very well for Helen and Jane to boldly put their faces and names on the line. But Dorie had something to hide.

And if she had to be a boy to do it, so be it.

In the moonlight she stretched out her hand.

What would a boy's hand look like?

She did not have any male friends—no truly close friends at all beyond Jack. She had had a few casual female friends at their boarding school, of course. Stella was the closest of those, but . . . Hard to have close friendships when you had an impossible secret. There was her cousin Tam, of course. But she hadn't seen him for seven years, not since the day she locked away half of herself. No matter. She did not want to look like a fifteen-year-old boy.

The moonlight picked out one of Jack's figure studies and Dorie jumped up. Of course. Not these, though—these were recent. Not good to look even remotely like someone she could run into in the next day. She went to her roommate's bedroom, where figure studies from her time in Varee were pinned to the wall—thanked her stars that Jack was not into modern art, but instead split her time between cartooning and beautifully rendered studies of people. She examined the latter until she found a largish pen-and-ink of a nondescript boy, fine-boned and thin. She studied it, thinking, there it is then. You lengthen the fingers, thicken the wrists . . .

In the moonlight her right hand reshaped itself until it had a more manly heft. As Dorie, her nails stayed long and perfectly manicured no matter how she bit and broke them; now she forcibly shortened them back to the finger. She looked at that hand, memorizing it, and then she set about to do the other.

It was hard, keeping the right hand changed while focusing on the left. She had done this years ago, but it was a tricky mental game, and she had not practiced in nearly a decade. She remembered from experience that if she practiced one particular look, it would begin to get easier to stay in the form without suddenly bursting out. But she did not remember how long it took to get that ease, and she could already feel the mental effort of holding one hand steady while she did the next, like a juggler twirling plates.

Dorie finished the left hand and looked at them both. Once complete, it was not much more difficult to hold two hands than one. She could recognize the pattern for both, reversed, sitting lightly in her mind. She held on to it as she stripped down to do the arms, the legs. Every inch—yes, every inch— until she came to the face. She stopped and looked in Jack's cracked mirror as she did that, sharpening the cheekbones, changing the shape of her nose and the thrust of her brow. In an odd way it was like sculpting, like her father used to do, except now she was the clay. She made her face less symmetrical than it usually was, a little rougher. She normally didn't tan, or burn, but she darkened her skin a shade now to look more outdoorsy. Chopped off her hair and colored it black. She had tried physically cutting her ringlets before, but when they had grown back overnight she had given up on the idea. She had not thought to simply transform them, back long ago when she had had the power. Of course, it was going to take an effort. She could tell. Every nerve strung alive with the balancing act as she looked at the boy in the mirror. Like a string of dominoes—if she let anything flip back to girl it would start a ripple effect; it would all fall down.

Carefully Dorie walked around the room, feeling her new center of gravity, keeping all her limbs intact. She felt as though she were a thin membrane holding back an ocean. She walked around until she was looking at the mirror again. Was that a boy who people would trust? Who the lab would accept? Was that a boy who could do things?

A cynical laugh slipped out into the moonlit bedroom. She was a *boy*—that was enough. They would actually look at her references. They would believe her when she said she could climb trees. They wouldn't tell her she couldn't risk her pretty eyes in the field.

There was a funny sense of rightness to her new face. It wasn't that she wanted to be a boy, but she had never felt right in the blond doll shape given her—the face that was unlike anyone she was related to. The face that never showed anything she did, good or bad—no sun, no scars, no laugh lines. This boy had character to his face. This boy looked like her family.

She had given him a thatch of wild black hair like her father's. A quirky, amused smile like her uncle Rook's—so what if they weren't technically related. Her nose—*his* nose had a very slight bump, as if he had been in a fistfight as a teenager. (She had.) It was too difficult to change her eyes, so they were still large and blue, but she shrunk the heavy lashes on them. She remembered how she had fallen from a tree when she was eight and in the woods with the fey, and not thought to turn blue herself on the way down. She had gashed her shin and broken her leg. The fey had mocked her, laughing, and showed her how to phase out and fix it herself. She had unthinkingly left the scar on her shin that day, but the next morning when she woke up her skin was clean and unblemished.

She put the scar back in now. Drew it from her knee, halfway down her shin, a long diagonal line. Her uncle's amused smile crept over her lips as she looked at her leg in the mirror.

She thought about modifying the face still more to look like her father, but then she thought better of it. Better to have her heritage be unidentifiable, so she could make it up. She would need a name, though. . . .

The door opened and Jack stumbled in, fumbling for a light. Her voice drifted out in song as she came closer. "Singing cockles and mussels alive, alive-oh—oh. Oh. Who are you? No. No!" She came and put her hands on Dorie's shoulders, laughing hysterically. "And I thought you were just going to cut your hair. It is you, isn't it? You're Dorie, aren't you? Else there is a very naked boy standing in my bedroom, looking like the cat who swallowed the canary. Who are you?"

Dorie's lips curved in her uncle's wry grin. "Dorian," she said.

Dorian Eliot rapped on the massive double doors the next morning, heart in mouth. She had thought she wouldn't have much *girl* to eradicate—but there were more things than she realized. More than just crossing her legs at the knee instead of the ankle. Or not crossing them at all and slouching down, taking up two seats on the trolley. Men did not care so much whether they took more than their fair share of something. They did not automatically stay on the edge of the sidewalk so others could pass. Dorie had spent the last seven years trying to blend in with what other human girls did. She was surprised to find how many of those things were specifically *girl* and not just *human*. Now she was going to have to unlearn all of those, because if you did any of those weakening maneuvers as a man, you became an obvious target.

It was still early, but it was going to be another scorcher. She was glad when a butler in tails motioned her into the cool drawing room. The interior was every bit as gaudy as the showy exterior had suggested. The house was not overly large, but what it lacked for in size it made up in peacockery. It was covered within an inch of its life with wood paneling, tapestries, oil paintings, gilt leaf woodwork. . . . The oil paintings and tapestries were divided neatly into two subjects: exotic animals and barely dressed girls. Her newly returned fey senses were overwhelmed by the scents: tobacco and sandalwood and cloves. It was a heady, dizzy feeling. She curled her lip at the excess. Malcolm hadn't even been obnoxious in person yet and already she wanted to pick up all his possessions in a whirlwind and send them out onto the street. Just one of those tapestries could feed a family of four for several months.

Out of habit, she scoped the room for anything edible, but all she found was a bowl of three lonely hard candies on an end table, next to a thick book wrapped in protective leather binding, tooled in gold. She took two of the candies anyway, then flicked open the book to a random page. "It is out of fashion for learned men to believe in basilisks. The only skeleton extant is dismissed as an overgrown wyvern. But in the small towns nestled in the mountains, the legend of the basilisk is very much real. . . ."

A squawk behind her and she jumped, letting the book fall closed as she turned around. A large purple and scarlet parrot sat on a golden stand in the corner, its brilliant feathers blending into the riot of color in the room. "Pretty girl," it said. "Pretty girl."

Dorie's skin crawled. "Hush," she said. She walked closer, studying its cocked head, its inquisitive eyes.

"Feed me? Pretty girl."

A noise from the doorway made her turn. A man who could only be Malcolm Stilby stood there. He was quite average looking—a bit thin and pasty—yawning in a splendiferous lounging robe embroidered with birds of paradise. He laughed at her discomfort. "He says that to everybody. Amusing, no? I've had men threaten to punch me for it." He shrugged. "It's just a bird."

Dorie straightened. "I hear you pay for animals," she said in her gruffest, most manly voice. She had modified her vocal cords as well, so she could not accidentally slip up and talk in treble. Nervously she wiped her palms on her trousers—Jack had borrowed clothes from a male friend for her—and held out her hand. "Name's Dorian Eliot." Malcolm kept his eyebrows raised, a carefully blank expression on his face, and she thought, oh, hell, what did I do wrong? Her mind raced, and then suddenly she remembered to add: "Fitzhaber sent me."

"Good, good," Malcolm said, finally shaking her hand. "Can't be too careful these days. Not technically illegal, but the silvermen are always looking for an excuse to shut me down under Subversive Activities. Jealous, I say. Birds in cages getcha birds on couches, ya know? But I envy you university men. A campus full of coeds these days, you get all the birds you want, eh?" He held out a wooden box and extracted himself a cigarette from it. "Last time Fitzhaber came we sat on this couch until three a.m. drinking whiskey and talking about his campus conquests. Really takes me back, ya know? Fancy a smoke?"

"No thanks," she said, wishing he would offer her a snack instead. It would almost make it worthwhile to be here. She had not known how uncomfortable it would be to listen to this kind of thing. This wasn't true of all men, was it? Was this what she would encounter from day to day? It would be a rough haul if so. But Dorian came from nowhere. He didn't have the credentials to waltz into the Queen's Lab. She was going to have to work her way up.

Malcolm did not seem put off by her unwillingness to spill the beans about the girls at school. Perhaps he figured it was only a matter of time and whiskey. From his dressing gown pocket he produced a bit of paper with penciled figures scrawled on it. "The list I give to all you chaps," he said. "Current pricing for horns and eggs and so on—subject to change, of course! Ya never know when the market abroad is gonna decide that ground-up *tortua* shells don't give them the . . . potency . . . they were hoping for, eh? And what would I do with a roomful of shells then. Certainly I got all the potency I need, but maybe you could use some, eh? Skinny-looking chap like you?"

"Right. The list. Got it," said Dorie. She turned to go. The contrast between this man and the Queen's Lab was stark and humiliating. Her top marks, her careful letters of recommendation—none of it mattered now. All that mattered was that she was a boy, and the magic words "Fitzhaber sent me." It's a job, she told herself. No worse than Jack drawing nudie pics. (Blood money.) It will pay the rent. Bring him some cast-offs, feathers and shed skins, that you don't mind getting for him. And then, you can use this to work your way up, until what matters again is your brain and your skill, what Jane always promised would be true.

"But never mind the list for right now, really," Malcolm said as she started for the door. "Keep it for next month. I've told everyone there's a two-week moratorium on everything on that list. What I really want are wyvern eggs."

Her heart sank. "*Live* eggs?"

"Yes, yes. Focus on wyvern eggs and don't bring me any damn other thing. The Queen's Lab is trying to corner the market on them—can't have that. We got just as much right to their benefits as anyone else."

Her attention sharpened. At least maybe she could find out what they were for. "Yes, those properties are interesting, aren't they?" she said, trying to draw him out. "I was just in the Queen's Lab the other day watching one hatch."

He took an eager step closer, and she tried not to back up. "In the Queen's Lab? I hear they have a machine for extracting the goo. Tell me, ya think it keeps it any fresher than scooping it out with a copper spoon?"

"I don't know," she admitted. She kept her stance wide and casual. "Does it really go bad that fast?"

"I'm told it stops working after a few minutes," he said. "I haven't tried one myself—get more money out of selling them *before* they hatch, obviously. But I sold one on to this blacksmith, and he's got one of the blue devils captured, and he said it only works on them within the first few minutes. Then it's no good; might as well be a chicken egg for all the good it does."

Dorie went cold from her head to her toes. Blue devils—that was fey, of course. Her voice croaked as she said, "What do you mean—*works?*"

"Well, kills them, of course. That's what this run on them is all about. Pure poison to fey." Malcolm took a long draw on his cigarette and said, "Well, look, Dorian. You bring me wyvern eggs and I'll pay you well, you understand? Don't worry if you have to take down the adults to get it. Eggs are what's important." He pointed at the number on the sheet. "Take that and double it."

Dorie shook with fear and rage as she trailed him to the door. Her fingers jerked out—a table ten feet away wobbled, its contents shaking. She managed to still it before he noticed. She twisted her fingers together to stop herself from destroying his library in a tornado of splintering rage. That would not help make the rent. "And nothing else?" she said tightly. "No hartbird feathers right now? Cast-off hydra skins?" Anything but live wyvern eggs.

"Bah," Malcolm said. A trail of smoke drifted behind him as he showed her out. "Got all the damn feathers I need. Come back soon and show me what you're made of." He pointed a finger at her. "You, me, whiskey, girls. I think highly of my boys who work for me. We have a grand old time."

"Glad to hear it," said Dorie. It was not quite a spit.

He smiled as she went numbly down the steps, fingers interlaced. "Just remember, Dorian. Wyvern eggs or nothing."

Chapter 4

STALKING THE WYVERN

In a small town out east I found the first sign of a connection between wyverns and fey. Here, it was well known that a wyvern egg, cracked by the light of the full moon and buried in your yard, would stop the fey from coming past your gate. (That the sheer difficulty of procuring wyvern eggs made this superstition impossible to test was considered rather beside the point.) But two towns to the north I found the corroboration in an attic, in an ancient set of decaying notebooks from the town's former wisewoman: *1 swallowe of the juice of the wyvern egg will kill the fey inside you,* it said. *But the remedie must be applied within 5 minutes of cracking the egg.*

—Thomas Grimsby, "Wyverns: The Fey Antidote?"
Collected Fey Tales

* * *

There was a reason everyone was paying so darn well for wyvern eggs, beside their recently discovered value. Wyverns were cranky, skittish, and elusive. They were devoted parents and kept a sharp eye on their nests. Dorie really had no idea how anyone had managed to get any eggs at all—it was nearly impossible to get close to the wary animals unless you were fey.

And Dorie was only half.

After leaving Malcolm's, she had hitched out as far as the major country road would take her. Then it was still a good trek up the side road that led into the forest that covered the base of Black Rock Mountain. Thankfully the higher she went, the cooler it became. The mountain was carpeted thickly in evergreens: tall fir and juniper and soft spruce. She had last been out here a year ago, tracking down some feywort for a sick friend in the history department. It was widely known as the best place to find wyverns—generally meaning, the place you most wanted to avoid during hatching season. The nesting wyverns could steam you with pinpoint accuracy—and would.

She was still in guise as Dorian, as only practice would make that shape perfect. Better to slip up while alone in the wilderness, rather than in the city. She stepped as carefully through the forest as twenty-two years of woodscraft and being half-human could let her, moving from stick to stick with no more sound than a falling leaf. Removing her fey side seven years ago had left her suddenly dependent on ordinary human senses and skills, and, frustrated, she had sharpened those to bring them back as close as she could to half-fey.

Now, with her fey side filling her bones, she felt bright as light, stunning, invincible. The pine smell filled her nostrils, and she could sense every robin, every sparrow, every tiny goldwing moth for several paces in every direction. It fizzled her head like wine. She had to remember how to let those senses fade out and focus on what was in front of her.

There was a clear track that the others must have been using—well, perhaps not clear to ordinary eyes, but as clear as a paved highway to Dorie. A flash of silver wing up ahead—she was close. She crouched to wait, to watch. There was a clump of wild sorrel by her feet, and she absent-mindedly plucked a handful of the sour leaves. It was definitely time for second breakfast. She had found the wyvern, but she still needed to find his nest. Silently she moved closer still—

—and the wyvern, alerted by who knows what, startled just enough to flit several trees farther on. It peered around, head cocked and angling with some sixth sense.

Damn.

Dorie sighed and rubbed her forehead. She still hadn't decided if she could really go through with taking that odious man a live wyvern egg. A live wyvern egg whose contents just happened to be deadly to half of her family tree. But the amount he was paying for one single egg would exactly cover their month's rent. And that would buy them a whole month, in which Jack might sell some paintings after her gallery opening tonight, or Dorie might find another job with her new-found boyness.

So, first things first, she had decided. Better see if she could put her money where her mouth was and obtain an egg at all. Decide once the egg was in her grasp what she should do. Maybe there was a third option she hadn't seen yet. Once she got the egg—*if* she got the egg.

But she was pretty sure she could. Especially now that she had her fey talents back.

Dorie's half-human, half-fey heritage made for an interesting mix of abilities. It was hard for true fey to hold a human shape for more than a few minutes. That was why, during the Great War two decades ago, they had killed humans with fey-infused shrapnel—then slipped in to reanimate the dead bodies. Most people died from the poisoned shrapnel. The few that hadn't—the ironskin—often wished they had. Later still the fey had figured out a way to purposefully attach part of themselves to living humans—and take them over.

Dorie couldn't take over anybody at all—not that she wanted to. But with her fey side back, she could change herself.

And more than just shape-shifting into Dorian. She could make herself be more like the smoky blue fey of her ancestry.

She did so now, thinning her substance until she was part blue, part human. Only half there on the ground. It was as far as she could go . . . but it should be far enough to get her close to the wyvern. It was like slipping into an old, familiar bathrobe. In this half-state she could get close to creatures everyone else only dreamed of getting near. She had frequently watched wyverns as a kid—just never tried to snatch their eggs.

The world went fuzzy as she thinned. Colors changed and mutated—some perceptions expanded; others went dim. She waited now until the wyvern calmed down enough to hop a few more trees over, finding its mate and changing places on the important eggs.

Dorie could now sense humans at a distance near the edges of the forest, fuzzy warm red blurs around the edges of her sight—though her senses were no longer quite the same as a human's. "Sight" was an approximation. There were fey, too, blue and cold and deeper in. She could vaguely "hear" them talking with each other on some wavelength that wasn't quite like human sound. Not that fey really talked. It was more like feeling.

But the key perception that changed, she remembered now, was her sense of time. Fey were ancient, and they did not sense time in quite the same way as humans. Everything sped up around her, while she slowed. She had the patience necessary to move quietly up to the wyvern, one centimeter at a time, not disturbing its quiet nesting.

She stopped a few feet from it, her body half-tangled with a tree, watching. Wyverns had been thought extinct before the Great War, but in recent years more and more of them had been spotted. She could not figure out how the researchers at the Queen's Lab had discovered the properties of the wyvern eggs, but the information was certainly moving quickly through the city, to judge by Malcolm. So much for Simons's puffed-up sense of secrecy.

Dorie watched the wyvern move and rustle, first slow, then fast, as she drifted in and out of the fey time sense. The morning ticked on. Any moment it would stand to stretch, spread its wings, sit back down. It was the perfect time to slide in with all the grace and speed of the fey—grab and be gone before it even noticed.

It started to stand—she pulled on her fey half, slowed all her senses down to a halt. Moved with sudden speed to the tree, where as it stood she saw that it had a clutch of three eggs. Good. She did not want to take its only egg. Her fingers slipped through the air, grasped one of the eggs, warm and slightly rough in her hand, pulled it free of the nest. A rush of glee spread from her fingertips, trickled up to her spine with an electric tingle, a mad rush, and she grinned. She was doing it. She was alive. Everything was brilliant.

It sensed her.

She was, after all, only half-fey, and it turned to stare at her with those liquidly hypnotic eyes. Adults were much darker than the babies; its pewter scales glinted like steel, like polished stone. Dorie felt as caught as a rat or bird. Surely she could break free from this, she thought, and yet somehow she did not want to. Her hand was half-hidden by the nest and she could not tell if the wyvern knew she was clutching its egg or not. Through tremendous will she slowly moved her hand holding the egg down to around her belly, where the pouch would be when she phased back in. It was like moving through molasses. Her mind lingered on the fact that wyverns were said to be related to basilisks, who supposedly had been able to kill you with a glance.

The wyvern cocked its head, studying her, watching her feeble attempt to get away. But it did not pounce, and she thought perhaps her fey side was standing up to the strain of its hypnotism. She did not know how long they stayed there, locked in connection with each other, neither one able to definitively make a move.

But the wyvern had more experience in the matter. It moved closer, its three iron grey talons creeping over the nest—and then something else caught its attention. A red blur that her fey senses knew meant *human,* creeping up from the side, hand ready to go into the nest. The red blur was . . . whistling?

Quicker than any human the wyvern's head turned, the steam boiling out in an arc toward the human's face.

Quicker than any human Dorie took that split second of the broken connection to *move,* to throw herself on the explorer who was about to get his face melted.

The searing-hot steam shot directly over her head as the two of them fell. She lost all her feyshift as they tumbled, cracking down hard on branches and bushes. Her hazy human impressions told her only that it was some guy she was falling hard on, some guy with a foraging pack that was now digging into her ribs as they finished landing, tangled in a clump of some sort of low but very poky evergreen. She closed her eyes against the prickles and rolled, not daring to feyshift to ease her way. Then she sat up, pulling green things out of her collar and looking desperately around for the egg. It was not in her hand.

From the middle of the bush came an oath so mild it could hardly count as one. "Criminy," said a woozy male voice. It put a lot of feeling into it, however.

The danger past, the prickles present, Dorie stood, thoroughly annoyed that someone was bungling her mission. "That was my egg, dammit," she said. She *needed* it, and this clod was probably some idiotic bounty hunter competing with her for Malcolm's money, certain he could pay off a sizable bar tab doing the impossible. The wyvern was standing now, wings spread, rocking back and forth and ready to shoot another bolt of steam if need be. She smacked the branches of the evergreen aside to see who had interrupted her quest, ready to lay a round of scathing abuse on the boy in the bushes—and froze. Her mouth opened with surprise to say—"Tam?" and then she saw how he clutched his arm, and she forgot to say anything at all.

She sunk down next to him, supporting his shoulders as he tried to sit up. He was looking at his reddened forearm, already blistering from the steam, and she took the opportunity to feel delicately all around the back of his skull, checking for lumps or blood.

"Criminy," he swore again, and she swallowed to keep from laughing, or perhaps crying, because that had been the most he would swear the last time she had seen him—when he was fifteen.

Seven years ago.

Tam looked straight at her. His wire-rimmed glasses were bent and dangling on one ear, and his wild mop of hair had escaped his hat. "You don't have any butter on you, do you?" he said. "It's good for burns."

"No," she said, and bit off a laugh. Only Tam would ask her for butter in a forest.

He grabbed her arm then and said intently, "You saved my life. Thank you."

So many things crowded her thoughts to say to him that what came out was the most banal: "I could find you some calendula for that burn, but you'd still have to steep it." Her face flamed as he let go of her arm, for he didn't recognize her. And surely he would, any moment, as soon as the shock wore off. And then . . . what? Would she be forgiven, the stupid things you did as kids forgotten? Or would he turn and go, and avoid her at every family event ever, and she wouldn't see him for another decade? Tam straightened out his glasses and retrieved his hat. He bent back to his arm, his battered old explorer hat (surely not the same one from back then!) now tipped down and shading his eyes. It rather floored her how he could look all grown up and still just the same, that same sweet, studious boy she had played with for so many years. She had seen pictures of him now and then—they were cousins in name if not one bit in blood—but not *him*. Not in the flesh.

Tam carefully peeled his damp cotton sleeve back from the rest of the burn, and she made a small noise in her throat at the sight. "Oh yes, *calendula incantata*," he said. "It is fairly good." He looked vaguely off into the distance. "Usually I burn myself on the toast and then butter is handiest, you see? Criminy."

"You can swear around me," Dorie said. "I don't mind."

"I never quite got into the habit," Tam said absently. "My father didn't care for it."

Dorie snorted. "What, when you were five?" His parents had both died when he was young, and she couldn't imagine his adoptive father, Rook, caring about swear words.

The vague look faded as he peered at her intently through his wire-rimmed glasses. "Yes, when I was five. How did you know that?"

Dorie was starting to feel annoyed that he still didn't recognize her. The stress of waiting for his reaction was weighing on her. Get it over with, already. Besides, how could he *not* know her? Seven years or no, she knew—much to her chagrin—that she still looked like that perfect china doll she had as a child. Blue eyes, pink cheeks, blond ringlets that grew back overnight even if she dyed them green and shaved half of them off . . . unconsciously her hand went up to touch one of those ringlets . . . and stopped. "I am a fool," she said in a low voice. "A complete fool."

Tam poured a bit of water over the blisters, then took a clean cloth from a pouch at his waist and began to cover the burn to keep it protected. "It's not your fault. I was testing out this story I ran across that wyverns could be tamed by whistling. Man swore up and down that his grandfather used to walk right up to full-grown wyverns by whistling the Danse in E Minor from the Midsomer Suite." He laughed ruefully. "It probably was a bit risky. Anyway. Rather my arm than my face, and I have you to thank for that. In a moment I would have been steamed pudding."

Oh no, it wasn't that she had aged. It wasn't anything like that.

She was shaped as Dorian.

Dorie plopped down on the forest floor next to Tam, took the cloth that he was vainly trying to knot with one hand. "Let me," she said. Her heartbeat slowed as she realized she was safe for a moment, that she could learn about what he'd been doing without risking finding out that he still hated her. Above them the silver wyvern settled back into its nest, not steaming them, but still on guard. Dorie carefully wrapped the cloth around Tam's forearm, her fey-enhanced senses picking up the scents of clean sweat and dirt. He had his sleeves rolled up and it was clear that, despite the spectacles and the absentminded professor air, he was rather more muscled than he had been at fifteen.

To distract herself from that she cast around for some small talk, and came up with: "Whistling?"

He answered her with a very creditable performance of a tricky bit from the well-known suite. The wyvern did, in fact, settle down, though it kept a watchful eye on them. Tam looked thoughtfully at it. "The thing is, there's often something to these old wives' tales," he murmured, and he pulled a faded leather journal from his vest pocket and began scribbling. "If I hadn't been rummaging around old attics in ancient crumbly houses, I wouldn't have my current job."

"Which is . . . ?" said Dorie, but she knew the instant he said it.

"Field work. For the Queen's Lab."

Dorie barked laughter. So she *had* seen him yesterday—it wasn't wishful thinking playing tricks on her. Tam looked sideways at her. "Nothing," she said. "Only I applied there"—ah, best not to mention yesterday. "Awhile ago," she finished. "After University."

"It's tough to get in," Tam agreed. "They only wanted me for my book—thought I was too scatterbrained for the field. I had to produce two copperhead hydras and a winged squirrel before they believed I could do the field work, and they still think I'm going to bolt into the nearest attic at a moment's notice." He shrugged ruefully. "Which I might." He looked up at the wyvern, which was watching them intently.

"Still doesn't help me with wyvern eggs. I don't know how anyone does it without getting fried to a crisp."

"They kill them," Dorie said bluntly, going off what Malcolm had intimated.

His kind face darkened. "Barbaric, troglodyte, stupid, stupid fools," he said, and he infused the epithet with enough venom to make it sound like a swear. "There's not an infinite supply."

Dorie shrugged. The topic made the blood boil in her veins, and she was unsurprised that it would do the same to Tam. She sat down, straightening out her boy's field jacket. There was a strange little lump in her belly.

His eyes narrowed behind his specs. "That explains how Henderson suddenly started coming back with more eggs. I told him it wasn't a contest. . . ." He suddenly pounded the ground with his good hand, his eyes growing wild. "I should never have taken this job. I need the freedom to pounce on whatever I find. And here they have me with a minder and metrics and—" His eyes unfocused as he stared off at something she couldn't see. "The woods are strange lately. First I saw a flight of purple swallowtails, and they're usually much farther north this time of summer. Then a clutch of yellow garter snakes I'd never seen before. That kind of pattern disruption is one of the signs, and yet—" He broke off. "Have you seen anything . . . big . . . recently?"

Dorie shook her head. "But I haven't been here recently." She ran her fingers over the lump in her belly, feeling it out.

He shook his head. "Old Pearcey is all 'wyverns wyverns wyverns', but I've half a mind to skive off wyvern-hunting for a day and whistle up the fey to ask them about it."

Dorie started at that. "You would . . . talk to the fey?" she said. "Willingly?"

The wyvern was restless, and Tam whistled again before he answered, something slow and mournful from the suite. "Sometimes more willingly than others," he said, staring up the mountain. "But I don't blame the fey for that."

Behind him, Dorie flushed again, and her fingers felt hot and numb. Any thought that she would reveal herself to him, that she would find he had forgiven her, was gone now.

He was obliquely referring to *her*.

To the summer seven years ago when she had traded him to the fey.

It did not matter that she had been fifteen, that she had not meant it all to go the way it happened. It did not matter how much she had tried to atone since then. What mattered is that unforgivable things were unforgivable.

Dorie listened to his melody until it ran out, and she thought of just turning and running. Seven years was not enough time to face up to this. But Tam turned before she could make any kind of decision, and in a normal voice he said, "At any rate, the lab would never know. After all, everyone *knows* it takes scads of time to track down eggs."

The distraction shocked her from her fugue. That's what the lump in her belly was. The egg. She had saved it after all. It had remained in her belly as she phased back into human form, as she tumbled from the tree.

Dorie ran her fingers over the lump, feeling it with great surprise. It made a hard little shape in there. A strange kind of pregnancy, for this girl who looked like a boy—and an ironic smile twisted on her face. What if she circumvented her whole dilemma with Malcolm Stilby, and gave Tam the egg? She was suddenly struck that perhaps she could use the egg to make amends. Tam could take it back to the lab, be the hero for a day.

But no. How would one egg, one day of praise, make up for what she had done to him? Her guilt was too big to atone, or at least, she had not figured out how to atone for it yet. There was something still to come.

Dorie let her skin go soft and blue under her shirt, pulled the egg free as if she was pulling it from a hidden pouch. "Pretty thing," she said softly to it.

Tam's face brightened. "You *did* get it! I'm impressed. Look, if it's just money you want, they'll pay you for it. We're making great strides studying what can be done with the eggs when they hatch."

Her spirits rose. Maybe this would be a good way out of her dilemma. "How much?" she said. Tam named a figure that was Malcolm's old going rate—i.e., half what he was now paying—and she pondered that. Perhaps their landlady would take that in good faith ... or if Tam left, she could phase into fey state, climb the tree and take a second egg, though she hated to do that to the wyvern pair.

"It's a fair rate," Tam added. "I'd make sure they didn't try to talk you down."

Dorie ran her fingers over the raised, glittery surface, thinking. She needed the money. She didn't want to sell to Malcolm. But what if she could parlay this one egg into a better future? "It's not money I want," she said slowly.

Tam looked puzzled, then lit up. "Oh. You want a job at the Queen's Lab." He leaned in. "Look, Killingsworth just left. Well, not left ..."

Dorie's eyebrows rose.

"Tangled up with a giant *tortua* while overseas," he admitted. "Came back with several bits missing. He'll be learning how to walk for a year. It's perfect timing." He pointed at the silver egg. "Let me see how close it is to hatching. It looks like it's started to darken a bit. A day, don't you think?"

"Less," said Dorie, relying on her fey intuition. She couldn't have said how she knew, only that she could tell from the way it thrummed in her hand.

"You bring that in this afternoon and I can nearly guarantee you Killingsworth's old job. At least for temporary—but you'd have a year to prove yourself and I don't see why you couldn't. I mean, heck, I didn't even see you up in that tree when I arrived, that's how good you were."

Breath caught. The Queen's Lab. Her, Dorie—*Dorian,* but small matter, she could proudly reveal herself to Dr. Pearce well *after* she had brought everyone around to her way of doing things. She briefly entertained a fantasy of leading a team of recruits into the northern mountains a year from now, on the trail of the mythical cave-dwelling ice monster. . . .

"Bother, social niceties," Tam said. He rubbed his hands on his trousers and stuck out his hand. She took it, feeling rather odd about the whole thing. "Here I am trying to offer you a job and I haven't even introduced myself. Thomas Grimsby. But everyone calls me Tam."

"Dorian," said Dorie. She had told Malcolm that her last name was Eliot—her stepmother's maiden name—but she thought she might as well avoid mentioning that for now, as it was Tam's mother's name, too. She changed the subject by saying, "What are you finding that can be done with the eggs? I mean, I know they're poison to fey."

"Well, you know the silvermen, I suppose? The silver eye in their palm—that compound came from us. The albumen left in the wyvern egg is part of the secret compound."

"That comes from you," Dorie stated, that heartbreak rising again. No wonder the lab had suddenly become so wealthy in the past year. What a fool she was to think they would hire her to do anything that might help the fey.

"From the lab, yes. The silvermen use it to drive the fey out of others, but regular folks are using it to keep themselves from being taken over. Defense, not offense. The fey aren't all evil—but the ones that are . . ." His face twisted with hatred, and her heart twisted in response. But it only made sense. Even without her mistakes, he had more reason to hate the fey than the average person—one had destroyed his father.

"They leave scars," she said softly. She was thinking of Tam, but she was also thinking of the ironskin.

Tam nodded, his eyes lighting again. "Yeah, you know about the ironskin? Get this." He adjusted his glasses and flipped open his journal to a page where he had pasted a photo—the modern black-and-white photos, not the blue-and-white of the old fey tech. It showed an expanse of skin—a belly, she thought—with an old, faded scar. "So the lab hired me for the wyvern research in my book, and stuck me in a lab where they were busy testing it on some captive fey." He saw her repress a shudder and he said, "I know. Believe me, I know. I've since got them to stop it."

She was warmed by the thought that he could have gone through everything he'd been through and still be more logical about the fey than the average man on the street. Something unclenched a bit.

"So the field work positions were still relatively new," Tam continued. "They'd been relying on a few freelancers. And there was only one person capable of bringing them fey—a blacksmith. Old guy. Massive. I told him how the wyvern albumen was dissolving the fey he'd brought. And he asked if he could watch the next set of tests—I didn't think much of it, except that he's a fanatic, you know? I understand that. Us fanatics are how discoveries get made. So I snuck him in.

"And then get this—apparently this blacksmith was ironskin himself. I was standing there with the freshly hatched egg and suddenly he hiked up his shirt. There was a horrible red scar—nasty looking. I'd never seen an ironskin scar but I knew it was fey all right. They seem to bubble and writhe. I was kind of stunned and then he took the albumen from me and he flat-out rubbed it on his scar. It steamed and hissed and I'm sure he would have been screaming if he weren't this crazy stoic blacksmith guy. But it cleaned out the fey." Tam showed her the picture again, of the faded scar that looked a decade old. "I took this the same day."

Dorie's eyes were wide. "No."

"Yes. Weird, huh? So you can see we'd be happy to pay you for the egg."

"The scar is gone," she said slowly. That the goo in the wyvern egg killed fey was disturbing, but this new implication was a sudden bright spot. If it could kill just the bit of fey remaining in a two-decades-old scar . . .

"Well, his skin was still technically scarred," said Tam, putting away the journal. "But there wasn't any fey left in it. He no longer had the curse to deal with."

"What about the others?" she burst out suddenly.

"What others?"

"The other ironskin. Are you going to take care of them?"

Slowly he turned to look at her. "*Are* there any others left? I mean, I only knew of one other, and she was fixed a long time ago." Her stepmother, Jane, he meant. Jane still had a bit of fey in her face, but it was no longer cursed, and it could not be removed without harming her.

Dorie nodded. "I know of at least one." The server at The

Wet Pig, with the curse on his leg, who was hungry every day. He could be helped after all.

His lips twisted sardonically. "More important, could they pay?" She saw again the boy she had known, the boy who was somehow sweet and cynical all at once. He was the one who had explained to her that a little girl who was visiting would shun her if she tried to impress her with any of her fey tricks—and when she had done them, and the girl had indeed called her names and run home, he had comforted her, and let her show him the fey tricks he had seen many times, until she finally fell asleep, tear streaked and exhausted.

"Oh," Dorie said, crushed. Another reason she had hoped to join the Queen's Lab, gone. She had wanted to find remedies for those who needed them. But what to do when the remedy was there . . . but not being given? She suddenly felt hopelessly naïve for not having realized that maybe research wouldn't be enough. Cures shouldn't be kept for those who could afford to pay. But how could she make those with control over the eggs see that? She cupped the precious egg in her shirt, keeping it warm. "Do you know—is any other part of the wyvern poisonous to fey? The outside of the egg?"

Tam shook his head. "We sacrificed some eggs to studies. The anti-fey substance in the white and yolk increases in concentration right up to the moment of the wyvern's hatching. So you don't get any benefits by disturbing its birth. What's left inside the eggshell as the wyvern steps out of it is the purest stuff there is. And yes, the only anti-fey substance appears to be the leftover albumen."

"What do you do with the wyverns afterward?" Dorie said.

"Sell them," Tam said, and his face darkened with conflict again. "They've never known anything but captivity, you know. If we can keep them alive past the first few days—which doesn't always happen; they're so stubborn and wary—then they go to zoos, mostly."

"And then no more eggs," said Dorie.

"They've never been bred in captivity, no," agreed Tam. "Look, I promise you it'll get a fair shake, though. More chance than if you sell it to some rich so-and-so who just wants to say he's got one and doesn't even know what to do when it hatches."

As usual, the inequity of everything stopped her words, dammed up her thoughts. She came up against the stupidity of the world and it was like someone had bashed her head into a wall. How could you think what to do in response to everything being unfair? Where did you start?

And why did it have to be Tam here, now, when she was failing to make things *right* in the world, as she had always told him so proudly she would do? She was out of things to say, which left her with wanting to shake his shoulders and say who she really was, and ask him if he still hated her. He couldn't, could he? Oh, but the time in the forest had changed him. His wild eyes, his wary expression. The damage had been started by the fey who impersonated his father, and continued by the cousin who sold him off because she thought it was the only way to fully learn about her fey side. Well, she'd learned all right. Betrayal on betrayal.

"Tam," she started, and then she heard how soft and beseeching and stupidly girly that sounded, and she quickly stood, arranging herself in the most manly way she could think of. "I'll think about your offer," she said gruffly. She eased the egg back into her belly as if tucking it back into that hidden pouch.

Tam jumped to his feet, too. "Let me give you my card," he

said. "I know I have one somewhere." He patted his pockets. "Oh bother, is there a place I can ring you?"

Reluctantly she gave him her landlady's number and told him to leave the message in care of Jack. At the sight of the two of them standing, the wyvern grew suspicious again. Although Tam started his whistle, the wyvern tilted its head upward, opened its throat to let out the strange ululating cry that would call back its mate.

"You'd better go," said Dorie. "One will nest and the other fight. You won't like that."

"You're right," Tam agreed ruefully. "Can we offer you a lift back to the city?"

"We?" said Dorie, dusting off and looking back at the nest. She was watching the wyvern—graceful, proud, silver—and then the next moment she wasn't. It was falling to the ground, a dart protruding from its scaled chest.

A woman about their age strode into the clearing. She was tall and broad-shouldered, scrubbed and fresh-faced, and was dressed in a trim jacket and slacks that appeared both expensive and tailor-made for clambering around the forest. A whiff of clean soap came drifting into the forest behind her.

"What was that?" Dorie spluttered.

"Tranquilizer dart. It was going to attack you," the woman said calmly. Her voice was crisp and educated, no nonsense. She reminded Dorie of the girls in the sporty clique in school— the sort with impeccable school spirit, top marks in every subject, stars in one or three sports and sadistically competent in the rest, and who occasionally could be found having panic attacks in one of the restroom stalls. "Clear sign of wyvern battle cry, *ja*? Next it would have torched Thomas's face." There was the barest hint of foreign lilt to her words.

"I had it under control," protested Dorie as she stormed

over to the felled wyvern. "It might have broken its neck." Or, almost worse for it—a wing.

The woman did not bother to respond. She strode past Tam and swung herself easily up the tree. Grabbed the two remaining wyvern eggs and tucked them in a special pouch. She was as tall as Tam—taller than Dorie, who made a slight, skinny boy. She did not think she could bulk up further without losing some of her solidity. She was used to being short, but being short was not a *thing* when you were a girl—she suddenly felt odd, being at a disadvantage for her presumed sex.

The woman swung carefully back down. Her casual athleticism felt like arrogance—she was not even breathing hard. Next she turned her attention to the felled wyvern, and ran her fingers along one wing while Dorie examined the other. She made a great show of double-checking Dorie's checking, before easing the tranquilizer dart free and patching the wound with a bit of cloth tape. Dusting her hands, she turned to Dorie, dismissing the adult wyvern as no longer her problem. "There were three hollows in the nest," she announced, looking straight at Dorie. "Did you already steal an egg?"

"If I had, it would be half as many as you," returned Dorie. She gently tugged the wyvern under some nearby bushes and arranged some fallen birch limbs in front of it.

The woman was not amused. She stalked over to Dorie and held out her hand. "All wyvern eggs have been declared the property of the Crown," she said, adding, "we will pay you a fair price." Dorie turned from her work, looking at her calmly, stubbornly, and the woman added, "And we will *fine* you that same fair price if we find you in possession of one." Still nothing, and the woman sighed, pulled out a medallion with a silver eye, and said, "Look. By the authority invested in me by the Queen's Lab, I command you to surrender the egg you have stolen. That is official enough, *ja?*"

Dorie gaped, words deserting her. "You? The Queen's Lab?" What did this woman have that Dorie didn't? Besides the ability to callously tranq wyverns, that was.

The woman appeared to have waited long enough. She took advantage of Dorie's shock to reach into Dorie's egg pouch herself.

But of course the egg was not there.

Dorie smirked and the sharp annoyance on the woman's face shuttered closed. She clearly felt she had been made a fool of, and detested it. Dorie was too impossible to deal with. "You might have said you didn't have it," she told Dorie, and then turned sharply to Tam, dismissing Dorie from her world. Dorie looked at Tam, wondering if he would say something, but although he gave her a puzzled expression, he did not. "Oh, Thomas, did you hurt yourself?" said the woman, finally seeing Tam's arm.

"I'm all right, Annika," Tam said, waving her off. "Dorian helped."

"What a terrible bandage," said the woman. "The University needs you in prime condition. You must return immediately." She pulled Tam protectively into her, a move Dorie was perfectly well used to seeing when in girlshape. She was still a boy, she thought. Maybe her cover was slipping. The woman glanced back at Dorie. "I would leave before the mate comes," she advised.

"Of course," Dorie said dryly. "Good-bye, Tam," she said. "Pleasure meeting you."

"Stop by the lab sometime," he said, still giving her that same puzzled face. He raised his eyebrows. "This afternoon would be an excellent time." With the unhatched wyvern egg in tow, he meant. Or what? Would he tell on her? Dorie did not care if they tried to fine or punish her, although it would be a nuisance to ditch her Dorian face and start fresh learning a new pattern. But it was Tam, and he hadn't told so far, and she owed him. He waited for her reluctant nod, and then turned to hurry along with the woman, their shoulders close and full of implication.

Dorie snorted. Wheeled sharply about and stormed out of the forest.

Chapter 5

THE LAST OF THE IRONSKIN (NEARLY)

Any other young woman would have sold the egg to pay the rent. But those young women had not had it drilled into them so thoroughly by their stepmothers that financial concerns must always come second to the *right thing to do.*
— Thomas Lane Grimsby, *Silverblind: The Story of Adora Rochart*

* * *

Dorie-as-Dorian hurried through the center of the city, through the heat and smog that choked the streets, thinking over that odd encounter with Tam. She had missed his requested appointment at the Queen's Lab as it was already well past afternoon—the Crown might have an automobile for Tam and that girl to use to go out into the country whenever they wanted, but Dorie hitched, and that took time and patience. Still, he probably would be there now. . . .

The newly built, concrete-and-steel Queen's Lab was near the University. She stopped and hung back behind a tree, out of sight, looking up at the symbol of all her ambition.

A job. Not just any job, but the most prestigious one in her field. Field work paid little enough—you were in it for the glory, weren't you? Or at least to be in service of Truth and

Learning, and in this case, the Crown. She rolled her eyes, for that was her least favorite bit of it. But set aside the fact that it would further her goals of helping people like the ironskin waiter for the moment. Be practical for once. It would mean a steady income, and no more swallowing her pride when her aunt offered her leftover clothes that hadn't sold at her atelier. No more poaching dandelions from city gardens—though truthfully, she didn't mind that as much as scrounging off her aunt. But mostly, getting paid to do what she did anyway— roam through her beloved forests, finding and exploring what other creatures were in some ways *like her.* And then using that knowledge to set right the damage her fey ancestors had done, either directly as with the ironskin, or indirectly by causing people to stay away from the forests that held their potential remedies.

And to get this job, all she had to do was show up, as Dorian, with the wyvern egg that was currently incubating in her belly.

It would pay half the rent. She could get hired on, find them another one; pay the other half. She could play along with all this "all wyvern eggs are property of the Crown" business, as patently unfair as that was.

Or she could help the ironskin.

Right now.

Now that Tam had told her what the wyvern eggs could do, she could see it. If that blacksmith had removed the fey in his skin, then she could too. Hadn't Jane told her a story of an ironskin blacksmith who had helped—not just Jane, but a whole bunch of ironskin? There must be other ironskin left in the city besides that waiter boy, others who didn't have the contacts or wealth to destroy the fey poison and return to a whole life.

She knew what the blood racing through her veins told

her. She wanted to try that goo for herself, help the ironskin *right now.* Her fingers tingled with it. She tried to think through what would be logical to do. Think of yourself first. Take this egg to the Queen's Lab. Pay off your own rent, so you and Jack don't end up homeless and eating dandelion stew.

But was that only her amoral fey side talking?

Because she could always take that waiter a different egg— couldn't she? He had waited two decades—he could wait a week or three more. But that girl today had been so insistent that *all* wyvern eggs were now property of the Crown, which meant the eggs would just be harder and harder to come by. And Tam was right—the Lab wasn't going to let their precious eggs go for free. The more she thought about it, the more the Queen's Lab had acquired a tarnish it hadn't had yesterday. Creating fey poison. Testing on fey. How could she look at it with the same blind eye?

No, she *knew* what the right thing to do was. Even if they didn't.

Dorie set her jaw and turned toward the bar.

Dorie-as-Dorian found a clean table in the corner of The Wet Pig and dismissed a couple of waiters' offers of assistance until she saw the young man with the ironskin leg limping out with an order for someone. He smiled at the customers, laughing and joking over the food, and she saw him filch a fried potato as he turned away. He shoved it in his mouth with a hunger she could easily feel, even if his curse was covered and technically not leaking to anyone. She raised her hand to get his attention as he came back, and he veered over to her table, eyebrows raised to ask politely how he could help.

"I'm not here to order," said Dorie gruffly, because she

didn't have any more money than she had had yesterday. "I wanted to talk to you. Can you take a short break?"

"Sorry, sir, but that's not really my thing," he said, his friendliness fading away behind a plastered-on smile. "Today's choices are on the board up there. Molly will help you if you're wanting to order."

Dorie reddened. "No, I mean. I'm here to help you. I had a tip-off, I mean. It's about your ironskin." She lowered her voice on the last word.

He looked skeptically at her but he didn't walk away. "Nothing to be done about that."

"Yes, there is," she said. She sensed he would run if she tried to force him to listen, so she kept her voice low, forcing him to lean in. "I know of one person who's been cured already."

"Come off it," he said, and turned.

"A blacksmith," she called after him as he limped away. Dammit. It would be wrong to mentally flip over a table and block his path. So very wrong. She groaned. How could she fix wrongs if the wronged wouldn't let her?

But he turned at that. Came back and stood at her table. Leaned over it and started wiping, as if pretending he was busy. "Do you know his name?"

Dorie shook her head. "But it was . . . it was a belly scar."

His cloth stopped moving. "Niklas," he said, and he no longer seemed to be talking to her, but to himself. "He saved us all, you know. Gave us a place to come to. Told us what was happening. Haven't seen him in years. . . . He's really been cured, then?"

"In the Queen's Lab," she said, hoping it would lend her credibility by association. "And I have the ability to fix you," she added, with far more confidence than she felt. "But I need to talk to you privately about it first." That was pulling her punches, because actually she thought the egg might hatch to-night, and in that case . . . But she couldn't spring everything on him at once. Work up to that. "It has to be tonight, and it can't be here. Do you have a flat?"

He looked at her for a long time. She was not sure if he was weighing whether to trust her at all—or if he believed that she at least thought she spoke truth, and was weighing whether or not to risk his own, long-buried hope. It struck her then what sort of fire she was playing with. Not a lark, not just a science experiment. Twenty years of misery and hope, pinned on what you think you could do, your first time out. But at last he seemed to reach a decision, because he named an address. "I've been here all day. Get off soon, when the dinner rush dies down. You could meet me then."

And then somehow she would have to get back for Jack's gallery opening. But that ran for several hours, so even if she missed the first few minutes, Jack would surely under-stand. . . .

"Okay," she said, and stuck out her hand. "My name's Dorian, by the way."

"Colin," he said. He didn't seem to know what to say after that, so he turned and limped back to the kitchen, washrag trembling in his hand.

Dorie was still in boyshape as she made her way to the wharf. She had been in boyshape since six that morning and her nerves were quivering with the strain. She knew from long-ago experience that every extra minute spent in a different shape would make it easier in the long run, but in the short run, she was nearing her limit. She had never spent this long as another person in one stretch.

Still, no point in changing back now. She was quickly realizing that half the point of boyshape *was* the wharf—the taverns, the back alleys, the slums. All those places she had avoided before, because *don't look at me* would only get you so far when you were tiny and blond and in a dress. Dorian was a skinny, undersized boy—but he also looked, and was, quite fast. His physique would not threaten anybody—but it was nondescript in a way that golden curls and dresses were not.

The silver wyvern egg was still nestled in her abdomen. Surely this was not how the other scientists transported their eggs. She grinned, imagining everyone at the lab with a belly full of yodeling eggs. Really, her belly was working surprisingly well as a carrier. She felt attuned to the egg in a strange way—she could feel its slow pulse as if it was considering hatching soon.

<<Wait,>> she told it mentally, much as a pure fey would do. <<Wait.>> It seemed as though her belly purred in response.

A cluster of rough-looking men spilled out of a tavern near her, heading to the next tavern. She took a breath and started sliding through. A hand reached out as if to clamp down on her skinny boywrist—looking for a violet to kick around a bit, no doubt. She fuzzed just a bit, turned her time sense into fast forward, took his hand, and pulled it just far enough to reach one of his fellow drunkards. She slithered through the group, turning back to laugh at the sight of the fellow drunkard's expression when he found he was holding hands with his drinking buddy. She could hear a brawl starting as she turned the corner.

The streets got rougher; the summer sun finally dropped into twilight, but there were no further incidents as she neared the wharf. The smell of sewage grew stronger as she approached the river, and she tried to dampen her fey senses back down. No need for fine precision now! Following Colin's instructions, she passed the statue of Queen Maud, swung down the second alley after that, and fetched up against an old iron door, a ground-floor room in a ramshackle old building that stank of mildew. This was going to be exciting, she could feel it. A bit giddy with her first rebellion in years, she knocked a shave-and-a-haircut.

Two bits were rapped back, which warmed her to him. The door swung open to reveal a hefty, ginger-haired man with a tooth-missing smile. His face was still guarded, but it was more open than she'd seen him since she had first said the word "ironskin."

"Dorian," Colin said. "You came. Was starting to think I'd dreamed it." He shook his head. "Stopped by Niklas's smithy on the way home. He weren't there, but a helper confirmed what you said. Can hardly believe it." His ginger eyebrows furrowed. "He said it had something to do with some sort of egg?"

"It does," Dorie assured him. Fire ran around her veins. "It's something the Queen's Lab and your blacksmith solved. And what they can do, we can do." She clapped him manfully on the back and followed him into his dim quarters. There was one dingy bulb hanging from the ceiling—the yellow electric light of human technology. In her parents' day there had still been clean blue fey tech, but now there was smoke and smog and electricity. The small room was clean and empty except for a table, two chairs, and a pot-bellied stove. The table had a cheap yellow-backed paperback on it, its spine cracked open. She had brought a small birdcage for the wyvern—a prop left over from one of Jack's paintings—and she set that on the table. Next to the stove was a stack of homemade shelves, piled high with various foodstuffs, and the scent of cooking grease lingered in the air.

"Gonna make myself a cheese sandwich," he said. "You want one?"

"Yes," said Dorie, for the last time she had eaten was foraging on the country roads between hitching back to the city. There was plenty to eat this time of year—mustard greens and blackberry bushes ran rampant through the ditches and you could always snag plums and apricots from someone's orchard, if you were quick—but food grew sparse as the smog and cement of the city choked it out, and she was ravenous.

"Good. Hate to eat alone and always am. Let me put my leg on then." Colin sat on a chair and picked up two large curved pieces of iron, rags for padding nestled inside. With a few practiced motions he clamped the two pieces around his leg and lashed them together until the leg was enclosed in a stiff iron brace. It brought back memories from years ago, watching her then-governess Jane wrap her face in an iron mask to block her young charge from the curse.

Ironskin.

Colin swung his way to the stove with his stiff, awkward walk, and now with the practiced movements of a trained chef, he had the bread toasted and the cheese melting on it in the blink of an eye. She could only imagine how much food he went through in an effort to appease the curse, and she thought that probably only the fact that he worked at a place where he could filch leftover food kept him alive at all.

"Busy day at the Pig," he said, flipping the sandwiches over. "Been filling in for a sick server. Ready to get back behind the grill."

"You should keep your ironskin off while you're serving," Dorie said. "Make all the customers hungrier."

He barked laughter. "I should at that. Park me in the center of the room till the wallets are emptied and the food all gone." If he wondered what the urgency for "talking" was tonight, what the timeline for his possible fix was, he was good at hiding it. He was too proud to ask, even though he knew she might have something that would change his life. Dorie respected that.

Twenty-three years since the end of the Great War. Twenty-three years, or more, of covering his scar with iron, to stop the curse from affecting others. Dorie's stepmother, Jane, had been cursed with rage when Dorie had first met her. Dorie had been five then, but she remembered Jane removing the mask for the first time. Even with her fey side to counteract it, she could still feel the waves of anger. Could feel how her human side wanted to rage against her governess in response. The ironskin were stuck with two choices: keep the ironskin off and poison everyone else with your particular misery; keep the ironskin on and poison yourself.

For more than twenty years. A whole lifetime, for Colin.

Small wonder most of the ironskin were gone now. Their curses had made them a casualty after the war—ignored, repelled. Hard to find reasons to keep going when you pushed everyone around you away. Immediately after the Great War, hundreds had gone to Jane's friend for help, that blacksmith Tam and Colin had mentioned. And now—she hadn't seen one in years, until Colin. There couldn't be many left at all.

Dorie looked at Colin again—despite the care lines etched in his face, he couldn't be much older than she. He must have been only a baby when he was wounded.

"Here you go, then," he said, sliding a clean plate with the sandwich in front of her. "What?"

"I was just wondering how old you were," Dorie said haltingly. "When . . . when your leg was hurt."

"Three," he said easily. "And just learned not to soil myself and now I was out of commission and back in nappies for two months till I could walk again. My mum was right pissed."

"Not to mention hungry," Dorie said in a low voice. No one had known that iron would block others from the curse until the blacksmith discovered it after the war. And then later still, Jane had discovered that keeping the iron on made the curse worse for the one who was cursed—it kept the poison in.

But here was Colin, wearing his brace to keep his guest at ease.

"Hungry, yeah," and he laughed. "My mum once took me to meet her employer when she was trying for a raise." He looked at her with a bright twinkle. "After ten minutes with us he was so hungry he would have agreed to anything just to get us out of there so's he could eat."

Dorie barked with laughter through bites of her sandwich. "The positive side to the curse! I never would have thought."

"Everything has a silver lining," he said. "Or an iron one."

Dorie set her cheese sandwich down and looked at him soberly. She was quickly warming to this young man who seemed so determined to keep a positive outlook on life. Feelings made everything so difficult. Was she doing the right thing, putting him to this risk? Her fingers touched the egg nestled in her belly. It purred in response and she thought, no going back now. "Well, perhaps you've already guessed the news I have," Dorie said. "Right here with me."

Colin sucked in air. "You want to fix me tonight."

Dorie nodded.

He stood and clunked a few paces. Sat back down. "Never

thought I would see the day," he said. He shook his head. "Don't even know what it will feel like. Always been hungry."

"Even when you're eating?" said Dorie.

Colin shook his head, temporizing. "There's a few minutes right after I eat. I feel all right for a moment. Not full, I guess, if full means you don't feel hunger. But I'm not *very* hungry. I can tell I'll want to eat pretty soon. But just at that moment, I can manage."

"That's a start," said Dorie. "It's like that, but . . . better than that." She grinned. "There's even *too* full, when you eat yourself silly and regret it. You might have that happen a few times before you realize you don't have to eat cheese sandwiches every five minutes."

"I'd like to see that," he said. He was controlling his excitement now, long fingers carefully positioned on the table. She felt a sudden rush of kinship with him. Though not cursed herself, she knew what it was to have to control a strange side of you, a ravenous, alien side. She had met an ironskin once, with Jane, long ago, on the street. She had only seen the poor man for a few minutes, but she remembered a miserable, barely coherent wretch. But Colin, she understood. He had found ways over the last two decades to stop the curse from poisoning his life completely. He had learned self-control far beyond what the average person had to do.

Because if he hadn't, he wouldn't be around anymore.

Under cover of the table, Dorie pressed her fingers gently against the egg in her belly. It was thrumming inside her now. The tenuous connection she shared with it knew what that meant. "It's getting close," she said. "Maybe an hour or two. I'm told the goo only works when it's fresh, so we'll have to work fast."

"You're *told*?" he said. He was sharp.

"Yes," she said, and silently watched him, waiting to see if he would back down from this experiment, tell her to get a new guinea pig. But he didn't.

"What about the little chick, then?" he said instead, which endeared him to her more. She hadn't expected him to ask, or care.

"We'll need to get food ready for it," she said. "Here's the tricky part. They need to kill right at birth and then eat the meat. Rodents will work if we can't get anything else, but ideally we'd get a bird."

He whistled. "Not a lot of time." And in the same breath, leaned down to unlash his leg. "Landlady has rat traps in the garret," he said. "I'll check there first."

"Well, good!" said Dorie, surprise plain in her voice. "I'll check outside. Be back in time, though, or it's all for naught."

"Can't have that, what?" he said, and loped through a door by the stove that apparently led to the rest of the building.

Dorie went out the door into the alley, wondering if anybody else she knew would put the welfare of a wyvern chick before their own like that. Or maybe all humans would, and it was only her amoral fey side who kept reminding her about self-preservation. Regardless, she wouldn't have faulted Colin if he hadn't—she imagined the thought of being released from the curse would be overwhelming. And then there was the time constraint—you wouldn't want to be off looking for a rat when the egg hatched, and miss your chance.

So Dorie had expected she would be the one to find something. Which she was easily able to do. She went down to the wharf and sharpened her fey senses until she could pick up the rats scuttling underfoot and the pigeons and gulls circling overhead.

Colin's ironskin put her problems into sharp relief. It was

clearly far better to be half-fey than cursed by one. Dorie's actual parentage was both disturbing and complicated—a powerful fey had had her human father in her clutches. She had taken over a female human body, and together they had produced Dorie. Dorie was half-fey—or a third? She was never quite sure how to do that math. Regardless, she was the only one she knew of. Until Jane had come, she had been quite wild as a child—as well as barely talking or using her hands. Even at five, she had been able to do some things a true fey could do—mostly odd parlor tricks like levitating objects and making pictures of blue light.

Dorie had barely known her fey mother—had never known the human body she temporarily used. Later, after the Fey Queen's death, Dorie had insisted that her father take her into the forest to learn from the other fey.

That had been . . . different.

Fey were not generally cruel—they had been pressed into the war by a determined leader. But they did not follow human morality, either. Perhaps she knew more about them than most, due to her time spent living with them, in her odd state as partially one of them. She had a certain understanding for some of their traits. They spent a lot of time drifting diffusely through the forests, enjoying the sun and rain and wind, but they also came together in more compressed states and amused themselves . . . sometimes with humans.

Dorie had run wild with them for several summers. But she knew whose side they really saw her on, in the end.

It was cooler down by the wharf, now that the sun had set. The sticky summer air made the city so miserable this time of year—the smog thickened, and the smells worsened. Especially down here, where the sanitation lagged behind the richer parts of the city. She could practically smell the individual rats and birds without the aid of her fey senses. A rat scuttled by, and it was so slow to her that she had plenty of time to consider grabbing it. But she let it go. She was feeling protective of the little wyvern in her belly. She wanted it to have a good first meal.

And then what? she suddenly thought. And then what will you do with this chick?

Certainly she couldn't keep it, even if they liked people, which they didn't. She didn't want to sell it, not to Malcolm or anybody else.

She would most like to take it back to the forest and give it back to its parents, and though that sounded ridiculous, she thought it might also have a chance of working. Wyverns weren't bird-brained chickens or turkeys. They were sharp—and they had few eggs to begin with. When she was little she had found an egg that had rolled out of a nest, and a wyvern nearby was yodeling at it, trying to figure out how to get it back in. Using her most nonthreatening gestures and calming aura, she had managed to convince the wyvern to stand down while she put the egg in the nest. It seemed to understand—at least, it had settled happily back down on its only egg, and it had not steamed her while she crept carefully away. She came back to check on the nest a week later, and again the wyvern did not steam her, though it watched her warily.

It was a reach. But it was worth a try, especially since this would be this wyvern's only chick left.

Except she didn't know if the wyvern had made it through the tranqing. And if it hadn't, then with the eggs gone, its mate would have no reason to hang around the nest. It would leave and start its life again.

This chick would have no home to go to.

Her belly thrummed harder and with a start, Dorie realized the egg was about to hatch. In sudden panic she wondered what would happen if it tried to hatch inside her. She could phase blue and let it out . . . but wouldn't the albumen react poorly to her fey side? She shuddered.

Dorie phased into her half-there state—keeping her belly fully solid—and shimmied through time and space to the end of the dock. Up the railing she went, and then her canvas bag was swinging over the grey pigeon there, and now she had it. Her momentum carried her back down to the ground, and she rolled and came up, turning solid as she went.

The bag rustled and beat. She tied the cloth handles in a knot and carried it back to the slum.

She arrived back just as Colin did. He was holding up her birdcage with a sorry-looking rat inside. Crowed triumphantly, "Got one! Leg's gone mangled in the trap but that's all right, ain't it?"

"The woglet won't be picky," Dorie assured him. "I've got a pigeon for backup." She swung her moving bag down and set it on a corner of the floor. It would be all right there. "Start water boiling," she said. "Drop this cloth in it. And hurry." He set the pot going while she turned away, and with her back to him, eased the egg carefully out of her belly.

The egg glinted under the yellow glow of the lightbulb. Silver like mica, flecked with shine. A hairline crack was about to form around the top, she thought, and then watched it happen and wondered how she had known. But that was how the other egg had started—the woglet chipping away with its egg tooth—so perhaps that's all it was. "Do you have some rags?" Dorie said. "Mine are in with the pigeon."

Colin grabbed a holey towel that she thought was probably his only one and laid it on the table. She mounded up the edges to make a nest and set the rocking egg inside it.

"Now when the woglet comes out," Dorie said, "it will have to rest for a couple of minutes. Get its strength back before it goes after the rat or pigeon. That's the point where we will take the goo and apply it to your leg." Her fey side took over from her human nerves, leaving her as steady as a rock and as cold as ice. "I need you to roll up your pant leg and wipe down the scarring with some alcohol, all right? Better be safe than sorry." She had been thinking over the process all the way home from the forest. Just wiped the albumen on the scar, Tam had said. It would hurt. It was little enough to go on—but for Dorie, it was enough. Her fey side would do the rest.

Colin found a small measure of cheap brandy and did as she asked, then said as easily as possible, "Gonna hurt like a sonofabitch, right?" She nodded and he slugged the rest of the brandy. "Wouldn't expect anything else from a twenty-year-old curse removal." There was a swallow left in the bottle and he held it out to her, and she drank it, because she had decided Dorian would do such things, even though she had never acquired a taste for anything other than beer.

Dorie turned back to the egg, for this was the moment, this was the point, and suddenly the crack around the top widened and popped off, and a triangular, silver-white head poked through, questing for the outside. Its eyes were mottled green, like some cats', and the bright silver scales ran sleekly over its head and neck, glistening with the precious substance used to grow it.

Colin sucked in air, and the head swung around, but it pointed at *her*. Suddenly the wyvern hatchling was looking at her with its large luminous eyes. No, not an it—a *him*. Wyverns were difficult to sex, and yet, somehow, locked in his gaze, she was sure. She remembered his parent catching her this morning. This wyvern was too little to really be able to trap her, but still, she felt the insidious pull. He made a low purring noise, turning his head, and the spell was broken. He went back to rocking, trying to get free of his shell prison.

"Is it . . . now?" Colin asked.

Dorie shook her head. If they didn't care about the wyvern hatchling it would be now, could be anytime they wanted. But you couldn't help a hatchling free itself without likely damaging it—that was true of any sort of chick or lizard she'd ever heard of. This little one had to free his own self from the yolk sac and the shell. It was a waiting game now, a knife's edge of just the right moment.

She looked down at Colin's leg, preparing herself for what she would need to do. She realized now that she had been slightly hungry ever since Colin came in with the rat, and now, in this close proximity to his curse, she was positively starving. No wonder he didn't have a close relationship with anybody. Carefully she leaned down to gently touch the scar, let her fey side feel the fellow bit of fey that lurked within. Even after two decades, the poisonous scars were angry, red, and raised, and they ran down the inside of his leg, from knee to ankle. The scars seemed to twist and move as she stared at them. It was a long scar. It would need every last bit of the wyvern goo. And every last bit of Colin's fortitude.

The woglet's trills called her back to him. From her limited experience with wyverns, they apparently made a variety of yodelly ululations, each more annoying than the last. This one sounded like a high-pitched kazoo and clearly meant effort. The egg rocked wildly back and forth and the wet silver wings suddenly came poking out of the top. The wyvern got one of them outstretched, then, exhausted, rolled over on top of his triangular head. "C'mon," crooned Dorie. "You can make it." She thought that might sound too feminine, so gruffly she added, "Let's go, sport." She retrieved her bag with the annoyed pigeon in it and set it down next to the table. The rat in its cage limped back and forth.

The other wing waved back and forth and finally stretched all the way out. The wingspan was surprisingly long for such a little creature. Then the wings folded up again and the wyvern got one leg out. His head naturally curled up into a ball and he rolled over again. His little stomach panted in and out as he ululated his annoyance with the situation.

Dorie felt every inch of her tense with the waiting. Beside her she could feel that Colin felt the same.

The wyvern warbled in little pants that sounded like an air raid siren as he struggled to free his foot. He hopped forward on one leg, kicking—and finally the other leg came free, and the egg half rolled away behind him. He plopped down on the towel, cooing, exhausted again.

"Now," said Dorie.

She grabbed the discarded egg. Stuck her solidly human fingers into it, cleaning it free of the albumen that had surrounded the wyvern—the yolk sac and leftover strands of nutrient goo. It felt like any normal egg, but she kept her fey side firmly locked away. Not a good time to discover what fey poison felt like to that side of her. "Now," she repeated, and Colin closed his eyes and she touched the anti-fey wyvern goo to the top of the red scar.

He shuddered and clutched his leg with both hands, letting out a muffled oath. She had hoped he could keep still—too late now if he couldn't. No time to tie him down.

Working as quickly as possible, she painted the raised red scar with the goo, working from top to bottom. The scar burned away in a puddle that was not quite goo or human or fey, but something strange in between, and she took the hot cloth she had boiled, and wiped it clean, as Colin gasped and his leg shook with the effort of holding it steady. As she wiped the ooze a blue steam roiled off the leg, lifted up and evaporated, eradicated. Colin pressed his lips shut as a thin whine escaped them.

When Dorie was done with the first pass she studied the leg. It wouldn't do to stop too soon and leave any trace of fey behind. She had to be certain to get every last bit of blue out. Where the scar had been was now a shallow inverted scar, a smooth depression of skin. It was angry and red from the treatment, but it was whole, and she looked it up and down for any stray ridges of the old, writhing scar. When she thought she had it she wiped the whole leg one more time with the hot water, making sure to remove every bit of the anti-fey goo. And then carefully ran her fingers along the skin.

Hardly daring to breathe, she phased her fingers into fey state, just a little, not enough that anyone would know. Like a magnet calling to iron, the fey in her fingers quested to see if there was anything left on the leg. If there were any blue left, she would surely feel it.

But the skin was clean. The albumen had worked. Her fey side had done something useful.

Her atonement, for this human, at least, was done.

Colin stretched his leg out, wondering at it. Dorie rocked back on her heels. This was no longer about her; this was about him. His reclaiming of his own body.

"Does it still hurt?" she said.

He nodded no, then yes. "Like a day-old burn. But not like . . . a moment ago."

It was a good sign, she thought. If it went like the black-smith, then it sounded as though the scar and the ache would both fade. And of course, no more curse.

That would be its own sort of adjustment, of course.

Dorie turned her attention to the new thing that needed her—the woglet who was now realizing he was hungry, as hungry as Colin had been. Hungry—and fierce. The little wyvern raised his head, swaying, looking at Dorie for confirmation. She stroked his head—she didn't mean to, but somehow she was there, doing it—and crooned, "Yes yes, little one. Kill something." She reached down and unlatched the birdcage, setting the rat free to slowly limp out and look around. Then untied the bag, letting the disgruntled pigeon burst free with a rustle of wings.

The woglet's head swung up, sensing the prey moving about the room. Unsteadily he spread his wings and crept to the edge of the table, looked down. The rat limped below.

The woglet flapped his wings and cried shrilly. Then he jumped off the table, gliding down on the new wings to land with an ungainly thump next to the rat.

The rat was twice the size of the baby wyvern and Dorie's heart beat fast in her chest. The contest seemed so uneven, even with the rat's injured leg. But the baby wyvern in the lab had done just fine, hadn't it? The rat crept away from the woglet. Again the woglet looked at Dorie for confirmation. She felt oddly moved. It was so unlike the behavior she expected from witnessing the cranky hatchling in the lab. "Go on," she urged him.

The woglet swung around to face the rat directly. Several lids around his eyes fanned open, expanding the apparent size of the woglet's eyes like petals around a flower. But that was not all the lids did. The scales on the inside were as shiny as mirrors. This was where the basilisk heritage came into play. It whimpered, a funny sound that in another animal would have meant an injury. Unthinkingly the rat swung to look.

And was caught in the woglet's gaze.

Powerless to move, the rat stood there as the tiny woglet advanced, step by step. The woglet trembled on the brink—he had never done such a thing, and the rat really was huge. "Go on," Dorie said again, and the silver-white head sunk teeth into the rat's neck for the kill.

There was a short sharp squeak, but the rat made no move to defend itself, even after the eye contact had broken and it lay dying. She felt a little sorry for the rat—it had never had a chance. The woglet had a strong power. His parents would have been proud. He would live.

"Bloody hell," Colin said softly.

The silver head bent to feed as the rat's eyes dimmed to flat black. The spell broken, Dorie turned back to find Colin avidly watching the scene, one hand absently massaging the skin around the old scar. The red was already fading to pink.

"Little savages," she agreed.

"So hungry," he said.

"And you?"

He shook his head and suddenly his eyes welled up. He harrumphed manfully and turned away, stomped toward his stove with the force of old habit. He slid a pan on the stove and stopped and looked at it wonderingly, and either the realization that he was not hungry or the brandy broke something inside, for the heretofore calm and collected Colin said, "Do you know what it's like to think about food all day long? To always be wondering how far you are from when you'll let yourself have your next meal? To turn down invitations 'cause you don't know if there'll be a way for you to get a sandwich at the right time, and if you don't get it, then what's the point of going anyway, 'cause you'll spend the whole time thinking about *food*? I can scavenge slop with the best of them. Sure we was always broke, but me mum would be horrified if she knew how often I've et from bins. You see a bun and it doesn't matter that it has ants crawling over it, you have to have it—" He broke off, swallowing more words, banged his pan on the stove, then flipped it over, let it go.

There was a moment of silence when Dorie did not know what to say. She supposed a boy might clap him gruffly on the back and hand him more brandy. A girl might pat his shoulder and let him cry. She, who had tended so carefully to the scars up and down his leg, did not feel comfortable doing either of those things.

He wheeled on her and said in a low voice, "I want to help. Tell me more about those you're helping."

"Oh," said Dorie. "Well. You."

Colin shook his head. "Am I really the first you've done? I thought maybe—but then you seemed so confident. Are you . . . you're sure it really is done then? It won't come back?"

"It can't," she said. "I can tell all the fey is gone. You can, too, can't you?"

He nodded. And then said again, "I want to help. You're going to do them all, aren't you?"

"Yes," Dorie said, because she felt in her bones that this had been her inevitable path from the moment she stole the first egg. Or perhaps from the moment she let the rest of her fey self back into her body. Her fey side could get the eggs that would help the ironskin. Her human side *wanted to*. She, who had been neither fish nor fowl, was suddenly the perfect person to solve this problem. "I will need to find the rest of the ironskin," she said. "And each one will be time sensitive. I have to wait and find a new egg, nearly ready to hatch, for each person. One egg—one scar."

He paced. "Could I help find eggs?"

Dorie made a face. "Not easily. They're hard to find and dangerous to get. And they're in the country." If this was going to work, she was going to work alone. Can't go blue with humans around.

"Dorian," he said, and he sat his hefty frame on the chair next to hers. "I want to *do* something. Surely you understand. You helped me. I need to help someone now. Have to make it fair."

She nodded, for she felt a similar force driving her every day.

He spread his arms. "I look around and see so many problems. These are the folks I've grown up with. Not saying any of us think we have the right to live like the Queen. But you read things in the papers about how the world is changing. Then I look around and see someone like my landlady's daughter dying of crimson fever."

Dorie shook her head. "There's a cure for that. No one's died of that for ten years." She saw his look and quickly corrected herself. "I mean, no one needs to die of that anymore. It's a tincture of feywort."

"Which you can get if you have the money for it," Colin said.

Anger rose through the bewilderment. This wasn't like the lost cure for spotted hallucinations last summer. Feywort was known and proven. "No one should have to pay for that. You can gather it in practically any forest where the fey have been."

"And how often have you seen it here in the city?" Colin shook his head. "You've a different outlook, growing up in the country. You live with all the old dangers—but you can get all the old cures."

"The fey lived right behind my house," Dorie said absently, and he grimaced. She pounded one fist into the other. "You're right. Let me think this over. There must be something we can do." She had been thinking too small today. Out to save the ironskin—atoning for her heritage. But there were more than the ironskin who needed her help. It wasn't enough to set the score even—well, as even as twenty years of living with the injustice could ever be. She needed to tip the balance toward what was good and fair. This had been what she wanted to tell them yesterday when she had applied at the Queen's Lab. And now she had that chance again. Get inside and find out what their secrets were. Where was the feywort going, if it wasn't available for the poor? Maybe they knew. What else had they discovered in the forests that they were keeping to themselves? What were they hiding? She had been too proud this afternoon. She should find another egg, go to them as Dorian. Get in the back door so she could use their work for good. Certainly no one else would stand up for the fey. It *had* to be her.

She looked up at Colin, who was offering himself a piece of bread, and then taking it away from his mouth, over and over, with a bemused expression.

Well. Perhaps she had done some good today. "I would need to *find* the rest of the ironskin," she said. "I only stumbled on you by chance. Do you know of any more?"

He nodded. "You meet over the years. You know each other. You lose some. But it's not exactly a group that's growing, is it? Bet there's maybe twenty left in the city."

Twenty eggs to find. Were there even that many wyvern pairs on Black Rock? She had never seen that many at once.

"Currently know the whereabouts of eleven or twelve of the ironskin," he said. "But between us we can find everyone else. You keep tabs, you know. Those of us that are left." He put the piece of bread down and leaned forward.

"Let me bring them to you," he said with quiet intensity. "I have one in particular that needs to be done straight off. The curse hit all along her spine. It's a tough one. She can't hold out much longer."

Dorie laced her fingers together. "I will warn you. Wyvern eggs are considered the property of the Crown now. Every one I bring you is illegal."

"I vouch for her that won't matter." He gripped the back of the chair. "Shoulda had you go to her first. Was too selfish . . . Please. As soon as you can. Promise?"

"I promise," Dorie said. What else could she do? "But look, it's not just her. With eggs being black market now, every one of your friends will run the risk."

"And you?"

"I would rather rot in jail than see those rich bastards make off with all our eggs," she said. Her intensity surprised both of them, and he looked at her for a long time, thinking impenetrable thoughts.

After a moment, he looked around and tried to smile with his usual manner. In a completely different voice said, "Did you know there's a pigeon in my house?"

A choke of laughter burst forth. "Damn, I forgot," said Dorie. She picked up the cloth bag and went toward where the pigeon perched on the windowsill, wondering if she could convincingly capture it without going blue.

And then a silver flash of wings streaked past.

The pigeon startled—the little woglet wobbled. They both fell to the floor in a tangle of wings. Dorie stalked over, saying, "Look, you're not hungry, silly thing. You have a whole rat you can work on. Let the pigeon go." But even as she arrived on the scene, the pigeon was dying, its neck snapped, its eyes open and fixed on the little wyvern. "That's nonsense," Dorie scolded the woglet. "You shouldn't kill what you can't eat. Show some restraint." The woglet looked up at her, green eyes liquid and warm. Then he sank his teeth into the pigeon's neck.

Dorie sat back down in the chair. "Um, sorry about the blood," she said. "And rat guts. If you want to boil some more water I'll help you clean up."

"What's it doing?" said Colin.

The woglet had his teeth firmly in the pigeon's neck and was dragging it backward, straining mightily on his new legs and flapping his still-wet wings. Through his clenched teeth he was humming, but she did not know what it meant. He had to stop several times, exhausted, but the teeth stayed closed and the hum continued all the way up to Dorie's feet, where the woglet finally let go of his prize and broke out into a full-throated warble.

"I think it's for you," Colin said.

Dorie looked at the woglet in shock, who was now attempting to climb her pant leg with his rather disgusting claws. The woglet warbled all the way up her leg in the pitch of a wounded yodeler. Once he reached her lap, he tucked his tail around his nose and folded his wings. The wounded yodel changed to a wounded snore. "It can't be," she said. "They hate everybody. I'm supposed to take it back to the forest and try to find its parents."

Colin grinned. "Think you're the father now. Hope you didn't have anywhere to go that don't involve a baby wyvern."

Only the Queen's Lab, Dorie thought in dismay as she watched the silver woglet snore. Only the Queen's Lab.

Dorie hurried along the paths to the University, still in boyshape, woglet folded in the crook of her arm. It was dark now, and the black buildings rose around her. At the building where her flat was she stopped. What on earth was she going to do with a tiny wyvern on her arm? If the Queen's Lab really was cracking down on them, then this baby was clear proof of her crime. She had not expected this problem. She had been expecting a cranky baby wyvern that she would have to stare down. Pop him all protesting into the birdcage, and take him back to the forest before he could get too cranky with the situation and steam his way out.

She had not been expecting him to sleep in her arms.

Dorie tucked her fingers under his belly, wondering if she could maneuver him into the birdcage after all. He could stay in their flat then.

Woglet protested and dug his claws in tighter. Dorie yelped and let that bit of her elbow fuzz out to ease the pressure. She brought her whole arm toward the birdcage, and he yodeled ominously. That noise would have their landlady in their room in a heartbeat.

She sighed. She could not miss Jack's gallery opening. Her first one in the city. The one that would set the stage for her whole career—the one Dorie had sworn in blood to attend.

There was no help for it. She was going to have a wyvern on her, and that's how it was.

Jack was sharing the space with nine other artists. They had gone in together to rent a space near the University that catered to this sort of thing: art shows and avant-garde theatrical performances. Now as Dorie approached it she saw there was a large crowd outside, and she wondered if the opening time had been delayed, for she was rather late. She had not had time to change clothes or shape; she was still Dorian, still in hiking pants and muddy boots. But apparently it did not matter, for at the top of the steps a man in uniform was taping off the doors.

Jack met her on the grass, ranting and out of breath. She was in red cigarette pants—Jack generally wore red—and a pile of handmade jewelry over a loose top. "One of the artists got us all shut down," she said. "We were open for all of five minutes and then all these silvermen come in and force everyone out. No one even made it to the back where my work was."

"I'm sorry," Dorie said. Curiosity overcame sympathy. "What did he show?" The men in Jack's collective outnumbered the women eight to two, so she felt safe assuming it was a *he*.

"I don't even know; he's been so secretive. I gather it was some sort of human figure but lit up with blue light." Jack wrinkled her nose. "Well, and obviously that says fey takeover now that I think on it. No wonder—he's been having a hard time of it since one of his mates got blued. I suppose that's why the silvermen are involved with a rinky-dink art show."

"Jack," said Dorie slowly. "*Blue* light. Like the artist was using a bluepack?"

"You mean like the ones we learned about in history class?" said Jack. "The ones the fey made to trade with us?"

"Not exactly *made*," said Dorie, swallowing, for she knew the bluepacks' disturbing history even if the textbooks had elided it. The bluepacks the fey had traded to humans had been split-up pieces of whole fey—punishments set by the Fey Queen. It wasn't known how she did it—it wasn't even known that that's what the bluepacks really *were* until long after the war, and the trade, were over. At that point there was little reason for it to become common knowledge. People had moved on.

But where could this artist have found a bluepack to light

up his sculpture? Surely he hadn't. Surely it was a gel or something. Otherwise . . . otherwise she did not know what to think.

"If only his works had been at the back, and mine at the front," said Jack, whose mind was working in quite a different channel. "We drew lots . . . ugh, this is so frustrating."

"So not fair," Dorie agreed. Jack was quite talented, as far as she could tell. She only knew a dilettante's smattering about the subject, but Jack's technique seemed to her to be doing something new and interesting. She was mostly doing nudes, but her colors! They were rich and flat all at once—you could not stop looking at them. "You shouldn't be punished for his mess. What can we do about it? Look, I'll go distract the silvermen, and we'll take down the tape."

"No no no," said Jack. She grabbed Dorie's arm, her bracelets clanking. "None of your pranks. As maddening as it is, logically I know the publicity will be excellent. Let the men do their stuff. They're confiscating all works to take back to the station. Supposedly the rest of us will get our pieces back tomorrow. I'm just keeping an eye out for when they start crating stuff up, because if they think they're touching my paintings without me present, they've got another thing coming." She sighed. "It's not the worst thing, to be part of a show banned for public indecency. But why couldn't it be at the *end* of the evening? Not to mention, then maybe someone would have had a chance to buy one, because our rent is due." She eyed Dorie meaningfully.

"Yeah," said Dorie glumly.

"How did the interview with the sleazeball go this morning?" said Jack.

"Horrible," said Dorie. She lowered her voice. "All he wants are wyvern eggs, and that's all the Queen's Lab wants, too."

She told Jack the price he was paying, and Jack whistled. "But they're living creatures, Jack! Not to mention deadly to the fey. I just can't take him anything living, and especially not wyvern eggs. I just can't. I know, I know, the rent . . ."

"Landlady actually showed someone our quarters today," Jack said. "I think it was all for show, but who can say."

"Well," said Dorie.

"She made the usual threats about tattling on us to my aunt and then said there better not be any more suspicious noises at night or the rent that we haven't paid would be going up. For someone who's always going on about morals she sure has a dirty old mind."

Dorie tried to think of helpful things to say, but couldn't come up with any. She thought it would improve her mood to sabotage the silvermen's work, but it sounded like Jack was not in favor of that idea. "Let me change back into curls and we'll go cadging free drinks to cheer ourselves up?" she offered. "After you crate?" She could feel her ethics slipping every moment.

Jack drummed her fingers on her arm. "The thing is, I wish it were me, you know? The one being arrested." She nodded at the inflammatory artist, who was being carefully handed into a black automobile, triumph on his face and flashbulbs bright around him.

"Mm," said Dorie. Like Jack, she was iffy on the value of the law, but she would rather escape to do whatever the heck she wanted another day. Jail did not appeal to her.

"It's really a wake-up call," said Jack. "I'm not pushing the limits enough. My technique is really doing something, I think, but that's not enough in modern times. It's subject matter that really gets them. But something *meaningful* to me. I have to find something authentic. . . ."

"Mm," said Dorie again, who had never thought of searching her soul to share it with strangers. There were so many ways she and Jack were in lockstep that it always surprised her to find the gulfs she could not cross. As far as Dorie was concerned, strangers were entitled to exactly nothing from her. They didn't need to know anything beyond what she presented.

The woglet in her arm stirred and made sleepy coos of protest at the noise around them.

"Is your arm . . . yodeling?" said Jack.

"Ugh," said Dorie. "I don't even know." Peering around for the silvermen, she pulled back the rags that covered her elbow and let Jack peek at the coiled ball of silver. "They're not supposed to . . . cuddle."

Jack sucked in breath. "Is that what I think it is?"

Dorie nodded as she covered Woglet.

Jack threw up her hands. "Ugh. Dorie, you know I love you, but seriously. Was that thing in an egg a few hours ago? An egg that would cover our entire rent?" Dorie nodded again and Jack said, "Sometimes I could just . . ." She made strangling motions at her best friend.

"And there's more," Dorie said in a small voice. "I saw Tam."

"Oh, honey," said Jack. And then, looking again at Dorie-as-Dorian: "Like that? Oh, honey." She put an arm on Dorie's shoulder. "Did you tell him who you were?"

Dorie shook her head miserably. After seven long years she had seen Tam, and he hadn't known her, and she hadn't told him. She didn't know how to say the long-buried story here, on the street with all the students and silvermen. She didn't think she could ever tell Jack what she had done. Jack knew Tam from way back, of course—Aunt Helen and Jack's aunt were old friends. Jack knew Tam and Dorie hadn't spoken since some fight at fifteen, but Dorie had never been able to tell her closest friend the details. She could still barely tell them to herself.

Dorie pressed Jack's hand where it sat on her shoulder. The sleepy chick was stretching now. Its cooing grew shriller. "He's probably hungry again," said Dorie. And silvermen everywhere. "I'd better get out of here." But before she could take off, Woglet stood and yawned, fanned his wings, and swooped to the ground. He was blessedly silent while yawning, as apparently he could not yodel and yawn at the same time. And then, back into the yodel as he strutted around, no doubt scaring off all the prey for miles. A gallery-goer turned to look and Dorie mentally encouraged them: *turn away, nothing here.*

Dorie lunged for Woglet, but he easily eluded her, then made a distinctly petulant yodel in her face that clearly demanded: *feed me, Mom.* No help for it. The little air raid siren would have to eat.

"I have a roll I nicked from the cheese tray before they threw us out," Jack said, searching her paint-splattered satchel.

"Only if rolls can be hypnotized," said Dorie. She closed her eyes and searched with the fey senses out around her. Something must be alive, warm, scuttling. . . . She tracked down a vole under a nearby bush, and, eyes closed to keep attuned to it, she moved unerringly around the edges of the crowd, Woglet screeching his silly head off as he strutted after her. In the back of her mind she thought how powerful that screech must be—maybe his eyes weren't the only thing that was hypnotic!—to make her do anything fey-related at all, no matter how invisible, so near this enormous crowd. But she could not see any other way to make him shut up.

"It's there, near that bush," she told Woglet, opening her eyes and pointing. She did not really think he could understand her, but this close he could probably sense the prey for himself. He quieted as he scuttled under the bush. The vole darted out, the woglet after it, and then he made a new sound, a warm cooing that one's mother might make, if one were a small and timid vole, and the vole turned to look, and was caught. The woglet advanced, step by step, until it was even with the vole, and then it pounced.

Belatedly Dorie realized that a small circle had formed around them—this interaction was rapidly becoming more interesting than arrested artists. Her encouragement to look away would only get her so far—she and the wyvern were being far too interesting. Woglet devoured the tasty parts of the vole in rapid succession, and Dorie knelt near him. "Come on back," she said with mounting frustration and fear, and with something long and stringy dangling from his mouth, he obeyed, flapping back to her arm. He tipped his neck up and with one long slurp sucked down the last morsel. Dorie-as-Dorian looked at him, exasperated fondness lighting her face.

And then all the flashbulbs went off.

Chapter 6

THE QUEEN'S LAB

Dorie is nine, and so is Tam. The pair of them run wild through the broken-down house, the house with the bombed-out wing that there will never be enough money to have restored. Not in her parents' lifetime, anyway. They run wild through the lawns, and then, as soon as they are sure Jane and Edward and Helen and Rook are no longer watching quite so closely, they go into the forest.

Dorie treasures these brief visits with her city cousin. There is no one else who understands her. Not only does Tam truly know who she is, he doesn't care. It doesn't matter to him. He doesn't run away from her.

For Tam, Dorie's fey side falls under the category of parental damage. His father, his real father, was in a drunken car accident when he was five, an accident that killed his mother. Then a fey took over his father and impersonated him, eventually destroying its host. So Tam remembers his father as first a lax drunkard, then a rotten dictator, and though he tries to remind himself the second one wasn't his father, it's all jumbled up and impossible to sort out. Sure, he was later adopted by Helen and Rook. But you carry those scars. And he knows that she carries her scars, and they aren't her fault any more than his are. In order to make peace with his own past, he has to make hers okay, too, or perhaps simply realizing that she, too, has a past, makes it easier for him to ignore his. He thinks that in some strange way her history is bound up in his, but he never says anything like this. All that happens on the surface, between them, is that they don't give two bits for each other's damage. They let it go.

And if sometimes Tam wakes screaming in his bed, she goes in to comfort him, and they don't wake any of the parents. And if sometimes Dorie pranks the maid or the postman, he just *looks* at her. And she makes it right again.

—T. L. Grimsby, *Dorie & Tam: A Mostly True Story*

* * *

Jack rousted Dorie from a hard-won sleep. She had been dreaming of her childhood, running wild with Tam, and now those memories melted away as she sat up. It was morning and the summer sun was already baking her side of the room. So much for the temperate climate—would the heat wave never break? "Woglet!" Dorie said, and then found him curled in a sunbeam, in a nest around her feet. *Girl* feet—she must have shifted back in the night. Woglet seemed not to care what state she was in. Mother or father—it was all the same to him.

"He woke me around six chasing down a mouse," Jack said. "And that's after the mouse he ate when we got home last night."

"Better than a cat?" offered Dorie hopefully.

"Here," said Jack, tossing a sheaf of newspapers on her bed. "You might as well see this now."

The front page of the biggest city paper was a clear picture of Dorie-as-Dorian, looking on in maternal—well, *paternal,* perhaps—awe as the woglet swallowed, bright wings spread wide. Dorie groaned.

"The good news is you're not technically in trouble," said Jack, plopping down next to Woglet. "The whole article went on about some new law that was passed on Monday making it illegal to own wyvern eggs. Wyverns *themselves* are not illegal. Yet. They asked one of the zookeepers to make an educated guess on how old your wyvern was, but the guy said he couldn't say for sure whether it had hatched that night or a week ago. Also they didn't know your name, although it was strongly hinted they were interested in finding out."

"I don't even know," said Dorie. She flipped to the continuation of the article to see if there were any more pictures, but there weren't. "I guess Dorian's kaput then. Time to invent a new persona," she added glumly. She looked up at Jack's expression. "Did we scoop your show?"

"I can't decide," said Jack. "Would we have made the front page without you? Or would we have been buried under a police report file somewhere? The show's only under investigation for now, but the sculptor who did the fey piece got booked under Subversive Activities. And you know what happens there—you never hear about the incident, or them, again."

"I'm sorry, Jack," said Dorie. She laid a hand on Jack's, but Jack dismissed it.

"Don't be. In a weird way I envy him. He had something worth fighting for, you know?"

"I suppose," said Dorie. A brief article below hers caught her eye—NURSES' STRIKE TURNS UGLY. A grainy picture showed one of the women struggling against a policeman in riot gear. They had framed the shot well—the woman looked violent, insane. She peered at it, hoping it was not her stepmother.

Jack thrust a scrap of paper into her view. "We're not done here," she said.

"And . . . ? What's the rest of it?"

"The Queen's Lab called," Jack said. "It was strongly suggested that you be there by nine."

"And the time is?"

"Eight forty-five," said Jack. She put her hands up. "Don't look at me—the landlady literally just brought the message up."

Dorie put her head in her hands and groaned. Woglet ululated happily in response.

The Queen's Lab was a five-minute walk from their flat. Dorie managed to change into Dorian and get out the door by nine-oh-five, which she thought was doing pretty well as Jack had insisted she clean up the remnants of the mice Woglet had left the night before. Jack was not particularly squeamish, but she said it was the principle of the thing, and she didn't make Dorie clean up after her models. Dorie said when the models started eating bits of mice they'd talk, and with one thing and another they both were rather grouchy by the time Dorian Eliot slipped out the fire escape and up onto the roof, and leapt the half-meter between the sheltering sycamores to the arts building, which was her preferred method of avoiding their landlady. Artists could always be counted on to leave the roof door open, and she sauntered down the stairs and out of the building.

At the base of the arts building, she let Woglet chase a vole while she nibbled on a clump of sorrel growing in the shade. Someone had left a half-eaten apple by a sketchpad, and she filched the apple and hurried Woglet along from his vole bits before the artist could return.

More than one student stopped them on their walk to see

the woglet live and in person. Several wanted to pet him, and Dorie-as-Dorian let them, wondering how Woglet would react. It was different every time—a small boy he let stroke his head, and a large professor he stood up and tried unsuccessfully to hypnotize. Once he snapped, and that person snapped at Dorie for letting her pet him, and Dorie shrugged.

At nine-twenty she strolled into the lobby of the Queen's Lab, outwardly serene, but truthfully with her heart in her mouth. Woglet was asleep again, digesting the morning's activities with a wobbly snore. The gatekeeper pressed his silver-sigiled palm onto hers with a yawn, then waved her through. He had done that on Monday, but she had not known the significance then. She walked through the steel door he opened, glad once again that what was poison to true fey was not always so to her. She didn't particularly *like* being in close contact with iron for very long, but it wasn't deadly. And now the wyvern goo—although she was not eager to try touching it in fey form, it seemed to not poison her as long as she was in human shape.

Everyone who happened to be walking through the area looked around when she came in. Some of them managed to go back to their missions, but a couple of scientists stopped and stared openly. She always cataloged them, automatically. Like Jack's artists' collective, the lab was highly gendered. It wasn't just the field work position—there weren't many women here, period. Still, the self-assured girl from the forest must be here somewhere.

Simons came hurriedly up to her, still looking rumpled and overworked, but decidedly more deferential to Dorian than he had been to Dorie.

To be fair, Dorian *did* have a woglet.

"Right this way, sir," he said. "Our lab director is very eager to meet you."

Dorie lingered, enjoying the sudden shift in power. "You know, I'd really love to see your wyvern facilities first, Mr., uh . . ."

"Simons. Are you sure that's the best idea? Wyverns are notoriously cranky, even with each other."

Dorie strode forward, strong and easy, toward where she remembered the lab was. She could get used to this. "Is it down this way, Simons?"

He hurried after her, trying to keep up. "Yes, but I'm sure the director will want to show you *personally*. . . ."

"Oh, but I'll want to make sure the facilities are adequate for the work I'm interested in doing."

Simons spluttered. "*Adequate*? This is the Queen's Lab—"

She was on the edge of gaining her goal when a commanding voice stopped them in their tracks. "That's enough, Simons," said a mellifluous voice. "I'll take it from here." Dr. Pearce clapped Dorie on the shoulder and steered her down the hall to his office. He gestured for her to take a seat, but she decided Dorian would rather stand than sit in that low chair next to his massive desk. She strolled over to the terrarium, forcing Dr. Pearce to tag along if he wanted to talk to her. The adolescent wyvern was back in the cage—but sometime in the last two days the little copper bolt had been replaced by an iron padlock.

"What do you think, Woglet?" she asked the purring silver ball in the crook of her arm. He stood on her elbow, poking his nose up with curiosity. The wyvern inside the cage fanned its wings dramatically and opened and shut its mirrored eyelids—display gestures of aggression. Woglet tried to fan his wings, too, and dug his claws into her arm as he overbalanced. She pried the claws off as she turned away from the cage.

"The question in all our minds, Mr. . . ."

"Eliot," she supplied.

"Eliot," Dr. Pearce filled in smoothly, while watching the wyvern display with a great deal of interest. "How on earth did you tame him? I'm pretty sure it's a him, by the way, though wyverns are hard to sex. You can just tell he's a fighter."

Dorie, who was sure Woglet *was* male, decided in that moment to refer to him as female as long as she was around Dr. Pearce.

She had in fact been turning the matter of Woglet's docility over, and she had come to the obvious conclusion that it must have been the time the egg spent in her belly that did it. The belly plus her fey side? Simply the belly? No way of separating the two for a proper study, regardless, and certainly no way of disclosing how it had been done. Dorie settled on saying, a bit pointedly, "Perhaps it was because she knew she had no parents or nest to return to."

Dr. Pearce shook his head and said, "Unfortunately, there have been other wyvern chicks found in that sad state. May I?"

Dorie tilted her elbow up, interested to see what Woglet would do—bite, hypnotize, or purr. He flapped his silver wings and began the shrill yodel that meant displeasure. Dr. Pearce put his hand out regardless, and as he did, she noticed the silver sigil marking his palm. It glowed brighter as it approached Dorie and Woglet. Woglet's yodel dropped an octave and took on a purry rumble. He actually let that man stroke his head. Dorie was taken aback.

Dr. Pearce saw her face and smiled. "He recognizes his womb," he said, showing her the sigil.

Dorie swallowed at this confirmation of what they were doing with the wyvern albumen. "I thought just the silvermen had those," she said.

"Silvermen first," he agreed. "First we protect those at most risk—policemen, scientists. Then those who can afford to pay the large initial investment fees—we need to support the cause somehow! But eventually, everybody. We'll be free of the fey menace for good."

"I thought iron did that," said Dorie.

"Better than iron," said Dr. Pearce. "Wyvern albumen, if you haven't heard, is actively poisonous to fey. Next best thing to the legendary basilisk eggs. With the sigil in your hand you cannot be taken over. Never."

"Well, that sounds just dandy," managed Dorie.

He studied his palm. "We've found that they glow around fey, but it's not as useful as we hoped, as they have a pretty sensitive threshold and glow around a number of other, non-fey things. Like your little friend here." He rubbed Woglet's head, who was cooing. "It's an area we're still studying." He stood. "But enough about that. Let's take a tour of the facilities, shall we?"

Under his personal escort she saw several labs stocked with what he assured her was the very latest equipment, and then a well-stocked storeroom full of things like hartbird feathers and vials labeled DANGER—HYDRA VENOM, and then he handed her off to a clump of researchers to poke around the wyvern hatching facilities while Woglet chased field mice from the lab's stores. She knew there was plenty more proprietary stuff she *wasn't* being shown, yet even this was so fascinating that she was still caught up in it at lunchtime when he popped his head back in and declared he was sending her out to lunch on the lab's expense.

"Along with the two field scientists you met yesterday," Dr. Pearce said, "since you've already met, and they're a couple of our best and brightest. Tam and Annika?" Tam loped over to meet them. Annika wore a tight-lipped smile on her athletic face. "Counting on you to woo Dorian," he said. "Tam is our golden boy here, the one who discovered the secret of the wyvern eggs—and no one can resist Annika's charms. Half the lab is smitten with her and the other half just doesn't know it yet." The young woman's forced smile did not change and Dorie had a stabbing flash of what it would have been like if she had accepted that liaison job here, as Dorie.

Dr. Pearce steered them out the front door, and Dorie was impressed at the sheer amount of force he displayed, while being only straight human. His attitude to her was different as a boy, and certainly better, but he was clearly the alpha male of the lab, in charge of everybody, boy or girl.

She and Tam and Annika found themselves out in the bright sunlight, blinking and at a loss for words. The cool lights of the facility had been giving her a headache, she now realized. Woglet emitted a pleased yodel at the sun.

"Well," said Tam finally. "There's the University cafeteria, but I doubt anyone wants boiled potatoes when Old Pearcey has deigned to comp us a meal."

"I would not eat there on a bet," said Annika.

"Noted," said Tam. "What about the Queen's Arms? It's close."

"No women allowed," said Dorie and Annika together, and Annika shot her an odd look.

"Ah, right," said Tam, a bit sheepishly. "You usually work through lunch, Annika."

"There are reasons for that," said Annika tightly. But she

softened and said, "What about The Wet Pig?" and so they went there.

Dorie had just been there as Dorian to find Colin, but then she had been distracted. Now she looked at it with a fresh eye.

The Wet Pig catered to students, particularly the free-spirited, breaking-boundaries sort of students, and women were everywhere in here, sitting around drinking ale with the men in cheerful, casual fashion. Dorie knew the place well, as it was one of the few places she enjoyed going while female, which made it extra odd to be going here as Dorian. It was also a perennial artists' hangout—a favorite of Jack and her gang. The old plaster walls had long since been covered over in several layers of murals from successive art students, the good ones left by common accord and the poor ones rapidly painted over. At this point it was practically a who's who of the artists who had passed through the nearby art institute. There was even one by Jack, and it was in fact of Dorie, head thrown back in a riot of laughing curls, pounding a table with a mug of beer. She sat down with her back to it.

It occurred to her that Colin might be working today, and she hoped he would have the sense not to say anything to her if so. She thought she had impressed upon him the need for caution, but . . .

Woglet jumped off her shoulder onto the wooden table, where the other two scientists looked at him with frank curiosity and seemed not to particularly care that there was a lizard near their food. She warmed to Annika a smidgen for that. Scientists were restful.

Dorie took the opportunity to order everything she had ever wanted off the menu—smoked trout, a plate of thick-cut fried potatoes, roasted plums, a pint of dark stout. Usually she stuck to the cheapest fare: bread and cheese and whatever ale was the house special. Tam and Annika, she was pleased to see, ordered food and drink in equal quantities, and the waitress looked glad to have someone besides penniless students to wait on for a change.

"So how did you get your job at the lab?" Dorie asked Annika, because it was the question burning on her tongue. "You must be one of the only women there."

"One of four," Annika said. "The only one out in the field."

Tam was holding out his fingers for Woglet to sniff. Woglet looked dubious. "Even Pearcey can manage to hire a girl when she's twice as good as everybody else." Dorie stiffened in response.

Annika brushed this off. She leaned into Dorie. "Not twice as good," she said intensely. "Twice as driven, perhaps. I wanted to continue working abroad with Thomas, post-University. But the fey are only here in this country. Thomas had to return home to continue his research." She spread fingers. "And here we are."

"You went to school abroad?" said Dorie to Tam. She had thought Tam had gone to University down in the south country somewhere—though he had had the marks to go to one of the top schools here in the city. Aunt Helen had been bemused but accepting.

Tam shook his head, and named a second-tier but respectable country school. "I followed my research," he said. He rolled up his shirtsleeves, exposing a neat bandage over the wyvern burns from the day before. "I needed access to the woods and small towns to write my book. And the sort of school where I could skive off for a week to chase a lead. A wild goose chase took me abroad, to Annika's school for a term. But I don't regret it." He looked away, apparently busy pulling his journal from his vest, but Dorie knew him well enough to see the hint of a smile that lightened his features. It stabbed her heart.

"I grew up here," put in Annika. "But for school, I wanted to see my mother's country. My colleagues thought I was crazy to leave the job offers I was getting there after University, *ja*? But you have the wyverns. You have the fey. And, you have Thomas." There was an unspoken "most of all" in that sentence. "His book was still in draft form then. I knew what he had found could change the world, if we got it into the right hands."

"Well," said Tam, demurring. He flattened his journal and began making notes, eyes on the baby wyvern.

"He is too modest," interrupted Annika. "He had what amounts to a history degree. Crypto-zoology? Who knows, who cares. I have the science background and as a woman, I will tell you I am used to being overlooked. Therefore I could see what others were overlooking here."

"The childish ravings of a lizard-loving lunatic," murmured Tam with amusement, apparently quoting someone. "I think that should go on the back of my book." He was more interested in rubbing salt on his fingers and holding them out to Woglet. Woglet licked the tips of Tam's fingers and purred. Tam made a note.

"At the time, I was working with a small team on that tranq formula you saw in action," Annika continued. "I brought Thomas and his book and the serum to Dr. Pearce, and made Dr. Pearce an offer he couldn't refuse." Her eyes narrowed. "And I don't mean what you're thinking."

"What then?" said Dorie. The waitress set their drinks down on the heavy wooden table, barely sparing a glance for the winged lizard. Another good thing about the Pig—standards were clearly so bohemian that they didn't care if their patrons had pets.

Annika nodded her thanks as she tried her drink. "Nice to be back home to a fine brown ale," she said.

"Although those cold lagers would be nice on a day like today," put in Tam.

"True."

"Annika, what did you do?" said Dorie. "How did Dr. Pearce let you in?"

Annika leaned back in her chair with her ale, studying Dorian. "I brought him proof," she said finally. "None of your little dolled-up girl scientists with their treasured letters of recommendation, tiptoeing in like a supplicant, expecting to be thrown out." Annika took a long swallow as Dorie sat on her hands and suppressed her temper. "I brought him a live northern vampire bat that I had defanged myself. And I brought him a sample of the tranquilizing serum you saw in action. Perhaps he could pass up the vampire bat. But only I hold the key to the tranqs. You have not invented anything like that here. We are not releasing the formula. I hold the upper hand." She shrugged her broad shoulders. "And that is all you need to do if you are a girl."

"I see," said Dorie. There was an uneasy feeling in the pit of her stomach. Perhaps the things she had always done to keep her fey side from being noticed, to keep herself from being noticed and commented on, had played right in to her submissive role in the interviews. What part of her was Dorie-hiding-fey, and what part of her was playing into the part that society had handed her? Perhaps if she had gone in two days ago as she had gone in today—with a wyvern chick, walking as though she owned the place. . . . The character of the person who hid, who tried to work behind the scenes, who retaliated not openly but through spilt teacups . . . that was not the character of this girl across from her. And where was the root of that? "Most women I meet aren't quite so sure of themselves," Dorie said slowly. It was a question, not a barb.

Annika seemed to accept the gentleness in Dorie's tone, for she said with some understanding in her voice, "I think I have had a different position by being half-foreign. It was . . . not always easy growing up. And then my mother would tell me stories of her country, how women there did everything men did on a daily basis. She was always pointing out hidden problems in society here that I might otherwise take for granted."

Dorie thought Annika's mother and her stepmother might well get along.

"It is hard," Annika said, and took a swallow of her ale, searching for words. "I love my country very much. But when I went abroad I saw different ways to be. They went through their revolution a hundred years ago, and now everyone is equal. My classmates would ask me how I could stand to live in a place stuck in the dark ages. There, it is commonly understood that the sexual and technological inadequacies here are why we have never been able to expand beyond our borders, why our efforts at expansion have always met with failure."

"Why didn't you stay there, if it was so great?" said Dorie. She was needling again, but perfect, superior Annika was getting under her skin.

Annika looked at her coldly. "You don't save something you love by running away. Besides, Thomas—"

"Yes, yes, Thomas," said Dorie. "Thomas and his mythical book. Can I pick it up at the bookstore, do you think?"

Tam laughed but Annika did not. "The Crown confiscated

the University printing and declared it the property of the Queen's Lab," Annika said. "Those of us who were smart enough to pick it up when it was first published keep our copies secret. When I first started corresponding with Thomas about joining him here—"

"You did?" said Dorie, raising her eyebrows. She was straight-out taunting now, but it was clear that Annika was busy engineering Tam's future to suit herself.

Annika stared her down. "It is purely the meeting of two scientific minds."

"Oh, of course," said Dorie, perfectly politely and not a bit insufferably at all. She leaned back in her chair like a man, legs stretching out into the aisle. Annika rolled her eyes and looked away. Tam stared off into something in his brain, lost behind his glasses.

Oh, it was all going just *beautifully*.

Over Annika's shoulder, Dorie saw Jack and Stella walk into the Pig with a man she didn't know. Jack was in her typical slim trousers and bangles, but Stella was in a flouncy blue dress she couldn't possibly have worn to the laundry. With relief at the interruption, Dorie excused herself to say hello. She strolled over to their table in the corner, grinding peanut shells underfoot, confident in her new male walk. She was starting to get the hang of this.

Jack had her pocket sketchpad out, and her most cynical-but-trying-to-hide-it expression on, when she looked up and saw Dorie. Her eyes brimmed with laughter as she recognized her roommate's boyshape. "Sit down, sit down," she said.

"I can only stay a minute," Dorie demurred. "I was only stopping by to say hi."

"Dorian, this is Peter Tomkins, from the magazine I was telling you about." From the arch of Jack's eyebrows Dorie could guess that was the girlie mag, which also explained how Jack and Stella were able to afford lunch—someone else's dime. "And my best and dearest friend, Stella." Dorie shot a look at Jack and found her with raised laughing eyebrows, daring Dorie to take offense. "We were just talking about me doing a series of sketches for the magazine with Stella as model."

Well. This should be interesting. Dorie couldn't imagine that Stella would really go that far—surely the two girls were just stringing Peter along to get a good lunch. "Pleased to meet both of you," said Dorie. She straddled a chair and leaned her elbows on it, trying to match Peter's laddish behavior. "Knowing Jack's skill and hearing so much about Stella's . . . talents, I'm certain those would be some good pictures." She was surprised to see forthright Stella blush, all the way down the V of her flouncy dress.

Jack glanced sideways at Dorie in the gesture she recognized as studying her for a sketch. There was a funny look on her face, though—Dorie was not sure why. Was she going too far in teasing Stella?

Peter reached across the table to shake her hand as the waitress set down their drinks. "That's exactly what I'm thinking," he said with a fellow grin. "Tell me, wouldn't you buy a mag with pictures of this little lady?"

"Like a shot," Dorie assured him. She watched the casual, self-assured way he held his ale, leaned his elbows on the table, and tried to mirror his gestures. Woglet hopped down from her shoulder and made himself at home among the saltshakers and bottles of malt vinegar. He peered into Jack's gin drink as if to sample it and Jack shooed him off.

"Now there's a fine fellow," said Peter, leaning forward. "I know a couple of mags who would be interested in getting their hands on pictures of him. I can put you in touch if you like."

"Oh?" Dorie said politely. She didn't want more people thinking wyverns would make good pets, but Jack jumped in.

"Peter, what a *fantastic* idea," drawled Jack. "I would buy *that* issue like a shot. Why don't you give me the names later and I can make sure to pass their contact information onto Dori . . . an here."

Dorie narrowed her eyes at Jack, who smiled innocently.

"Can I see him?" said Stella. Her heavy blond hair fell forward over her eye as she held out her hand for Woglet to sniff.

"Careful," said Dorie. "They're not known for liking most people." But Woglet leaned down his triangular head and delicately licked her outstretched fingers. He flashed his mirrored eyelids at Stella in a way that meant he definitely did like her. "Well," said Dorie.

"I grew up with a lot of animals," said Stella. "My parents had a farm." Dorie recognized that as a slight stretching of the truth as in fact Stella's parents were in service to a wealthy gentleman farmer. In the girls' cataloging of how a decade ago they wouldn't have been able to go to their respective schools, Stella's was even more so, as in the olden days her class would have been thoroughly against her as well as her gender. She wondered if Stella was trying to impress Peter so he would raise their fee.

"You raised a lot of chicks, didn't you?" said Jack. "Maybe that's why Woglet likes you." Woglet delicately picked his way around to study Stella's cocktail, claws tapping. He flicked his tongue at the side of the glass and warbled at it.

"Oh yes," said Stella, putting her hand over her glass. "Bottle-feeding goats, hand-hatching chickens—there's always someone being orphaned on a farm."

Dorie perked up. "Did you ever build an incubator by

chance?" she said. "I'm going to be tracking down a few more of these guys for the Queen's Lab, and"—she couldn't keep them in her belly, not if she didn't want to acquire more pets—"I thought a little portable device might be helpful for bringing the eggs back. Just a little box with a lightbulb and a battery."

"I never did, but I bet I could," Stella said eagerly. The engineering, mathy side of her clicked on and Dorie could practically see the wheels turning as she made calculations.

Peter looked thoroughly bored at the turn the conversation had taken. "Surely your lab will have incubators," he pointed out to Dorie. "Don't bother my cover girl's head with such things."

Stella laughed this comment off. "But he's probably right," she said to Dorie. "They'll have something better than anything I could do. Gosh, it would sure be easier if we had the fey batteries like back in the old days. Compact, clean . . ."

Peter smiled lazily. "I wouldn't call them the old days if I were you," he said. "You might be surprised what we'll start to see soon enough."

"What is that?" said Jack. "Social regression, reduced opportunities for women and the poor? I expect we're already seeing it. Backlash."

Peter waved this aside. "No, I'm talking about something much more interesting." He leaned in. "Through the other editors I hear about the latest things hitting the streets, often well before the papers. Some boring like the overcrowding at the hospital or, what was that kerfuffle last week about? You know, about the belligerent women."

"About women being turned away from the public boxes in Parliament?" said Jack, with the smile that said she was not amused but dammit, she was broke. "When they were trying to listen to the bill that plans to roll back women's property rights?" Dorie's stomach sunk again at what Jack was doing for them.

"Yes, yes," said Peter. "Well, much more interesting to my mind is what's coming over the wire about a . . . certain sort of technology we used to have, shall we say. A very clean, *blue* sort of technology."

Stella lit up. "If trade has started up again, it would be wonderful. We've studied the old energy in class—so far superior to anything we've managed to create yet."

Peter smiled in a way that looked unpleasant to Dorie's eyes, if not to anyone else's. "Yes. *Trade*," he said. He leaned back in his chair, a finger to his lips. "You didn't hear this from me, but word is for a very nice fee, certain wealthy gentlemen in this city are able to buy themselves a very nice sort of energy that lasts . . . *forever.*" He shrugged. "Nice to be rich, eh?"

Dorie felt pale from head to toe. She stood, retrieving Woglet from Stella's drink and excusing herself with all the politeness she could muster. It was mostly limited to smiling and handshaking, as the words were getting stuck up behind her tongue again.

Stella smiled sweetly at her, and Peter told her to buy a copy of the issue with Stella in it.

Jack shook her hand and held it for a second. "Dunno what it is, Dorian," she said. "But seems like every time I see you, you've changed." She casually slid the sketchpad over in front of Dorie. "We'll have to get together more frequently."

"Yes we will," said Dorian. There was a funny feeling sinking to the bottom of her chest as she looked down at the sketchpad on the table. It was all too clear from the sketch what Jack meant.

The bump on her nose was gone, and her hair was curling into tiny black ringlets.

Shaken from this double blow of news, Dorie found the restroom before she returned to her seat. She willed her body to calm. Men did not tremble. And surely Peter was mistaken. The fey were no longer selling bits of themselves for energy—that had been a punishment from the old Fey Queen, long before the war. And how else could it be happening? You couldn't forcibly split a fey . . . could you?

She stared at the doors to the two restrooms, lost in thought, before she finally realized she was supposed to open the men's and go through it. The women's was quite modern in comparison—literally so, as it had only been built in the last twenty years as the Pig cast off its reputation as an old campus boys' club and opened its doors to the second sex. She had not known the men's would be that disgusting, and it only had one tiny splotchy mirror above the sink. But it was enough to look in and see what the sketch had told her. She was not keeping a firm enough grip on *Dorian*. Her mother's imprint was leaking through.

There was no one around, except Woglet. Quickly she put the bump back on her nose, firmed up her jawline, straightened her hair. Hoped it was dim enough in the bar that no one would notice the slight changes. She looked at her ears, trying to remember if they were the same or different, and shook her head. She was going to have to get Jack to do her a quick sketch of Dorian—a reference point.

Their food had arrived by the time she got back, and Dorie picked up her fork and stared at it. Almost without meaning to, she said suddenly, "Have you heard of any rumors in the lab? About any sort of new technology?"

"New technology happens every day," Annika said coldly.

"Well. Anything particularly *clean*? Anything new on the energy front?"

Tam shook his head and Annika just shrugged.

The rest of the meal passed without incident, if also without any particular pleasantness. Tam was lost in his head, stuck on some puzzle, and Annika shut down Dorie's feeble efforts at politeness. Eventually Dorie gave up and ate her food.

Back at the lab, she was shunted into Dr. Pearce's office to wait for him. Before he had been attentive; now she had to cool her heels. Which meant they were going to talk actual numbers next. Woglet flew over to examine the caged wyvern, and Dorie distracted herself by seeing if she could snap one of Dr. Pearce's pencils from across the room. The cool lights that were everywhere in the lab were giving her a headache again, and she put the unbroken pencil back in its tray.

When Dr. Pearce finally walked in, he sat down across from her at his lovely desk and launched in without preamble. "Let me lay it on the line, Dorian—I can call you Dorian, can't I? We need a man of your talents around here. Someone who can bring us back the test cases we need. I would appeal to your love of country, but I sense that an upwardly mobile man like you might be more interested in . . . shall we say, more monetary rewards." Dr. Pearce looked pointedly up and down Dorie's neatly patched jacket and she stared levelly back at him. "I hate to do anything so gauche as talk numbers, but let's see if this sort of thing is up your alley, shall we?" He took an already prepared piece of paper from his pocket and slid it across the desk to her. It was a penciled list of animals with prices next to them. "That's in addition to a monthly stipend," he added.

The numbers were already a touch higher than Malcolm Stilby's, but Dorie knew that if he had written these before she walked in the room, it was just a starting offer. And regardless, if you looked like a boy, they expected you to bargain. She barely glanced at the paper, then slid it back. "Double it and we'll talk," she said. He looked pointedly at the patches on her borrowed boy's jacket, and she said, "We all have our little foibles, don't we?"

He sighed and said, "This lab is in service of the Crown, Mr. Eliot. We subsist on funding."

"And on the wyverns you sell to collectors, and the new protective compound to the wealthy, and—"

"Consider if there's anything else I could throw in to sweeten the deal," he said. "I noticed you eyeing Annika. We brought her in to secure Grimsby, but I'm sure she wouldn't mind having two of you to take care of. You might need an assistant to help you handle some of the cases. . . ."

"Not Annika," she said before she thought. "Tam."

"Ah, that's how it goes, is it?" Dr. Pearce mimed zipping his lips, and said, "I am the soul of discretion. Let's say one point five on the numbers, and your very own, personally chosen assistant. And"—he raised a finger, forestalling whatever Dorie would have spluttered to this—"a special bonus if—no, *when*—you bring us one hundred eggs. We are in great need, Mr. Eliot, and those bastard underground brokers like Malcolm Stilby are not only beating us to the eggs, but they don't care a bit what kind of damage they do getting there. I can tell you're a bit of a bleeding heart yourself, though you try to hide it. Let me assure you, crooks like Stilby are a far worse threat to the wyvern population than anything that goes on here. Now, are you with us? On the side of truth, justice, and a bit of cash for yourself? What do you say?"

"Yes, yes," Dorie said. "Of course I am." Her headache was throbbing and she would have agreed to anything at that point to get out of there, even working with Annika. She had finally realized what was bothering her about the blue-tinged lights in the lab.

The entire building was lit with fey light.

Chapter 7

CATCHING SILVER

Dorie is seven, and she has convinced her father to take her into the woods, to see what the other half of her heritage is like. Her father is easy to convince; he is still shredded from what the fey did to him. She knows that, even at seven, and she knows that she contains all of his guilt, and all she has to do is push and pull in the right way and he will tell her what he knows.

What he knows is this:

He himself was taken by the Fey Queen when he was a young boy. Most fey are too indolent to take humans. They drift through the trees. They bask in the sun. But the few fey who are strong-willed cause all the fey tales one hears, back in the human world. This one took him when he was a small boy. Put her hooks into him, and he drifted along with them for several decades, aging at a snail's pace.

It is said when the fey release humans back into the world, they send them with a gift, and it is so—if you count being impregnated with fey substance a gift. It is both power and curse, and it was what allowed the Fey Queen to retain her hold on Dorie's father, even after he had been let go.

He has no fey in him anymore. Jane has driven it from him, leaving his hands crippled and scarred, but human again. He is aged; no longer beautiful, no longer talented. They would have no interest in him, and even if they did, Dorie could protect him. He knows this, she knows this. She knows, too, even at seven, that it is a hard thing for her father to go back into the forest, to introduce her to the fey. To let her meet them, to let her go.

She makes him do it anyway.

If you think that children don't think about their moral compass, you are wrong. This is the thing seven-, eight-, twelve-year-old Dorie struggles with, over and over, the thing that she has constantly turned to Tam about and said, is this thing that I do, wrong? Is this *fey*? And Tam does not know what to say. For when he does something wrong, where can *he* place the blame?

Still, whatever this human thing called compassion is, Dorie thinks she doesn't have it. Somewhere along the way, whether from Jane's rantings about right and wrong, or from her own determination not to be amoral like her maternal line, she has developed something else. A strict sense of what's fair.

Life mostly isn't fair.

And *she* hasn't always been fair.

It is perhaps her great mistakes in this arena that make her more determined to not fail each next time. It is not *nothing* when she errs. It is proof that she is rotten, fey to the core. And so each time she fails she becomes more rigid, and Tam watches it happen, and sees her struggle, and thinks she must be human from head to toe, to care so much.

And yet, to know Dorie is to know she pranks. Even Tam knows this, though he never expects it to happen to him.

No, with the strict sense of what's fair she has fought for, you only trick those who deserve it. The wealthy who don't deserve their wealth. The policeman who abused his power. Those above, who would trample those down below.

And when you betray someone who doesn't deserve it?
You are lowlier than the lowliest worm.

—T. L. Grimsby, *Dorie & Tam: A Mostly True Story*

*   *   *

Thursday morning Dorie woke herself bright and early, a habit she had trained herself into during those first rough months of prep school at fourteen, when you never knew who was about to do what to you for being different. Her headache had ebbed. She wondered if the blue lights in the lab had really physically given her the headache, or if it was just her subconscious saying: *something is wrong*. Because as far as she knew, the fey were not trading. And that whole building was tinged blue, the blue of clean fey energy that Jack's magazine contact had been hinting at in the bar.

Still, she had no proof that something was wrong. The fey had been absent for nearly twenty years. And yet, they were being seen again occasionally, weren't they? That incident in the bar with the silvermen proved that. Before, when the fey had infiltrated the city, it had been due to a strong leader. And when there had been trade before, that, too, had been due to a strong leader. Perhaps two decades had been enough time for a fey to rise again, directing the other fey in what to do. Perhaps that fey was making deals with people like Dr. Pearce. Perhaps she had been wrong to think that the fey were the victims here—perhaps there were wheelings and dealings she was not privy to.

She shivered in the light of the summer sun. Perhaps she would swing by the City Hospital on her way into the lab and see if her stepmother was still there.

And then it would be time for her new job.

Her new job with *Tam*.

As Dorian.

Woglet stretched like a cat and rolled over, still snoring. Dorie groaned. She needed to see Jane as a girl, with no woglet, but then appear at the lab as a boy, with one. How was that going to work? She nudged a sleepy Jack and said before her roommate could fully wake up, "I will be back in ten minutes. Woglet is still asleep. You'll be fine."

"Dorie," mumbled Jack threateningly, but Dorie pulled on a dress and hurried over to the hospital, filching an unattended slice of bread and jam off a patio table on the way.

The nurses' strike was still going when Dorie arrived. Sparse but determined, she would call it—a dozen women in the white dresses of their profession, keeping vigil in sensible shoes. Dorie found Jane down at the end, talking at length to an older man who clearly just wanted to go into the hospital without having to think too hard about workers' rights at that particular moment.

Dorie took pity on him. "Jane," she said, catching her stepmother's attention.

"Dorie!" said Jane gladly, and gave Dorie a poky sort of hug with a sign that read TOMORROW IS TODAY. "How are you doing? How did your interviews go on Monday?"

"Mmm, they'll let me know," temporized Dorie. "I actually came to ask you a couple questions. Have you . . . have you heard anything about a certain sort of energy coming back into use?"

Jane compressed her lips and looked around. "Take a sign and walk with me," she said.

Dorie picked up one that read BETTER CARE FOR STAFF MEANS BETTER CARE FOR PATIENTS and fell in line. Her stepmother had not changed much since Dorie was five—she was still thin and neat, still with a white lock of hair that showed where her fey curse had blighted her cheek and forehead and scalp. Her cursed face had long ago been replaced by a perfect one, infused with fey and embedded with strips of iron to keep her safe. The iron was long gone, but a crisscrossing pattern of reddened lines showed where it had been. Up close, Dorie could see where the grey hairs now streaked the dark hair.

"What did you hear?" said Jane.

"Rumors at first," said Dorie quietly. "But then I saw—the lights in the Queen's Lab are all tinged blue. Not yellow; blue. Unless it's simply a new invention it seems awfully suspicious." She wrinkled her nose. "And it gave me a splitting headache. Does that seem possible?"

"We still had bluepacks at Silver Birch when you were little," said Jane, "and I never noticed you complaining. But that doesn't necessarily mean anything." She darted a glance at Dorie. "Do you remember me talking about a blacksmith named Niklas? Who helped the ironskin?" Dorie nodded. "His hatred of the fey continues to grow more intense," Jane said. "Leading him into places that . . . I just don't know. He spent the first five, six years after the war just working on a machine that would destroy the fey. And when that failed, he turned his attention to other avenues. I heard a rumbling a few years back that one of those avenues might be the energy problem." She shook her head. "I have not seen him in a long time."

"The blacksmith," Dorie said, realizing. "He's been cured of his fey curse. Did you know?"

Shock filled Jane's face. "What do you mean?"

Dorie realized belatedly that that subject was going to open so many things she didn't know if she could tell her stepmother yet, about Tam and her boyshape and the wyvern eggs. Certainly she didn't want to say any of it out in the open, on the street. She backed up a step and managed, "I mean, I just heard . . ."

Jane looked hard at her former charge. "Whatever you learn, come tell me about it," she said. Her attention was drawn then by a mother with two children walking toward the hospital. Jane stopped to tell them about the overcrowding, the long hours, the overworked nurses making unnecessary mistakes. She got the woman to sign her name to the clipboard another nurse carried, and Dorie fidgeted impatiently, certain everyone walking down the street was looking at her in her curls and dress.

"How's the strike going?" Dorie said, when Jane turned back to her.

"Not well," said Jane. "When the police came it scared most of the nurses back into the hospital." She nodded at the other women holding signs. "They gave them a twenty-four-hour ultimatum to be back on duty. We have had some nurses come back and march on their days off, but it's not really getting the hospital where it hurts." She shook her head. "Everyone's for it, but no one wants their face splashed across the newspapers. They want someone else to do the dirty work."

"Not everyone is as brave as you," said Dorie. "Getting thrown in and out of jail is more dangerous for those . . ." like herself, she thought, but she finished up, "well, those with families, for example."

Jane got a funny look on her face and she bent her head close to Dorie's. "Have you seen your aunt Helen recently? The twins?"

"No," said Dorie. "Why?"

Jane shook her head. "I've heard rumblings," she said. "Your uncle Rook is a good man in Parliament. Always willing to fight." She shook her head. "I don't know what's going to happen. But I know he's someone you can count on to stay and face trouble. That's what we need there. More people like him."

From down the street Dorie saw the police returning. Hastily she shoved her sign into her stepmother's hand. "I'd better go," she said. "I'm late. For a thing."

She could see disappointment in Jane's eyes, but all her stepmother said was, "Be strong."

Dorie made it to the lab panting and out of breath, but on time, in boyshape, with Woglet on her shoulder. She was disheartened to find that Annika was waiting in the auto for them, but it turned out Annika was only going as far as some nobleman's country home. "I was warned about this, *ja*? That the token 'lady scientist' would be sent to do fund-raising while the men went off to slay dragons. Well, I haven't turned the tranq formula over, so there's that. And I won't until I get the research needed to complete my book."

"Maybe Pearce sent you because you know so much about wyvern research?" Dorie said hopefully.

Annika shot her a sour look. "He sent me because this man likes blondes."

There was an odd push-pull with Annika. How was it possible to feel sympathy toward another woman, a smart, strong woman, fighting the same fight you were—and yet to heartily dislike her at the same time? This must be another bit of her fey side coming out, Dorie concluded. Surely an ordinary human woman would readily form a sisterhood with this woman. Or siblinghood, or whatever you called it when one person was a girl and the other nominally a boy. She would have to do better.

After that, they mostly drove in silence. Despite the warm summer day, they kept the top up and the windows nearly closed to contain Woglet. The stink of petrol fumes in the hot auto made her feel nauseated. Woglet crawled up and down the seats, hanging on with his pinprick claws. Sometimes he got too far away from where Dorie sat in the backseat, and fanned his silver wings into Tam's field of vision as he drove. Dorie apologized and collected Woglet, but it didn't deter his exploring.

It was a relief to finally reach the place where Annika was going, a grand country house very close to the turn-off to Black Rock Mountain. Dorie watched Annika's stiff back go up the steps to the door and wondered if she should ever go back to being female.

"Rum go, I suppose," said Tam, perhaps thinking similar thoughts. He was the only boy she knew to even think these things, but then, he had been raised by Aunt Helen and Rook, and that surely explained it. Aunt Helen did not go off on lecturey tangents about women's rights the way Jane did, but still, in her own subtle way, you could tell what was and was not acceptable behavior.

"Are you two . . . you know. Seeing each other?" Dorie asked abruptly.

Tam casually turned the wheel and got them onto the bumpy side road that went straight up, zigzagging back and forth. "It is purely a meeting of two scientific minds," he said in a decent approximation of Annika's accent. Which, though amusing, did not entirely answer the question. "Why, do you think she likes me?" he said easily. "I don't ever understand the signals. Maybe she likes you. Or Pearcey. That would be entertaining."

"Er. Well," said Dorie. "I mean, just curious."

Tam shrugged as he drove. "I confess she seems a bit prickly when you're around," he said. "But I'm told sometimes that's a good sign. Any particular place you want to try? Good leads on possible nests?"

"I actually want to see if Woglet will go back to his parents," said Dorie. "It would be better for him." She fidgeted. "One of the stories in your book suggests they might."

Tam lit up. "Dorian! You read it! What did you think? I'd like to have more feedback from someone who's a strong field naturalist to begin with. Before the Crown decided it was valuable and locked it away, I'd gotten very little feedback on it. I think because it's such a mix, you know? Interviews, transcripts of old herbalist knowledge, stories . . . but it's all primary sources, and you never know where the next insight is going to come from. I was hoping someone would surprise me by connecting dots I haven't yet. But the few people who did read it dismissed it as a book for children, and the ones who didn't were stark bonkers—conspiracy theorists and that sort of thing. It was a real relief to have Annika's unconditional support."

"I've just read a bit of it," Dorie said, which was true. "I only borrowed it from the lab yesterday." *That* part was a lie—Aunt Helen had given a copy to her several months ago, when he'd first published it through his school. She hadn't been brave enough to crack it until now.

"Well, the bit about the woglets is in the Glass Mountain story," Tam said. "But that story is often retold, and though I encountered lots of variations from the oral storytellers, the part about the princess returning the hatched wyvern to its parents was always in there. I started thinking more seriously about that once the eggs became valuable at the lab."

That nudged her memory. "Dr. Pearce said the wyvern goo was the next best thing to basilisks. Is that in your book?"

He looked at her sharply. "Pearcey was talking about basilisks?"

"In a theoretical sense."

Tam nodded. "That's an even older story. You know the story that basilisks can opto-paralyze us? Well, legend says they can do the same to the fey. Once upon a time there was a warrior who was granted the power of the basilisk—the story never says exactly where the power comes from, but it's certainly clear where it goes—in his eye. The eye turns silver, and then he can control the fey."

"The silver eye," she said. "In the silvermen's palms."

"A nod to that story," agreed Tam. "The idea that we could rise up and have dominion over the fey."

Why did you never tell me that story? she thought. But perhaps he had not wanted to scare her, as kids. Anyway, "Basilisks are mythical," she said.

Tam stopped the auto at the entrance to the trail. The engine rumbled to a halt as he looked at her. "Would you think I was crazy if I said I was actively looking for one?"

"Noooo," said Dorie slowly. "Not given the other things you've uncovered. But in the stories, they're huge. Monstrous. Wouldn't someone have seen them?"

"Some historians think that they might have had a periodical life cycle, like cicadas," Tam said. "A couple of the Old English epics refer to the 'hundred-year blindworm.'"

"Basilisk larvae?" said Dorie, raising her eyebrows.

"I know, it sounds nuts. We don't have much to go on. The only possible skeleton is from the seventeenth century. It's only about four feet from tip to tail, and the current fashion is to dismiss it as an overgrown, misshapen wyvern—or even a hoax."

"I've never seen that," she said, "and I've been to the Natural History Museum a bunch. Is it not on display?"

"Nope. Once it was downgraded from 'definite basilisk' to 'possible basilisk' to 'possible mutant wyvern' it got sold off during the Great War when funds were scarce. I hear it's in a private collection somewhere. I'd give my eyeteeth to see it."

"You and me both," said Dorie.

"Well, assuming it's even the skeleton it's claimed to be, then it's the one the naturalist and fortune-hunter John Pendleton brought to the king. He swore it was a baby basilisk and that he had mortally wounded the mother, who was at least thirty feet long. That's how Kent painted him in the famous picture of Sir John and the Basilisk—because Pendleton was knighted for killing the poor thing, you know. But Pendleton couldn't produce any proof that there had been an even *bigger* creature, so opinions were divided, even at the time. At any rate. Some sort of offset cycle could potentially explain why basilisks turn up simultaneously in multiple sources, and then not again for a long time. But there are signs that are supposed to herald them coming. The historian Christopher Mills has copious notes on the strange creatures that appeared that summer. And now, this summer . . . well. The yellow garter snakes I've never seen before. The swallowtails that are too far south."

"But migration patterns are changing," pointed out Dorie. "The heat from the factories and the mining down south have been changing things. One of my professors last year kept talking about it."

"True," said Tam. "That could be all it is."

He stepped out of the car, and Dorie followed him into the fresh air with a profound sense of relief. The clean pine scents washed away the petrol stink and nausea from the drive.

There were tire tracks all around the point of entry to the trail, not just theirs. Tam's face darkened. In a low voice he said, "I come and find eggs, and then more and more people come. I'm contributing to a slippery slope." He looked sideways at her as he tugged on his explorer hat, eased his leather jacket over his bandaged arm. "But you were probably a mercenary before the Queen's Lab, so perhaps we're not on the same side on this issue."

"No," Dorie said, feeling very glad she hadn't taken Malcolm anything. "I wasn't."

"I don't know what to do," Tam said. "How to make up. There's a line between responsible research that helps people and then . . ."

"Yeah," she said gruffly, grabbing her pack. Woglet flew onto her shoulder as they started into the forest. He seemed extra alert, and she wondered if he recognized this part of the world somehow.

"I don't know," Tam said. "I feel like I can trust you with this, even though Pearcey would haul me off under Subversive Activities. I . . . don't agree with everything the lab is doing." Immediately he looked like he regretted having said it and he laughed at himself, embarrassed for saying something so open and naïve. "Just the side effects of having my life saved, I guess. Run off at the mouth. Don't mind me, Dorian."

But he could trust her. He *could*. Except where he couldn't.

The tree canopy grew thicker and darker as they pressed deeper into the forest.

They reached the nest. Empty. Her heart gave a sudden irrational leap. She did not want a baby wyvern, dammit. Woglet poked his triangular head into Dorie's eardrum and burbled. "C'mon," she said. "I'm putting you in the nest anyway, so you can see what you think. Maybe the smells will tell you something." She climbed the tree as straight human, and let Woglet crawl off her elbow and into the deep nest. He turned around a few times. Stood up and let out a sharp cry that was clearly meant to call somebody. Then turned around again, and apparently satisfied he had done all he could do, started purring.

Dorie and Tam looked at each other, wonderingly. "Well," she said at last. "Maybe they'll come back for that."

Meanwhile, you never passed up an opportunity for free food, so she slithered down the tree and poked around until she found some purslane and a double handful of wild strawberries. She was never quite certain which of the three hundred varieties of mushrooms were perfectly safe, so when she found a clump, she resorted to the trick of letting her fey side take over, her fingers exploring the caps and stems in a faint blue glow that she shielded from Tam. Edible, her fingers said, and she gathered a few and sat down by Woglet's tree, rubbing the dirt off of them as they watched and waited. She offered one to Tam, but he peered at it through his spectacles and demurred. He had never been as good a forager as she, and he was wise not to trust a strange mushroom if he couldn't identify it for himself. He did take her up on the offer of strawberries, and she poured half of them into his cupped palms. They sat companionably, their fingers red with juice.

It was so nice just sitting with him, like back in the old days, that she almost told him then. Almost said who she was, almost transformed to prove it. But she looked at his solemn face behind the glasses and did not. Tam of old was so slow to trust. And yet here he was, eating strawberries with her like they were old friends.

Perhaps it didn't hurt that she had started the introduction by saving his life.

The lie was a big knot in her chest, but after seven years without him she couldn't bear to give him up so soon. Just one more day. One more adventure.

Tentatively, feeling him out, she said, "So . . . what if we could make up for this somehow? What if . . ." She took a breath. "What if there were a few ironskin left, that could be helped by the eggs?"

Tam pondered. "A few like three? Like a hundred?"

"Like twenty."

"I suppose they could apply through the lab for aid, but I'll warn you the lab isn't into charity."

"I figured as much," Dorie said. "It seems unlikely that help would come from that source." She watched Woglet poking around and purring, while waiting to see if Tam would come to the same conclusion she had. It was much cooler up here in the mountains, under the forest canopy. The glints of summer sun that filtered through were pleasant instead of merciless.

"You think we should help the ironskin," Tam said slowly. He laughed ruefully. "Forget just *saying* I disagree with things. This would get us locked away for years."

"So that's a no?"

He looked at her. "You've only been there one day and you're already pointing out where I've fallen into the slippery slope of just paying attention to my research and nothing else." He cocked his head. "Who *are* you?"

But she was spared from answering this by a rush of silver wings. "Duck!" she shouted.

They took cover in the low trees and brush the best they could, Tam shielding them with his jacket. There were suddenly silver wings everywhere, crackling and snapping as the wyverns turned and swooped. Great fighting yodels broke out all around them, screeches and shrill calls, and the occasional bolt of errant steam shot past.

"Is this about us or him?"

"I think they're here to protect Woglet!" whispered Dorie. "They don't know from what." The wyverns settled in a loose circle on the trees around them and she held her breath. It was a beautiful sight—all the curved silver bodies arranged in the branches. They seemed to be waiting for something, looking from one to the next. Finally, one wyvern swooped down to where Woglet was, and the others purred in unison. Dorie almost leaped out to protect her hatchling, but Tam grabbed her arm, and she remembered in time what they were doing. She waited, watching, until she saw the bit of dirty tape on the grown wyvern's chest. It must be his parent, then— mother or father; who could tell? It had a darker silver marking like a mustache and she decided to consider it the father. He glided in for a landing and settled on a branch near Woglet's nest, cooing in a distinctive pitch.

Woglet jumped to his feet. His purr took on a yodelly flavor. With a snap his wings fully extended into a fighting display.

Dorie did not recognize this behavior. Well, she did, but she didn't expect it from day-old wyverns reunited with their parents. Woglet circled the nest, wings puffed up to make himself look larger. "You called your dad," she whispered. "What did you expect?" But Woglet did not seem to know what to do with the wyvern he had called. The instinct of being a lonely woglet in a nest and summoning a protector was one thing. What to do with a large wyvern on your doorstep was another.

The parent wyvern, who had initially been welcoming, now became wary. Had it made a mistake? Was this some other, unrelated chick? The coos took on a more irritating whine. The father cocked his head from side to side, peering at the forest floor. Then he jumped out of the nest and glided down, claws extended to snatch a vole. He launched back to the nest, live vole extended to Woglet.

Woglet looked sideways at the vole. He lifted one foot, then the other.

Then he jumped and glided all the way down to Dorie, burying his muzzle in Dorie's elbow.

"What am I going to do with you?" she asked the wyvern, and it wasn't really rhetorical.

"That's done it," muttered Tam, as several more wyverns came down to explore the two humans crouched in the bushes. Woglet trotted out, rearing to a fighting position, and Dorie frantically grabbed him around his little warm belly, tucked him into her armpit where he yodeled unhappily. She did not want Woglet's attack posture to get him killed. The father wyvern glided down and looked at all of them inquisitively. It made the distinctive coo one more time. This time Woglet spat.

Dorie looked at Woglet, now cuddled in her arms, then looked up at the father. The father looked at Woglet, Woglet looked at Dorie, and Dorie looked at the adult wyvern. They stayed like that for a long time before Woglet's purrs turned into snores.

At that, the father wyvern seemed to decide it was official. He launched himself off the ground and into the air, all the other wyverns following behind. They tore through the trees, Dorie and Tam taking cautious steps behind them, through piles of blackberry bramble that had not been cleared for decades. Silver wings led them on through the struggle, and then all at once, the trees and bushes suddenly cleared away and the two found themselves at the top of a tall ravine. The wyverns swooped down and then up, curving around the mountain, and settling into a distant clump among the trees on the cliff face.

They watched the dark silver blur coat the side of the mountain, disappearing one by one as they blended into the mica-flecked rocks and silvery grey scrub. Woglet launched himself from Dorie's shoulder, circled around once, and flew back, as if waiting for her to hurry up.

Tam looked at Dorie, a challenge behind his spectacles, man to man. "How good are you at climbing?"

It was a nasty hot trip down, picking their way through the thorns and scree. Woglet mostly flew around their shoulders, though once he spotted something he wanted to eat and flew off to nab it. For a hatchling with no parental guidance, he seemed to be getting the swing of things.

They made it to the bottom, where the summer remnants of a creek ran past in the sun. Feywort was running wild all along the creek, and she said, "Wait a minute," and used her little knife to gather a double handful for Colin's friend. It was flowering this time of year, and usually you could see the little blue bells of the flowers running up and down the mountain. But not this year. Just bare swathes of grey rock in its place. Feywort apparently *was* scarce, then, but where was it going? Unless it, too, was falling victim to the changes that were affecting the swallowtails and snakes Tam had seen.

They forded the stream at the stones, stopped at the other bank to let the wyvern drink. Dorie cupped her own fingers in it to have a swallow herself, but the water, which was generally clear and potable even in summer, was sharp and tingling on her fingers, and she let it fall away. She usually did not bother to bring water with her any more than food, and she swallowed against the dryness that tickled her throat.

"Pressing on," she said, and they began their way up the other side of the ravine, weaving through the birches and evergreens. This side of the ravine was still in the tail end of morning shadow; a welcome relief from the summer sun. And then—

"Wait," Tam said quietly, putting a hand on her shoulder. He pointed way down the ravine, down to the south.

There were fey there.

The blue drifted along the scrub in the ravine, disappearing in and out of the foliage. With her half-fey heritage, she never felt the instant dread you were supposed to feel. Despite everything, Dorie was filled with a sense of wonder at the sight of her wilder kin.

"They look so innocent," Tam said quietly as the blue flickered on past and vanished.

She shifted uneasily. "Tell me the stories you've learned about the fey," she said. "The strange ones. The ones nobody knows."

"A long, long time ago, the fey and humans were not at war," he said, starting to climb again. "Never exactly allies, but not at war. You know there was trade until before the Great War?"

She nodded.

"Long, long before that, there's stories of humans and fey living in close quarters intentionally. The fey would invite humans into the woods—not kidnap them. The humans would return a century later, enriched by the trade. Or so they say."

"Go on," Dorie said. She hooked her arm around a birch, hefting herself upward. She never needed nor wanted help climbing, but it was funny not to have someone offer. Restful.

"There's a very unusual story that I only ran across once," Tam said. "Most of the stories are repeated, changing from town to town. You can sift out the kernel of truth that the story grew from. But this one I only heard once, from an old woman in the northernmost forests, who was said to be fey-touched herself. Neighbors claimed she had lived two hundred years—spending one of those centuries with the fey."

"What did *she* say about it?"

"She was evasive on the subject," he said, looking off into space. Finally he added, "But that's common. She said that this was an old story among the fey themselves. That even to them it was a myth, an ancient rumor. Their story goes that there's more than one world. That major events create a bend, a fork, and worlds splinter off."

"Wow," said Dorie, trying to wrap her head around the idea.

"I recorded the story and forgot about it," Tam said. "I ended up not including it in the book—there wasn't room for everything, and I'm more interested in the stories that mention animals, so I focused on those. But then I was talking with someone from the physics lab and he happened to mention this thought experiment they have—something called the Multiple Worlds theory. It's the same idea."

"Wow."

"Except there's one more wrinkle. I pulled the story out to look at it. As far as the fey are concerned, the theory is only applicable to them. If you don't know, back when we were using bluepacks for everything, they didn't work the farther you got outside the borders. Like you go to Varee and poof, your flashlight is dead. Fey only live in this country—fey power only works here, too. Which is strange, but it was never fully explored. Perhaps there's a central point in our country—perhaps a larger concentration of fey in the middle somewhere that affects individual fey, perhaps all the fey draw their power from some central nexus—I don't know."

"Okay."

"So this fey story claimed that these world turning points only come about due to them—due to large changes in their history. Now, solipsism is nothing new. And how would they know how many worlds there are? Except the story says there is a link between the worlds. Sort of like the nexus that spiders out from the heart of our country, there is a central point between the worlds that they can access."

"So the fey can know more about these other worlds? But then surely there'd be more stories about this idea."

"Right. The story implied it was hard to cross over. Because—and mind you, this is the only story I've ever run across about this—the story says that, millennia ago, that's how the fey got here. That they spanned out from one world that had them in it and they crossed over to a few other places, including here."

"An origin story," breathed Dorie.

"If you like," said Tam. "Like all origin stories it leaves out as much as it explains. Where did those first fey come from in the other world?" He shrugged.

"Did you ever talk to the old woman in the north again? After you heard that this was a real theory from your physics friend?"

"I tried to, but it wasn't until a year later. She had passed on." Tam sighed. "These stories are being lost all the time, due to the fact that people think of them as fey tales. And sure, does the story of the beautiful sleeping princess with the good fey and the bad fey fighting over her tell us much about anything? Well. Mores, perhaps. That even the fey can disagree. But then you happen on something like the story about the wyvern eggs and that's a major breakthrough right there."

"It makes you wonder what else you could learn from spending time with them," said Dorie. She had done just that for several summers. But she had been interested in her own story, in what she could do, and had not thought to press them for their myths. When had Tam thought to do so? Had it started when he was with them?

"It's not always worth the price," he said somberly. "Don't

think I'm hogging my sources, but I wouldn't try it if I were you."

They came up out of the ravine and he put a cautioning hand out. "Look."

Above them, several dozen wyverns soared. Silver wings flashed, and yodels trilled at irregular intervals, like demented birdsong.

"The real question is how we get some eggs away from them," Tam said in a low voice. "I know you're good, but are you fifty-some-watching-wyverns good?"

The real problem was she wasn't one-human-watching good. She couldn't phase blue with Tam there.

"We passed a sort of cavelike thing as we climbed," Dorie said. "You take Woglet—if he'll go—and the pouches and stay there. I'll bring you eggs and you protect them."

"It's hardly fair for you to do all the dangerous work," Tam protested.

"I can't get *any* eggs with Woglet," she pointed out. "Not to mention that your arm is still recovering from the steaming." She grinned. "You can fight your legendary basilisk when we find it."

"Deal."

Woglet was in fact leery of this new arrangement, but once he found a garter snake hiding in the back of the cool little cave he settled down to investigate that.

Tam safely out of sight, Dorie made her way to the cliffs and began to climb. She didn't dare put the eggs in her stomach again—one baby wyvern was enough. So she actually did need Tam to stay behind in the cave.

She was lucky. It was a good time of year and there were a number of nests with clutches of three and four eggs. Wyverns were clean animals, but this many together at once left a faint acrid tang to the clearing. Still, better than petrol. Dorie phased in and out of blue, slowing and speeding up her timesense to get close to the nests. She was getting pretty good at avoiding triggering the wyverns' gaze. In the end, she was able to get eight eggs without taking more than one from each nest, and she brought them all, one at a time, back to Tam, who wrapped them up and coddled them in his portable incubator. Another benefit to bringing Tam into this—she would not need to have Stella rig up something for her. With eight eggs carefully packed into the incubator, they had run out of padding—no one had ever gotten more than three at once, as Tam kept saying—and the wyverns were getting restless, so they left.

They retraced their path, tramped up and out of the ravine, hot and dirty. Woglet had gone from flying back and forth like a crazed bat to sleeping curled on Dorie's shoulder, tail in a chokehold on her neck. His triangular head poked snores straight into her ear.

"When do you think they're going to hatch?" said Tam.

"Two to three days for most of them," Dorie said, "except that there's one that's going to hatch tonight, probably midnight-ish. So either we sit around at the lab tonight with that one, or—"

"Or we take it to an ironskin," Tam said. He took a deep breath. "Do you know one we could help?"

"Yes," she said. "My contact does, anyway. Through him we can reach all of them. I was thinking . . ." She hesitated, then pressed on. "Four for us, four for the lab?" Besides the symmetry, the bonus for bringing in eggs, split between her and Tam, would then just cover the rent.

"We'll already be heroes for bringing home four on our first day out," he mused. "They'd never guess that we found *eight.*" He looked up at her and nodded, decision firming his face. "Let's do it."

They agreed to meet at ten and pressed on, talking through the logistics for their secret adventure. It had all gone so well that she thought maybe now was the time to tell Tam the truth. It had been just like the old days—the two of them on some grand and glorious expedition, bringing home twigs and birds' eggs. Except now the twigs were feywort and the eggs would cure four more of the ironskin. They were in dirty sweaty harmony, and she looked sideways at him and found him grinning. Perhaps something of the same thought was going through his own head, for he said, "You know, Dorian, this has been a really good day."

"Yes," she said. "It has." And then suddenly added, "Let's not tell anyone about their nesting place, shall we? I don't want them to be disturbed."

"Of course not," he said. She beamed and then her smile fell as he added, "Well, Annika. But other than that."

"Right. Annika."

"You don't like her very much, do you?"

Dorie couldn't answer that honestly. Finally she managed, "She's very smart."

"And forthright," he added immediately. He looked down at his hands. "I don't know what your past is like, but I've been burned by dishonest girls." His voice fell away. "Well. One girl."

Her heart was pounding in her ears and her throat choked with guilt. "Maybe the girl made a mistake," she said.

He shredded his leaf and let it fall away, turned and grinned wryly. "And maybe all girls are deceitful and I should have known better. That's why when you find someone like Annika, you appreciate it, is all."

They came to the edge of the woods then, and right on cue, there was Annika, stretched out on the ground, making a careful drawing of a blue feywort that was growing at the edge of the woods. "You found some eggs, *ja*?" she said, carefully tucking her pencil away in a case and pulling out a penknife. "I stayed through lunch, I stayed through tea, but when he started to encourage me to stay the night I dumped my raspberry fizz on him and hiked up here."

Dorie laughed in spite of herself. Tam offered Annika a hand up from the ground, which she waved off. With her penknife, she sheared the plant she had been drawing at the base of the stem and wrapped it in a cloth, its bells trembling. A drop of sap welled out, bleeding onto the cloth.

The way back was more convivial than the way out. Despite her trying afternoon, Annika told them all the details with a candid bluntness that verged on having a sense of humor. Tam shared the full story of their adventure—minus the actual number of eggs they had found—and Annika sounded duly impressed. Annika even unbent so far as to say that perhaps they should finish with a drink at the Pig, but Tam demurred before Dorie had to decide whether or not she could enjoy sitting there with the two of them, unable to afford even an ale to take the edge off.

"It's Thursday, isn't it? My mother's having a cocktail hour for her Young Women's group at eight and I promised to help serve," Tam said.

"Oh, *them*," said Dorie. She had a standing invitation-slash-order from Aunt Helen to go, which she had never actually followed through on. It sounded dreadful—all those girls she had never understood during prep school, now grown up and married well and using family money to feel like they were accomplishing something. No one actually down in the trenches, no one she understood. "I mean. That sounds nice. What do they do?"

"Oh, it's chiefly eating canapés and discussing how to improve the city," Tam said, not in a dismissive way. "Annika, you'd be more than welcome. In fact, my mother would be thrilled if I brought you." That hung there for a moment while they all thought about what it meant. Tam coughed and added, "Dorian, I'm afraid I'd be persona non grata if I brought someone of the—erm, inferior gender along."

"Of course," said Dorie, all manly and casual while her heart broke inside. Annika go? Tam inviting Annika? Here she was bonding with Tam, and now she was going to be too late to ever make up.

There was a rare moment of hesitation to Annika's self-assured demeanor. Then stiffly she said, "I think I would like to come, then. If you are sure I will not be intrusive." She looked down at her dress, now dirty from the forest floor. "And I must change."

From the backseat, Dorie saw Tam's posture relax slightly, his shoulders unclench, his back unbend. He laughed. "Me too, or my mother would kill me. I'll meet you in front of the lab at a quarter to eight."

Chapter 8

DOING GOOD

Sept. 9: Though difficult at first to believe, the most likely answer seems to be that this poor, cursed girl is seeing a variety of possible futures. It is a confirmation of Dr. Rochart's Many Worlds Theory, from a most unexpected source. When in fey trance, the subject (Alice) frequently speaks of a scene where men with "silver on their hands" storm the forests around Black Rock Mountain, and systematically decimate the fey. At first I would reason with her, and remind her that the fey were eradicated after the successful "Great War" two decades ago. Continued scans have turned up a grand total of three fey in the years since, each of which was quickly dispatched. But she insists, and now I let her tell me what she sees, for it is all too clear these sights are happening somewhere—at least in her mind if nowhere else.

For now, we have decided to leave the fey substance on her shoulders. This is a hard decision, but with the fey themselves gone, there will never again be such an opportunity to learn.

—Dr. Tamlane Grimmsby, *What Alice Saw*

* * *

Dorian Eliot stood in front of the mirror and relaxed every finger, each knee, each ear, until she was plain Dorie again.

Her "date" to meet Tam was not until ten, but damned if she wasn't going to that cocktail hour as well. Just, not as Dorian. She took a quick sponge bath—her Dorie shape was automatically clean and shiny and smelled of fresh air after a rainstorm, but she *felt* dirty.

The real problem was what to do with Woglet. He was Dorian's charge, not Dorie's, and in particular she couldn't let Tam or Annika see him. There was the old birdcage, but she could only imagine Woglet's yodels if she tried to leave him alone in the flat in that. Landlady would be thrilled. Woglet had gone so well to Tam this afternoon, but Tam would be there tonight, and not able to watch a woglet.

In the end, the best she could come up with was a large patent leather handbag that had been a hand-me-down from Aunt Helen's atelier. Dorie wrapped the precious blue-belled feywort up and slid that in an interior pocket, since she would be seeing Colin after. She had left a note for him at The Wet Pig. Then her boy clothes in a tight bundle, and then Woglet himself. She used her fey senses to catch another of the omnipresent mice, and dropped it in, and let Woglet go to town. That should knock him out for a nice nap.

She did not know what you wore to cocktails with a Young Women's League, so she pulled at random one of Aunt Helen's dresses, figuring it would show she tried. It was pink with rosebud buttons and a little lacy cape thing over the shoulders and she thought ugh, what the heck, and put it on.

It was going to be hard to go out the window with a purse full of woglet. Dorie braved the noisy house stairs as quietly as possible, wincing at each creak and bang.

It was not quiet enough. The landlady heard and jumped out in billowy nightgown and fuzzy slippers to lecture her on the rent, and additionally remind her of the house rules about curfew, which Dorie, going out at eight in that hussied-up pink dress, was very likely planning to ignore. It was a lecture Dorie had heard too many times, and it finished up with, "and if you didn't live with that nice Miss Jacqueline, you'd be out on your ear."

"I know, Miss Bates. I'm sorry, Miss Bates."

The landlady harrumphed. "Maybe you will be anyway. Today's the fourteenth and your rent is two weeks past due. I put up with a lot for the sake of my dear friend Alberta, a sweeter lady never lived. It's not her fault she has a niece with questionable taste in roommates. But friendship won't pay the rent."

"I really am sorry, Miss Bates. Look, I just got a steady position, I promise. We'll have the money soon."

Miss Bates poked a bony finger at the rosebud buttons. "And where is that?"

"At the—" But no, that was Dorian Eliot's job, and Miss Bates was quite capable of calling to check them to see if they really were employing a Dorie Rochart, which they emphatically weren't. "I can't say."

Miss Bates drew herself up to her full height of five foot one. "And just what sort of boarding house do you think this is, missy?"

"No, no, I promise it's nothing immoral," Dorie said desperately. "I just mean it's not official yet, and I don't want to jinx it."

The finger jabbed higher. "There's strange goings-on here, missy, and don't you think I don't know about it. I think if that rent isn't on my doorstep tomorrow by noon, I'll be talking to my dear friend Alberta just to let her know what's going on with her niece and that niece's friend."

"Nothing's going on!" said Dorie. Of course that was the

moment Woglet started to poke his head up from the purse. She shoved him down, remembering the extra charge for pets. "I'll ask for an advance at my new job; we'll get the money. . . ." She retreated to the front door.

"Those kind of jobs don't pay in advance," Miss Bates said sourly, determined to have the last word. She whirled and retreated to her rooms in a billow of floral cloth. "Shoulda started a boarding house for boys, my mother always said. Know where you are then. But no, I thought, girls would be so sweet and *moral*. . . ."

Dorie hightailed it for the trolley.

The rent. The rent was all her fault. Her stubborn stupid pride—she didn't want to take eggs to Malcolm, she didn't want to beg her aunt for money. But she couldn't let Jack fall into a hole through her stupidity. Jack would have had her half of this month's rent ready, if she hadn't had to pay Dorie's half last month. She groaned. There was nothing for it. She would have to man up and ask Aunt Helen to loan her the rent. It would be better than jeopardizing her new job.

The lace on the dress was scratchy, the snoring handbag awkward. She longed to ditch this outfit for her field clothes and a free woglet on her shoulder. But she only had to make it a short trolley ride over to Aunt Helen's. Well. And then, through the party. Damn, she was starving. There had been nothing in the cabinets except Woglet's mouse. Dorie filched a double handful of mulberries from one of the campus trees and got on the trolley without incident, her fingers stained purple with juice. She dampened down her aura as the conductor passed her—no one's here, move along—and avoided paying the fare. She had forgotten how simple it was, having all her fey powers back to smooth her way. No one even gave her a second glance until she stretched both feet out in front of her, taking up the aisle. A few shocked glares reminded her that a) girls didn't do that, and b) she had unthinkingly put on her dirty hiking boots. Another glance down told her she had gotten a smear of purple mulberry on her pink waist. Dorie tucked her feet back under her chair and hunched her shoulders. Smaller, smaller.

Aunt Helen lived in a nice but comfortable part of town, with old fruit trees in the front gardens and kids playing tag in the quiet road. She had two other children besides her adopted boy Tam—twin ten-year-old girls. Dorie had always been fond of her cousins, so she had stopped in frequently in the last four years she had been in the city attending the University. With Tam at school in the country, Dorie had been fairly sure of not encountering him. Now, though, she was planning to meet him. As herself. What was she doing? Perhaps she should turn and go, meet him at ten as Dorian, as planned.

But no, she wanted to test the waters. She wanted to *know*.

Dorie knew the location of all the fruit trees on her route— one was a plum tree across the way from Aunt Helen's, with sweet black-purple plums that dangled over their brick wall. She stopped there in the summer twilight, her fingers closing on the plum. As she touched the fruit her whole arm tingled, like a jolt from faulty wiring. She let the plum go and stared up at the tree in disgust. Some sort of poison, clearly—those new-fangled pesticides coating the tree. But she was hungry, so she touched it again—and recoiled again. Her fey side was not going to let that one pass. Woglet stirred in her purse as she massaged the tingle from her fingers.

"Dorie!" shrieked a voice from across the street, and another said more sedately, "How do you do, Cousin Dorie?" The girls were on the small side, being a quarter *dwarven* through their father, her uncle Rook, but not so much as to make them stand out. They had Helen's copper-blond hair and their dad's laughing eyes. Though identical, they seemed to deliberately form their characters in opposition to each other—Rose liked pretty dresses and books, and Violet liked to be dirty and blow things up. Still, more than once Dorie had caught Violet reading in the garden, and Rose helping Violet to create an explosion. Dorie often suspected their established characters were part of some deeper mischief against the grown-ups.

"Girls!" Dorie said in delight, and one grabbed her free hand and the other her skirt and swung her toward the house.

"Mother will be glad you finally showed up," said Rose.

"Only a half-hour late," said Violet.

"Better late than never?" said Dorie.

"It's all right," said Rose. "They haven't got past the stage where they congratulate one another yet. It's boring. We're supposed to be in bed."

"Pfft, bed," said Violet. "How can we sleep when we're going on an adventure tomorrow? We're all packed."

"Packed? Where are you going?"

"Somewhere fun," said Rose.

"Somewhere far," chimed in Violet. "And we're never coming back."

"They don't think we know," Rose added, more seriously. "It's a dead secret."

"Never?" said Dorie. Surely this was one of the twins' games.

Rose grinned, launched into an old children's song: "Never sits upon an old oak tree . . ."

"Singing of a fairy fey so free . . ."

"Never falls and tumbles down . . ."

"Boom, boom!" they shouted together.

"But try to focus, Cousin Dorie. The canapés are still to come," said Violet. "Cucumber and cress."

"Tuna and olive."

"Pineapple and frog legs."

"Gorgonzola and little green newts."

They opened the screen door and shoved her in. Dorie stumbled in, hand automatically going to her purse to keep it from swinging and waking Woglet.

A whole roomful of women, dressed to the nines, looked her up and down.

Surprise flooded Aunt Helen's dear face at the sight of her wayward niece, and Dorie felt answering guilt. Surely she could have come to her beloved aunt's beloved charity thingy before now. All the help her aunt had given her over the years, and she couldn't come sit nicely for a few hours and eat canapés? What was wrong with her?

Helen rose to greet her, immaculately dressed and not a glimmer of reproach on her face for Dorie's ratty boots and stained pink dress. Was her lovely face set with strain, or was that Dorie's imagination, spurred on by the twins? "Please join us, love," she said, and she squeezed Dorie's hands. "We were just discussing the new plans for the hospital. So many good ideas in this room."

Dorie nodded mutely, her words deserting her as usual, and looked for a seat. The windows were open to catch the evening breeze, and several of the girls wielded pretty paper fans. Everyone was in a perfectly pressed cocktail dress, or at least a sleek skirt. Nobody had rosebud buttons. Maybe she had gotten that wrong, then. Just how long ago had Helen given her that dress? She sighed, tugging on the scratchy lace on her shoulders. See, this was why she didn't come to these. She could find plenty of things to say one-on-one to Colin, as

Dorian. Or to Jack, as herself. But a roomful of perfectly turned-out women? She thought back to Dr. Pearce's suggestion that she be the liaison for the lab, and she snorted. He couldn't see past her blond curls to see what she would really be like when confronted with a group of people she was supposed to charm. Dorie was emphatically not charming.

She took the last remaining seat, a delicate wooden chair with a finely embroidered cushion. Half of the embroidery was blown away and the rest of the cushion was covered with scorch marks. Violet had been here.

"We were just discussing the overcrowding at the Mercy Hospital this summer with the Young Women's League," said Helen. "We're trying to raise funding for a new wing."

"It was state-of-the-art when it was built," another woman put in earnestly. "But that was almost fifty years ago. Population has finally bounced back after the war and is climbing all the time, especially among the lower classes. It is our humanitarian duty to have adequate facilities."

Dorie nodded sagely as if she had a clue about the hospital facilities and looked around vainly for the promised canapés. She hoped some of the canapé recipes were the twins' little joke and not an actual description of the menu. She rather liked frogs' legs, but newts with Gorgonzola sounded a bit . . . slimy. Ah, there was one tray at least, right next to a thin blonde who was ostentatiously ignoring it. Dorie cradled her wyvern-stuffed purse in her arms and tried to creep across to the cucumber sandwiches. They were on the other side of the room from her, so it turned out that creeping was impossible. All eyes followed her as she clumped her way across the room.

Might as well be hung for a sheep as a lamb, thought Dorie, and she took the entire plate of sandwiches. "Thank you," she said politely to the girl, who was trying hard to pretend this wasn't happening. Dorie tromped in her boots back to her blown-up chair and sat down with the plate, balancing it on her purse. Down at the other end of the room she saw a broad-shouldered girl sitting stiffly with her own sandwich and for the first time she felt mildly pleased to see Annika.

The thin girl next to Dorie cleared her throat. "We're discussing what sort of gala we should hold for the potential donors. A buffet luncheon? A cocktail hour?"

"I think a brunch in the garden would be classic and delightful," said another.

"No, we want them to *drink*," quipped another.

"Morning cocktails are the best cocktails," drawled another. "Speaking of . . ." She waved her fan languidly at a man who had just poked his head in through the swinging doors, holding a silver tray. Gone were the boots and dirty jacket, even the explorer hat. He had on a nice suit, and he looked about as uncomfortable in it as Dorie felt in her pink dress. Still, the sweet, dreamy face behind the eyeglasses was all Tam, and a number of the girls in the room perked up. He started serving at the other end of the room from Dorie, and she willed her galloping heart to slow. All too soon, he would work his way around, and then see her. . . . Dorie stole a glance at Annika to see what her face revealed. Her expression was calm, her posture stiff. But Annika, too, watched Tam as he smiled and served the champagne coupes.

"Girls, we'll take a break for a few minutes," said Aunt Helen. She nodded at Dorie. "Could you help me bring in the chocolates, please?"

Dorie clomped her way over, following Aunt Helen into the kitchen. As the door swung shut behind them, she was surprised to find her aunt enveloping her in a tight hug. Tears hovered in the corners of her aunt's eyes. "What is it?" Dorie started, but Helen put a finger to her lips, pulling away.

"Help me sift the powdered sugar," she said in a loud voice, and then, bent next to Dorie's ear as they worked. "We're leaving tonight," she said. "Rook's under investigation under Subversive Activities." Her fingers shook the sugar. "Ever since he got elected he's been a thorn in the establishment's side. He's been too prominently working against this bill that would roll back many of the protections for women that have been passed in the last twenty years. He got a tip-off that they're trumping up charges against him and he could be hauled in any day—officially they can only hold you for forty-eight hours, but we know several people who've disappeared into the system. We have the girls to think of—we can't risk it."

Dumbfounded, Dorie nodded.

Helen's face softened. "I tried to get your parents to come, but they won't. If you want to go, be here at eleven. We can't wait—Rook has *dwarvven* contacts on the border to meet us. If you're not here, we go."

The misery Dorie felt at the idea of losing her city family must have showed on her face. All she could do was run her finger back and forth under the pink lace, searching for relief.

Helen took a second look at her niece, and then a laugh suddenly broke through the worry. "Oh, honey, did I really saddle you with that dress? You look like . . . I don't know, a greyhound wearing bows. There's a reason it didn't sell five years ago. Promise me you'll get rid of it before you bring shame on my shop."

Dorie nodded. She stared at her aunt, willing her to change her mind and stay, but she could not find words, here in her aunt's kitchen, surrounded by several dozen girls. The swinging doors opened as two girls whisked in. One pulled a stack of cocktail napkins from a drawer, the other reached for a spritzer bottle and dishcloth, both with the ease of long familiarity. "Out of napkins, Ms. E.," said one, and, "Julia's spilled her wine again," said the other, as they whisked back out.

Dorie stared after them, feeling that they had usurped some role in her aunt's life that she should have been there for. And now her aunt was leaving.

"Is Tam going, too?" was all she could think to say.

Her aunt looked at her sharply, as if discerning what was really going through Dorie's mind. "No," she said. "I asked him tonight, but he says he's found his own good fight. He looks happier than I've seen him since that summer you two were fifteen and went camping in the woods for three months. Drove all the grown-ups wild, you scamps," she added with a laugh. "But Rook and I know what it's like, to finally find something worth fighting for. We can't make him leave it."

Leave the ironskin? Or leave Annika? Dorie did not dare guess which.

Conversation billowed around the room as Dorie returned to her seat, and she sat for a moment and just watched her cousin. He was bookish but not shy, not awkward like she was. He was more comfortable by himself in the woods—he did not glad-hand or crack jokes as he handed around the drinks, but he had an innate kindness and gentleness that was clearly very attractive to the more perspicacious unattached girls.

Dorie's heart beat in her throat and she kept a firm grasp on her woglet-filled purse as Tam bent to offer her the silver tray. From across the room she could feel Aunt Helen's eyes on them—Aunt Helen knew none of the details, but she certainly knew they hadn't spoken in years. His sweet brown eyes met hers as he handed the champagne coupe to her.

And then, there. There was that moment of recognition she had been expecting in the forest that first day.

He knew her.

Seven years were nothing. Her blonde curls and blue eyes were the same and he knew her.

There was a moment of stillness, when time seemed to slow just as it did in fey time. And then the champagne coupe passed into her fingers, he nodded briefly at her, and passed on.

Her heartbeat refused to slow. She clutched her champagne coupe. No one was looking at her, not even Aunt Helen now, but she felt as though all eyes in the room were looking at her from the inside out: her boots, her woglet, her beating heart.

Time stayed slow until he passed out of the room with the champagne coupes. She reminded herself that she was starving, and felt her senses slowly calm as she ate another sandwich, then two. He was gone, he was going, he was gone. She could never tell him who she really was. He despised her. Eat another sandwich, Dorie. Smile.

Fifth tiny sandwich in hand, Dorie looked around and remembered why Aunt Helen had wanted her to come. Nearly all the women laughing and holding champagne coupes were around Dorie's age—the Young Women's League. She wondered how many of them had to work in the morning. There were a few older women, like Aunt Helen, who were included as mentors for the group—women familiar with fund-raising and charity work. She remembered her aunt saying she wanted Dorie to meet some of her peers who were also interested in doing Good Things. So here she was, finally at one—and it sounded like it would be the last. Not that she would have come back anyway. Not with him here.

Oh, it was miserable. So hot and stuffy, and that damned

lace shoulder blanket scritch-scritching on her neck. Dorie ran her nails under it, squirmed in her seat like she was one of the twins. Why did doing good have to be so ... so ... indoors?

"I had the best Dead Dwarf at this quaint little hotel in Varee," someone was saying.

Several pairs of eyes turned on the woman. "We don't call them that anymore," scolded one. "Nowadays you say 'Spicy Tomato Cocktail.'"

"Oh, poo. They still call it a *douarven mort* in Varee. Slightly more evocative."

"Why do you want to build a new wing?" said Dorie suddenly.

All eyes turned on her. "Excuse me?" said one woman.

She stopped and swallowed the bite of her sandwich and tried again. "I mean. If the problem is overcrowding, maybe we're attacking this at the wrong end. Maybe there's a way to stop people from needing the hospital to begin with."

"We can't just turn people away," said one.

"No, wait. She means we should prevent people from getting sick."

Someone laughed in disbelief. "Nice trick, that."

The wall of mute frustration started rising up. Dorie tried to swallow it back down and let the words come out. "Crimson fever," she mumbled.

"Is solved."

"Not among the poor," said Dorie obstinately.

"She's right," put in another woman, someone Dorie didn't know. "There have been bad outbreaks this summer. Didn't you read the figures I obtained from the hospital? That's part of this overcrowding we're seeing."

"And thus the long hours, and then the nurses' strike. Did you hear they sent in police to break it up? *And* scabs."

"Who'd want a scab nurse?"

"Who'd want the city hospital?" came the sarcastic dismissal.

"We're getting off track," complained the blonde across the room. "We're here to discuss funding the new wing."

"This isn't about what would be nice in a perfect world," someone said condescendingly. "It's about what we have the ability to accomplish. The government is doing everything they can with the feywort they've got. It's carefully monitored and controlled. We can't just make more feywort out of thin air if there's a run on it."

"But *why* is there a run on it?" said Dorie, but no one was listening at that point. Woglet was stirring in the purse from all the chatter rising above them. Any minute he would poke his head up and they would all see a baby wyvern. Dorie wedged the empty sandwich plate on top of the purse opening.

Across the room she heard the blonde say to her neighbor, "Bother this. It was all going so smoothly until the peasantry walked in." Dorie's face flamed.

"This is all irrelevant," cut in someone. "Let's get back to planning the menu and drinks."

"Damn the drinks," said Dorie, way too loudly. It cut through the din. Woglet reared his head, knocking the plate onto the floor with a crash. Dorie pushed him back into the purse. The feywort for Colin was in there and she pulled it out, waving it. "There used to be acres of this stuff growing wild—why on earth should it be hard to get?"

A trim brunette who until then had been silent stood.

"That's interdicted," she said quietly. "All feywort is the property of the Crown." She came toward Dorie, peeling off a short white glove as she did so and flashing the palm of her hand around the room.

Inscribed on her palm was a silver oval with a circle in the middle.

Everyone was shocked into silence, looking at the two of them—some with confusion, some with vicarious enjoyment at Dorie's predicament. The brunette's occupation didn't appear to be common knowledge. Someone reached for the brunette to pull her back and then stopped, realizing her friend was different than she had thought.

Dorie backed up, knocking the little chair over. "Acres and acres, all gone from the mountain. . . . You don't understand the first thing about making a difference. You're not out there on the front lines. You don't have a clue. . . ." Woglet began pushing his head through her fingers. He grew warmer, building up a head of steam. She wasn't going to be able to keep him hidden much longer, and the brunette was advancing. Desperate, Dorie said, "Is that a mouse?" and with her mental focus made a fallen napkin twitch and scurry from under its chair to under the blonde's chair.

The blonde screeched, and pandemonium ensued as half the women tried to get away from the supposed mouse and the other half tried to catch it. A wall of women filled the space between Dorie and the approaching brunette. Annika looked at them as if they were all mad.

Dorie used the chaos to slip out the front door. She caught sight of Aunt Helen as she made her escape. Helen watched her niece go with a rueful expression. "Sorry," Dorie mouthed. "Sorry."

* * *

After all that, it was a relief to change back into Dorian. She found a secluded spot in the park, and with her best *don't look at me* on, stuffed the lacy pink dress into her purse with Woglet and put on her boy's clothes even as she reshaped herself. The clothes were dirtier than she was—was that smudge mouse guts from Woglet's meal?—and she thought that she was really going to have to get a change of clothes for her alter ego. She sighed as she realized she had not asked Aunt Helen for rent money. But how could she, with her aunt and uncle fleeing the country? They had far bigger concerns than where Dorie was going to live next month. Maybe she could bring herself to sell the woglet that was going to hatch tonight, though she felt sick at the thought. But to whom would she take it? Malcolm only wanted eggs, and he wasn't likely to hand over his sources. Besides, how could she do it without Tam knowing?

Colin was first to their meeting place. Dorie pulled out the feywort as she approached, holding the blue flowers up like a trophy of war. The relief on his hefty face was palpable.

"Better tuck it away until you have a chance to use it," she said. "I don't think the average joe on the street can tell one herb from another, but if you run into one of those silver-palm goons . . ."

Colin nodded soberly and the feywort disappeared into his satchel. "If you're able to get any more, I can take them where they'd be most help."

"Next time out, I'll bring you all I find," Dorie promised. Woglet poked his head out of the purse, peering around at the wharf. Colin extended a finger, but Woglet ignored it.

"Shall we go then?" said Colin.

"We have to wait for my colleague," Dorie said.

"You told someone else?"

"He's trustworthy," Dorie said. "And he has better access to the lab equipment than I do. He's got the portable incubator, and a cage for the new chick." She lowered her voice. "We have four eggs for you. We'll be able to do three more people tomorrow night, if you have them."

"They'll be ready," Colin said. He lowered his voice as well. "Be careful. Think someone was following me when I left the Pig last night." He shook his head at her expression. "Haven't told anyone, of course not. But I'm afraid I took off my brace—didn't occur to me anyone would be watching a cook at the University tavern. But if someone *were* paying attention, and if they put two and two together . . ."

Dorie nodded. "So far you and Tam are the only people that know. And the other ironskin you've told, of course." She cocked her head. "You didn't tell them *how* it's done, did you?"

He shook his head as Tam appeared out of the mist and Dorie lost track of whatever Colin was about to say. Tam was back in his explorer clothes, his hat tilted down against the humid fog. "You must be our contact," he said as he approached. "I'm Tam." Dorie noticed he left off his last name, presumably as protection.

"Colin."

"Let's go, then."

Woglet flew to Tam's bag with the incubator in it, perched on top of it as if he knew his kin were inside. Maybe he did. Dorie returned Woglet to the handbag, wishing for the moment that everyone in town had a woglet, so no one would notice hers. It suddenly occurred to her that boys didn't carry purses, either, but neither Colin nor Tam had appeared to notice. Of course, Tam had the practical focus of the absent-minded scientist. If he *had* noticed that Dorian was carrying a handbag, he had probably thought, what a clever vehicle for woglet transportation.

She thought that he must be upset about his parents fleeing town. She looked sideways at him, wishing there were a way that Dorian could find out about it, so he could sympathize, lend a friendly ear. Yes, and then after that, she could find out about how he'd seen Dorie tonight, and did he still hate her, and so on. The flights of fancy grew elaborate. But Tam's face was closed off.

They followed Colin along the water to an even grungier and nastier section of the city. In sharp contrast to Colin's flat, this girl's place was filthy. She apparently shared the small room with three other people and a crying infant. A large man in an armchair—a father? a boyfriend?—eyed them suspiciously as Colin explained what they had come for, but he made no move to stop them. The two other people—an old woman and a pre-adolescent boy—were noisily playing a card game while the woman rocked the cradle with her foot.

The man grunted and jerked his head toward the back, apparently not caring what three boys were there to talk to the girl for. They picked their way around rotting floorboards till they reached a flowered yellow sheet hung as a curtain across one corner of the room. Two shapeless mattresses lay on the floor behind it, and sitting on one with her knees tucked up in her worn dress was a girl.

Colin knelt and took her hand. "Alice," he said gently. "Alice girl, these people are here to help you."

Like Colin, the girl was young to be ironskin—she must have been an infant when she was cursed. She was like a baby bird, all bony and fragile, unaware of the wider world. Her hair was uncut, snarled in long blond loops.

"What's her curse?" Dorie said quietly to Colin. Not that

they could be heard over the wailing baby and the arguments from the card game.

He rubbed his jaw. "Alice hears voices. People who aren't there."

"And she's been like this for twenty years? Since she was a baby?" Dorie sucked in her breath. Did this girl even have a chance of getting better?

"You have to help her," said Colin, perhaps seeing her dubious expression. "Please."

Dorie nodded, and Tam said, "Where's the scar?"

"Neck and back." Colin blushed a bit as he stood. "Look, you're the doctors. I'll duck out and find some food for the chick."

"Shouldn't be too hard around here," Dorie muttered.

"Be brave, Alice girl," Colin said. He hesitated as if he wanted to add something else, but couldn't think of anything to say. He pushed his way out of the yellow curtain, leaving Tam and Dorie alone with the girl.

Tam hiked up the knees of his trousers and sat down cross-legged with the incubator. He brought out the well-made implements Dorie had seen at the lab—copper spoon and vials and so forth—and began preparing a little nest for the egg to hatch in. Dorie turned her attention to the girl huddled on the mattress. She set down her handbag and Woglet poked out a curious head. "Can I look at your back?" Dorie said gently.

"They march in," said the girl. "They march in with their spikes and cages and they glow with silver eyes."

Dorie narrowed her eyes. "Who marches in?" she said. "Is this something you're seeing right now?"

Alice turned vacant blue eyes on her. "Your egg is talking to me." She reached a hand toward Dorie's stomach.

"Whoa," said Dorie. She sighed. "Can I look at your back?"

The girl turned to the wall but made no other reply. Dorie carefully unbuttoned the top few buttons of the back of the girl's dress to see her shoulder blades. The scar wrapped around from the front of her neck and ran down the length of her spine, as if it were a snake coiling around her throat. As with Colin's, it writhed along its length. Dorie let her hand fall away. "When this egg hatches, I can fix your curse," she said. "But it will hurt a lot. Do you know what I'm saying?"

"The cages hurt," said the girl. "The men leave them in the cages. They chase the basilisk through the mountains."

"Wait a minute," said Tam. "Are you seeing a basilisk?" He set down the copper bowl and looked carefully at Alice. "What does it look like?"

Dorie stopped herself from saying, what does it matter what this girl's imaginary basilisk looks like? Because this girl did have a fey curse, after all. And as tempting as it was to dismiss her ravings as madness, Dorie had far too much experience with the strange possibilities that fey substance could bring you.

"Big," Alice said succinctly.

Tam looked disappointed, as if he had hoped for something else. He took off his explorer hat and ran his fingers through his hair, settling it back into place. "Well, let's see how the wyvern egg is coming along."

"Like iron and copper and silver, all mixed together," Alice said, staring at a point over Dorie's head.

Tam jumped on this. "How many claws do they have?"

Alice stared off into the wall as if actually examining basilisk claws. Even Dorie, with her long experience of fey matters, was unnerved by it; she wanted to turn and make sure there was not, in fact, a basilisk behind her.

"Four," Alice said finally.

Tam sucked in breath. He pulled his notebook from his

pocket and began making notes. "Do they have a forked tongue?" he said. "Are they in pairs, like wyverns? Can you see eggs?" He drew breath. "Alice, Alice. *Where* do you see them?"

Alice focused on Tam. "Through the mountains," she repeated. "The men chase the basilisk through the mountains. It's a mother basilisk."

Tam scribbled this all down in great excitement.

"Why does it matter what her basilisks look like?" said Dorie.

Tam's pencil point broke. "Criminy," he said with feeling, and pulled out his penknife to fix it. His eyes were bright with discovery as he explained to Dorie, "Because if you look at the National Portrait Gallery at the famous wyvern paintings, most of them have three toes. Like wyverns."

"So?"

"So if my theory is correct, it means those people never even came close to seeing a real basilisk. They looked at Rodanthe's technical drawings of dissected wyverns and they extrapolated from there." He flipped furiously through his notebook and spread open the pages to show Dorie. She leaned over his shoulder, trying not to let their nearness affect her. She was Dorian, Dorian, Dorian.

There was a long list of dates in the notebook, with notations. "Writings and paintings about basilisks crop up in clusters," Tam said. "But there are other mentions of them, too, which obscure the true data. A lot of people *claim* to have seen them. But there's really only one person who we can probably verify as true, and that's Sir John that I was telling you about. Because he took the whole carcass to the king in 1656, and loads of people wrote about that. Plus it was on display long enough for Kent to see it, to paint his famous picture of Sir John and the Basilisk—but the fourth claw isn't really obvious in the picture, unless you're looking for it. And then Hoglarth came along sixty years later, and he painted the *other* famous picture due to the nubile maidens in it, but *that* basilisk clearly has three toes. Everyone copied that, or they copied Rodanthe's wyverns. But I went to the gallery, and the Kent painting has four toes. Do you see?"

"Um," said Dorie, trying to assimilate this rundown of basilisk art history. The baby had finally stopped screaming and there was silence from the front room, as if the others were listening in on this lecture. She wondered what on earth they would make of it.

"It can't be coincidence," said Tam. "I think her visions are of real events. And I think it's verification of my theory that the four-toed basilisk sightings, in art and writing, are the real sightings. Not the *hundred*-year blindworm." With his sharpened pencil he struck through the misleading dates, scribbling down numbers next to the pattern that emerged. "*Ninety-seven.*"

"But you don't have any basilisk sightings in the last century. You crossed them all out."

"Add 194 to the last sighting in the eighteenth century," he said, "and—"

"This year," breathed Dorie as he wrote it.

"That's why I've been looking for them. And why I'm inclined to believe the signs Mills mentioned—the disruption in patterns of the small creatures. And now . . . her."

Alice had resumed rocking, shaking her head, drawing back in on herself. The noise in the front room began again as the large man apparently joined the next round of cards.

"Is this what Colin was like?" Tam said to Dorie.

"No," said Dorie. "His curse was hunger, is all." The only other ironskin she had met was Jane, and she couldn't tell him about Jane. He was looking at her, so excited, so curious, so dear, and she should tell him about Jane. Not here. Tomorrow. Tomorrow she would tell him. "Your blacksmith wasn't like this, was he?"

"No." Tam gently touched Alice's shoulder. "Hey. You'll be all right. As soon as we put this stuff on, you won't have any more visions."

"No more basilisks then," Dorie said in a low voice.

He looked troubled. "I wish I could ask her many more questions, of course. But it's not right to leave her like this. No matter what I could find out."

Dorie nodded. She did not know what else to say, for she had her own strange feelings about changing the girl. Certainly the girl was not living a normal life. But then, neither was Dorie. She had chosen once to give up her fey side. She wasn't going to do it again. Was the girl able to make that choice? Where was the line between curse and part of you?

As Dorie sat and watched, the egg started rocking, the little wyvern raring to go. Woglet clambered all the way out of the handbag and perched on the handles, warbling at the egg in encouragement.

Colin burst through the curtain, mouse dangling by the tail. He dropped it in the little wyvern cage. "Am I on time?" Alice turned her fragile face up to him, smiling, and for a moment, a real person broke through the confusion and visions. He knelt and pressed her hand. "I'll be here to help you," he said.

With a series of smart taps, a chick burst through, a pugnacious tilt to his shoulders. "Hey, little guy," Dorie said. "Hey, Buster." Under Woglet's watchful eye, she shepherded the baby wyvern into the cage with the mouse. He spat misty air at Dorie's fingers as she nudged him along. Once inside the cage, the mouse caught his full attention, and he paid no attention to Dorie closing the door behind him. He had a crooked tail that flapped as he zeroed in on the mouse.

Tam had scooped up the eggshell and was carefully scraping out the goo with his copper spoon.

"Do you want to do this?" Dorie said gently to Alice.

Hand in Colin's, she nodded and closed her eyes.

Dorie and Tam looked at each other. Dorie rocked back on her heels as Tam leaned in.

"I'll take the lead on this," Tam said. Despite not knowing that Dorie was part-fey, he still sensed her ambivalence to changing the girl's fragile state. Apparently he was more sure of what would be right for the girl—that what would be right would be to get rid of the fey. And it was true—then she would be able to think for herself. Dorie just did not know.

She sat on her hands and watched as Tam smeared the goo around the girl's neck and down her spine, erasing all traces of the fey inside her.

Chapter 9

ALL THE THINGS WE HIDE

Dorie is fourteen, and so is Tam.

Tam trusts no one, but he trusts her. When you have been fooled by someone disguised as your father, you are slow to believe anyone else. He opens up to her about the things he cannot at school. At school he is self-contained and distant, but it's known he can hold his own in a fistfight, so they let him alone.

Which is good, because his choice of subject matter doesn't help him stay under the radar.

Tam reads fey tales. All of them: Beauty and the Fey Beast, Rose-Red and Violet-Blue, Bluebeard, Queen Maud and her Pirates, everything. He reads the ones that humans wrote; he reads the ones that *dwarvven* wrote. And when he is visiting Dorie in the country, he goes around to the old women in town and drinks their chamomile tea and listens to them spin out the stories they knew from their childhood. He has heard some new ones this way, and he ambles home, staring past his spectacles into nothing, and tells them to Dorie. Dorie's heart beats the most then, for it is as if he is telling her stories about herself. Dorie's father always stops himself if he starts to talk about the fey, and Jane thinks telling the old tales gives them a power they shouldn't have.

But Tam tells her, tells her all of them, and they soak into her bones.

It is one of these tales that goes with her into the forest.

It is one of these tales that leaves Tam there.

—T. L. Grimsby, *Dorie & Tam: A Mostly True Story*

* * *

"You get paid every two weeks," the accountant said patiently. "That's perfectly reasonable to work with your budget."

"Except it's taken me long enough to find a job that I'm behind on my rent," said Dorie, trying to sound calm and not desperate. It was Friday morning and the black clock above the accountant was inexorably ticking onward. "I have till noon to pay it. Isn't there any way to get an advance—just this once?"

"It sets a bad precedent," said the accountant. "Do you know how many bar tabs we'd be covering for you boys if we did that?" She shook her head with an air of finality. "I'm sorry."

Dorie trudged down the hall, wondering if she would have looked more fiscally responsible as a girl. Or if the female secretary would have had more compassion for one of her own gender.

No use second guessing. Tam had kindly offered to take the wyvern chick from last night, so that possibility was out. Really, if she didn't want to be homeless, there was only one option left. Malcolm. And she would have to filch one of their three remaining eggs from Tam's incubator, and how could she possibly explain that to Tam?

"Dorian," exclaimed Dr. Pearce, giving her a hearty slap on

the back. "Well done, old chap. First time out, and you and Tam brought back a better haul than anyone else."

Dorie nodded, then said hopefully, "Yes, and I was wondering if I could get my bonus for those. . . ."

Dr. Pearce looked vague. "Oh, I'd check with Elsie in accounting. She rules the roost, you know—whatever she says goes." He clapped a hand on her shoulder and steered her down the hall. "But look, you must know about our little anti-fey treatment by now, yes? We're making a protective solution from each wyvern egg you chaps bring back. One egg stretches to protect about twenty-five people. There's a long waiting list as you can imagine, but Tam told me about your little sighting of the fey yesterday. We need to get the two of you safe and protected. You're our two most valuable naturalists."

Dorie tried to demur. "I'm sure I'll be fine. I always have been."

He stopped and eyed her seriously. "Now, Mr. Eliot. You know as well as I do that this isn't just about *your* safety, but the safety of everyone in the lab, in the city. If you or Mr. Grimsby were to be . . . compromised in the field, we would all be at risk. Tam tells me you think the first egg is going to hatch day after tomorrow, and you seem to have an eye for these things. So let's see, that's Sunday—the boys in the lab will make up the protective solution right away—so Monday morning we'll have you and Grimsby treated straight off. Sound good? Good."

Dorie smiled uncertainly as Dr. Pearce strode off down the hall.

She was outside Tam's door. She didn't have one of the copper medallions, but the door was ajar, and she gently pushed it open to the sound of arpeggios.

Tam was standing on his desk, directing a whistled aria at a spiderweb. He broke off as she entered, leaning down to make a penciled note. "You wouldn't think there'd be a connection between wyverns and house spiders," he muttered, running a spiderwebby hand through his hair. "Maybe all fauna just really like the Midsomer Suite. . . ."

Dorie came in and shut the door behind her. "I need to borrow the incubator with the other three eggs," she said. "For, um. Tests. Before tomorrow."

Tam pointed a distracted finger at where the incubator was hidden behind a pile of papers. Just like that. "Let me know what you turn up."

She couldn't do anything but nod mutely. He trusted her. Oh, heavens, he trusted her.

"Tomorrow is Saturday, isn't it?" said Tam. Dorie nodded. "Well then. We'll take all four wyvern chicks back to the country and try the catch-and-release with unbonded woglets." His eyes lit up behind his specs. "Such an opportunity. Do you mind if we poke around and see if we see anything matching that girl's stories?"

About the basilisk, he meant. "Why not?" She picked up the incubator and moved to the door. She had promised herself last night she would tell him today. She should tell him now, before she left with those eggs in tow. Because he trusted her. "Buster still doing okay?" she said instead.

"Quite belligerent," Tam said. "Only acknowledges me with hisses. Unresponsive to whistling, but he liked the piano." He looked somewhere past the spider, unfocused. "I suppose if tomorrow is Saturday, today is Friday?"

"It must be."

"If you're sure the next egg won't be ready till dawn, then I'm going to be out late tonight." He did not look at her.

"No, dawn tomorrow it is," Dorie managed. He must be meeting Annika. For a late, late date. Her heart sank to her ribs. "See you then."

He whistled as she left the room, eggs in tow.

She couldn't take an egg to Malcolm Stilby. She couldn't.

But what else was she to do?

At eleven-thirty Dorie left the lab and walked all the way to Malcolm's, fire raging over her choices. At the end of his block she stopped, sat down on a bench. She was a traitor if she took him an egg—a traitor to the Crown, to the fey, to the ironskin. To the wyverns. To Tam. To herself.

But if she didn't take him one she was a traitor to Jack, who didn't deserve to lose her apartment over Dorie's moral conundrums.

She stood, walking briskly toward the front door before she could change her mind. She was at the bottom of Malcolm's steps when she stopped again. Woglet cooed on her shoulder, rubbing her ear, and she reached up to pet him. Her fingers skritched behind his wings and he burbled, and she knew it was no use. She couldn't go through with it.

She turned, and as she did, the door opened and the tall butler from the day before gestured her inside. Inside she could clearly see Malcolm Stilby.

Rage smeared his face at the sight of her wyvern, and as quickly was gone.

But Dorie knew what she had seen. She backed up a step.

"Come in, come in, Mr. Eliot," he said. "I want to discuss with you the small matter of your picture in the newspaper." His voice held implicit threat and she took one more step away.

"You can discuss it with me on the front step or not at all," she said gruffly, trying not to let her voice shake. There was no way she was going in there, especially not with a baby wyvern and three eggs. Oh, why had she even tried this?

"Mr. Eliot, be reasonable," Malcolm said. He came to the doorstep, wrapping his lounging robe tighter. Given that it was now lunchtime, she wondered if he ever changed out of it. "I am a perfectly understanding man. I do not own you, nor any of those who work for me. No contracts, no penalties like the Crown would impose. I just am curious why, if you were not interested in bringing me the . . . items we mentioned, that you would have come to me at all. I very much dislike the idea that someone is spying on me, you see."

"I wasn't," said Dorie. With an effort she remained calm, careless. A sure-of-himself young man. "This was an accident," she said, pointing at Woglet. "I was trying to bring you an egg I found, but he hatched before I could get back into town."

"Ah," Malcolm said. He looked calmer now—pulled a loose cigarette from his pocket and lit it. "You have to forgive me, Dorian. I heard an odd tale this morning from one of my other boys. Some drunk man came wheeling into a tavern where they were last night, going on about a couple of boys who'd just healed his daughter with some sort of flying lizard egg. But I suppose, come to think on it, I saw your picture with the wyvern in the paper on Wednesday morning, and this is Friday. So your wyvern could hardly be from the egg that hatched last night."

"No, it couldn't," said Dorie. "Obviously." She was relieved that she had had Woglet in the purse when they entered Alice's flat last night. Angry at the girl's father. Colin had sworn the family to secrecy—they had been there to *help*! And now . . .

"Well then," Malcolm said. "Were you coming to bring me something?" He nodded at the incubator in her hand.

"Uh, no," Dorie lied quickly. "I was just on my way out to the forest for the day to try again. Coming to ask you if you knew anything about, um"—she threw out the first creature that came to mind—"basilisks?"

Malcolm laughed. "Find me a basilisk and you can ask for the moon. They've been extinct for three hundred years. Wishful stories in that *Fey Tales* book to the contrary."

"Oh," said Dorie. She thought back to her conversations with Tam. "I heard there was a basilisk skeleton somewhere. In some collector's house."

Malcolm nodded. "Malformed wyvern, the scientists say these days. I think they're wrong. It's the real deal—just long dead. I mean, some people used to wonder if they hibernated. Because they would disappear for decades, and then be spotted, and then disappear. But this is my profession, to know what's out there, eh? And I think two centuries without a basilisk seems like no more basilisks. But I'm always willing to be proven wrong . . . in this sort of matter, anyway. Hey, do you want me to unload that wyvern on your shoulder? Rate's a good deal less than an egg, but he looks like a pretty healthy specimen."

"No, I'm good," said Dorie, taking one more step away. "I'm actually hoping he can help me find more eggs."

Malcolm snorted. "Good luck with that," he said. His eyes narrowed as she turned to go down the stairs, and she wondered if she had really covered her tracks. "Oh, Dorian," he said, as she reached the bottom. "Do let me know if you need any help, won't you? I'm always happy to organize a team to go into a prime location."

She swallowed and nodded.

And as soon as she could, she blended into a crowd with

her best *don't-look-at-me*. Looked over her shoulder all the way back to the lab.

Dorie trudged back to her desk, despondent. The landlady's deadline of noon had come and gone, and she had failed. Walking to Malcolm's and back had taken more than a standard lunch hour. She had told the lab she was headed to the library for research after lunch, and nobody really checked up on you, but still, she should look like she cared about her new job. They had set aside a corner of an office for her and she should spread some papers around it or something. Not that any of it mattered. All she wanted from the Queen's Lab was the chance to get back out in the field.

Well, that and the rent.

She was miserable enough that she thought telling Tam now couldn't possibly make it any worse. She would return the incubator to him and tell him. But he wasn't in his office—had gone off to do some research, she was told. She wondered if he'd gone to the Portrait Gallery to look at that basilisk.

Somehow she made it through the afternoon. She waved off offers from scientists heading out to enjoy the weekend, and tramped back to their flat. How much longer would it *be* their flat?

Dorie sighed as she trudged up the stairs to their room, the temperature rising as she climbed. The smell of linseed oil drifted into the hallway and she opened the door to find her roommate working on her latest canvas. The canvas only partially obscured the nude girl draped on the armchair in the middle of the room, asleep in the late afternoon sun.

A laugh broke through Dorie's gloomy day as she shut the door. "And I just got reamed out for *my* morals, Jack. Our landlady only tolerates me because of that 'nice Miss Jacqueline.'" Woglet launched himself from her shoulder and glided down to the armchair.

"I am a nice Miss Jacqueline," Jack said calmly. "Don't drop your foot, Stella."

"Are you almost done, Jack?" Stella said sleepily. "I've got to get to my evening tutoring." A coo from Woglet made her suddenly sit up and notice Dorie, and her look of shock made Dorie realize she was still in boyshape. Stella blushed as she grabbed her clothes, but all she said was, "You might have knocked."

"I am so sorry," Dorie said, embarrassed by her forgetfulness. She turned to face the door.

Jack snorted as she set down her brush. "Yes, yes. You can go. Can I get one more session tomorrow sometime?"

"Sunday I can," Stella said. Dorie could hear her unhurried motions as she dressed. "Will you get the passes for me for next Friday, though? My mother's in town and I swore in blood I'd take her to your aunt's nightclub."

"That should be easy, since I'll have to be there all week," said Jack in a voice packed with meaning. "I'll even comp you a drink."

Dorie wondered what exactly that meant. She didn't like the sound of it.

"That would be lovely," said Stella, and then in a raised pitch to Dorie she drawled, "You're safe now."

Dorie turned around to find the tiny girl fully clothed in shirt and skirt, patting Woglet on the head. Stella had regained her composure, and Dorie thought it likely that she was the red one now.

"Toodles," Stella said, and sauntered past Dorie and out the door, waving her fingers.

"I think she likes you," said Jack as the door closed.

Dorie reddened further. "You know what Stella's like."

"I do," Jack said quietly, returning to her brushes.

Dorie went to look at Jack's canvas. It was another beautifully rendered figure study, like all of Jack's work. From the angle you couldn't quite tell if Stella was *dwarvven* or if it was just a big armchair. "That's funny," said Dorie. "Because scale is such a thing with Stella—I mean, the Pig has stools, but not all places think about the *dwarvven,* you know? Like the post office, or the desks at school. And then does she need help with a trolley seat, or if we're not around, is she going to bat her eyes at some man, and so on. But you can't tell what the scale is here."

"Hmm," was all Jack said.

Woglet hopped over to the cabinets, where he had been having good luck finding mice. Dorie plopped down in the vacated armchair, thinking about their finances.

Finally Jack said, "My aunt stopped by this afternoon."

"Oh."

"Yeah. Miss Bates telephoned her about the rent. We're through, Dorie."

Dorie slumped.

"Aunt Alberta will cover our rent, but I have to start training under her."

"You can't do that. You're so talented."

Jack threw her brushes into the cup. "So what? I can't get a break. Even the nudie mag won't pay what we owe. I've been scrounging food off of friends, I'm out of Alizarin crimson and lampblack *and* white; how can you do anything without white now and then? I tried to go paint by the harbor but with the heat wave everyone who can afford to buy art fled the city for the shore, and I can't afford fare to go to the shore.

Forget trying to have a breakthrough. I can't paint, period. We're through."

"I'm sorry," Dorie said helplessly, over and over. She had had Jack's salvation in her hands and she threw it away for her own pride. She might have broken down in tears, even, except Dorie Rochart did not cry. She gouged her temples with her fingers until the pressure behind her eyes subsided. She looked up to find Jack looking at her with reluctant sympathy.

"Well," said Jack. "Water under the bridge. I can still paint in the afternoons when The Supper Club's closed. And my aunt's going to teach me to drive her ancient car—maybe we can borrow it and get out of this hot city for a day off." She put a hand on Dorie's shoulder. "I know you've been trying. You're exhausted, too. And it's got to be hard staying a boy all the time—isn't it?"

Dorie nodded.

"Look. My aunt's breaking me in easy," Jack said. "She could have started me off today with maraschino cherry negotiations, but instead she wants me to go listen to a musician for the club. I mean, it's not all altruism—she keeps promising Uncle Léon she'll go on a date with him occasionally instead of putting out fires at the club and she never does. Point is, you're coming with me. We'll go get something to eat."

"All right," Dorie said with relief. She had not realized till that second how tense the strain had been. She let go, sagging, and her muscles and joints and bones melted, reshaped, softened back up into little blond Dorie. She had never been so happy to see her porcelain doll face, and at the same time, there was an overlay of regret as Dorian's wry charm with its broken nose and banged-up leg melted away.

Perhaps, when all of this was over, and she was ready to be simply Dorie again, she could be not *simply* Dorie, but a changed Dorie. She could meld the best of both worlds: be a girl again but with the stamp of her heritage on her face, with the marks of her life visible.

"There," she said to Jack, and Jack laughed.

"I know you've gotten used to Dorian's clothes—and heaven knows *I* don't care if you go in drag, but at least go in drag suitable for a club."

"Ah," said Dorie. "Right." Jack herself was busy pulling a flared red dress out of the tiny shared closet, so it looked like dresses were the order of the day. Dorie grabbed the first dress she touched on her side of the closet and put it on. Another of Aunt Helen's discards that hadn't sold, but they all were. In the first place she didn't care about fashion—even if she had had money she wouldn't have spent it on clothes—and in the second, thanks to her fey mother, it didn't matter whether she cared or not. Dresses reshaped themselves to her—or more accurately, her body reshaped itself to them. Minor adjustments, but enough to make anything remotely her size look tailored to her.

This dress seemed much better than the lacy rosebud one. It was chartreuse silk, with a fitted bodice and short flared skirt. Jack watched with amusement as Dorie's cleavage recontoured itself to fit. "That's a terrible shade for a blonde," Jack said. "Or it should be. Except your skin even changes—did you know that? Picks up slightly different undertones."

"Oh?" said Dorie indifferently.

"Only an artist would notice, I suppose," said Jack. She tossed her paint-spattered trousers on her bed. "Every time I paint you I have to adjust the colors I use for the underpainting. You're like the perfect model for someone to never get bored with—if you liked sitting still, that is."

"Stella's the perfect model," countered Dorie. "After your

eighteenth job of the day all you want to do is sleep in an armchair. Although I could really go for that, too."

"Yes, where were you last night?" said Jack. She had taken all her bracelets off for painting, and now she loaded them back on.

"With Tam," said Dorie reluctantly.

Jack wheeled around to look at her. "As Dorie? Or as Dorian?"

"Dorian," she said. "Except then I was also at Helen's house as Dorie, and he saw me. As me."

Jack was shaking her head. "And you didn't tell him, did you?"

"No."

"Ugh. Dorie. This kind of thing never ends well."

"Ugh, I know!" Dorie had two nice-ish pairs of shoes and she dug them out of the closet. "Navy heels or copper flats?"

"Flats," said Jack. "How is he? I haven't seen him since he left for University."

Dorie shrugged. "He's written a book. He works at the Queen's Lab." We're kind of doing something we're not supposed to do, and I don't want to drag you into it if I don't have to. "Are we ready?"

"Yes," said Jack. "Since you don't need to do any hair or makeup. Seriously, how do you do that?"

Dorie groaned as she popped Woglet in the leather handbag and pushed out the door. "Oh, honestly, Jack, after however many years you know it's not on purpose. I don't even want to talk about hair and makeup. It's a relief being Dorian, you know that?"

"As long as you can stay in his shape."

"It's getting easier. Your sketch helps."

"Good!"

A couple of boys whistled as they went past and Dorie remembered that as a girl she dampened her aura, shrank back, fell away. Of course, when you were walking next to a tall girl with a fiery red dress and mile-long, satiny-dark legs, you might not be able to fall away. Boys were going to whistle no matter what.

"I think . . . ," Dorie said slowly. "I think after this is all over, and I can just be a girl again, I want to be a different girl. Even if it's more work to stay in a different girl shape."

"Go on."

"It's like . . . who I am on the inside has never matched with my outside, you know? I don't recognize myself when I look in the mirror. Changing to Dorian was the first time I ever started to like what I saw."

"Do you mean you want to stay a boy?" Jack said neutrally.

"No," said Dorie after consideration. "No, I'm a girl inside. Just a different girl." She turned to her friend. "I wondered if you would help me make a sketch." The heat was ebbing as the sun sank behind the buildings. The sky was the perfect fading blue of a late summer twilight. "I'm not artistic like you. I cobbled Dorian's face together out of memories and your life-drawing sketches. I want you to help me create a Dorie I would like being. One who looks a little like my parents. One who's got her choices written on her face, for good and bad."

"I'd be honored," Jack said seriously. "But when you say your parents, do you mean—"

"I mean my dad and my stepmum. Yes. Not genetically accurate but . . . yes."

"It's a plan," said Jack. She shook Dorie's hand as they arrived at the club. "I'll use that photo on your desk and come up with some ideas for you."

Dorie undampened her aura as they walked up to the front of the line. "We're here on behalf of The Supper Club," started Jack, but the sturdy bouncer waved them through before she could finish. In short order they were installed at a tiny table near the kitchen, with a decent view of the performing space. Dorie didn't realize how starving she was until Jack told her to order whatever she wanted.

"I think staying a different shape takes it out of me," said Dorie. "I eat like a horse as Dorian. Or I would, if I could find enough dandelions."

"What have we been doing to ourselves?" said Jack. "The artistic life—maybe it's just not worth it. Look at you, having to make choices between selling off wyverns and paying the rent. Me selling dirty pictures. How is that artistic integrity?"

"We'll make new plans," said Dorie. "Refuse to compromise. Never surrender."

"Oh, I dunno," said Jack. "Life is full of compromises. Maybe art is, too. Maybe this whole thing is foolish."

"No," said Dorie firmly. "The bright side here is working for your aunt—"

"The man—"

"will *free* you from having to compromise your art. This is a temporary setback. You will work for your aunt for a bit and whatever business skills you learn will be useful if you want to open your own gallery."

Jack perked up a bit. "There's that."

"You'll have your artistic breakthrough on the weekends, that's all."

"Week*days*," Jack pointed out. "Club hours."

"And I get paid in two weeks. A lot can happen in two weeks."

Jack took a deep breath. "I won't jump off a bridge tonight, then."

"Or marry some doughy millionaire."

Jack laughed ruefully. "I don't think that's ever an option for me. The millionaire would be followed shortly by the bridge." She pulled her sketchpad from her satchel and set it on the table. Her pencil touched down as the first player, a thin cellist with long hair and beard, entered. "All right, Mr. Cello," she said. "Do your worst."

"Worst," unfortunately, turned out to be predictive. One cellist, two "musicians," and four drinks later, Jack had a sheaf of mocking cartoons but nobody to hire for her aunt. Additionally, the screeching of the cello had started Woglet yodeling in harmony, and Dorie had had to step outside until that act was over. Now he was curled on her lap on a napkin, deigning to eat bits of chicken from her plate.

"Well, that was a waste," said Jack.

"Hardly," said Dorie. "Your aunt gave you money for dinner and musicians have been comping our drinks all night."

"Cheers," agreed Jack, clinking her empty glass against Dorie's.

As if alerted by the motion, the waitress appeared behind them and deposited two more drinks at their table. "From the cellist," she said with a knowing grin.

"It's amazing how fast the word gets around about who we work for, isn't it?" said Jack. Under her breath: "Too bad the cellist was so lousy."

The waitress rolled her eyes. "And you don't have to listen to him every time there's an open night."

"Tell me," said Jack. "Is it worth sticking around for anybody else? Between the cellist, the drummer, and that girl who was singing and accompanying herself on harmonica . . ."

"It has been dismal, hasn't it?" agreed the waitress. "It's usually much better. It's the summer curse—beautiful nights make people busk on street corners or chuck it all and go to romance. But the next guy is good, I promise. He doesn't come often—has a real career I gather, unlike most everyone here who wants to 'make it.' Stay for him and you won't be sorry."

"Sure thing," said Jack, lifting her full glass. "Have to, don't we?"

"She was cute," said Dorie, as the waitress left.

"Not my type," said Jack.

"Not Steeeella," said Dorie, who was feeling tipsy.

"Hush, the pianist is coming on."

"If he's anything like the cellist a little noise would improve—" Dorie started to say, but then she saw the pianist and stopped, mouth open.

Tam.

"Wait, isn't that—?" said Jack. Dorie flapped her hand at her to hush.

He was in the same sort of clothes he wore every day—canvas trousers, boots, that battered leather jacket. He had, thankfully, taken off his explorer hat, and his sun-streaked hair was wild.

The cellist had worn a suit. The harmonicaist had worn an evening gown. Yet no one laughed. Quite the opposite—quiet settled over the noisy club.

In the silence one finger fell, striking the ivory keys precisely, and the note rounded and shaped itself through the silent air. Another, another, and then both hands were pulling an unfamiliar melody from the keys. Unfamiliar—and yet not; as it stretched and pulled like taffy into the air the criss-crossing melody pulled familiar memories into her mind—the forest, the wyverns, the eggs. Standing in the clearing with Tam and watching the wyverns swoop down to the nest. And then the melody took another turn and it began creeping along, guilty and ashamed. Stealing and thieving, and next to her Jack shifted uncomfortably in her chair.

Dorie was feeling pretty uncomfortable, too. This was how Tam felt, she could tell. This was how she felt. Eggs for research—a step up from Malcolm. Stealing them for the iron-skin. A step up again, perhaps. And still you felt guilty.

Well. Tomorrow would tell them if they could return the new wyvern chicks back to their families. That would make up for a lot.

She sat in silence—the whole nightclub did, even Woglet—until he was finished, and then there was a sea of applause. He was last—how could anything top that?—and the wait-ress said, he's too good for us, you know, and Dorie agreed, while Jack just sat and stared past her sketchpad with no sketch of Tam.

Jack was silent as they left, tramping home through the darkness. Finally she said, "It felt like he just reached into your head and pulled something new out of it."

"Sure," said Dorie, who did not really understand the artis-tic process, but understood that Jack liked to think about it. "I had no idea he liked to play the piano. I don't remember him doing that."

"Play *and* compose," pointed out Jack.

"And write contraband books, and do field work better than anyone except me. Makes you wonder what else he's hiding."

"We're all hiding something," Jack said. "You don't talk about being half-fey."

"Jack! Hush."

"And when you're a boy you don't talk about being a girl."

"Please be quiet, or I'll—"

Jack talked over her. "It's not just you; it's me, too. How often do I go around telling people I like girls?"

"Our friends wouldn't care."

"Oh, our friends. You mean the rebellious artsy anti-culture types? We live in a bubble, Dorie. Get beyond that and people would throw me out of their living rooms."

"Really?" said Dorie. "I mean, maybe if you were being all forthright and saying to folks 'I want to kiss girls' over and over. But like you could move in with Stella and be old maids together and no one would ever bat an eye. You remember our aunts' friend Frye, right? We used to play dress-up in her attic? Well look, she's been living with some lady singer for a dozen years now."

"And they still just call each other 'friends' in public," said Jack. "That's a separate issue, that two women in love aren't even considered dangerous enough to lock away, like two men are."

"Ugh, I don't even get your point," said Dorie. "You can slide under the radar. Aren't you glad? I mean, look at Stella. She can't hide being *dwarvven*. She has to face it every day, that stools aren't big enough and some bigots are still anti-*dwarvven*. Et cetera."

Jack wheeled on Dorie. "Yes. She has to live as who she is. That's what I like about her. Can you imagine Stella hiding anything about herself?"

"No," said Dorie. She couldn't help but add, "Which means she probably doesn't like girls, you know."

"Dammit all," said Jack. "I know that. After ten years, don't you know I know that? Who cares about love, though.

I'm on the verge of something important. An artistic breakthrough." She seized Dorie's arm. "You can't live a lie and
expect your art to be truthful. This is the integrity we were
just talking about. You can't hide things. It all has to pour
out, just like your cousin in his music. I could hear a story in
there, you know? I always thought that was bollocks, getting
stories out of instrumentals, but tonight I could hear it. He'd
done something he regretted, and he's still thinking about it,
so much later. Who can't resonate with that?"

"That might just be universal," agreed Dorie.

"I have to go home and paint," said Jack. "I have to go right
now."

"Jack!" said Dorie. But Jack was gone, her heels click-
clacking, her candy-apple dress disappearing into the night.

Chapter 10

DUSTING

Dorie is fifteen, and so is Tam.

Tam wants to hear what the fey themselves tell. Such a thing
has not occurred to Dorie. She asks the fey about things that *are,*
but Tam wants to know about things that *were.*

Dorie takes the guilt onto herself, but still. It is *Tam's* choice to
go into the forest with her.

Tam's choice to meet the fey. To be surrounded by them.

To drink the blue liquid, when it is offered.

To stay.

—T. L. Grimsby, Dorie & Tam: A Mostly True Story

* * *

"I'm still reading your book," said Dorie to Tam. "Did the
old lady in Middleford really say 'opto-paralyze'?" It was early
Saturday morning, and they were walking through the streets
to the next ironskin, last two eggs safely in the incubator. They
had already tracked down one ironskin at dawn, and then
Tam had ferried the new woglet back to his flat to join a
cranky Buster in his cage. Dorie had brought back the three
eggs and not told Tam why she had taken them, and he had
not asked. On the other hand, he had not volunteered any

information about his extracurricular activities last night, so perhaps they were both hiding something. As soon as he told her he was a concert pianist, she would tell him that she was Dorie Rochart. That would put that off nicely.

Tam laughed. "No, 'fascinate' is the older, less scientific term." The incubator was disguised in an old canvas bag; he shifted it from one hand to the other. "Crypto-zoology still doesn't have a wide acceptance, even with the discoveries presented by the wyvern eggs. So you choose the words of your stories very carefully. I kept all the exact transcripts, of course. I included as much of those as I could. But sometimes I had to reinterpret for the scientific mind—if I wanted anyone to take this project seriously at all."

Dorie nodded. They had followed Colin's instructions and were at the address now. Despite being in the slums, it was not a flat or back room. It was a white door in a small building of shops, with the symbol for "hospital" discreetly painted just above the doorknocker. The building was shabby, but markedly tidier than surrounding buildings, and the paint on the white door was fresh. A small sign showed the Saturday morning hours for the clinic. There was a woman behind the desk, and two women waiting on chairs, and that all made Dorie feel rather comfortable until she realized they were looking at *both* her and Tam as outsiders. A heavyset woman with a kind face betrayed no dubiousness, however, and ushered them back to a small white room to wait for the second ironskin of the day.

Her name was Dr. Moira O'Donnell, and she was a women's doctor for the poor.

Tam was setting out the incubator as the doctor entered. "It's close," he was saying. "She'd better not stop to take out an appendix or something."

"Or something," Dr. O'Donnell agreed dryly, shutting the door behind her. She studied them, then guessed correctly, "Tam? And you must be Dorian. Please, call me Moira."

She was a little older than them, perhaps early thirties. She was also the first ironskin Dorie had met who was not on the edge of poverty. She was a lean, striking woman with freckles, a mop of bright ginger curls, and a pleasant, no-nonsense expression. It seemed likely that any woman willing to first fight her way through the male-dominated University system to become a doctor and then come down here and work in the slums must be exceptionally no-nonsense.

"Where's the scarring?" said Dorie. The question was becoming familiar.

"Abdomen," said Moira. With no touch of uncertainty, she unbuttoned her shirt to reveal a slender mesh of iron wrapped around her stomach, below her modern brassiere. "Before you ask, it's depression. I decided long ago that I was going to ignore my suicidal thoughts." Her eyes glimmered with a touch of mischief. "Letting the patients have them would interfere with my practice."

Dorie snorted, and then the motion of the egg caught her eye. "Rocking," she said. "We won't keep you from your practice for too long. It's nearly ready."

"Were you followed?" Moira said.

"What?" Dorie looked at Tam.

"I am a physician," said Moira sharply. "Do you think I'm going to let you test some random herbal remedy on me without checking it out first? I thoroughly examined Niklas, Colin, and Alice. Along the way I learned that the eggs are now interdicted, and you two risk yourselves by coming to me. As a women's doctor who helps everyone in . . . need, you may well believe I and my clinic are quite familiar with risk, and I am indeed grateful to you. But that doesn't mean the risk has to be any more than necessary."

"We were cautious," Dorie said finally. "As far as we know, no one knows about our extra activities yet. But we were cautious all the same."

"Good," said Moira. "Now explain the process to me. I'd like to do it myself."

"It hurts," said Dorie.

Moira threw her a look.

Dorie explained how the procedure would go, finishing up with, "And that's why we usually advise a slug of gin." Over at the egg, the woglet's eyetooth was just cracking through. "Tam, if you want to wash up, I'm going to need you ready with the copper spoon in about two minutes."

Tam ducked out, and Moira looked at Dorie with a sharp eye. "There's something you aren't telling me."

"It's going to hurt?" offered Dorie.

"I mean, about you. You're carrying around a physical secret. It's none of my business and I won't pry. But I just want to let you know, we don't only treat women here at my clinic. There are others in need of care who don't feel they can go to a regular doctor, for whatever reason. Sometimes it's because they have certain private differences that make them uncomfortable." Moira let that lay there as she un-self-consciously prepared her stomach for the procedure.

"You mean like a . . ." Dorie couldn't think of the word. "You mean, like a person who's both sexes?"

"That is certainly one possibility. There are a number of people who feel at risk trying to find a physician for one reason or another, and we try to help them all here." Her words held a coded message that Dorie had never had occasion to listen for. She was not a regular human with "differences."

Nor was she a woman in trouble—for she was slowly starting to gather that that was the major risk that Dr. O'Donnell was alluding to. The reason why the clinic kept a low profile, and stayed on high alert.

Dorie shook her head, stood, walked around the room. There was a small metal frame that contained a picture of Dr. O'Donnell with her arms looped over the shoulder of another woman. A treasured picture; the person well loved. But the picture was old, sepia, and they were only Dorie's age in the picture. Yes, the two women could have just been friends. But somehow it reminded her of Jack, and Jack's intense relationship with her girlfriends at school. . . . Dorie let her fey intuition flow out around Moira, who was watching her. "How did she die?" she said.

"Cancer," said Moira, and though her face did not change Dorie could pick up the loss buried deep behind the eyes. "She was an artist. She was too young."

Dorie watched Moira's face. "I am not really a boy," she said.

Moira nodded. "You don't have an Adam's apple, for one thing."

"Oh, heavens, I forgot." Dorie's fingers flew to her throat. "Forgot?"

She might have told this kind, perceptive woman everything then, but Tam walked in, and with the slightest shake of her head she implored Moira not to say a word. The egg cracked, diverting everyone's attention. The triangular head pushed through, then the shoulders. This one was a fighter.

Tam brought the small cage with the lab mouse in it and set it next to the baby wyvern. It seemed to spur the little chick to greater efforts. Out came the wings. Out came the tail.

And then the egg cracked all the way and a baby wyvern

was advancing on the lab mouse, mirrored eyelids folding out. Dorie reached for the eggshell, scooping out the goo with the copper spoon into a little copper bowl.

"Wow," said Moira. Murmured, "I'll need to disinfect that table. . . ."

Angry voices from the pavement as Dorie scraped the egg-shell.

"Someone's here," Moira said, with the instant response granted from long familiarity with raids. "They're either after us or after you, but I'm guessing you. Regardless, I need to alert the staff."

"You need to put this on," contradicted Dorie. She turned with her copper bowl to Moira, her voice rising. "It only works within the first few minutes."

Moira strode to the door, flagging down a nurse. In calm tones she gave the evacuation command, then returned inside. "Hand me the substance," she said. "I can do it. You take the evidence and go out the back."

Dorie handed the goo over to the doctor, but stood her ground. "You need me to make sure you're clean." She nodded at Tam. "Take the hatchling and go. She can fascinate her mouse outside."

Moira sucked in her breath as she began to paint the first of the goo on the scar.

Tam was already gathering everything. He whistled at Dorie's shoulder, and to her surprise Woglet launched from her shoulder and flew to Tam's. "Fewer wyverns the better," Tam said to her surprised face, and a bit of mischief glimmered behind his glasses.

"Will wonders never cease," said Dorie as Tam left the room.

The scar was half-gone now, steaming away as Moira continued her careful, deliberate painting. "Distract me," she said through clenched teeth as she worked. "Tell me why I need *you* to make sure I'm clean. Some sort of ultraviolet monitor you run over me?"

"You don't miss a thing, do you," said Dorie. "Why haven't they knocked down the door yet?"

"Proper procedure," said Moira. "We have a big burly nurse who stands at the door and insists on paperwork whenever they want to inspect. Between that and a sympathetic sergeant on the inside, we haven't had a serious problem yet. You didn't answer my question."

Three-quarters down, and the sparkle on the goo was fading. Dorie scooped some up and started from the other end, ignoring Moira's intake of breath. "Doctor-patient confidentiality?"

"We'll pretend the patient normally operates on the doctor, sure," said Moira.

Dorie took a breath. It wasn't ever going to get any easier to say this. But maybe, you had to start trusting someone, somewhere, if you didn't want to live your whole live as a lie. "I'm half-fey," she said.

"How interesting," panted Moira, and even through the pain it was with the expression of someone who's heard it all. "You must promise to come back sometime and tell me all about it."

Dorie nodded. "I suppose . . . I might like that."

"I thought you might." Moira unclenched her teeth as the last bit of scar fell to the goo. "That's it, isn't it?" She took the hot damp towel and wiped her belly clean. "And then I'm rubbing you down with alcohol," she muttered to it.

"Let me see," said Dorie, and as soon as the wyvern goo was completely cleaned off she ran her fingers from one end of the scar to the other. But Moira had been thorough. The fey was gone.

Footsteps outside the hall.

"Oh, crap, no time," said Moira. She gave Dorie a gentle push onto the chair, and pulled her lab coat back on, getting the most imperative button done up over her unbuttoned shirt.

In that split second it occurred to Dorie that the men were probably looking for two *boys*. With a deep breath like a plunge underwater she released Dorian all at once, becoming curvy and long-haired there on the chair. Moira's shock registered only for a second before her professional doctor face returned—this woman was quick-witted enough for anything.

"And that's the sort of care you'll need to take with your lady parts," Moira said loudly as the door opened and men burst through. "Do you mind? This is a private room."

The man in front blushed as he scoped the room. "It's clean," he said. "The boys must have gone out the back."

"Do you mind?"

"Er. Sorry, miss." They stormed off as Dorie breathed a sigh of relief. Moira watched in fascination as Dorie carefully turned herself back into Dorian, a longer process than the reverse.

"You're in for it, you know," said Moira. "It's not all fun and games trying to elude them. They're throwing folks in jail right and left."

Dorie nodded as she stood, her dirty men's clothes now fitting correctly again. "I know," she said soberly.

Moira stared across the room. She might have been looking at that picture, or a jar of cotton, or anything at all. "If you have anything to set right, I'd do it sooner than later," she said.

Tam had gotten away safely. Dorie met him at the agreed-upon spot, and they looked at each other as if assessing damage, then continued on. The last ironskin for the day was out in the country, not far from the spot where the wyverns lived. They took the train, and Tam had wired ahead to rent them bicycles at the station. Dorie promised to pay him for her share in two weeks and mentally chalked up another debt.

This ironskin was an old man, and he yelled and cursed while they fixed the scar on his hand, and then grouchily threw them out before his wife got home.

"I don't think he's going to change much, scar or no scar," said Tam.

"I'm surprised his wife has stayed with him all this time," said Dorie. "Habit, perhaps."

They started in on the long bike ride down the road to the mountain turnoff. The humidity was getting oppressive, and the sky overhead was grey with a tinge of green. Dorie hoped they might finally get rain, and a break from the heat wave. Woglet rode on Dorie's shoulder, but the four newest wyvern hatchlings were in covered wire crates they had brought from the city, now precariously wired and balanced on the bikes, along with the portable incubator. "Quite the caravan," Dorie said once, but then the road got steep and it became too hard to talk.

The woglets in the carriers were all very grumpy by the time Dorie and Tam had trekked down the ravine and up to the caves where the wyverns lived. They spat their baby version of steam at their carriers—which luckily was not hot enough to do anything except make Dorie's and Tam's hands slippery.

Dorie and Tam set down the cages and unlocked them. Instantly the four silver hatchlings clambered out. "Well, here goes nothing," murmured Dorie. Woglet flapped his wings.

She and Tam retreated to the bushes to watch. She had no idea which chick belonged to which wyvern. Would they know?

The little wyverns seemed to feel at home on the mountain. Buster strutted into the clearing, the others hopping a little behind him. A couple of adult wyverns poked their heads out. One began circling. The little wyverns started the same yodeling that Woglet had in the nest when Dorie had tried this scheme. Dorie held her breath.

One wyvern came. Then another, then another. She had taken eight eggs from the nests, and before long there were exactly eight parents—the other eight remaining behind on the nests, presumably. They settled in a group around the strutting chicks. Then, one by one, each parent made a distinct vocalization.

When the third wyvern yodeled, Buster perked up his head. He wagged his bent tail like a new puppy and hopped forward, echoing the sound. Dorie was surprised to find tears in her eyes as the parent and chick called to each other, crossing the distance between them. The bonding that had mistakenly happened between Dorie and Woglet now happened here correctly, as the parent wyvern nuzzled his offspring.

The calls continued until the other three parents had found their woglets. Perhaps the chicks were familiar with their parents' voices from their time in the eggs, for each one seemed to recognize a yodel meant exclusively for them. Woglet appeared to be as interested in the process as the two humans, and he mewed, shifting his feet back and forth. "You could have done that," Dorie whispered, but Woglet did not seem agitated, merely curious.

The disappointed wyvern parents returned to their nests, but the matched parents stayed with their offspring, encouraging them to find something to fascinate and eat before returning to the nest. Dorie thought they might want proof that their child could do the fascinating necessary of a wyvern, for the parents all watched the process with an eagle eye.

Tam and Dorie returned to their cave on the side of the cliff. Dorie read Tam's book, and Tam scribbled in a notebook, lost in thought. It was a good hour later before they felt things had relaxed enough that Tam could watch Woglet and Dorie could return for the remaining eggs they needed for the ironskin. She climbed out of the cool cave and instantly felt the humidity again, a hot pressure that soaked her to the skin even without rain. Slowly she looked up at the beautiful nests of silver wings and felt torn in two.

She had proven that the baby wyverns could return home, and this bore her up. The eggs they clandestinely took today would not have to be shared with the lab. But the raid at Dr. O'Donnell's this morning—the risk. Could she swear that all the children she took today would be returned home safely?

Yet, how could she not finish saving the ironskin?

A distant crack of thunder urged her to action. Dorie went as quickly as possible, retrieving the eggs and taking them to the cave, and before long she had the eighteen eggs necessary to complete her goal. They were able to slip away, move carefully out and down the ravine. The ravine was dry now, the little bit of water that Dorie had tried the other day, gone. They set down the incubator and crates to shake out their hands and Dorie said, "They could have all gone back then. All the ones the lab took. They could have gone back."

"Yes," said Tam, and then they were silent, looking down the ravine to where they had seen the fey on the first day. The first drops of rain splattered on the dusty creekbed. Far down the ravine she could sense the fey, out of sight.

They were standing there together, and they were so in harmony that Dorie thought now, it has to be now. I have not told him but I must, for it will weigh on us forever.

"I have something to tell you," she said, forcing the words past her lips. "It's difficult."

"Something new you want to take to people?"

"Something about me. I'm not . . . I'm not exactly who you think I am." I'm not *what* you think I am, either.

His eyes stayed on the far end of the river, which was good. She didn't know how she would get it out if he stopped and turned to look at her. "Go on."

"I know . . . I know you've been hurt in the past by people pretending to be someone other than they are." His empty hands trembled, but he said nothing.

She took a deep breath. "I wanted to tell you that first day but I thought you would still hate me. My name isn't Dorian. I'm not even really a boy. I'm . . . I'm your cousin. Dorie."

Tam backed away, behind the crates, balling his fists in his pockets. "That's not funny," he said. Thunder cracked and the drops fell faster. Tam pulled his hat down, hiding his eyes.

"I know it's not funny. It's just . . . true. I wasn't having any luck getting work as a girl so my friend Jack suggested I try applying as a boy. I just happened to meet you the first day I was trying it and then I didn't know what to do."

"This is just the sort of prank my cousin would try to pull," he said in a low voice. "Seduce some poor unsuspecting boy and convince him to pull jokes on me."

"I would not," said Dorie, stung. Seducing was not part of her nature, no matter what she looked like. How could he believe that of her?

"I thought . . ." Tam turned away, picking up the crates and lashing them inside one another as if for something to do. "I thought we were friends."

We are, she thought. I mean, I want to be. That's why this is so hard to say. I wanted to tell you. The words would not come.

Tam strapped the incubator and crates to his back and prepared to climb out of the ravine. He pointed past her, down where he had been looking. "If you're telling the truth, then there are your friends. I'd keep company with them if I were you."

She turned, but though she could sense the fey down there, she could not see them. And then she heard a whistled song curl past her ear. Not the Midsomer Suite, but something more like what he had played at the club the night before. An eerie, *calling* sound, and just as the song at the club had made her think of betrayal and loss, so this clearly said, *come to me, come to me.* . . .

Blue.

First a haze, then a fog. Coming from the end of the ravine.

She turned to him, but he had broken off the song, and was climbing, away from her. "Tam," she said, but he did not stop.

The rain came then, as he climbed and climbed. It thundered up the dry ravine, came through the whirling wave of blue. Rain did not bother the fey; they mingled with the clouds and rain and thunder, coming toward her.

"Tam!" she cried, as he disappeared over the top of the ravine, back into the forest.

Woglet nuzzled her ear.

"Come on," she said, and there was a great horrible open cavity in her chest. "We might as well go meet them."

The blue scarves thundered around her and she gave herself to them. She did not recognize any fey that she had met before, but they recognized the fey in her. Woglet flew among them, interested, and they made space for him and let him be. Her sadness and shame loosened as the water washed a summer flood down the ravine.

With their help she faded out, not just halfway, but all the way blue, and turned over and over with them, floating through the trees as if she were pure fey. Dusting, she had always called it. Dissolving into motes of blue. She could feel herself spreading out, mingling with the others, reaching through the rain and trees and sky. She was part of everything, and she could see how you would come away with the fey and drift like this forever.

Long ago the fey had had a strong leader. The Fey Queen had pooled through the fey consciousness, mingled with them, brought them humans to play with, gave them things to do. Ordered punishments as she felt necessary. She had been that leader a long time. Subsequent attempts to replace her had failed.

Now the fey had no one.

And they were dying.

That is what they told her as they drifted: they told her of loss, of separation. This one had been taken, that one had vanished. They did not know why or where. They knew that they were all growing weaker.

<<Why were some of you in the city?>> asked Dorie, in the way that fey "talked." <<Was it for trade?>>

<<We do not know. There is no trade. No one has gone to the city intentionally.>><<We promised a girl named Helen, once, a blink of an eye ago.>><<Too soon to have forgotten our vow.>>

<<But I have seen a human taken over by a fey,>> said Dorie.

<<A desperate one, perhaps.>><<A captured and escaped one.>>

The Great War had started partly because the Fey Queen had been trying to resist the industrialization that was poisoning the land, the water, weakening them. And now . . .

It did not matter how long you lived, or how bored you were when you thought you still had thousands of years in front of you. And what was boredom, to a fey? A long holding pattern, a restless sense that the sunlight was not as clean, the air not as pure. The old games of intermingling with a human for a century or so and letting them go was no longer fun, no longer rejuvenating.

They were dying, and vanishing, and they wanted the old world back.

<<You could do something about it now,>> Dorie told them. <<You could take back the city.>>

<<No, silly girl,>> they told her. <<We promised.>> <<We promised.>> <<We promised.>>

Dorie twined and twirled. <<I will help you,>> she promised. <<But you must tell me how.>>

In answer they turned her over and over, rolled her along, and up and up the mountain. Woglet flew behind them, darting in and out of the blue, apparently unperturbed by either the rainstorm or the fact that wyverns and fey were supposed to be antagonistic.

They went higher than Dorie had ever been. The rainstorm was fading now, sweeping through. Everything was cool and washed, and little rivulets ran down the tracks and ruts beneath them. She was not sure how she would get down from the mountain, if she wasn't entirely blue. As they drifted, she could hear the same thoughts rippling through the blue: <<our circle has come>> <<the center has appeared>> <<a way to everything.>>

There were caves high up on the mountain when they finally touched down. The rain was at a patter now, a few straggling drops. There was a circular clearing there, in the mud. Blasted looking. Nothing was in it—no trees, no grasses, not even the invasive ivy that pervaded the lower levels of the forest.

The fey did not go through it, or even over it. They stopped well back from it.

<<Our center,>> they said, and she said, <<But you can't go in?>>

<<We need help to go through.>> <<We need help to go home.>> <<We no longer can enter the way.>>

They disentangled from her and she solidified to human and moved around the visible scorch marks, looking inside. It did not look strange, except for the fact that everything was dead. No mice. No birds. Woglet swooped around the circle, looking at it with curiosity.

The fey moved around Woglet, thrumming with interest. <<He is a little one,>> they said. <<The big one came through, opened the way. We can go when the big one goes.>> <<If someone keeps it open.>> <<Yes.>> <<Yes.>> <<And then we all go.>> <<All at once.>> <<Forever.>>

<<Where would you go, forever?>> she said.

They thrummed as if they did not know how to explain, or were trying to find the imagery to describe it. While they hovered, Woglet burst through the circle and went straight in, swooping around in aerial acrobatics.

It distracted Dorie from the fey. "Come away from there," she told Woglet, as she went after the silly thing . . . or tried to. There was a nasty cold feeling at the edge of the barrier that didn't want her to cross it. She pushed a little, and felt it push back in waves.

Panting, she stopped and looked at the circle again. Perhaps it was not just plain air after all—perhaps there was in fact a slight shimmer. Especially if she looked at it sideways, with fey senses.

Yes, from that angle there was more than just a shimmer. There seemed to be things moving inside. Woglet, yes, but with her fey vision she thought she saw birds flying through, and then, more strangely, a shimmering version of herself. Was it a mirror? That Dorie was in field clothes like her, but . . . her mouth grew dry. That Dorie was in *girlshape*. What was she seeing? That Dorie walked through the blasted circle and vanished as she crossed the ring that held This Dorie back.

"What are those," she said to herself, but the next thing that happened was she saw wings, huge glinting wings, far bigger than any wyvern, pass through the circle and vanish like the Dorie. She turned to inquire of the fey, but they were scattering at the sight, zipping off in all directions into the forest.

She swallowed and turned back—the huge beast crisscrossed the circle again and was gone.

Woglet turned his head, apparently tracking the enormous thing's passage. It was so big it could eat him like a snack, and

Woglet wouldn't have a chance of fascinating something that size, not with those enormous mirrored eyes it had—

Her heart dropped into her belly.

It was a basilisk.

Tam was right. They had returned.

"Woglet. Woglet!" she shouted, and when he didn't return she gritted her teeth and pushed herself through the thick air. It felt like forcing your way against a head-on wind. Another shove and she was through the barrier. She straightened— was hit with a sharp wave of dizziness. The circle, the forest, went in waves around her; she was on the deck of a ship and everything else was an ocean in a storm. In the haze she saw a flash—a fey, two, three, flickered in front of her and then were gone. The air around her was blue and howling—far worse than any thunderstorm. She cried out and sank to the muddy ground, putting her head to her knees, waiting for the dizziness and visions to subside.

Slowly, slowly she stood up inside the circle, looking around for Woglet. He was splashing in a puddle, apparently com- pletely unaffected by the strangeness of the circle. Where was the basilisk she had seen? Dorie took a half-step toward her wyvern chick—and was again buffeted by the same vision of the fey. She swallowed hard against the dizziness and opened her eyes, watching to see if she could sort truth from illusion, for surely there were no fey in the circle, were there? They had gone. But without another human with her, she had no way of telling if these visions were affecting her human side, fey side, or both.

She moved her head very carefully, then held it still even as the nausea threatened. The fey appeared through a mist, clearer and clearer. The blue swatches swam through the air in front of her. And then—they contorted, twisted. She felt a pull like keening, deep inside. They strung out and melted into a million particles. Gone.

The wings flashed back again through the circle, and this time she was seeing them full on, not sideways with fey senses, but clear and visible. Steam curled from the beast's mouth; the silver eye oriented to stare down at her—she shrieked and rolled, grabbing Woglet and fetching up hard against the barrier. Her panic was affecting her—did she need to be human or fey to get back out of the circle, or some mixture?

The basilisk swooped back as she thought that perhaps her fey side could slip out, slither around whatever strange thing this was, and she let one finger go thin and blue as she pushed against the boundary. Her head spun, she was going somewhere and she was staying here. She was melting into droplets and her head whirled, as if all the thoughts were bouncing around, fetching up hard against her skull. If only she hadn't told Tam—she could be with him right now. If she had told him the first day—maybe she would have discovered he'd forgiven her long ago. He would have asked her to Helen's meeting, not Annika. . . . The tip of her finger was spinning out, out, out, pulling the rest of her, melting—

Pain pulled her back.

Dorie jumped back, panting. The blue outline of her hand was missing the tip of a finger. It still felt like it was disintegrating, even not touching the barrier. She made her hand go back to human and nearly fainted from the pain. The tip of her index finger was gone, halfway down the nail.

What. The. Hell.

She stared at the circle's barrier, stared it down.

She had gone in as full human; she could get out that way. She wasn't willing to believe anything else. She steeled herself against the nausea and illusions, and in full human mode with Woglet safely under her arm, she pushed through the reluctant barrier until she burst through the other side, dizzy, panting, through. She sat down hard, breathing and trying to find her equilibrium.

Now that she was out of the circle she saw things she hadn't noticed before—chiefly, something that looked like a track leading away from the circle, up the mountains toward the cave. The remainder of the rainstorm outlined the track, trickling down its ruts, down the mountain. She looked more closely at how the track side-winded and thought, yes, it really does look like the track of a massive tail. Carefully she stood and followed the track, staying off to the side, in the bushes. Woglet squirmed out from under her arm and clambered with pinprick claws to sit on her shoulder.

A half-hour up the track she stopped. Sunshine picked out a wet clearing in front of her, and behind it a large cave, large enough to contain the giant basilisk she had glimpsed in the circle.

Inside the cave she could dimly see three eggs, nestled in a pile of leaves and branches.

Each egg could have comfortably held Stella.

She stared at Woglet. "What is this?" she said, and Woglet chirruped inquisitively. Cautiously she crept to the cave, fey senses extended for a return of the creature she had seen in the circle. She laid her good hand on the nearest egg, wondering if she could sense its state as she had with the wyvern eggs.

A thrumming deep inside her belly, like the vibrations of a bass drum. Tiny motions from the egg. It was going to hatch soon but not today—Tuesday, she thought. She checked the other two, but they seemed colder, a bit further from hatching.

A noise alerted her, and she scuttled back to the bushes, holding Woglet so tightly he squealed.

But it was nothing—a flash of green wings; a bird she did not know. The blood in her damaged finger was pounding more insistently now. The cut was bloodless—it looked like an old wound. But it felt like a new one. She let her finger fade to blue, where it still hurt, but in another way that was more mental than physical. At the moment she thought she would rather deal with some mental pain than actually have to look at the sheared-off tip of her index finger.

Woglet nudged his head against Dorie's ruined hand, whimpering. "I don't suppose you have any butter?" she said, a catch in her voice. He nuzzled into her arm and the yodel-whimper sank into a purr that thrummed through her bones and did seem to help. "Come on, then," she said. "We still have to figure out how a human gets down from here."

Chapter 11

GOING HOME

...the old woman said it was common knowledge in her village [of 18 people] that the yolk of the wyvern egg was poisonous to fey. But as for applying that knowledge, well, it was a question of who bells the cat. She further stated that, just as the basilisks were much larger, more terrifying cousins of the silvertailed wyverns, so the yolk of their egg was known to be proportionately more powerful. A tincture of the yolk, applied to the eye, would not only grant complete immunity from the fey, it would enable the viewer to opto-paralyze the fey just as regular basilisks opto-paralyzed humans.... Sadly, no basilisks have been reported in two centuries, so this theory is impossible to test.

—Thomas Grimsby, introduction to "Rose-Red and the Basilisk," *Collected Fey Tales*

*   *   *

Dorie was hot and tired by the time she had found her precarious way down the mountain. She was bone-sore, dying of hunger, and her finger was throbbing like fire. There was no help for it. She had to sleep, and eat something more substantial than dandelions, and that meant she had to go home. The rented bike was still there, and she headed down the muddy hill and farther out into the country.

Night was falling as she reached the dilapidated old manor that was Silver Birch Hall. She had not done a four-hour bike ride since she was a teenager, roaming around the country, and her legs ached and her rear was sore.

Dorie banged the hoop doorknocker with her good hand until the door creaked open and a small liveried figure with a cane and long grey braid opened. "Hi, Poule," said Dorie. She waved the same dirty hand at the old butler. Woglet mewed.

Poule looked at the slight boy standing on the doorstep with first one sharp eye, then the other. "Come on in, Dorie," she said.

There was dinner, a bath for her and Woglet—Woglet took to it surprisingly well, splashing mightily with his silver wings—and then at length Dorie found herself in girlshape in one of her old dresses, in the faded old piano room, explaining herself to two dubious parents.

"Believe me, I'm thrilled about the ironskin business," said Jane. "But why do you have to do it as a *boy*?"

"Well," said Dorie. All her clever reasons seemed to have deserted her along with Tam. "I wasn't getting anywhere as a girl. And now I am." Poule had put some sort of cool gel on the hand with the damaged finger, and bound it up to keep the gel from getting on anything. She wondered what was in the medicine—feywort? It did seem to help. She rested that hand carefully on her lap.

Jane shook her head. "I understand, of course," she said, in a voice that clearly meant she didn't really understand, not at all. "I just wish you could fight the battle as who you *are*. Not disguise yourself. That just lets them keep thinking they're winning."

"But they *were* winning," said Dorie. She was hot and tired and the road dust was making her eyes itch and water. No, she had washed her face, hadn't she? It must be something in the air.

Her father came and held her close. "I think it's very brave," he said to Jane. "And very clever." But her father always said those things. Dorie was not naïve enough to think it meant that only her father could possibly understand her, that she was special and unique. No, she understood all too well that he simply loved her too dearly to ever think ill of her. She could probably tell him the whole truth about Tam and have him not say one word of reproach.

Jane also loved her, but Jane had standards.

And if she didn't live up to Jane's standards, then she had to think seriously about who was right and who was wrong and what she truly believed.

It would be so much easier to believe she was always right. That's what her father thought.

Dorie rubbed her eyes with the back of her good hand. "Did you know Aunt Helen and Uncle Rook left town?" she said. Her parents just looked at each other. "Why didn't you go, too? Are things really that bad? You should have gone with them."

"You can stay or you can run," Jane said, but Edward put a hand on her knee, and her face softened.

"In war, everyone has to make the best choice for their family," her father said. "Helen and Rook have two little girls. There isn't much I wouldn't have done for you."

She felt like she would dissolve at that, but what she said was, "Do you think this is . . . war?"

"It's a different kind of war," her father said soberly. "This war isn't fought hand to hand. This war isn't equitable."

"Does war have to be equitable?" said Dorie flippantly.

But her father answered her seriously. "People in the city are trapping the fey en masse. Led by that blacksmith—"

"Niklas," Jane said quietly.

"I couldn't stop your stepmother from investigating, once you tipped her off to what you'd been hearing." Edward looked at Jane proudly, and Dorie's heart clutched at the sight.

"You were right," said Jane to Dorie. "He's been working on a new machine the last five years." Anger suffused her thin frame. "And I found out where the feywort is going, to boot. Denying it to those with crimson fever—using it for this! For this, Dorie! They're *splitting* the fey just as the Fey Queen did when she was supplying us with bluepacks long ago. Clean energy for all—only this time it isn't voluntary. It's slavery. And it doesn't have an end date, which bluepacks had back in the old days. Bluepacks lasted a few years until their servitude was up, and then the bits of fey wriggled free and went home to be whole again. But this? Splitting them forever? This is—"

"Genocide," supplied Edward.

Jane nodded, her fingers unconsciously going up to touch the old red lines of her face. "I have always hated the fey. I never thought your father should have taken you into the woods. But this . . . I can't condone this."

"We're practically alone in the fight," Edward said. "Those of us who speak out are hauled in under Subversive Activities. And out here in the country the wounds are still too fresh, even twenty years later. We get turned away from shops. They see me as a sympathizer." He spread his crippled hands. "But genocide?"

"It is strange to find myself on the other side of the fight," admitted Jane. "And yet not so strange, for we have always loved you."

"Morals aside," said Dorie, "shouldn't you run? If you're in danger from the country, danger from the city? Wouldn't it be safest to go abroad for a few months?"

Her parents looked at each other, then shook their heads.

"We've worried you," said her father. "We want you to understand what's going on, but don't worry about us. We're safe out here. We're forgotten."

Jane shook her head. "We're not forgotten, not really. But I won't run, either."

Dorie could tell this was an old argument between the two of them. She thought how odd it was to have been on her own for so long that they could have an old argument she didn't recognize. For a moment she looked at them with fresh eyes— the wrinkles beginning to weigh down her father's face, the grey streaks and white lock in Jane's hair. "Good night," she said gently, and kissed the two of them, and headed up to her old room at the top of the stairs.

She meant to sleep just a few hours, then head back into the city. But her body betrayed her; she slept until almost dinner. There would be no trains from here this late on Sunday. She bowed to the inevitable and followed the real sleep with a real dinner: great heaps of potatoes and cheese and whole milk and half of a chicken Poule had insisted on killing for her. (Poule was also very pleased with Woglet's mousing skills, and said he was welcome anytime.) Dorie had hoped a night's sleep would make her parents more tractable on the subject of leaving the country, but it did not, and when she finally went up to her bedroom on Sunday night it was with a sense of foreboding.

Sleep was slow in coming. At last she got back out of bed

and opened the window, looking out into the pitch-black forest that came up to the back of her house. It was quite cool, now that the heat wave had broken, and she breathed the air with relish. She was seized with the sudden whim to go outside. Martha, the maid, had washed her boy clothes, and Dorie put them on, thinking through where she would go. Perhaps she would go tramp through the forest as she had as a child; perhaps she should leave right now and hitch back into town. She stared into the night, pondering, remembering everything that had happened there, remembering everything she had messed up with Tam.

She stayed awake for so long she heard the men burst through the front door.

Dorie was alert in an instant, shoving her feet into her boots and tying them with her mind as she ran into the hallway. Yes. Silvermen, their glowing palms readily visible in the moonlight. She cast about, searching for something to throw at the intruders. Three shabby old curtains hung around the foyer below her; she ripped them off and tangled them around the men's ankles. That slowed them down—for a second. Her parents came stumbling out behind her, slow humans running into the hall. "Go," she shouted at them. "Run!"

But they didn't. She knew they wouldn't, and she was proud of them even as she was frustrated—what could they do? Her father was a painter with crippled hands—he didn't even hunt.

The men were untangling themselves now, heading for the stairs, silver palms extended and glowing in the presence of Dorie. With a presence of mind that suggested she had thought through this scenario, Jane upended an entire bag of Dorie's childhood marbles on the stairs, momentarily stunning the men again. In the chaos, Dorie mentally pulled an oil painting of her father's off the wall and smashed one of them over

the head. "Sorry," she called to her father. "I liked that one."
She looked around for something else to throw, but all she
saw was the old chandelier. It was well bolted to the ceiling
with iron—she couldn't budge that. But it had once run on
fey power, and so the lower links were copper. Perhaps she
could loosen those. . . .

"Martha is taking the auto and heading for town," her
father shouted in her ear under the clatter. "Run to the back
and meet her."

Dorie gripped his arms and said, "No, listen to me. You
run. They can't catch me."

He shook his head ruefully and said, "I won't leave Jane,
she won't leave me, and neither of us will leave this house.
You see how it is."

"It doesn't have to be," she said, uselessly. Surely sometimes
discretion was the better part of valor—surely sometimes it
was better to lie, and hide, and work within the system. He
smiled at her, as if divining her thoughts, and Jane grinned
savagely and threw an armful of books, one by one, at the at-
tackers.

They were foiled by the age of the house—the foyer had
long since stopped being perfectly level, and the marbles had
all run through the missing curtain into the back hallway.
The men were approaching cautiously, but they were on the
stairs again. The one in front seized Jane—and then Woglet
flew into his face, biting and scratching, until the man let
go, trying to protect his eyes. Jane kneed the man in the
distraction.

Dorie got back to working on that copper ring of the chandelier just as Poule came hurrying down to the foyer, rolling
some enormous cylindrical contraption. The old part-*dwarvven*
woman moved slowly these days, but she hobbled as fast as

she could. The men ignored her, which was their mistake. Poule flicked a switch, and soap foam began to spray out of the nozzle. An invented carpet cleaner, perhaps, repurposed. With frothy accuracy it sprayed into eyes and mouths and noses.

One of the silvermen realized that Poule was more dangerous than she looked. Shielding his face, he crossed the foyer and landed a blow to the gut that knocked the wind from her, toppled her to the floor, unmoving. "Poule!" shrieked Dorie. She redoubled her mental efforts with the copper ring, until she twisted the last bit away, and with a push in the right direction, managed to drop the chandelier squarely on the head of the man who had hit Poule. He crumpled to the floor with a satisfying crash.

It was good but it wasn't good enough. The other men had seized Jane and Edward now. Edward went gracefully and with an air of hauteur; Jane kicked and bit for all she was worth. The last two men were now approaching Dorie with ropes; they obviously thought the little blond girl would be an easy catch. She smirked, planning what damage she was about to cause. But the man holding Edward seemed to be the one in charge, and he said, "You idiots; didn't you see her drop the chandelier? She must be fey-ridden." He tossed a pair of iron handcuffs to the man advancing on her. The eye on their palms glowed silver.

"Go," shouted Jane, and her father smiled sadly at her.

Dorie backed up through the door to her room, Woglet returning to her side. The men grinned as they came close.

And then there was nothing for it but to leap through the open window and fall, fall, turning half-fey and rolling as she went.

* * *

She did not know where to go, and in her despair found herself fleeing into the cold forest behind her house, looking for fey to help her fade out to blue and help all her human worries vanish. But the fey were not there, and as if in a bad dream, she ran wild and half-fey through the woods, searching for her old companions. Woglet flew behind her, cooing in concern.

They were not in the fey ring, where she had once met her mother. They were not in the stand of silver birches that ran along the creek, where she had first gone with her father to meet her other kin. She ran until she reached the place she had never wanted to go back to at all: the old copse of pines where she had taken Tam that summer.

They were not there, either, and she sank to the ground, panting and exhausted. The ground was cold and dark and wet and there is nothing, nothing left of the fey.

She spreads her fingers in the needles and as if that fey loophole has taken her through time, she is back there, and it is sunny and golden where the light slants through the trees. She sees another Dorie, she sees another Tam, but this time she recognizes them all too well. Dorie has blond curls, Tam has a crisp clean explorer hat, and they are both fifteen.

Tam is excited, for he has tried to talk to the fey, but they laugh at those who *want* to find them. Today Dorie has promised an introduction. He turns to her, eyes shining, and takes her hands.

Dorie has butterflies in her stomach that twist and turn into giant basilisks. She has never been truly accepted by the fey. They say she is too human, that she cannot understand their games, their caprices, bright against the backdrop of the lazy drift of time. Impatient, fifteen-year-old Dorie perhaps cannot. But at the same time, she is not fully human, not accepted there, and she thinks again and again when she is teased: fine, I didn't want to be an ordinary girl anyway.

She spent all last school year plotting her escape and now, here at the start of summer, she has come with a special request. She has asked the fey: *How can I be more like you? What can I trade you? I want to be all fey, as much as I can.*

Older Dorie knows what they answered, but does not want to face it, not just yet. She looks at her younger self and wonders if seven years has made any difference in her understanding of time. Perhaps being here, right now, is the strongest suggestion that it has. Fey senses are different than human. They spread over centuries, and perhaps a slow dip into past memories is commonplace.

She would pull back from this memory, but it drags inexorably on, and sick fascination compels her to stay.

For what the fey answered was, <<Bring us that boy with the funny hat.>> <<Your cousin, the one who charms the birds with his whistle.>> <<Bring us Tam.>>

That Dorie, young Dorie, tells herself that she is only giving Tam what he wants. He has begged her to talk to them. He has his notebooks, he has his pencils. He wants to know the stories they tell. He wants to be with them, to drift with them, to *know.*

He does not know what he is asking, not really. He does not know what it is to be a human, taken by them. To go into the forest, where they will entwine him with blue and time will pass more slowly than it does outside, one day for every three. Where the blue fey will start to solidify, in contact with him, and they will amuse themselves with games with him, entertain themselves with his gifts. Where everything around him will be strange and full of illusion.

And she does not really know what she is giving him. She

does not really know if it is for him or for her that she holds his hands in response and leads him backward, a step at a time, deeper into the circle of pines.

He stops her before they are quite in the middle, and she thinks perhaps that is the sign to turn back. She can sense the fey hovering, so very near, and she thinks that is why he stopped. That he, like she, has regrets.

Instead he cups her cheek and kisses her, and she dissolves and breaks apart as if she is all fey, turning blue.

But no, when she pulls back she finds she is all too human, looking into those dear brown eyes.

That's when the fey she has summoned finally come.

That's when they hand her the blue cup that looks like water, and she looks at him and gives it to him, and he drinks down the fey substance that will let the fey take him and keep him.

He thinks this is just an afternoon of talking.

She never has to see the betrayal on his face when he finds out it's for a year.

This Dorie pulls back from the past, into the night, and she is crumpled on the ground, broken. There is one fey above her now, two, three. No more, but that is something, and they take her gently and help her fade into nothing.

<<They have taken everyone.>> <<They are gone,>> they say, and Dorie, lost in her own past, at first does not understand. They are flying quickly now, racing toward the mountain, and they transmit horrible sensations that ratchet her bones, a stretching, pulling feeling like pain.

Then it all stops, and she goes tumbling into the ravine where she and Tam fought only yesterday morning, Woglet tumbling down next to her.

It stops.

Dorie sat up, looking around. The fey that brought her here had vanished. She climbed up the ravine on the wyvern side, looking for the blue. There was an awful smell of petrol and she felt as though she were climbing through memories again, but this time not her own. They were impressions of ripping, of burning, limb from limb. And another smell, a stench far worse than fuel. Her eyes were stinging by the time she got to the top.

The silver cliffs of the wyverns had been desecrated.

Adult bodies were strewn everywhere—mangled and torn in the vicious fight to protect their eggs. She ran to the nests to see—empty. Systematically emptied one by one, and the remnants casually strewn down the cliff. Only the eggs had been considered of value, although here and there she saw wyverns shorn of their head or wings—grisly trophies taken back. Not even the babies she and Tam had brought back had been spared. She recognized Buster's bent tail and knelt beside him, petting the cooling body.

Night turned into predawn as she cradled the baby woglet. The first blues streaked the sky above. Woglet lifted his head to the sky and yodeled. It was a new sound she had never heard before, a hollow cry as the black became dawn.

Chapter 12

SUBVERSIVE ACTIVITIES

Nov. 3rd: Sometimes the subject switches from the stories about the extinction of the fey to stories about the extinction of wyverns. Or feywort, or goldmoths, or copperhead hydras. I need hardly mention that none of these have existed since much after the Great War.

Sometimes the subject finds a happier note. This morning she spun a long tale of lonely ice monsters who come down from the mountains at night to dance with pretty girls, and where their dance takes them, they leave footsteps of bluebells and snowdrops.

It is hard to say which of these visions is more fantastical.

—Dr. Tamlane Grimmsby, *What Alice Saw*

* * *

Dorie managed to hitch on the Monday morning milk train—after changing back into boyshape—and it was still early when she reached the city, eyes burnt and hollow. She had thought it through on the train, and the only way to get the rest of those eggs finished was to warn Colin to prepare. Presuming Tam didn't hate her so much that he would refuse to give her the ones they had collected. She rubbed her eyes. She should tell Tam about the basilisk. She owed him that much.

If he believed her.

The misty morning air swirled around her as she banged on Colin's door.

"Dorian," he said with surprise, blinking sleep away. "Do you have something about to hatch?"

"Sort of," she said. "Can I come in?"

He ushered her into the small place and she sat wearily down at the table. Her shirt, which had been briefly clean, was now streaked with dirt and wyvern blood. It rustled as she sat, and she remembered that in the midst of that awful descent, she had stumbled on some feywort and tucked it in her button-down for safekeeping. She pulled the blue flowers out now and gave them to him, and he put them in a jar of water.

Woglet curled in Dorie's elbow, head drooping against her shoulder. "We have all the rest of the eggs," Dorie said quietly. Colin sucked in breath. "But five of them are hatching tonight, and we won't be able to make it around to everyone's in time. Can I trust you to gather the next group of ironskin together?"

"'Course," he said.

"But listen, I want you to know what you're in for. You know how dangerous this is getting? They found the doctor's the other day. The goons raided us. We got away, but . . ."

Colin nodded soberly. "I'll be careful."

"I don't know," Dorie said. "Have they noticed at your work? Maybe you should put your brace back on till this is all over."

Colin shook his head. "A good idea, but when I woke up the morning after you fixed me and I weren't hungry, I sold the iron for scrap. And good riddance." He stood and paced. "If the last few days have taught me anything, it's that you have to stand and fight. Hope comes along when you least expect it. You have to fight for your cause."

"I understand," she said. She stood and shook his hand. "I'll see you an hour after midnight."

After that, she went straight to the central police station to try to find out where they had taken her parents. She plunked Woglet in the shrubbery across the street so he could find some breakfast and hoped he had the sense to stay in the shade. She dusted her hands, preparing to cross the street with her nice, easy, boy stride, head held as high as if she couldn't possibly be the least subversive—and then she saw *herself*.

It couldn't be her, of course.

She peered through the morning traffic, the passersby, trying to catch a glimpse of the girl descending the station steps. It really did look like her—Dorie, not Dorian, no less—in a blue dress and corkscrew curls, looking satisfied.

Dorie ran across the street, insouciance forgotten. Who was that? It wasn't *her*, obviously. She was currently Dorian and that—That Dorie was nothing, nothing—some trick of the light that made some passerby look like her. She wheeled, searching—but That Dorie was gone, disappeared into the crowd.

Had going into that strange circle in the forest left her with aftereffects? Had hurting her finger hurt her mentally, that now she was seeing things? This Dorie shook her head, trying to clear it. She had been awake too long, was all.

The bored clerk inside the station looked down at her and said that he couldn't give that information out to just anyone, and what was the young man's relationship to the people about whom he was inquiring?

"I'm their—" But she stopped short. "I'm their nephew?"

He peered dubiously over his spectacles. "Well, 'nephew,' the best I can tell you is that those detained for questioning under Subversive Activities are not being charged with a crime. They are merely being housed in a comfortable space to answer a few questions. The Rocharts will be released within forty-eight hours—provided, of course, that they are *not* charged with activities against the Crown." He shut his book with a snap. "And with that you will have to be content."

And with that she would have to be. Unless, of course, she whisked that book away from him to see if it had any further information. Or dumped his tea down his jacket, just because. Or even went outside and came back as Dorie to see if, in this case, being a girl would get her further than being a boy. She suddenly looked hard at the clerk. "Did a girl with blond curls just come in here?"

"No."

A trick of the light. She eyed that book, but it was under his hands and chained down besides.

"Forty-eight hours?" she said.

He looked sternly at her and repeated his admonition. "Provided they are not charged with activities against the Crown."

The lab was quiet when she walked in. Two hours late. Heads turned to track her dusty progress and she thought, what? Perhaps I should have taken a shower. If the landlady hasn't kicked us out completely. She looked down at her boy's clothes and saw besides the dirt and blood on the shirt, there was smeared blood on her right pantleg. She wondered what the clerk at the police station had thought about that.

But no, it was more than that. Whispers followed her down

the hall as she passed open doors. Her night had been horrible, but surely no one knew about it. Her hand sneaked up to feel her rough chin, her cheeks—wasn't she still Dorian?

It was Annika, of all people, who pulled Dorie into her closet of an office and made her sit. "Where have you been?" she whispered.

"Field work?" said Dorie.

"The lab's in an uproar," said Annika. "There was a contraband egg given out over the weekend—they traced it to a women's clinic by the wharf, but the trail has gone cold. They think the doctor might have been administering the albumen to a patient—but they encouraged her to return to answer a few questions, and the word is that she's been most unhelpful."

All they have to do is pull up her shirt to find the truth, thought Dorie, but she was glad to hear things hadn't come to that pass. "So what's the problem?" she said, heart heating up her chest. "The egg could have come from anywhere."

"Sure," said Annika. "Except Dr. Pearce checked his sources and they all claim not to know about it. And since they're only in it for financial gain, they are probably telling the truth when it comes to charity clinics, so that points the trail back here. Anyway, there's more."

"More."

"Well, that was Saturday, you see. A reward was put out. All this happened very quickly. And then a father brought his daughter in last night—turned her over. Said she was a former ironskin. Wouldn't say anything else—took his money and ran. Not exactly the sort of civic-minded poster child one could hope for, is it? The girl's really out of it—poor thing. Keeps rambling about these strange dreams she used to have. Shameful treatment. I don't think she really knows she's cured.

But she says two boys and a girl came to her. The girl was beautiful and half-fey."

The room wheeled around her. Dorie gripped the back of the chair and said casually, with everything she could muster, "But what does that have to do with the lab?"

"Already marked me," Annika said ruefully. "I'm the only girl; better check that I'm not half-fey, *ja*?" She held out her hand to Dorie. Inscribed on it was a silver eye. Her palm was red and angry from the process. "And because the three of us have been so busy together gathering eggs—"

Dorie could not process the irony of this. Somehow that fey-touched girl, Alice, knew Dorian was a girl. Thus two boys and a girl. Tam, Colin, and Dorie. Not Tam, Dorian, and Annika. And here she was being suspected of the very thing she had done, simply for the quirk of fate that had put those two trios together.

"Tam's in there now," Annika said. "Next you, and then you will be safe from the fey, too."

Dorie nodded numbly. "Of course," she said, and her tongue stopped there. She should run. She should hide. But Dr. Pearce walked past and saw her, and seized her shoulder.

"Excellent. Thank you for finding our lost sheep, Annika." Annika smiled tightly at the director and Dorie could not then have said whether Annika had been trying to drop her a friendly warning, or whether she was simply holding Dorian for Dr. Pearce. Or both. "You're up, Mr. Eliot. Young Grimsby's all done and busy healing. No fey in him."

"Healing?"

Dr. Pearce propelled Dorie down to the main lab room, where a number of young men in white coats whisked around and pretended to be busy so they could stay and watch. A new baby wyvern strutted around in a cage, yodeling its displeasure. I could have taken you back to the forest, thought Dorie. And now . . . Did the lab even know what had been done out on Black Rock? It couldn't have been the lab; it must have been someone sent by an angry Malcolm, determined not to be cheated. The desecration . . .

"Right hand," someone said, and she held out her bandaged hand and Dr. Pearce demurred. "Left, then."

Two men spread Dorie's hand open on the table and held it there. "We've tried this on someone who was fey-ridden," Dr. Pearce said conversationally. "It was quite dramatic. Everywhere we tattooed the silver, the fey began to leak out as if bleeding out through a wound. It smoked away as it hit the air, destroyed for good. Of course, it was too late for the poor human it had taken over."

"I suppose it would be," said Dorie. She was not fey-ridden, she was half-fey. She had carried the egg in her belly and caused no harm. She had touched the albumen with a human finger and had no problem. If she focused hard and kept her hand human, she could make it through this.

She thought.

Besides, there were ten of them, and all her chandelier-crashing tricks would only get her so far.

Could she go half-fey and squirm her hand free? But that would blow her cover and they would haul her off for sure. They likely had their suspicions about Dorie Rochart, after that incident last night. But no one yet knew about Dorian Eliot. If she wanted to stay free, wanted to finish curing the ironskin . . .

The metal tattoo gun lowered itself to her palm.

Desperate, the bottled-up words leaked out. "I saw traces of a basilisk."

The tattoo gun was lowered for a second. "Go on," said Dr. Pearce.

Ugh. She hadn't meant to tell him. It was *Tam's* basilisk to study. At least Pearce had lowered the tattoo gun. "Large wings, mirrored eyes—it couldn't be anything else. High up the mountains. Nearly impassable." Eggs due to hatch tomorrow—but no, perhaps she wouldn't say that quite yet. She didn't want him to send a team of twenty up the mountain. "You won't be able to find it without me. I'll need my team."

He drummed his fingers on the desk. They were still pretending that this process was routine. He wasn't *sure* there was anything feyish about her, after all—he would hardly like to falsely accuse his brilliant new naturalist. And now she had something he dearly wanted, presuming she wasn't lying. Of course, if she were fey-ridden, she'd be likely to lie, wouldn't she? She saw all that pass through his head, and her gambit fail.

"Fantastic," he said smoothly. "You and Annika and Tam can go first thing tomorrow morning. Just as soon as we make you safe."

And then the silver tool pressed down.

It hurt like a needle, like a shot, like being jabbed with a tiny hot knife.

But it was a tattoo. And she presumed that was how it hurt everybody. She focused on her palm, focused on keeping it solid. The pain ebbed and flowed as the needles thrummed more easily over fatty flesh, then bit into tendons, outlining the eye. She was human, she was human, she was human.

Nevertheless, she stared at her hand as if expecting to see her other half leak out the silver eye.

They were halfway through the tattoo before it became clear that nothing untoward was going to happen. No fey was going to burst out of her hand, thin and blue. Dr. Pearce clapped her on the back. Their eyes met and there was disappointment there behind the smile. He really didn't like her, did he. Perhaps he didn't like anybody, only what they could do for him. "Excellent," he said blandly to Dorian's smirk, as if there had never been any doubt about her humanity. "Henderson will supply you with ointment for it. Looking forward to hearing the news about the basilisk, what?" He moved off, and so did the surreptitious watchers.

Dorie held on until the tattoo finished, then struggled down from the stool. Woglet balanced on her shoulder as she made her unsteady way out of the lab room, out of the lab. She held out her red and silver hand as she went, and those who had silently watched her come in now silently watched her leave, "proof" that she was human writ clear on her palm. She met Annika's eyes, but Annika made no move to talk to her.

Tam was waiting for her outside. He seized her arm and walked her down the street, away from the building. Cheerfully waved at a fellow lab guy: "We're off to lunch." Boys did not really grip each other's arms like that; they gripped shoulders, and suddenly she thought that perhaps he might believe her.

"Look," Tam said in a low voice as they got out of sight. "I couldn't stop Pearce from grabbing you. You must believe me."

Dorie nodded.

"I mean. If you *are* my cousin—" He sighed. "Dorie and I have had our problems, but I wouldn't want anything to happen to her. When she left me in that forest . . ." His hat was off and he ran his fingers through his wild blond hair till it stood straight up.

"I didn't mean to," she said hoarsely. "I mean I did, I but I repented. Oh, how I repented."

He looked down at her, his eyes full of an old misery.

"I hated being human. I wanted to be one of them. They said I could if I brought you, and you wanted to go."

"For a day! A week! Not for three months. And time passes so strangely there, it felt like a year, and as far as I knew I was there forever, with nothing to think over but how much you must despise me to have done it."

"I know! I know," she said in a rush. "I was stupid. I was wrong. It didn't even get me what I wanted, which was to be all blue and vanish into the forest *with you,* and never come back." He looked startled at that thought. "The fey haven't had a real leader since we were little, but the strongest ones, the ones who made me the offer for you, basically said, congratulations, your cold betrayal makes you more like us." She slumped, her fingers curling against the memory. "They *were* going to take you for a year, a real year. I played along like I *was* cold and careless until I learned how to split all the fey out of me. Then I told them your parents were going to murder me and I'd better trade to get you back. They said in exchange, they would take your love for me. . . ."

Tam rounded on her. "How could you know all that?" He seized her arms. "How could you know all that, and still not know that they couldn't possibly take—" He broke off. "You have to be Dorie. You *have* to."

Her heart took a sudden irrational leap. "I *am,*" she said. Her hands were shaking from the tension.

Tam wheeled her off into the trees in the park. His dear brown eyes looked down into hers. "Prove it then," he said hoarsely. "Show me."

"All right." She held out her left hand and willed it to change back to Dorie's dainty one.

Nothing happened.

He kept watching. She consciously relaxed, took a breath, tried again. "It's not working—" And then sudden realization struck her. She turned her hand over to show the silver eye on her reddened palm. "I . . . I can't," she said. "I think . . . I think the wyvern goo stops me."

The softening vanished; he was hardened to her again. None of what she'd said meant anything. She was some boy, playing a joke on him, making him look like a fool. "Convenient."

"Oh no oh no oh no," she said. Did it block everything? She whirled, reached out mentally to flip a park bench and nothing happened. Ruffle the elm leaves. No. Her hand again, the other, bandaged hand. A foot. No.

Another breath. She could deal with the loss of lifting trolley tickets and scooting things along—she had done without most of her fey self for seven years.

But if she couldn't change back? If she was stuck as Dorian forever? "I don't want to be a boy," she burst out, and watched him take a step back. She shook her head. "I know you don't believe me. Why should you. But I am Dorie. It's all true. I know everything. I know you saw me in Dorie form at Aunt Helen's the other night. I know how Dorie showed up in a nice dress and *these old boots,* and caused a riot while trying to hide the fact that she had Woglet. I know you ignored me."

"You're well coached," he said.

"I know how we grew up together," she said, the words flying out. "Summer after summer. I know the stories we told about the fey. I know how after I betrayed you, I hated myself for years and years. I locked my fey half away the day you were freed. I locked it away so I could never hurt anybody again." Her hands curled on the memory of all those years without half of her self. Tam just looked at her, and she said softly, "I know that my parents were taken by the silvermen last night. They should have left town with yours."

He started then, for no one knew that Helen and Rook were on anything but a vacation at the shore. But then he shook his head. "Dorie told you that, too? She must think more highly of you than you deserve."

"It's true! I'm Dorie, I am."

"And I'm a three-legged albatross, and I almost believed you," Tam said coldly. "Guess you're a better liar than I am."

He turned to go and she stopped him and said, "But wait. Aren't we still a team?" She lowered her voice. "Five of those eggs are going to hatch tonight."

He stood a moment, thinking, his eyes hidden behind his glasses. Then, "I think we'd better divide and conquer."

Except you can't test to make sure the fey is all gone, she thought, but she stopped herself. Who knew if *she* could do that anymore. Anyway, "We can't," she said. "Need one person to do the albumen, other to be on wyvern duty." Sure, she had done Colin all by herself, but now—? "We can't risk anything going wrong."

Tam nodded reluctantly. "Do you have the next address?"

"Colin's gathering them," she said. "One hour after midnight."

"Don't think it means I want anything else to do with you," Tam said. "I just want to see the ironskin taken care of. Before everyone's thrown in jail. Then we can comfortably avoid each other for the rest of our lives."

He stalked off and she sank to the park bench, Woglet crawling around her shoulders. Her hands hurt and she didn't feel as though she had the energy to move one centimeter.

That's when she saw them.

Herself. And Tam.

She saw the two of them walking along the meandering path in front of her, hand in hand. She rubbed her eyes, staring. What were these visions? She must be going mad. That Dorie had not made any changes to her face, but her hair was straight and dark brown, like Jane's. That Tam had his explorer hat tipped back, and they were laughing.

They stayed on the path, but they walked right through a couple strolling by. Dodged some invisible couple she could not see. That Dorie turned toward Tam, letting go of his hand for a minute, and Tam winked out. Then she touched him again and there he was, pulling That Dorie close into his arms.

Could she hear them if she went closer? What would happen if they overlapped? Could That Dorie see her?

This Dorie crept off her bench. She reached them, reached to touch That Dorie's arm, but her fingers passed right through. That Dorie did not even notice her. The couple kissed, and That Tam touched That Dorie's cheek, gently. Holding hands, they turned down the path until they rounded the corner and disappeared from sight.

Dorie ran all the way home.

She needed a friend right now. She needed someone's shoulder to cry on, not that Dorie Rochart cried. But Jack was not there. There was a note saying that she was on duty at the club and Dorie could mooch dinner if she came. But she had nothing better to wear, and her one pair of Dorian clothes were disgraceful, and she couldn't be Dorie.... Lost in a fugue of despair, she exchanged her field jacket and shirt for an unfitted striped button-down of Jack's. Tucked in with a belt, her hair combed, she thought Dorian could pass muster. It didn't matter. She was losing Tam. She had lost him. She made it to the club, where all the men were handing hats to the hat lady, and she certainly didn't have a hat, and she stood, stuck in the lobby, unable to decide what to do next, because her head was only filled with Tam, Tam, Tam, and there was nothing left to make a decision about nonexistent hats.

Jack was working the front of the club and she said, "Oh, honestly, not like that, really?" and hustled Dorie back to the hat lady, and informed her to fit Dorie with one of the spare jackets and ties they kept around. A humiliated Dorie watched in the mirror as the hat lady even tied the tie for her. The Tam loss was supplanted with Dorie loss as she watched her identity dissolve in front of her, into squared shoulders and sober navy ties.

If there wasn't a way to get the goo out . . . she didn't want to be Dorian all her life. She didn't want to be a boy all her life. It had started as almost a lark, a lark with a serious purpose. She was always going to go back to being Dorie. Even with her plans to adjust Dorie's face a bit—that was her, that was Dorie. What would she do if she stayed stuck as a boy? She looked at herself in the mirror, the fine but boyish features. Ever-youthful. It seemed entirely possible her face would never age; that she would always look like the portrait Jack had done of her to refer back to.

But more—what kind of life would it be to be stuck as a boy, a human boy? Would she be always alone? She quelled the rising panic and tried to think rationally. Stella liked her. Could she marry Stella, live with her? No, she could hardly imagine it. Besides the fact that Stella was her next-closest friend after Jack, there was just simply the fact that Dorie didn't like girls, not like Jack did. Could she find a boy who liked boys then? More precisely, some boy who liked a boy who was really a girl? Perhaps, but the law was not fond of that sort of thing, not to mention society. She had blithely told

Jack no one would care, but it was a different thing to be facing it herself. It would mean hiding out forever, or being brave forever, fighting a fight she had never expected to have.

She crumpled. It would be slightly ironic to go from hiding one thing to hiding another. Not to mention that the only person she had ever liked that way was Tam, and he didn't like her in any iteration, and that was that.

A waitress showed her to a table way in the very back corner and said, "You can have anything on the cheap section of the menu here, as well as the house ales or wine. Also Jack says keep that lizard out of sight." Dorie ordered a stout and tried to focus on her three entrée choices, each of which cost more than she'd ever paid for a meal. She curled up her napkin and set it on the chair next to her for Woglet and told him sternly to go to sleep. Someone was playing piano, beautifully but not near as interestingly as Tam. She downed her ale and her food and some more ale and tried to figure out where they had taken her parents, and if Tam was going to hate her forever, and oh, stars, please stop remembering that you're stuck as a freaking boy.

Jack and Stella arrived before Dorie's meal was finished, but well after three ales had been consumed. "Ugh, I'm taking a break for five minutes," Jack said, shaking her bangles. "Aunt Alberta didn't say there was this much *standing.*"

"You stand when you paint."

"Time flies then."

Stella lugged a barstool over from the wall and cozied up next to Dorie. This is it, thought Dorie tipsily. You're stuck as a boy forever. Maybe this is what's supposed to happen. Could you possibly like Stella?

She tried looking at Stella through someone else's eyes, some imaginary macho man. The girlie magazine guy, perhaps. Stella

was tiny and curvaceous, and those were traits that men supposedly appreciated, at least, judging by Stella's raft of boy-
friends. She had fine features and big black eyes, and certainly
she was not lacking in the brain department, either.

Stella leaned on her shoulder and Dorie tried hard to find
it appealing. She looked across the table at Jack, who was ex-
ploding with suppressed laughter.

That didn't help.

Gently she set Stella straight on her barstool. "I'm sorry,"
she said helplessly.

Stella looked confused for a second—such things did not
happen to her—and then she brightened. "Oh," she said.
"You like *boys*. That's all right, then. I have the perfect person
to introduce you to." She waved across the room to a slender,
good-looking young man laughing with his friends. He waved
back. Stella started to wave him over, but Dorie grabbed her
arm and stopped her.

"It's no use," said Dorie, because as cute as the boy was, he
also did nothing for her. She could not imagine kissing him
any more than Stella. All those years in prep school when
Stella had picked up a new boy from who-knows-where every
week, and Jack had nursed a hopeless crush on Stella while simultaneously having year-long intense and argumentative
relationships with some girl from the hockey team or debate
squad—Dorie had just never *gotten it*. Perhaps, she thought
wistfully, she had imprinted on Tam just as Woglet had imprinted on her, and there was nothing more to be done.

"Look, Stella," Dorie said finally to her puzzled expression. "There's something I should have told you a week ago."
Jack coughed and Dorie amended. "Something I should have
told you years ago. But I've been chicken my whole life."

"I didn't know you years ago . . . ?" said Stella.

"Hush," said Jack. "She's coming out of the closet."

"She?"

"I'm Dorie," said Dorie. "And I'm half-fey."

There were a lot more drinks after that, as Stella digested the news with a great many exclamations and "oh, that explains this one thing that one time." Jack had to drift in and out, checking on the front of the room, but she seemed amused enough by the situation to want to come back and catch the next round of exclamations.

"But you can't tell anyone," Dorie cautioned. "This silver eyeball on my hand is supposed to prevent fey from walking among us. At least from taking us over. That's not me, of course, and I guess I have my answer on what it does to someone half-fey." She looked at her hand ruefully. "It stops me from using any of my abilities—including changing back to Dorie."

Jack came back then, just in time to hear this last bit of news. "Really," she said. "Dorian forever? How horrible."

"You're telling me."

"I mean, Dorian's all right for a lark. But to be stuck that way? Ugh, I'd go insane."

"You're not helping," said Dorie.

"Sorry," Jack said contritely, and cast around for a new subject. "So I just heard from one of the artists in my collective. The authorities checked our confiscated work and decided we all pass muster, though we were strongly cautioned about aligning ourselves with 'radicals' in the future. So, the new opening is Wednesday night, and the publicity should be great." She put down her sketchpad and looked sidelong at it. "But, uh, I have some new pieces to put in the show."

"That's wonderful news," said Dorie.

Stella chimed in agreement. "Can we see?"

"Mm," said Jack. "Two days from now."

Jack must be working on the pieces at her aunt's, if they're that private, Dorie thought. Speaking of . . . "You should probably stay at your aunt's for a couple of days," she said, rubbing her fingers through a water ring on the table, not looking at her roommate. "Just . . . just in case."

Jack raised eyebrows. "And you?" she said.

Dorie shrugged. "I can jump out of three-story windows. You can't." A lurch in her belly reminded her that this was no longer true and she hastily continued before Jack realized. She wasn't going to bring doom to Alberta's house, too. "Club management and new paintings." She looked carefully at her oldest, dearest friend. "Are you getting any sleep?"

Jack snorted. "What's that?"

"You know. It hems up the raveled pant leg of et cetera, et cetera."

"Maybe once I get this maraschino cherry nonsense sorted," Jack said with a sigh. "I keep doing the sums and they keep coming out nonsense."

"Gosh, I'll help you with that," said Stella. "Why didn't you say the word?"

Jack's eyes brightened with realization. "You. Are a lifesaver. Look, if you could do some work for me each week, I'd comp you all your meals. And send you home doggie bags for breakfast."

Stella got the look of doing sums in her head before she said, "Done." Followed with the caution, "Don't expect I don't eat a lot just because I'm a cute little *dwarvven*."

"Wouldn't dream of it," said Jack.

After all that it was after midnight, and Dorie made her tipsy way through the streets to Colin's flat. Five ironskin would be cured tonight, and they would be that much closer to their goal. The rest of the eggs were safely at Tam's flat—this whole project could be wrapped up by the time her parents were released from jail. They would all go home and Dorie would settle down to a nice career as Dorian. She would get the hand thing figured out in due course. When your options kept getting more and more limited, the choices left to you looked pretty good, and right now, getting everyone out of jail and being done with illicit activities sounded pretty good.

Two more days. That's all she needed.

That's when she saw that the door to Colin's flat was wide open, torn from its hinges, smashed on the ground. Beyond it lay a body, still as ice.

Chapter 13

BASILISK

Of all blows this was the worst, for she had led Colin into this trap, as surely as she had led Tam into his.

—Thomas Lane Grimsby, *Silverblind: The Story of Adora Rochart*

* * *

Despair came first. She stepped over wreckage, her gaze sweeping the room. The table was broken; the jar that had held the feywort lay broken and spilled on the floor. The feywort was gone. There was only one body. He lay in the middle of the room, sprawled back. He had been defending the room when he went down.

The body was tall and hefty.

It had ginger hair.

She knelt beside him. "Wake up, Colin. Oh, please, wake up." His hands were bloodied—he had fought. Her fingers hovered under his nostrils—nothing. She touched his hair and her hand came away wet with blood. Whoever had smashed in his skull had done a good job of it. All that remained was to verify the pulse, and it was gone.

Anger came next, sweeping away the despair like a summer storm. She wanted desperately to mentally reach out and smash things, to wreak her anger on the room. But she could not, stymied by that silver eye in her palm. Slowly she rose. The table had broken during the fight but the chair had not, and that was about all that had belonged to Colin. Methodically she reached for the chair, picked it up in her two hurting hands, and slammed it into the broken table. Again, and again, until the manic energy wore out and she crumpled down in a heap in the middle of the wreckage.

There was a broken sprig of feywort under the chair. The blue bells trembled as she picked it up and then at last the tears started to come. Dorie Rochart did not cry. But perhaps Dorian was strong enough to.

It was in the middle of her weeping when Tam walked in.

He had the incubator with him.

Unthinking, she ran to him, flinging her arms around his neck. He stiffened, startled for a moment, and then gently he stroked her short hair. Then he stepped back and held out the incubator to her. "I got here early," he said soberly. "We got the five eggs that were rocking out and set them in a towel nest. The ironskin were all here—nervous as you might expect. I realized I was short one mouse and I stepped outside to look for one—taking the incubator with the other thirteen eggs with me. I got back, and—" He gestured around. "I was too late. I saw the goons hauling away the five ironskin for 'questioning.'"

"He said he wanted to fight," Dorie said. She rubbed away the tear streaks on her face. "He did."

"Are my aunt and uncle really detained as well?" Tam said. He did not say "your parents," but he did not say "Dorie's parents," either. Perhaps he was meeting her halfway.

"Forty-eight hours," she said. "From last night."

"We'll hope they hold to that," he said. He looked down at

Colin again. "I wish there were something we could do for him. . . . But the best we can do is make an anonymous tip-off to the police."

"In case the goons don't report their own dirty work," she said bitterly.

Tam looked at her. "Were you two . . . close?"

She shook her head. "I just met him a week ago." She sighed, for she did care a great deal about Colin, even though she had only just met him. His bravery and spirit had worked its way into her affections, and she was sobbing about him the way she might have about Stella. She knelt down next to the still body and gently tucked the broken feywort between his hands.

Cared for him, yes. But the way Tam meant? No, there was only one person whom she cared about like that. "No," she said, looking up at Tam. "Not like that."

In the near-darkness Tam looked at her for a long time, but all he said was, "We'd better get out of here before they come back."

Dorie stayed awake long enough to mark the approximate time on each egg with Jack's paints, and then when morning arrived she went through the streets to Dr. O'Donnell's clinic. She was relieved to find the ginger-haired doctor had been released from questioning and was back on the job. She waited in a back room, not very long, for Moira to come in.

Moira's gaze went immediately to the incubator, and the whole tale spilled out.

"I'm so sorry to hear about Colin," she said when Dorie reached that part.

"Well, and he was the focal point of this," said Dorie. She

rubbed her eyes. "He was the one organizing all the ironskin. But he said that each of you knew a few; that together every-one was known. I'm hoping you might know a place to start."

Dr. O'Donnell slowly nodded. "I do know most of them," she said. "Maybe all. I've treated a number of them over the years. Who did you say was picked up last night?"

"I don't know," admitted Dorie. "I never met them." She named off the other ones they had done, and the doctor nod-ded that she knew each of them.

Finally Moira said, "Here's what I can do. I will use my contacts and get you a name and address for each of the re-maining ironskin. But I can't let them be treated here and have thirteen wyverns here. I'm sorry."

"I understand," said Dorie, who did, but was still disap-pointed. "But the information will be invaluable. Thank you."

"It's not that I don't believe in your cause—goodness knows I do." Moira's hand dropped to her belly. "Have you ever been depressed?"

"I . . . I don't really know," said Dorie.

"The metaphor I like is a wet wool blanket," said Moira. She turned to the window. "Every day you wake up under this wretched thing. You can't see in front of you. You can't see the sun. And every day—in my case, at least—you have to tell yourself that the blanket is imaginary. That someone else put it there. That it doesn't belong to you; it's not your job to carry it." Her fingers touched the pane of glass. "And then one day you wake up, and it's no longer weighing you down." She turned. "I can still feel the aftereffects of twenty years with it," she said. "But you just don't know, unless you've been there. . . ." She sat down next to Dorie and gently squeezed her forearm, just above the bandage. "I will help you as I can,"

Moira said. "But I have to keep the safety of the women here in mind. It's my life's work, you see. It was the only thing that kept me going, day after day under that blanket."

Dorie pressed Moira's hand in response and said, "I do understand." Then she pulled her hand away, uncertain how one was supposed to handle extended human contact. "Can I leave the eggs here for one day? I have one more day in the field, and I'm afraid my apartment has been compromised."

"You know *this* location has been compromised," said Moira. "Another reason not to bring the ironskin here." But she relented. "We have a safe room that hasn't been found yet. One day."

"Thank you," said Dorie, and she turned for the door.

"You look somehow . . . more boyish than you did before," Moira mused. "Different clothes?"

Dorie swallowed. "That must be it."

Dorie made it to work on time, which felt ironic, given that her attendance record was really the last thing she cared about right now. She had remembered on the walk over that she'd only managed to tell Dr. Pearce about the basilisk and not Tam, so she went straight to his office to try to tell him. But Dr. Pearce's secretary stopped her and told her she was expected outside with Tam and Annika for field work, which meant Tam already knew, which meant he had yet another reason to consider her a rotten, secretive liar.

She was running on three hours' sleep and her head was pounding from the ale at The Supper Club the night before. The tattoo on her left hand stung, and her right index finger had moved on to itching. Wearily she piled into the staff auto with Tam, who looked tired and impassive, and Annika, who looked fresh and wholesome and ready to run a marathon.

Dorie gave Tam directions to where she had seen the basilisk, and he nodded, and did not say anything else to her.

Annika was giddier than Dorie had ever seen her. She chattered happily to Tam about a coffee date they had apparently had on Sunday night while Dorie was off fighting goons at Silver Birch Hall. Dorie tried to stick the cloth of Jack's shirt in her ear, but it wasn't very effective. Eventually she curled up in the backseat and passed out.

She awoke to find them driving on the last of the switchbacks that led up the mountain. Tam's knuckles were white with concentration as he maneuvered and tried to avoid wearing out the brakes. At last he stopped and said, "I can't take it any higher, if we want to be sure of getting out again."

"I can find my way from here," Dorie said as they got out of the automobile. Except she didn't have her fey tracking to fall back on. Still, she had spent seven years practicing her forestry skills with no fey senses. She wasn't flying completely blind.

"Do you think Dr. Pearce really believes we'll find a basilisk?" said Annika.

"He's hoping against hope," Tam said grimly. "If even half of my collected stories are true . . ."

"Of course, Dorian may have been misled," said Annika. "Sometimes the threat of pain makes people say funny things." She raised her eyebrows at Dorian. "Or perhaps you saw an overgrown wyvern?"

Dorie ignored this needling. "She had three eggs, each as tall as my waist," she said. "The first is due to hatch today. If we make it in time, Pearcey will have all the proof he wants."

The other two looked wonderingly at her. "Better step up the pace, then," said Tam.

They walked hard for a long time into the forest, Dorie

leading the way and Woglet darting forward and back. With the heat wave gone it was finally cool again, doubly cool for being in the mountains on a morning. But they were walking up tempo, uphill, bushwhacking a trail, and before long they all had their jackets off.

Though Dorie did know where they were going, there were a lot more fits and starts than usual. A lot more pauses and considerings. She was aware that her keen edge was gone, and Annika was getting scornful. Tam was looking at her when he thought she didn't notice, and considering.

"You're sure this is the way?" Annika said pointedly after a dead-end that took them to a ridgey dropoff.

Dorie did not answer. She patiently backtracked and pressed on, and then suddenly said, "Look."

A large blue bird with iridescent feathers flew overhead. As they watched, the bird shifted, chameleon-like, blue to green as it flew against the trees. Then it vanished.

"I have never seen a bird like that," said Annika. "How could a bird that big be uncategorized?"

"How could you not find a basilisk, when they're supposedly as big as a trolley car?" said Dorie. She looked down at Tam, who was scribbling rapidly in his notebook. For a moment their eyes met. "Things get weird the closer we get to this place. Come on."

It was another hour straight up and another hour around the curves. Dorie felt lost in a dream. Her fey senses were gone, but something else was drawing her on like a lodestar. It was as if she were being called home. She was not surprised when she started seeing wisps of blue out of the corners of her eyes. It was another half-hour before Annika spotted them, and who could tell about Tam? He was keeping his cards close.

Annika came to a dead halt the first time she saw one, spreading her arms out to defend the other two. "They're everywhere," Annika said, realizing. "This is where the basilisk albumen would be helpful."

"I thought your precious eye things would defend against the fey," Dorie said scornfully.

"Defend. But not attack," said Annika. "The wyvern albumen keeps you protected from the fey. But supposedly the basilisk albumen would allow you to *control* the fey. The stories all say—"

"The fey won't hurt us if we don't hurt them," said Dorie. She was tired of pretending to be human. "Buck up and come on."

The blue fey were inquisitive today. They drifted closer, watching the small party move closer to the center. It was comforting for Dorie to be around that part of her that had been cut off, but she could see Tam growing cautious and Annika growing angry. Annika kept her silver palm in front of her like a shield. Dorie stuffed hers in her pocket.

At length they reached the burned-out hole. Dorie wondered if she could touch it now that she had the wyvern goo embedded in her palm, but she didn't exactly feel like trying. "Careful," she cautioned Annika as the other woman moved closer. Annika poked a stick through, and then gently touched the ring with a finger. Nothing happened.

"Whatever did this, it's gone," Annika said.

Dorie was dubious. With her right hand, the one that had been so painfully disintegrated, she touched her pinky finger gently where the barrier would be.

The barrier was still there for her.

But it did not hurt.

She pushed gently, and felt the barrier mold around her.

She could see through it. She stepped through, expecting at least the dizzying vertigo, but no, that was manageable now. The center of the ring was still, and the outside . . . She turned back and saw Tam split into a number of different Tams, all poking around the edges of the ring. There were multiple Annikas, too, though not as many. And there—the many Dories.

She was a hundred Dories, she was a thousand. She was here with Tam and here with Jack and here with Jane; she was in the city, she was in the country, she was dead, she was alive, she was in jail and in asylums and on thrones. She saw those Dories she had seen since her visit here the first time: satisfied Dorie with the yellow curls, Dorie with straight brown hair and Tam at her side.

She stepped out the other side, letting the visions fall away. Tam and Annika were looking at her funny. "Did that hurt?" said Annika.

"No," said Dorie truthfully.

Annika followed Dorie's example and stepped into the circle. Nothing seemed to happen. "You looked kind of . . . blurry when you were in here," she said. "Wouldn't you say so, Thomas?"

"Yes," he agreed.

"Do I look blurry?" said Annika. "I feel nothing abnormal." Tam shook his head. Annika looked at Dorie. "What did you feel when you were here the other day?"

Dorie sidestepped this. "How long did you say the basilisk cycle was?"

"Ninety-seven years," said Tam.

"I don't think they have a larval form, or anything like that. I think they came . . . through here."

"*Through* here?" said Annika. "From where, the ground?"

Dorie shook her head, reluctant to say what she was thinking. It sounded too crazy. But how else to explain the multiple Dories she'd seen ever since she lost a bit of her substance to the circle?

Tam looked at her with his mouth slightly open. "You think they came through from somewhere else," he said.

Dorie nodded curtly. Whatever this was, she didn't want to explore it with Annika around. Besides, if that basilisk egg was going to hatch, she wanted to see it, potent goo or no. "Basilisk trail," she said shortly. "This way."

The other two followed her through the circle and to the trail. Great bare patches in the forest, where a tail might have dragged back and forth. Reptilian spoor, mostly buried under a bush. You did not need to be half-fey to follow this track. Tam had his notebook out, and he was taking notes, kneeling to measure the footprints and take samples. He flipped back and forth between the page with his dates, calculating and wondering. "There's always a reason to have a long cycle," he said. "To evade predators, or to find food. . . . How long do you think the circle's been here, Dorian?" He peered through his spectacles at her, past her.

"I don't know," she said. "I only found it Saturday." He refocused on her then, remembering Saturday.

"Ah. Right."

"The wyvern egg-laying cycle is about a month," said Annika. "Do you think it could have been here that long?" Long enough for a cautious basilisk mother to come through, and lay her eggs, and wait. . . .

The three moved quietly, cautiously, now that they were close. At last Dorie whispered, "Stop," and flung out her arms and made them crouch down. Just in front of the cave was one of the giant eggs. A fresh track behind it showed it had been recently nudged those few feet out from the cave, into the clearing.

And the egg was rocking.

And of course that was not all. If there was an egg, there must be the . . .

Their mouths fell open as the largest creature they had ever seen touched down in the clearing, wings kicking back dust. It was the same general shape as a wyvern, only much, much bigger. If Woglet was a bright silver, then the basilisk was a mixture of all metals: iron and copper and silver, all mixed together and glinting in the sun. She was a magnificent creature—clearly the victor of numerous battles, for there were places where the hard scales were broken, and there was a ridge of scar tissue under one wing. The mirrored shades around her eyes were so large Dorie thought she might fall under her spell even with no attempt on the basilisk's part to hypnotize. In her mouth she carried a deer, which she set down before the egg, casually snapping one leg when it tried to flee.

Dorie swallowed. They were going to try to get the goo away from *that*?

Back in the cave she saw the outlines of the other two eggs—a clutch of three, similar to the wyvern. As she looked closer, she noticed more details today. The eggs were fully buried inside a nest of branches and leaves and what looked like several sheepskins, possibly with sheep parts still attached. Unlike the wyvern pairs, this basilisk, at least, was on her own. At least at the moment, Dorie reminded herself, looking suddenly around. The staggered hatching gave each woglet a chance to have the parent's full attention for the fascinating attempt before moving on to the next. What did you call a baby basilisk, anyway? A boglet?

The egg was rocking and Dorie turned her attention back to

it. The now-familiar sound of the eggtooth chipping away—only much, much louder—filled the air. A few more pecks, and there was the triangular head poking through.

It was much like the woglet hatchings after all. They watched as the newly hatched basilisk hypnotized the deer, then tore into its belly. It wobbled happily over to its parent, who ushered it to the cliff's edge for a first flight. No time like the present, apparently.

Dorie came back to earth to find the other two quietly arguing.

"We'll pack it away in the copper," said Annika. She unpacked a small copper spoon and a series of vials from her pack. The spoon seemed laughably small next to the egg. "If we hurry, perhaps we'll still be able to test it when we get to the lab."

"That's five hours from here," said Tam, working with his own spoon. "The most the copper has extended the five-minute shelf life is an hour. There won't be anything left in five hours."

"It's a basilisk," pointed out Dorie. "The albumen may have different properties—we know it's probably stronger."

They ignored this. "Someone had to be the first to try the wyvern albumen," said Tam, "and someone is going to have to be the first to try this."

"Thomas, it's a story," said Annika. "The basilisk albumen in the eye is just a *story*."

Dorie sucked air between her teeth. He couldn't really be suggesting that he put that stuff in his eye, could he?

Tam looked up at Annika, his face inscrutable behind his glasses. "I thought you believed in my stories," he said.

Annika looked at him for a moment. Then, without turning

her head, she said, "Dorian? Let's cut to the chase. You're clearly the best trapper of the three of us. Bring me a rabbit—and do not argue. Just do it."

"But—" said Dorie. Annika just looked at her. Dorie sighed and went just out of sight so she could turn half-blue, and then remembered she couldn't and kicked a tree stump, wondering just how she was supposed to catch a rabbit as a human. Behind her, the other two hurriedly scraped the goo into copper, looking around every other second for returning basilisks.

"You are too valuable to the Crown," Annika said quietly but firmly to Tam. "I was hired to make sure you did not get into trouble. *I* will test the basilisk albumen."

"I can't let you do that," said Tam.

"I believe in your research," she said simply.

"They're stories," he cried out, suddenly finding himself on the other side of the argument. "They point the way. We can't always take them literally. What if it burns your eyes; what if you go blind?"

"Thus the rabbit," said Annika. "I will watch it for five minutes. Then I will take the test. I have eyewash with me if I think I need it."

Dorie wasn't that much of a trapper without her fey senses. Anyway, there wasn't always a rabbit around when you needed one. She set Woglet down on the ground and said, "Find me something." She didn't have much hope that he actually understood her, but he was still growing like crazy and used every opportunity to hunt, so she hoped that it would work out regardless. She watched him watch the ground, and when his eyelids flicked out to fascinate something, Dorie swooped down and grabbed it. "Sorry," she told Woglet. "Find another for yourself, okay?" She took the wriggling field mouse back to Annika and Tam, who had just finished cleaning out the egg. "Let's get out of here though, can we?"

They hiked back down to a safe distance—downwind, just in case the basilisks were smellers, though Dorie didn't think they were—and set up camp in a cave too small for a basilisk. Woglet swooped in after them, curious about what they were doing with his mouse.

"Not as reliable as the rabbit," said Annika, "but it will do." With her usual cold-as-ice expression she dipped her gloved finger into the egg and patiently waited for the right second to coat the mouse's eyes with albumen. Dorie shuddered.

The mouse squealed, then went limp. Well, that's done it, thought Dorie. But then the mouse started moving again. Annika set it down on the floor and it scampered around their feet and out the cave door, handily avoiding obstacles and seemingly none the worse for the experiment.

"Annika," Tam tried again. "That's hardly a valid field test."

Annika smiled softly at him. "You can't stop me, Thomas. If you try it, I will try it, too. It might as well be only one of us." Her face was an implacable mask as she touched her finger to the egg and put one drop in the corner of her eye. She sucked in a painful breath, but Dorie never saw regret write itself across her face. Annika held her breath, eyes closed, counting out the length it had taken the mouse to calm down, while Tam readied the eyewash, seemingly prepared to force it on her in another second.

Annika opened her eyes. The left one was still pale blue against white. The right one was solid silver.

Dorie forced down a yelp, as well as the useless question burning on her lips: *Can you see?*

Annika turned her disturbing gaze to Dorie, and Dorie

was unable to look away. Was that due to its strangeness? Surely she could pull away if she wanted to. But she didn't.

"I can see," Annika said slowly. "I see . . . faint blue shimmers. Some far, some near." She blinked at Dorie, her gaze remaining there for a moment. Then slowly she looked away. "I get a sense that there are fey across the ravine, in that direction."

There *were* fey over there. Dorie could sense them, even without her other fey powers. She shivered. What new advantages was this going to bring to the city?

"Do you see regular things, too?" said Tam.

Annika closed her normal eye. "Regular things look a little less . . . solid," she said. "The mountain is fairly solid, but the trees are a tiny bit blurry. Animals blurrier still." She looked around. "Do you see any birds?"

Dorie silently pointed to the nearest, a jay half-hidden in a larch above them.

Annika was silent for a moment. Then she said, "So that's what that red blur is." She looked down at the two of them. "You're a red blur, too, Tam." She opened both eyes, closed the silver one, then went back to closing the blue one. "Can I opto-paralyze you?" Annika mused, turning the force of her silver eye on Tam.

Tam felt himself all over, a probing expression on his face. "I don't think so," he said, then suddenly laughed. "No, I'd have to be fey, wouldn't I?" Now that the immediate danger for Annika had passed, he was giddy with another of his myths being proven. "We'll have to find the fey and try."

"That seems dangerous," put in Dorie. She wasn't sure she wanted Annika to have the chance to find out what the basilisk in her eye could do.

"No, we must," said Annika. "Pack up and come on."

Annika pushed her way through the forest and Dorie and Tam had to follow. Tam looked excited; Dorie felt ill. They reached the spot where they had seen the fey—the blue mist was still hanging around, minding its own business as far as Dorie could tell.

"Annika," she said again, but Annika advanced on it, silver palm out just in case her eye should fail. The blue drifted, then stiffened. A mirror of Annika's face formed, painfully slowly—the fey was attempting to talk to them, Dorie could tell, and it didn't even have enough knowledge of human conventions, or images stored away, to form some other face. Sick horror twisted inside.

"Hellllp me," it said slowly, the fey communication transmuting into a language the humans could understand. Woglet gripped Dorie's shoulder, his pinprick claws digging in.

"Please, Annika," Dorie managed again.

An unexpected source backed her up. "It doesn't mean any harm," Tam said. "I've been around enough of them to tell."

"They all can cause harm," Annika said coolly. "Anyway, it's science."

"I caaan goooo," the fey said again. "Let me goooo."

"Show me where there are more of you," said Annika.

"Really, don't you think we should—" said Dorie.

But Annika didn't even bother to tell her to shut up. "Take notes for me, Thomas," she said crisply. "Opto-paralyzing for more than five seconds appears to nearly immobilize the fey. The eye with the basilisk is fully open. Next I intend to see if I can release the paralyzation field just enough to have it obey a command. I will attempt to find out if this is a physical constraint—lowering the eyelid partway—or a mental one."

The fey tried one more time. "Help uuusss," it said, and the face turned toward Dorie, who felt her heart bottom out. She did not know what to do or say without exposing herself, so she did nothing. Slowly the fey turned away and started to drift through the trees.

They followed the blue mist. Annika's eyes were at half-mast, the silver one a half-moon reflecting light. The fey moved slowly, painfully, and then it rounded a clearing and they saw hundreds of fey.

And a large silver machine.

"Duck," said Tam immediately, and he pulled Annika under cover. It broke the connection between her and the fey, and she shot him a sour silver look as they crouched in the leaves. An act that could be parsed two ways, thought Dorie, but she could not try to analyze it further just now. All her attention was on the field: the fey, the machine, the silver-palmed men.

Like the basilisk tail, the machine had left a track through the forest. Trees and bushes were felled behind it as the men had bushwhacked a way for it to come into the fey-heavy clearing. The machine hissed and let off smoke, but the fey, who normally would be repulsed by both things, hung around it in the clearing as if held there by a magnet. One of the silvermen had a long hose with a funnel, and he was cautiously maneuvering it close to the fey.

"What do they think—" started Dorie.

Tam said angrily, "Down, I said," and pulled a shaking Dorie back down behind the bush. She grabbed an unprotesting Woglet and cradled him close, keeping them hidden.

The man with the funnel had to get very close to the hovering fey to get them into the suction tube. It was a lengthy process even with the fey staying close to the clearing; maneuvering around the other hanging fey, carefully getting the hose to one particular fey. Eventually he got one, and with great whirs the blue was pulled into the machine. Horror filled Dorie's chest. She wanted to run down there, *do something,* but Tam's grip was tight. Another man stood at the back of the machine, where he carefully took small blue packages and tucked them away into a well-lined case. Dorie could hear the shriek of the fey death—no, not death, though perhaps it would be kinder—as the fey was split into bits, each bound with some sort of silvery substance to keep it contained.

Then one of the blue bits escaped from the back of the machine, wriggled free into the air.

The machine croaked to a halt and one of the silvermen shouted, "We need another egg!"

From a portable incubator just like Tam's, the other man brought an egg out. He was wearing heavy gloves. "We've only got a few of these left," he said. "Damn Stilby wants an outrageous sum for the haul he got. They were still negotiating when I left this morning." He carried the egg over to the small copper funnel on the machine—and then cracked it on the side, dropping shell, goo, wyvern chick and all, straight into the hopper. Dorie shut her eyes, but she was too late to unsee it. Woglet struggled, and Dorie clamped him firmly under her armpit. She opened her eyes and stared the little wyvern down, willing him not to yodel his distress. Her mind could not stop replaying the scene and envisioning her Woglet being cracked into the hopper.

"Dammit," said a man down below. "We'll need twice as many eggs just for those we've captured today." He gestured at the fey hanging around the clearing. The first man restarted the machine and they began pulling the fey again.

"The wyvern albumen," said Dorie, her hands shaking. "It isn't just for protection. That's what they're using to permanently split the fey."

"Clean energy forever," said Annika, and her voice rang with something so awed that Dorie knew then, if she hadn't before, that they were on opposite sides of this issue. She looked down at the vials in her palm. "I expect the basilisk albumen might stretch farther, *ja*? Be many times as powerful?"

"You can't," said Tam.

Annika stood, looked down at the two of them. The silver eye reflected the one in her palm. She was a symbol of everything the Crown hoped to find—the beautiful girl channeling the legendary basilisk. A figurehead in truth. "There are moments," she said, "when you are given the chance to prove whose side you are on. You cannot play both sides. You cannot hide," and she threw a cold look at Dorie. She held out her hand to Tam. "You have the chance to come with me and be part of this. We will let them know we found it together. It is the missing piece they need—the basilisk albumen, more powerful than the wyvern albumen. Show them what you would do for your country."

Tam looked at Annika for a long time. At last he said, "I think we have different ideas of what we should do for our country. I cannot lie, even for you. If you go down there, you are a different person than I thought you were."

"Same to you," she said softly. And then she marched out of the trees, down to the men, who stood, both repelled and fascinated by the pretty girl with the silver eye. They had no fey in them and yet they might as well have been paralyzed as she strode up to them and pledged her help.

Dorie looked down at Tam, who was still watching Annika, betrayal written on his face. "Come on," she said gently. "We'd better get out of here."

They trudged back to the burned-out circle to gather the

rest of their things. Tam was silent the whole way. So was Woglet. "They're wrong to do that," Tam said at last.

"I know," said Dorie.

They sat on a stump and looked at the vortex. "Do you think the circle lasts as long as the basilisk is here?" Tam said.

Dorie nodded. "I think it explains where they go to. They come to a safe hatching place, and then they return."

"And this place was safe for thousands of years," said Tam.

Dorie spun scenarios. "Do you think there are no humans where they come from? Or lots of them?"

"Perhaps there are lots of fey," said Tam. "The way the fey and wyverns are enemies. Fey and basilisk surely are as well. They don't seem to have a fear of man—that would lead me to think there aren't any at home. But the question is, where is home?"

"Do you promise to believe me if I tell you?" said Dorie.

He looked at her and she knew what he saw. Scruffy, quirky Dorian—in looks completely unlike his porcelain cousin. Someone he had thought he could trust, when he had stopped trusting Dorie long ago. His life had been a series of betrayals—how could he trust one more time? "Perhaps," he said.

"When I was here on Saturday," Dorie said, "I went into the circle. But it was different than it was today for me. I saw so many things I felt sick. And then, I let my finger go all blue and touched the circle, and—this." She unwrapped the bandage from her right hand and showed him the bloodless, perfectly healed missing tip of her finger. It had finally stopped itching.

"I wouldn't think that sort of thing could happen to you," he said.

Did he mean, because she was half-fey? She wasn't ready to press it. "Since then," she said, "I seem to see other Dories."

The notebook was out. "Go on."

"I think the basilisk *is* from another world. And not just another world. Another timeline. One of those worlds that splinters off at the changes."

"That's the same story—"

"You collected in your book, I know. I know. I didn't steal from that; I'm corroborating."

"Multiple worlds," he said with awe. "Another fey story proves to be true." He looked again at her finger. "But why didn't anything bad happen today?"

"I don't know," she said. "It only happened last time when I went fey. And this time—" She held out her palm with the silver symbol.

"You couldn't," he finished.

"But I did feel something strange." She stepped back inside the circle again. She looked out at the ring. There were the multiple Dories, a blur of Dories. But if she concentrated . . . She stepped up to the edge of the circle and tentatively put her left hand to it, the one with the wyvern goo embedded in it. The basilisk was somehow able to control this portal. Focus it, to use it as a stepping-stone between the worlds. Could the wyvern goo help her do the same? Thinking of the basilisk, she focused on that. Where had the creature come from? She envisioned it—its metallic coloring, its massive wingspan. Its four toes.

She could feel something then. Traces of the pathway. She sought out that vision and it was as though the rest of the worlds stopped turning, until she was looking at only one— the side of the mountain, just like her own. The sight was overlaid on her own mountain; they fit together in a blurry picture. But the basilisk's mountain was crisscrossed with many tracks from basilisk tails. In the distances she saw more of the creatures, diving and swooping. No, this was definitely not her world. And then—blue. She almost jerked away, but she held still. The fey, masses and masses of them, drifting across the mountain path. More fey than she had ever seen at once here. Perhaps it was a world where the Great War had never happened.

Or where the fey had decisively won.

She pulled her hand away and looked at Tam. "If the basilisk could go through here, why not the fey?"

He pointed at the missing tip of her finger. "I think you already proved they can."

She clenched her fist, thinking of the systematic destruction under way in the forest. The fey had once been a powerful enemy. But that was then and this was now. "It's the only way to save them. They have to leave here—forever."

Chapter 14

BELIEF

Perhaps the betrayal at fifteen is what led Tam down the path to betrayal himself. Or perhaps it was earlier, when a fey took over his father and betrayed him in that way. When that fey taught him how to lie.

—Thomas Lane Grimsby, *Silverblind: The Story of Adora Rochart*

* * *

Talk was all very well, but how to get all the fey in the country to the circle? More important, how to do it before the basilisk returned home and the circle closed for good? Dorie and Tam trekked upward again to feel the eggs, and she guessed that the last one would hatch Thursday afternoon. On the way down the mountain she found a small cluster of fey that had not been seized by the men with their machine, and she warned them about it, and told them to tell other fey to collect near the basilisk. But she was not really sure how much of the conversation got through to them. It was very hard to converse with fey without being able to slip into her fey side herself; they drifted back and forth and she wasn't sure they listened at all.

It was well after midnight when Tam dropped her off at

her flat. Bone tired, she stumbled as she got out of the auto. "Hey, easy," he said, and came around and helped her up. His glasses reflected the streetlight as he squeezed her bony boy-shoulders. "We'll make it," he said.

"Yeah?"

"Get some sleep. What time do we have to start in on the ironskin tomorrow?"

"Six," said Dorie.

"Well. Get a few hours' sleep, anyway. I won't have the car—I have to turn it in. We'll be walking."

She nodded and turned, wearily dragging her feet toward the stairs.

"Hey," he said. "I was thinking. You might not have to keep that wyvern tattoo on, if you don't want it."

"Yeah?"

Tam held out his palm with the tattoo on it. "You might be able to abrade the tattoo off. Lose a few layers of skin, but . . ." He shrugged. "How far down does the poison go, you think? Bloodstream or surface level? It could work."

She stared at him, smiling, and he gave a half-smile in response. "Don't get your hopes up."

"I won't."

He got back in the auto and closed the door. "Dorie?" he said as she reached the stairs, and she turned, one more time.

"Yeah?" she said.

"Take care."

The car was around the corner before she realized he'd called her Dorie.

Moira had been true to her word—not that Dorie had doubted her for an instant. When she went to retrieve the eggs the next morning, the secretary handed her a sealed envelope. Inside were the list of names and addresses for every ironskin left. Dorie thought how ironic it was that those left had led an ignored and dismissed existence for twenty years, but now that they could be fixed, this list was suddenly as dangerous as a copperhead hydra. They would have to work carefully and fast to get each person aligned with an egg in time.

There was no time for niceties. Dorie split the eggs and the list with Tam. She roped Stella and her apartment in to care for the baby wyverns—she hated to do it, but there was no one left to ask, and Stella was not the sort to get flustered.

She had split the list geographically with Tam—though most ironskin lived in the slums anyway—and they began crisscrossing the route, moving with caution. They were helped by the fact that at this point, nearly everyone knew they were coming. She rather thought their underground network had supplied them with more names than the government would know; still, they found three flats already ransacked and the ironskin gone.

They had thirteen eggs left, nine of which were hatching today. Ten ironskin. One was a little old lady whose curse was on her hand, and was fear. She lived alone and refused to wear iron, and also refused the treatment. "I've lived with it twenty years, and it's my best defense against prowlers," she said.

"But perhaps you have children you'd like to see," said Dorie. "Grandchildren who are too afraid to come."

The woman smiled and patted Dorie on the head and refused to answer. "You save your egg for some young pup who needs it," she said.

The egg was in fact near to hatching, and Dorie ran all the way to her next stop, the wyvern chick cracking through in her hands as she burst through the door.

As careful as Dorie was, she couldn't shake the feeling that she was being watched. She felt lost without her fey ability to shake pursuit, to blend in. Still, she finished the last of her list without incident. Tam had finished his, and with a profound sense of relief they trudged up the stairs with their last two woglets to Stella's flat to collect the rest.

Unlike Colin's flat, Stella's had not been ransacked. It was as neat and orderly as the *dwarvven* girl liked it: everything in miniature, everything properly pressed.

But the woglets were gone.

And Stella was gone.

Only one of Stella's small chairs, overturned on the carpet, gave a clue that anything untoward might have happened.

This time Tam reached for Dorie, put his arm around her shoulders. "We'll get her back," he said.

Dorie wanted to relax into his arm, but she pulled away. "I have to tell Jack," she said. "I have to tell Jack." That triggered the memory that it was Wednesday and that meant tonight was the revised gallery opening. "Come on," she said.

The gallery was packed. People were spilling out of the building onto the front steps and down and for a moment Dorie thought the show had been shut down again. But no, the doors were wide open—it was just the crush of people moving in and out. Someone posted at the door was barring the way, keeping the hordes to a reasonable level, and clearly loving it. Scents of sandalwood, of cigarette smoke, of many many people, drifted around the throng. Dorie pushed her way through up to the door. She was planning to dampen down her visibility and sneak in, and she was all the way to the front before she remembered she was stuck as plain visible Dorian, and she couldn't smooth things along.

The gallery attendant looked down at the slight man hoping

to squeeze under her arm and her eyes widened. She drew back from Dorie—took a step back, even. Her face was a peculiar mixture of salacious excitement and fear. "Go right on in," she said.

Dorie was puzzled but she seized the chance. She pressed her way in, Tam following behind.

There was a painting just in front of the entrance, the first one you were meant to see, and Dorie stepped carefully through the crowd, peering around shoulders and hats. Was it the fey piece again—people coming to see for themselves what had been alluded to in the newspaper?

But no, she did not see that sculpture's blue light anywhere. The painting in front of her that held pride of place was a true painting, a real painting, and it was by Jack.

It was the painting of Stella, the one Dorie had seen Jack working on the last week. But it had changed. Jack *was* doing something new.

It was a new style. Jack had had barely any time to put her three new paintings for the exhibit together, and that was obvious to Dorie in the mere fact that it was of necessity a departure from Jack's regular, labor-intensive work. But there was not a lack in the paintings themselves. It was a mix of Jack's most gorgeous painterly qualities: the beautifully realized lines, the transparent colors. But they were sparsely used, and were combined with Jack's other side, her cartooning, caricatured, grotesquely exaggerated sketches. The two combined to make not only a painting style infused with energy, but a treatment of subject that was entirely new to Jack's work.

The tiny *dwarvven* girl was in the big armchair. But Jack had exaggerated Stella's small size; she had exaggerated the armchair's bulk. That offhand comment of Dorie's was here, writ large. Around Stella you saw a world that was not meant to suit her—a world designed for anyone but her. Simple every-day items were placed in such a way that you saw how she had to adapt, all day long. The real Stella never complained. But to Dorie, it hit home for the first time how hard it must be for her friend. In life Stella had been simply asleep—here the sleeping posture showed her to be wrung out with exhaustion.

It captured—not just Stella, but her place in the world.

Without noticing it, Dorie had moved closer to the painting, fingers stretched out as if to touch her friend. Without noticing it, the space around her had cleared for her.

She turned now, and all around she saw faces shot through with expressions similar to the gallery attendant: shock, excitement, fear. The crowds parted from her on either side; a long hallway of empty space opened up and she walked down it, heart beating more and more wildly.

There was a painting at the end of her walk.

A tall, wide painting, the biggest one in the collection.

Snatches of conversation met her ears before the speakers saw her and stopped. "It's this Jacqueline girl that's the real deal." "A start of a new movement." "Will be imitated for years to come." And then, "Do you think it's really true?" followed by the sharp hiss, the drawn-out breath, "Loooook, it's him . . . her . . ."

The painting was of Dorie. Of Dorian. Of something peculiar and abnormal and *fey*. It was both sides of her, fractured down the middle, pulling each other apart. Dorie on one side, with her blond ringlets and downcast eyes. Dorian on the other, with his bent nose and wry grin, Woglet perched on his shoulder. As the figures were pulled apart they were revealed to be hollow.

In between blue smoke rose up.

It was obvious that even if people wouldn't have immediately recognized her face as the young man in the drawing, there was only one person in town with a pet wyvern, and she/he was here tonight.

Dorie backed away, Woglet yodeling and flapping his wings for balance at her abrupt motion. The sense of betrayal mingled with something else, something peculiar. Relief, it felt like. She refused to feel it. Betrayal, that's what Jack had done.

There were silvermen moving through the crowds as she backed up. One more painting caught her eye—a painting of Jack, the size and shape of a mirror.

Jack had not spared herself.

It was an oval picture of Jack in paint-splattered cigarette pants and bangles, kissing a girl who was not Stella. Jack's eyes were not on the girl; they were looking back out at the viewer. Daring them? Or just, steady. Frank. One hand held a paintbrush, and it was coming toward you, the hand and brush wild and all out of proportion, devolving into a brush-stroked sketch. It was sweeping the fourth wall away, coming for you, going for the next painting, the next truth.

And there was Jack herself in the crowd, and her eyes met Dorie's as if to say, I'm sorry, and Dorie could not feel any anger toward her best friend, but still, the silvermen were coming, and Stella was in jail; her parents were in jail, Aunt Helen and Uncle Rook had fled—

They were on her then, and Dorie tried to run, but she could not wriggle free. She tried to fade, but she could not become unnoticed. She could not turn over some trash bins to slow them down, she could not blind them with blue light. She was well and truly caught, and she could never disappear again.

Dr. Pearce was the first to come visit her in jail. No, not jail, what was the Crown's preferred term for their fancy new security building? To be fair, her room had a nice bed and a shiny desk and a terrible painting of flowers and looked more like a hotel room than a dungeon. They had not reached the building till late last night, and so she had had a good night's sleep for a change. She should have been too worried to sleep, but it turned out she was too exhausted to worry. This morning, a man escorted her to the restroom and back, and now it was breakfast time in her nice not-jail. She could see blue skies and clear sunlight and the Queen's Lab through the narrow window. But Woglet was missing, the door was locked, and there was some of that new one-way glass all along one wall. The blue tint of fey light was everywhere. Jail would do.

If she had known Dr. Pearce was supposed to be the good cop, she might have been more cooperative. Or not. He got her back up at the best of times and this was not that.

After pretending to be impressed with her double interviews as Dorie/Dorian—but actually needling her in a supercilious way—he moved on to other areas of persuasion, appealing to her sense of justice, which he mistook for a sense of duty to her country.

"Now certainly, the fey energy won't work outside the country," he was saying. "But it'll transform our country into something great again. If we can lick the energy problem here, we'll be much stronger. And think about your beloved poor. This would clear up their pollution, their smog. Clean air. Clean living. Fewer poor in the hospitals with lung problems, or overworked from the factories—fey energy can take their place. People will be free to innovate."

"And it's only at the cost of subjugating an entire race," filled in Dorie.

Dr. Pearce scoffed. "Come, now. Don't be so dramatic. They're not even really people."

"Decimating another species—I suppose once the fey are all subdued, you won't ever need wyverns again. Might as well be gone."

"Whatever you might think of us, we did not commit that particular atrocity," said Dr. Pearce tightly. "More likely it was one of Malcolm Stilby's goons, tracking *you* up to the forest." He rose and said, "Perhaps you'll like Annika's line of questioning better." The malice in his tone suggested she emphatically would not. At the door he turned and said, "Oh, and I'm curious, Miss Adora. Show me how you switch from boy to girl." There was something so salacious in his eyes that it gave her real pleasure to laugh in his face and show off the palm of her hand.

"You stopped me from changing back," she said. "Sucks to be you."

After that, there was quiet for a time. She wondered if her parents had ever been released, or if they were going to be brought in as bait. She wondered what had happened to Stella, and if they had managed to supply her with something comfortable to sit on, or given her the standard-issue human-sized rooms. She wondered if she should be mad at Jack, who had refused to compromise her artistic integrity to keep her out of jail. Hadn't Dorie refused to sell an egg to pay back Jack, pay back the rent she owed? She wondered which was worse. The silvermen would have caught up with her eventually. She wondered about Woglet. She wondered about Tam.

The door buzzed and Annika came in with lunch. She sat down in a chair and looked calmly at Dorie with her mismatched eyes while Dorie ate.

Dorie refused to be unnerved. When your week had been mostly subsisting on dandelions you ate your soup and bread and enjoyed it, no matter how many basilisk stares you got.

"You knew, didn't you?" said Dorie. "After you put the basilisk in your eye. You knew I was part-fey."

"I couldn't be sure," said Annika. "But I had very strong suspicions." She flipped a page over in the notebook she always carried. "I was hoping to examine you myself. Before turning you in, of course."

"Of course," said Dorie. "Another chapter for your book. I suppose you'd like to have a matched set with Tam. *Collected Fey Tales* at one end, *Collected Half-Fey Tales* at the other, and husband Tam serving champagne at your cocktail parties. Full of the most blindly nationalistic people, of course, the ones who say 'praise the Crown' every other sentence and mean it."

Annika was unflappable. "Don't worry about my book. The research I gather today will be more than adequate. Besides, the Crown comes first." She narrowed her eyes at Dorie, considering. "I know that with this eye I have full control over true fey. What I want to know is, how far does that extend with you?" She opened her silver eye and stared down at Dorie. "Move your right hand," she said.

There was a small tugging feeling. But it seemed to be blocked, somehow. Her hand did not move.

Annika's shoulders slumped a fraction even as her eyebrows knitted together. "I don't believe that it has no effect," she said. "Merely, I have not mastered the application." She tried again, but still nothing. This time she got up and paced, thinking. "I don't mind telling you that this does not meet my hypothesis," she said. "My hypothesis was that it would work on you halfway—sluggishly. The fey in you should still react to my command."

Dorie shrugged and went back to her soup. "Iron doesn't work on me, either," she said. Which wasn't quite true—it did, ever so slowly, wear her down, make her sluggish.

"That's right," mused Annika. "There are things that can interfere with the process." She whirled, looking at the one-way mirror, then back at Dorie. "Your hand," she said. "You told Dr. Pearce the wyvern in your hand stops you changing. I wonder if it interferes with the basilisk eye."

Dammit, why had she given Pearce any information? His nastiness had gotten the best of her after all.

"Beats me," said Dorie, but Annika was already at the door, calling through the peephole for iron, copper, and more wyvern albumen.

Annika tried a number of things while Dorie got more and more furious and was unable to do anything about it except plan what she *would* do if something worked. The door was locked with those fancy buzzing locks they had at the Queen's Lab, but the medallion she had seen used by the silverman in charge was a different size and shape than the ones used at the Queen's Lab. They had not given Annika a medallion, so Dorie could not try to steal it. They were locked in here together. But there was a narrow window, if she could break through it. Maybe with that trash bin there. She was almost slight enough to fit through, and she could fuzz out a bit around the broken edges. What was this, the eighth floor? She could always go half-fey as she fell.

If something worked.

Around teatime, Annika decided the only recourse was to try to take the wyvern tattoo out of Dorie's palm. After consultation with the other room she came back with a handful of steel wool and an iron file. "Please understand this is purely scientific," she said to Dorie, and carefully she scraped away at the reddened palm, obliterating the silver eye.

The scraping seared and burned as her tender skin sloughed away. Blood welled up and dripped on their nice desk. She thought she might faint. But she could feel her power slowly wriggle free. Tam had been right. She didn't need all the wyvern out, just enough. She whimpered wholeheartedly about the pain and concealed her excitement. Annika stopped regularly to see if the treatment was working. Finally, about halfway through, as Annika leveled her silver eye to focus on her, Dorie closed her eyes and swung for Annika's jaw.

It was not a brilliant punch, but her right hand did connect, and then she was running for the window, eyes closed and fey senses extended.

They caught her after she broke the window but before she could wriggle through. They gave her a rag for her hand and silvermen peeled her eyelids back with tape and then finally, Annika was able to say, raise your right hand and have Dorie obey.

Annika walked Dorie around the room, testing the motions and scribbling in her notebook. Finally Annika sat Dorie in a chair and got to the deeper purpose in her role working for the government.

"What was your purpose with the wyvern eggs?" she asked, and Dorie, to her horror, found herself answering. "Very good," said Annika. She called in a secretary to take notes as Dorie went through all the details of her work with the iron-skin. Annika was thorough and the questioning went on and on and on. Once Dorie tried to use her partial fey power to manipulate Annika, but Annika threatened her with iron hand-cuffs and she was unlikely to ever break free of those, so she stopped. Her left hand throbbed. She fuzzed the edges of it blue to keep the pain manageable, so she could think.

Dorie tried to elide the fact that Tam had helped her, to keep him from getting into trouble. It was working pretty well— and then it dawned on her that Annika was intentionally helping her, never asking questions that would reveal Tam specifically. She hated to collude with Annika, but there was really no choice. They knew she had worked with another boy—she shifted the blame to poor Colin.

Still, what of it. The ironskin were done—except for the ones they had taken into custody. Dorie and Tam had done all they could do, and if the silvermen wanted to hear the details, there was not much that would hurt the former ironskin now. She answered as carefully as she could while trying to see what she could do to manipulate the wyvern in her abraded hand to act as a stopgap. She was in the unusual position of now wanting the wyvern goo to succeed. Annika's gaze could keep her from moving physically, but there was still stuff Dorie could do inside.

That's when Annika shifted into grilling Dorie about their work in the forests.

"You know all this," said Dorie. "You were there." Annika ignored this. "And why do you care anyway? You've got your machine to trap the fey."

Annika looked levelly at her. "Because all the fey left in the country will not be enough to supply all the energy we will need. And Thomas said that you had a theory that you could reach other worlds, with more fey."

"Tam? What do you mean, he told you?"

Annika smiled the smile of the girl who knew she'd won. "You don't think our little spat in the clearing meant anything, do you? Thomas Grimsby is, and has always been, the eyes for the Crown. We were pleased when he got you to trust him so easily."

It was a blow to the gut. Annika couldn't possibly be right—could she? Was this his revenge—his own betrayal? Was this the good fight he had told Aunt Helen he had found?

Calm and confident in her success, Annika pressed on, asking more questions about the circle the basilisk had come through, probing Dorie to find out exactly what her take on it was.

Dorie omitted, evaded, threw out sullen answers and sarcastic jests as much as she could. Dinner came and went and she was now too angry and upset to eat it. It sat and cooled until they finally took it away again.

Tam came in partway through this exercise and began pointing out when she was evading the truth. Annika beamed at him; Dorie felt a profound misery all over at this confirmation. She shot him one angry look, and then started answering in the other languages she had picked up a smattering of in prep school, stopping when she found one Annika clearly didn't know.

Finally, an irritated Annika called in one of the silvermen and commanded him, "Bring in her parents." There was another wait while the man went to obey. Pain and fear alternating with boredom—what a wretched combination. It was growing dark outside. How long would she be in here? Would they keep her day after day, until they wore her down? Of course, if they started in on her parents, she didn't think she would last very long at all. Jane would exhort her to try, but she would crumple.

Finally the man buzzed open the door and crept back in, looking worried. "They were released after forty-eight hours in detention," he said. "An administrative error."

"Fools," said Annika. She glared at the man as if wishing her silver eye could affect humans as well.

"She has another friend in custody," said Tam. "Her name is Stella—not sure of the last name, but she's *dwarvven*. Brought in last night. I called over and had her transferred to this building this afternoon."

Dorie glared at him.

"Excellent," said Annika. She smiled approvingly at Tam. "You were right about removing the tattoo, by the way. That was key." He gripped her shoulder affectionately.

"May you burn in a furnace," Dorie spat. "May you choke on a thousand bug guts. May a copperhead hydra bite your fingers off."

"Easy," said Annika. She was too self-contained to smirk, but Dorie could see it lurking behind the veneer. She stretched and said to Dorie pleasantly, "I'll let you think about whether we should call Stella in while I go freshen up. Now, I'd like you to tell Thomas everything you can about this 'way through' that you were traitorously planning to send our energy source through."

"Don't see what good it would do you," said Dorie.

A winning Annika apparently enjoyed sounding pleasant. "Well, obviously, if you were planning to send the fey through to meet other fey, then surely it would work in reverse."

Dorie was too stunned to respond.

"Just think of the resources we could mine from these other worlds!" said Annika as she went to the door. "Not just energy—we could get anything and everything we need." A half-smile cracked her face. "Just think, Dorie. They might even call you a hero."

Annika shut the door behind her and Dorie cradled her torn hand and thought of names to call both of them.

"Easy, easy," Tam said. "You probably need to freshen up, too." He turned to the one-way mirror. "I'm going to escort the detainee to the restroom." Carefully he fastened the iron handcuffs on her wrists and then, once secure, the door buzzed to let them out.

Tam led her down the hall to the restroom. It was now

pitch-black through the windows at the long end of the hall-way. The blue tinge to the lights seemed more prominent with the sunlight gone. The headache had long since returned, al-though it was drowned by the throbbing of her palm.

Once inside the restroom, Dorie looked at Tam warily, and he blushed. He looked away, fumbling with his pockets for the key, and then unlocked her iron handcuffs. They clinked into the white sink. From his jacket he produced a familiar-looking copper vial.

"Is that the basilisk goo?" she said, and he nodded. "And what? More experiments? In secret?" Her hand throbbed and she set it on the cool tiles of the counter.

"I've been using the time since they captured you to make a quick experiment of my own," he said. His jaw set. "I tried the basilisk albumen on one of the captured fey in the lab."

Her heart threatened to break at this frank admission. "And?"

"I wouldn't have done it except for you!" he burst out. "But nothing. It didn't kill the fey. It didn't harm them, Dorie. I ran some tests and it's still perfectly active. And it didn't harm them."

"I don't understand," she said. "I thought it was just a stron-ger version of the wyvern goo. We saw what Annika could do with it."

"They're different," he said. "The stories all say stronger, but that's not really it. Wyvern albumen kills fey. But basilisk albumen controls them without harming them. I think that if you used it, you could control the fey in this building."

"So I could control *me*," she said sarcastically.

"You could control the lights. The power. The magnetized locks. The alarms. This whole building runs on fey power, Dorie. You call the fey to you and we can walk out that door."

Dorie looked at him with astonishment.

Finally he sighed and said, "Annika and I have both been working for the government for a couple of months. Old Pearcey knows all about it. What he doesn't know was that I was . . . a double agent, I guess you'd say, except that implies I have a team, which I don't. Mother had gotten wind of this business with enslaving all the fey, and she and Dad encouraged me to get as close as I felt comfortable to try to find out what was going on."

He uncapped the vial and she stared at it. "Even if you're right." *Even if you're telling the truth.* "I don't really *want* to have that power. I don't want to be like Annika."

"I don't think we're going to be able to walk out of this building without it," he said. "The stairwell door is locked, and so is the door to Stella's room."

And they couldn't leave without Stella. If Tam was telling the truth, he'd had her transferred here specifically so Dorie could rescue her friend. Her fingers closed on the glass.

She wanted to be convinced of his honesty, oh, how she wanted to. Her heart beat a mile a minute. Was this the ultimate betrayal? There was not much albumen left in the vial—he was probably telling the truth that he had tested it on the fey.

But what had he really found out?

She tilted her head back. One drop hovered on the tip of the vial.

Dorie watched it fall.

Chapter 15

THE WAY THROUGH

Fey substance is a mixed bag. It can be a curse, or a blessing, or both. When the fey took Adora's cousin, they were bound to give him something in return. Perhaps she did not realize, for she was caught up in self-blame. But the fey work in their own ways, and they keep their old bargains. Everything had to be fairly paid for, including a young man with a voice like the birds whom they had tricked into staying with them.

—Thomas Lane Grimsby, *Silverblind: The Story of Adora Rochart*

*   *   *

The basilisk albumen felt strangely cool in her eye, like putting aloe on a burn.

She did not grow dizzy, or faint, or die. It did not even sting, as it seemed to have done Annika. Small blessings.

Everything shimmered silver as the albumen settled in. Dorie shied away from her reflection in the mirror. One more step away from her self. She focused on the lights; located the bluepack running them. If these bluepacks were like the ones they had seen the men making in the forest, then they were different than the old bluepacks, which were not bound by anything other than honor, by the Fey Queen's order to be split. These were enveloped in a coating of feywort and wyvern substance and who knows what else in such a way that the bit of fey could not wriggle free. It must be a very small proportion of the wyvern goo, she thought, to bind without killing. Or perhaps the coating *was* killing the bound-up fey, very slowly. Wouldn't that just be ironic?

But basilisk goo controlled the fey. Controlled it when it could no longer control itself. She had to believe that—she had to believe in *him*. She focused on the bluepack that ran the bathroom lights, and *pulled*. The blue bit of fey wriggled free from the copper casing, from the wyvern coating.

As it did the lights flicked off and they were left in darkness, except for the faint blue shimmer of a bit of fey darting around, excited to be free.

They had done it. It would work.

Tam seized her arm in the darkness. "You've got it," he said fiercely. "Now act natural." He propelled her out of the restroom and down the hall to another locked door. "Call the fey out of that," he said. She did, and the magnetic lock broke free. Tam pushed the door open to reveal a small girl perched neatly on a stool, writing busily in a notebook. One lock of her ponytail swung around her face, but otherwise she did not look a bit inconvenienced by being in confinement for a day.

Stella looked up as Dorie stepped inside the room. "'Bout time," she said, pushing the lock of hair behind her ear. "Dorie—your eye!"

"Long story," Dorie said awkwardly. "Let's get you out of here."

Stella cocked her head at Tam as she shoved her notebook into a large purse. "I know you, don't I?"

"This is Tam Grimsby," said Dorie. "My cousin."

"Technically," said Tam. "Not by blood."

"Of course," said Stella. "You came by the school a few times. Boy, that was a long time ago. What were we, fourteen, fifteen? We all thought you were so cute." She hopped off the stool, swung her heavy purse onto her shoulder. "I convinced them to let me keep my differential equations homework," she said, "although they seemed to think I was writing secret codes. Honestly. Do they think the fey *cipher*?"

"When we leave the room, the stairway is to the left," Tam put in. He looked a little blushy. "Dorie, you unlock it. Head down. We're on the eighth floor—count your turns so you don't end up in the basement. They don't expect anyone to be able to leave this level, so if we make it to the stairwell we should be all right. There was only one man by the entrance when I came in. More of a greeter than a guard."

"That's all?" said Stella. "Where are the guys with guns?"

"That's the old building. We wouldn't stand a chance there," said Tam. "This building is reserved for political detainees. No rough stuff."

"Escaping would be so gauche," muttered Dorie.

Tam poked his head out and then motioned them to hurry. They were at the stairwell when Dorie heard a noise from down the hall. A man from the room next to hers was just stepping out into the hallway. Their eyes met. "Hold up there," he said. He started toward them.

"The stairwell, Dorie," said Tam, but she ignored him. She reached out to all the lights in the hallway and began pulling on them as quickly as she could. She loosened them, one at a time, until the hallway was black, except for the flickers of darting blue.

Then she opened all the locks.

The doors buzzed as the locks broke open. Murmurs—shouts. People spilled out into the dark hallway, bumping into each other as they attempted to take advantage of the confusion to leave.

"Now," Dorie said, and unlocked the stairwell door.

They tumbled through, and Dorie pulled the lights from the stairwell as they ran, so the man would have a harder time following them if he made it through the crowd. The three reached the bottom along with the sparkles of blue. Tam peeked out the door. The greeter was still sitting by the door—but standing around the desk were several silvermen, looking as though they had just come in. "The detainees' floor," one was saying politely, but firmly, to the greeter.

The man led them to the elevator, his medallion out. "They're on eight," he said. "I'll buzz you through."

"We should go when their backs are turned," whispered Stella. Her set expression was lit by the dim fey light.

Dorie shook her head. "Better idea," she said. The elevator door closed behind the men and the floor numbers began counting.

The bits of fey flickered around them as she concentrated. She had often maneuvered things she could not see before, using her fey senses to locate them. Now she extended those senses to catalogue all the fey in the building: lights, locks, elevators, everything. Eight might be the only detainees' floor, but throwing the whole building into darkness would add to the confusion.

As would stopping the elevator between floors.

One by one Dorie pulled on the bits of fey and felt a mental pop as they came free.

Shouts rang out through the building.

"Let's go," Tam said grimly. He pulled the two of them through the stairwell door and out into to the dark lobby. Dorie bumped straight into the man from the front desk, and saw his eyes widen in fright at her blue halo of tiny lights. He yelped and ducked. Dorie called the bit of fey from the front door lock to them and they went through. The little bits swooshed out behind them, darted out into the night sky.

An ancient but impeccably maintained black auto was at the bottom of the steps. "This is us," said Tam, and he held the front door for Stella, motioning Dorie-as-Dorian to get in the back. The rag around her palm was starting to redden, and she was careful not to place it on the ancient upholstery. The light of the streetlamps picked out Woglet, curled in a tiny silver ball on a towel in back, sound asleep and apparently none the worse for wear. The auto roared around the corner before Dorie registered who was driving.

Jack.

Dorie bounded up from the backseat, grabbing the back of Jack's seat with her good hand. "Ugh, Jack, how could you? That painting! I mean, it's tremendous, true—were you in the papers?—but didn't you think what would happen to me?"

"Don't grab the driver," put in Tam. "She's still learning. Jack, that's a pedestrian."

Jack was in fact still learning, but apparently her only concession to being a beginner was not to drive slowly but rather to swerve a great deal at the last second.

"And you were in the show, too," said Dorie to Stella. "Did you see you? No, you couldn't, you were already locked up."

"Why, was I indecent?" said Stella.

"Turn left here," said Tam. "No, not *here* here, wait for the road."

"You *told* me to do it," said Jack to Dorie in the rearview mirror. Her face was lit with the streetlamps as they flickered past. "Never compromise." Her chin was out and there was a queer expression on her face that seemed to say she wanted to make up and be obstinate all at once.

"Around the lorry. Around!"

Dorie recognized the feeling because she felt the same. "Ugh, I didn't mean it like that," she said.

"Ugh," returned Jack.

"Ugh!"

The two girls glared at each other in the darkness until suddenly they both burst out in giggles.

Tam looked at them as if wondering whether their laughter was hysterical, or contagious, and if so, should he do something about it. "Left again."

Jack reached back with one hand and squeezed Dorie's where it sat on the headrest. "But I *am* sorry," she said. "I didn't exactly think about the potential jail part. I was so focused on getting somewhere new. It was like I could see it all before me, what to do, unrolling like a carpet, and all I could do was run faster and faster down the carpet, trying to get to this *new* place. I ran so fast I didn't stop to think."

"You're speeding," said Tam.

Jack hushed him. "You're being an old lady," she said severely. "We're in flight from the police. Who cares how many lampposts we bump into?"

"Your aunt, for one," he retorted.

In the back, Dorie caught Stella's eye and they laughed. "I'm sorry," gasped out Dorie. "It's just, it's like old times. Those couple of years when we were fourteen and fifteen, and all in school together, and Tam's school was only a quarter mile away—"

"The midnight feasts," said Jack. "Tam snuck into one or two of those."

"And never got caught, thank you very much," said Tam. "Even the time I had to dress as a girl to get in. But I had to, because you'd forgotten—"

"—the cake!" put in Stella. "Of course, that was *you*! And it was Dorie's birthday, and your father sent you something, something he'd made, what was it. . . ."

"Jane sent you a stack of books about inspiring women doing inspiring things," said Jack. "I remember that."

"A tiny book of flower pictures he'd painted," said Stella. "All from the woods behind your home."

"Say, I remember that," said Tam. "What happened to that?"

"Those horrible girls from the west dormer happened to it," said Stella. "'Accidentally' spilled tea on it. It was a soggy mess."

"But then I 'accidentally' spilled molasses in their wardrobe," said Dorie. "Do you remember them trying to figure out how I'd gotten in, when they were on the fourth floor, and one of them was always guarding the door?"

"*I* couldn't figure it out," said Stella. "I guess now I know."

"Those days were fun," said Jack with satisfaction.

"I remember I was sorry when we stopped seeing you," Stella said to Tam, gently tapping on his shoulder.

There was silence. Dorie's hand started to throb again.

Tam said, "Perhaps we should bring you two up to date on the ironskin and where we're going."

Jack stared hard at Dorie in the rearview mirror. "What have you done to your eye?"

"It's a long story," said Dorie. "We've been helping the ironskin, with the wyvern eggs."

"The interdicted wyvern eggs, that cost as much as our rent? Those wyvern eggs?"

"Yes," said Dorie.

"Just checking," said Jack.

"But now we have to help the fey," said Tam.

"The fey that we fought in the Great War? The fey that cursed those ironskin you're helping?"

"Yes."

"Just checking."

Tam filled Jack and Stella in as they drove, simultaneously directing Jack. At last they stopped by the wharf, and Dorie saw they were at the clinic.

Tam led them up the fire escape to the apartment over the clinic. He knocked on the door, first quietly, then impatiently, until at last Dr. O'Donnell came to it. She shook her head at the gaggle on her doorstep. "I'm sorry, Dorian," she said. "I thought we discussed this. I can't shelter you all here." But she didn't close the door.

"Her hand," said Tam.

Dorie held out the bloody rag, feeling embarrassed and hopeful.

Apparently that was all the excuse she needed to help them, for Moira barely glanced at it. "Downstairs," she said. "Back door." She disappeared back inside, and they trooped down the fire escape to the back. In a minute Moira was there, letting them in by the light of a small electric flashlight. Blackout drapes hung over all the windows, and she took them to a back room, similarly shaded. "You have made a mess of this, haven't you?" she said to Dorie as she unwrapped the rag. "And your eye?"

"Long story?" said Dorie.

"I think I'd like to hear it," said Dr. O'Donnell.

"That goes double for me," said Jack. She had her pencil and pad out and was sketching the scene. Moira's gaze flicked sideways, cataloging what Jack was up to, and returned to Dorie's hand.

So Tam went through the story again. Partway through there was a small knock on the back door. "That will be my aunt and uncle," he said. "I told them to meet us here so we can get them to safety."

There was a flicker of exasperation from Moira at that.

Dorie looked up in relief as her parents came in, safe and sound. Jane hurried to Dorie's side. "Dorie, your hand. Your eye!"

"Long story," chorused Jack and Stella. Moira glanced at Jack again, and a laugh escaped.

Tam finished catching everyone up and Dorie took over.

"So we think we have a way to get the fey out of here," she said, "so they'll be safe. We're not entirely sure if it will work, but it's the best chance we've got. But the bigger problem is, how do we get all the fey to the basilisk center in the next twelve hours? With the basilisk goo I can set them free where the men have captured them. But we can hardly sneak into every building in the city that has fey light—even if we had an accurate list. And then, there's fey in forests all over the country. Should we just try to save as many as we can?"

"The fey need a calling tree," said Stella. "We used those out in the country for emergencies. So you can telephone one and they telephone the rest."

Jack snorted at the imagery, but Dorie turned bright eyes on Tam. "You *can* call them," she said. "What's that you whistled in the forest?"

He shrugged. "Just a little something the fey taught me long ago," he said, and then stopped, his eyes unfocusing. "No, not just that," he said. "They said I could use it to call them."

"And you did," said Dorie. "You used it on Saturday."

"Not just then," said Tam. "They said I would know when I needed it."

Everyone turned to look at Tam. Dorie thought you could have heard a pin drop in the room. Tam wet his lips, and then, into that total silence he softly whistled the eerie, calling tune Dorie had heard on Saturday. It made even her, want to come closer, and closer.

The door to the room opened, and Jane, who had stepped out to use the restroom, came running in. Her beautiful white face with its fine red lines seemed to glow. "I felt something," she said. "What is this?"

Tam broke off in horror. "I've seen this," he said. "You have fey in your face. We tried calling it out a long time ago, when I was little. Me and my mother. You couldn't breathe—"

"Her face is not skin," put in Edward. "It is clay, infused with fey. She's one of the last ones left. She needs the fey to animate her face."

Moira looked at Jane with stark disbelief.

"Long story," said Jane.

"You can't take away her fey," said Dorie, heart pounding at the thought. "She needs it."

Tam snapped his fingers. "The masks. The full iron masks, like my mother used to wear. That would block you."

"That should do the trick," agreed Jane. "But where would we find them tonight? I don't want to go to Niklas's again, even if he has them. I don't trust where he's ended up."

Dorie was white. "I don't care. If you can't save my mother, we can't do this. We won't call a single fey if it's going to hurt her."

Jane wheeled on her. "You have to. This is more important than just me."

"No, no, no," said Dorie, and "Absolutely not," said Edward.

"Besides, wasn't there another woman left in the same

boat?" said Tam. "I remember she had the same name as an herb. Aloe? No. Calendula something, that's it."

"And you have to think of her," said Dorie to Jane.

"I forbid it," said Edward.

Jack laughed and cut across the chorus. "Is that all that's stopping us from saving the fey? Theater people never throw away potential costume pieces. Frye still has several of those masks in her attic."

It was a long trek up the mountain, especially after having just done it yesterday. Dorie's thighs ached and her palm burned.

They made it to the entrance by dawn. There they stopped, and Tam turned back to face the city, so far off it was only a smudgey glow in the dark blue sky. He whistled.

The song came through her bones and said, come with me. Come, be with me. Come to Tam. She set her jaw as it pulled on her, wanting her to run to his arms. Come to me. Come.

Resolutely she turned to face the city, standing next to him, alongside of him. She raised her arms, feeling the cool morning air against her Dorian skin. There was hope now, she thought. She could finish abrading her palm, get all the wyvern goo out. Become Dorie again. She could try.

But that was not yet.

For now, she sent her tendrils of thought out, extending her senses, farther than she had ever done before. She felt each caught bit of fey, and with the basilisk power she released them, set them free. And they came to Tam's call. From the city they came, and from beyond the city they came. Those near that heard his call echoed it to those farther, and farther, just as Stella had suggested. Tam whistled until he was out of breath, and then he took her hand, and they tramped into the forest together.

They stopped several times for him to catch his breath and repeat the call. As they got farther up the mountain, they began seeing the blue fey. They came swirling toward Tam—if a mist could fall into formation, then that's how they looked, Dorie thought. And up they went, up, up, up, Tam and Dorie, and farther behind them, Jane and Edward, because they had refused to leave Dorie, and Woglet flying back and forth around them all.

They began seeing traces of the trail as they neared the ravine. The trail of humans. It was a thick, obvious trail, that had come as far as it could by automobile, and now met up with the footpath and started walking. Tam followed the signs of the trail until he found the two vehicles, loosely covered by scrub. "Can't be more than eight thugs, I guess," he said. "I suppose they think that's enough."

"Isn't it?" said Dorie, looking at their paltry group.

"Well," said Tam. "We do have them." He pointed at the fey.

Dorie shook her head. "They promised Aunt Helen, remember? They don't want to fight. They just want to go home. Their new home."

They slowed as they climbed higher, nearing the basilisk circle. Went cautiously. The sun was high now, and warm. It was clear that the men were well ahead of them, and they did not know what weapons they possessed.

That's when Annika came down the trail, picking her way around the ruts and carrying a white flag. "Dorie," she said. "Delighted to see you looking so well. And Thomas." Her frosty voice betrayed her with a slight crack on his name.

"If you want to do something good for once, you'll stand aside now," said Dorie.

Annika merely raised her eyebrows. "I was rather hoping to give *you* one last chance. Be the hero to your country that you were meant to be. I'm not interested in glory."

"Ha," muttered Dorie.

"Merely that things be done right, *ja*? This is our chance, Dorie. Think of it. Clean air, clean skies. Pay all our debts. Better living for everyone—not just the wealthy. Everyone. Our country—strong, proud, secure. Forever."

Dorie stood her ground. "At what cost?"

"Give it up, Annika," Tam said. "She's never going to help you destroy the fey—from this world or any other."

"Oh?" said Annika. Her eyebrows raised and Dorie wheeled.

Two silvermen had ahold of Jane and Edward. They were manhandling them up the path.

"That's a white flag?" said Tam.

"You expected honor among spies?" said Annika coolly. "And now, Dorie-Dorian, if you would be so good as to open the portal and find us a pathway to a new world? One with plenty of fey, please. You managed to get all those here." She nodded nonchalantly at the pale blue army around Dorie and Tam. Have to give her credit for bravery, thought Dorie. "So you can bring some more back this way. About twice as many ought to do it, I think. For now."

"The basilisk will go home and the circle will close," Dorie said. "There's only a 'for now.' Not a next time."

Annika rolled her eyes. "Men are heading to tranq the basilisk even as we speak. I spent this morning adjusting the serum and I feel confident that I have the dose correctly formulated. The basilisk will not be going home." She wheeled and strode toward the circle. "Come on, then."

"Don't do it," said Jane.

Annika laughed as she walked. "Oh, she'll do it."

"I don't even know if I *can* do it," Dorie protested. They stopped at the circle.

"I suggest you try," said Annika.

"Don't," said Jane again, and Annika sighed.

"I assume there's a reason for the iron mask?" Annika snapped her fingers and one of the silvermen raised Jane's mask to the top of her head. Annika closed her human eye and focused with her silver one. "Yes . . . The less fey there is, the harder it is to see, but I think—I think I do see it there, shimmering around your face. This should be an interesting test case." Annika narrowed her eyes at Jane and slowly, slowly, Dorie saw Jane's hands rise to her own throat.

"Don't!" shouted Dorie. "I said I'm going." But Annika was lost in scientific exploration.

"You can do that, too," hissed Tam.

Of course. Dorie focused on Jane, and just as slowly, she saw her hands begin to lower.

Annika broke off, staring at a smug Dorie. She narrowed her eyes, thinking, and then she shrugged. "You can't keep your eyes open forever, can you? We have more men, and blindfolds." She crossed her arms. "I think your mother will make an excellent test subject. And I have a lot of tests."

<<Help us,>> Dorie said to the fey. But the fey just hung there, waiting.

<<We can't.>> <<We promised.>> <<We can't.>>

Dorie slowly moved into the circle, desperately running through her options for a better solution. She still didn't even know if she could manipulate the worlds. Still, if she could find the right world, surely she could send the fey through before Annika stopped her.

But then Annika would make sure that Jane was locked up for the rest of her life. Not to mention Dorie, too. But what were the two of them against an entire race of beings? She knew what Jane would say to do.

Dorie put her hand up to the boundary of the circle and felt the strange dizziness again, as she started seeing those other worlds, other possibilities. A world with no humans and lots of fey. That's what these fey wanted—that's where they wanted to go, to join the others.

That's what Annika wanted, but for the reverse reason. A world to pull all the fey from.

Dorie looked and looked, and then, through the circle, she saw something that she thought was part of a different world at first.

The silver wings of a basilisk.

"What are you looking at?" said Annika. "Did you find something?"

Behind the basilisk Dorie could see the silvermen Annika had sent, fallen on the ground like dolls. It had paralyzed them with a glance; dropped them to the ground. Heck, it might have even killed them—she could not tell if they were breathing. One had remembered his lore and taken a mirror—it lay broken on the ground.

Annika saw the fallen silvermen. She turned and faced the basilisk with her own silver eye. Her human eye closed as she reached for her tranq gun. "I'm your mirror," she told it. "You can't win against me." The gun leveled and aimed.

There was a loud clunking sound and Annika crumpled.

Jane stood over her, iron mask in hand. Behind her her guard stood, paralyzed by the gaze of Woglet. His little wings were flapping mightily as he tried to keep his vision in place.

The other silverman let go of Edward and grabbed wildly for Woglet.

And then— "Look away!" shrieked Dorie to her parents

and Tam. The two silvermen fell to the ground as the mother basilisk's gaze swept the group impartially. Her heavy head swung back and forth and then stopped, apparently satisfied that the remaining humans were not going to try to impede her access to her portal. The mirrored scales around her eyes retracted.

Dorie breathed heavily. She looked around at the waiting fey. The basilisk coming ever closer. She closed her eyes and shoved her hand back up against the circle.

She knew what she needed to find. All those other Dories from other timelines came swirling around, walking through her, clustering around her.

But the timeline she wanted was the one with no Dorie at all.

The one where the humans had lost twenty years ago, or perhaps even before that. The world where the fey had won, and if there were any surviving humans, they only existed in pockets, scraps, caves. That was where these fey were going. All of them, all of them, forever. She would be so lonely without them, and she despaired, but she kept looking, for this was the only way to save them all.

There were fey around, watching—a blue circle all around. Tam had sung to them, and they had answered.

Dorie melded herself into them, for the last time. <<Are you ready,>> she said, and <<Are you sure you want to go?>> <<Yes.>> <<Yes.>> <<Yes.>>

Her fey senses extended through the circle, through all the fey still streaming into the forest, and then she saw the humans there far back at the trail entrance just beginning to make their way up the treacherous and steep mountain. Annika's backup. Dorie saw them coming, just as the fey-touched ironskin Alice had shown her in the visions.

They marched into the forest. They marched in with their

long copper poles and their iron cages and their woven metal nets and in every hand glowed a silver eye.

And there was the way, there was the world, and she just had to bring the fey in and tell them to *go*. She turned, ready to call the fey—but then there were the great silver wings again and she faltered. The basilisk family was coming now, the basilisk and her two babies pushing their way from the cave toward the circle. The third egg had not yet hatched, but the disruption around her nest had caused the mother to abandon her original plan and bring the first two hatchlings in first. She spread her enormous wings at the sight of Dorie, standing in her center, and again her great mirrored eyes opened.

A basilisk's gaze was nothing like a wyvern's. Dorie could not move, felt as though she could not even draw air into her lungs. It came into the circle, and as it did, it triggered the way to open behind Dorie. It drew back—was it going to steam her before going home? Dorie mentally braced herself.

And then Woglet flew off of Dorie's shoulder and straight at the mother basilisk, yodeling and steaming his baby steam.

The mother basilisk blinked, and Dorie was free to step out of the basilisk's way, move to the edge of the circle. The basilisk looked at the tiny woglet—so much tinier than her own babies, and seemed to shrug, dismissing them all. With her head she nudged her two hatchlings, encouraged them to go through.

On the other side of the circle Dorie could see into the world that she had selected, that the basilisk had opened. It was another mountain, like here. But there were all sorts of swooping creatures on the other side, ones that had gone extinct here years ago, from hunting and trapping and poaching. And beyond there she saw fey, drawn to the vortex to peer through and see what they were missing.

"Not a lot," said Dorie under her breath, and she extended her hand outside the circle, and braced herself, and told them all to come.

And they came.

They came like a great storm, barreling through Dorie's conduit from this world to the next. The basilisk took little notice of them now; she had sent her two chicks through to the waiting mate on the other side, and now she was going back to wait for the last one to hatch. The blue fey poured in as Tam whistled. The men came closer.

The great mass of fey seemed to gain acceleration as they went. The whistle was calling them, but more, it was pulling them together into a great chain of fey, something stronger together than they were apart. Even with the wyvern goo bottling her own fey up inside, Dorie felt the insistent tug urging her to come with them, to go, go on through.

Dorie looked at her dear stepmother, with the iron mask covering her face, standing there, braced against the fey storm. There was something like victory on her face, or the feel of your teeth bared in the wind. She was watching the fey go, and she was staying.

It seemed as though hours went by. Dorie's arms were shaking from fatigue now, as the last basilisk chick finally hatched and was prodded by its mother to the circle. She was spread-eagled—one hand in the center and one hand outside of the ring.

The silvermen were coming, closer and closer.

But the way was open and the fey were going through and they were going to win.

That's when she realized that Tam was being pulled, step by step into the circle.

There was pure terror on his face, and in that moment he looked for *her,* his eyes met *hers,* he called out, "Dorie!"

But she couldn't stop it. Not now. The mother and baby basilisk were through now, but the way was still open for the fey. The storm was being pulled through her; she was the conduit, and if she left the circle now, the remaining fey would be stranded here in this world. "What is it?" she cried into the face of the storm.

"I don't know," he managed. "It's pulling my hands."

Jane turned then, and her eyes met Dorie's. They knew someone who had been taken by the fey. Who had returned with a fey gift in his hands. A gift that enhanced his natural talents—in that case, sculpture. Edward's brilliant masks had been a gift from the Fey Queen herself, infusing his fingers with pure blue fey substance.

Why had Dorie never thought that Tam might have been sent home with a gift? She had even heard it for herself.

"Your piano playing!" she shouted at him. "Your composing! It's not yours!"

"Of course it is!"

She shook her head, and then, as he was being pulled through the circle and into that new world, she grabbed him and held on for dear life. She was not going to let him go again.

She had no fey power to hold him. So she held Tam, willing the vortex to simply suck the fey out of his hands and let him go. But it pulled on him and in the maelstrom she could see him change to all manner of different Tams, in different clothing, different hairstyles. Smiling, laughing, angry, clever. All the other Tams on the timeline, and still she held him as the fey in his hands tried to pull him through to join the rest.

But the grip of her hands was not enough to offset the great mass of inertia pulling him through. All the basilisks were through. Most of the fey were through. There was no help for it. One human could not hope to win against the mass of all the other fey in the universe.

But she did know how to take the fey out of someone. Hadn't she done it to herself? It would not have worked with Jane or Calendula—their faces were no longer human, would not work without the fey to animate them. But Tam would still be Tam without his composing. She could do it—if the wyvern goo in her palm didn't stop her. There was that last little bit of wyvern left in the tattoo on her hand. She tore away the careful bandage that Moira had done. She linked her arm through Tam's, pulled the penknife from his pocket, and, giddy with the thought of the pain, scraped the last of the wyvern tattoo off her palm.

It burned, oh, how it burned.

It burned all the last bit of silver away, and then she was free to use her power to set Tam free once and for all. Keeping her arms wrapped around him, she reached down with her fey side into his hands and began pulling it out in long blue slithers, letting the fey do what it wanted and go out into the other world. It grew harder as she went and at some point she realized Jane was screaming from outside the circle.

She couldn't think why, but it was getting harder to think. She felt so faint, but the blue was coming out of his hands and still she held him.

And then it was all gone, and as she sagged against Tam she understood what Jane had been yelling about.

Her own fey side had been freed by removing the wyvern. And now it, too, was crackling away, too, going, going, out of her fingers and toes and the ends of her hair, vanishing into the ether.

The fey were almost through now, every last bit of them, and that included her.

The blue storm raged through her, and as it went it sucked all the last bit of her blue right along with it. It drained from her fingers and ears and toenails. It sucked away all the changes she had made and it turned her back into Dorie, bit by bit, unchangeable golden-haired Dorie with the curls and the lips and the skin that would never mar.

She sagged in Tam's arms where she held him, and now he held her as she slipped to the ground. The hole was closing— the fey were gone for good and forever. Tam leaned down, ear to her mouth, as she tried to say something. She hardly knew what she wanted to say until the words forced themselves through her lips like they, too, were leaving her body.

"I will fight," she said as he held her. The world grew black around her and she thought that perhaps the irony of slipping into it while finally realizing that life was for fighting was amusing, at least to someone not her. At any rate, she had stopped running in time, hadn't she? Stopped hiding, stopped pretending. She had saved them all, all the fey, forever and ever, and Jane, too, and Tam. She had done something with her life. So it was okay if the black closed in.

The words came through one more time.

"I will fight."

Epilogue

In one timeline the silvermen caught her before she could reach the circle, stopped the fey from going through. That world has clean energy for the whole country; surely there they call Adora Rochart a traitor, and burn her in effigy once a year at summer's end.

In our timeline the silvermen did not catch her. No one did. Tam did not forgive her in time, and so she went through the portal with the fey, left all of us behind, and we are poorer for it.

But I like to think that in another timeline they did not catch her, did not catch the fey. They went and she stayed, and perhaps she made things up with Tam, for he had always loved her, even when he thought he shouldn't.

—Thomas Lane Grimsby, *Silverblind: The Story of Adora Rochart*

* * *

Dorie.

Five, six years from now. Ten if she's unlucky.

She is standing in The Supper Club, now Jack and Stella's club, for Alberta has retired and the good friends are running it together. Stella does the books and charms the guests, and

Jack books the acts and wrangles over maraschino cherries, for it turns out she has a head for that after all. During the week-days Jack paints canvases that are steadily rising in value, and next year, or maybe five years from now, she'll be opening her own gallery, a certain redheaded doctor by her side. They'll sell Jane's paintings as well, and Jane will finally see a career of her own start to blossom.

Dorie's hands have healed, as much as they ever will. They are the descendants of her father's hands, mangled and scarred, but she doesn't mind as much as she might. She doesn't often go to The Wet Pig these days, but when she does, she looks at the picture of laughing Dorie, two perfect hands wrapped around her ale and her head thrown back in a riot of blond curls, and she doesn't miss that girl, the girl who never changed.

She wears her hair long and dark brown these days, a twin of her stepmother Jane's. Her nose has a bump from where she broke it in a fight when she was twelve. Her leg has a long scar from where she broke it when she was thirteen. She has a wry smile like Uncle Rook, and freckles like Aunt Helen, and she doesn't have to work very hard to keep any of these things in place, but she does, just a little, and that's okay, because she *can*.

Because a trickle of her fey side came back to her.

There was nothing for a long time. It was a long convales-cence for her. Losing half of yourself is a serious undertaking. Dorie spent three months in bed, and the next eight months sitting on a stone bench at the old Silver Birch estate, sitting just inside the woods and looking for something that did not come. The silvermen came at first to threaten her, then came less and less when it became increasingly obvious that Dorie

TINA CONNOLLY

could not only not reverse what she had done, she could
do nothing more at all. The palms with their silver eyes did
nothing. The application of wyvern goo did nothing.

Annika was brought in once to examine her with her basilisk eye; she said merely, "She's clean," and then pivoted and
left without saying another word to Dorie. Dorie heard later
that Annika had been promoted to second-in-command at
the Queen's Lab, despite the fact that what had temporarily
been a superpower was now a mere curiosity. What use a
basilisk eye if all the fey were gone, after all? But Dorie did
not care what happened to Annika, not even enough to
gloat.

Tam had not been entirely absent during that time, the
time when she sat on a bench in the forest. He spent the first
three months she was in bed reading to her, bringing her tea,
telling her stories of the city. When she finally came to terms
with the fact that she might be human forever, she got up
from bed and moved to the bench in the forest, and said she
didn't want to see anybody.

So Tam left.

He went around the world, tracking down myths and looking for things. He sent Dorie letters from every port: long
handwritten stories he had heard, about ice monsters and
feathered rocs and great tentacled kraken. There was still
magic in the world, if she would see it. But Dorie did not care
much for ice monsters if she wasn't one of them. In vain
Helen tempted her with outings in town. In vain Jane reminded her that she had chosen to stay and fight. In vain the
letters came.

And then one day, as if it had taken all that time for her
other half to find a way between the worlds, she woke up

with the faintest, vaguest thought that she could sense people standing just below her window. A few months later and she could jostle her teacup without touching it. She spilled the tea all over Aunt Helen's new rug that day and cackled with delight. Aunt Helen, who had been wearing a worried face for the last year and trying to hide it, smiled at the sight. Even Woglet—who was by now really too big to be sitting in people's living rooms like a fancy knickknack—flew around and around in circles, knocking over the rest of the teapot.

It keeps coming back, a very little at a time, as if the opening between the worlds is a fraction of a hairsbreadth, and it all has to come through in a very thin crackle of blue, back to where it belongs. One day there is enough to sense which mushrooms are poisonous. One day there is enough to make a blue light dance at her fingertips. It might take twenty years to all come back, but it comes.

On the day when there is enough to put the bump back on her nose, she finally answers one of Tam's letters. She sends a postcard from the village to his last known address, and waits for it to be forwarded on, and him to book passage on the next ship home. When he arrives at Silver Birch Hall he draws the postcard from his jacket pocket, now faded and sea-struck and bent, and shows her the two words she had written weeks and weeks ago. "Come home," it said, and here he is.

He sits down on the old stone bench at the edge of the forest; the two of them sit there together.

"And then I had my own journey," Tam says, "for I didn't want to make music anymore. It didn't come out the same. I put into port and burned all my old scores." He takes her ruined hand. "But then I thought of all you'd lost. And how if I couldn't fight for what I had, how could I tell you to? So I started over. I'm studying composition and theory and technique. And I play again. Perhaps . . . not like I did. But what is ever like it was?"

"Perhaps some things could be like they were," she says. She takes his hands, and presses her fingertips to his. There is kindness and warmth and simple understanding there, and just perhaps, maybe there is something more as well. A faint trickle of blue—not too much, for she does not have that much—coalesces on her fingertips.

He pulls back. "No," he says. "I can't accept their gifts. Not now that I know what it was."

She sets her fingers to his, and when he still seems reluctant, she leans forward and sets her lips to his, and for that he is not reluctant at all. When she pulls back she says, "There is no *them,* not anymore." Her voice trembles, firms. "But there is me. And just sometimes, only sometimes . . . I would like to share with you. Would you like that?"

He takes her hand and kisses her again and the world spins around and now she is back in The Supper Club, because all that is a real dream, a true dream that has happened long ago, and here she is at the table, watching a dear sweet man in glasses and a battered leather jacket take the stage. He sits down at the piano, and a little bit is her gift, but the rest is him, as the music swells around them and tells everyone a story of long ago.

It is the story of a Great War that split a country in two.

It is the story of a girl who was ironskin, and tried to help a small damaged child, and learned terrible secrets.

It is a story of a copper-haired girl who paid too much for beauty, and fell, and got up, and fought.

It is the story of a girl who was caught in the war, who paid to save a people with half of herself. Tears run down that girl's face as she sits in The Supper Club, and listens to her love, and considers what next to fight.

Acknowledgments

Many thanks to Caroline Yoachim and David Levine for reading the earliest draft, to a bunch of folks on Codex for answering random questions like what a tattoo in your hand would feel like, Neile Graham who has not yet been thanked for catching errors in *Ironskin*, Tinatsu Wallace for the chained-up copperhead hydra, Super Agent Ginger Clark and the Curtis Brown team, Super Editor Melissa Frain, Amy Saxon, Leah Withers, Susannah Noel, Irene Gallo, Larry Rostant, and the rest of the Tor team, Rosalyn Landor for her incredible voice work on the audiobooks, Peter Honigstock for always making the Powell's events go like clockwork, my family for giving me a week to hole up in Eugene and write while they toddler-wrangled, Dad for reading the third draft, Mom for catching typos, Eric for, really, just all kinds of help and support, and finally, sweet little baby #2 for only eating half of my brain and not all of it.

April 2014
Portland, Oregon